Praise for *Unreasonable Doubts*

"Thrilling and informative, a superb novel that should be read by all those interested in how our criminal justice system really works."
—Kenneth R. Feinberg, former administrator of the 9/11 Victims Compensation Fund

"A wonderful debut novel, it's a legal thriller with substance—a page-turner that will trigger introspection and reflection."
—David Lat, editor-at-large, *Above the Law*, and author of *Supreme Ambitions*

"A delectable book about a charming and savvy young lawyer dealing with demanding personal and professional issues of enormous interest to any reader."
—Floyd Abrams, author of *The Soul of the First Amendment*

"Reyna Marder Gentin's *Unreasonable Doubts* takes you behind the closed doors of lawyers' offices and courtrooms . . . A compelling look at the legal system with vivid and unforgettable characters who will keep you up at night, worrying about them."
—Jimin Han, author of *A Small Revolution*

" . . . intelligently written. . . . There is something in this story for everyone, and if you are like I was, the ending is going to be worth the wait."
—*Reader Views*

". . . [a] page-turner love story and legal thriller."
—*bookscover2cover*

"A compelling, aptly named novel about a young lawyer's search for clarity and fulfillment in her career, love relationship(s), and spiritual life. Reyna Marder Gentin, a former lawyer, is, without a reasonable doubt, a writing talent that is headed for a promising career as an author."

—MIRIAM AROND, former editor-in-chief of *Child* and *American Health Magazines*

"Reyna Marder Gentin has written an intense, intriguing, captivating, suspenseful and riveting novel that is extremely thought-provoking."

—*LINDA'S BOOK OBSESSION*

"The crisply written *Unreasonable Doubts* moves quickly and keeps readers on the edge of their seat with dialogue that rings true. Author Reyna Marder Gentin knows her stuff and displays that in her debut novel."

—ANDY GOTLIEB, *Jewish Exponent*

"*Unreasonable Doubts* is a cleverly written crime drama, blended in with mystery, intrigue and romance."

—*CHICK LIT CENTRAL*

"Well-developed characters, fast-paced plot, clear, straightforward writing. A joy to read, even when it was keeping me up way past my bedtime."

—JACQUELINE FRIEDLAND, author of *Trouble the Water*

"*Unreasonable Doubts* is terrific! The allure and the danger are palpable and the resolution is surprising yet entirely satisfying. Lots to think about when you finish."

—BARBARA SOLOMON JOSSELSOHN, author of *The Last Dreamer*

"Gentin gives us a little legal drama, a little psychological thriller, a taste of crime story, and lots of romance. Best of all, she gives us characters who come to life as real people who will stay with us long after we close the book."

—*READERS' FAVORITE*

"A blend of drama, romance, and legal suspense, Gentin's novel is engaging and fast-paced, immediately sweeping you into the tale."

—*Dayton Jewish Observer*

Unreasonable Doubts

Unreasonable Doubts

a novel

REYNA MARDER GENTIN

SHE WRITES PRESS

Published 2018
Printed in the United States of America
ISBN: 978-1-63152-413-4
978-1-63152-414-1
Library of Congress Control Number: 2018937318

For information, address:
She Writes Press
1563 Solano Ave #546
Berkeley, CA 94707

She Writes Press is a division of SparkPoint Studio, LLC.

Interior design Tabitha Lahr

For Pierre, Ariella, and Micah,
who had no doubts and gave me courage.

"There is nothing so whole as a broken heart."
—Rabbi Menachem Mendel of Kotzk (1787-1859)

CHAPTER 1

"Liana, you have Randy Napoli from the *New York Law Journal* on line one. Want me to ask him what it's about?"

"No, thanks, Tony. You can put him through," Liana said. She and Randy had the kind of friendship that sometimes flourishes when both parties know that it exists only in cyberspace and they'll never actually have to meet. When Randy needed an angle or had a legal question, Liana would provide background information, off the record. In turn, he had written a number of articles on Liana's cases, and even when she lost, she came out looking good. It was a win-win situation.

"What's up, Randy?" Liana asked.

"One of your clients got rearrested. I'm working on a story." Randy didn't make much small talk.

"Which one?" Liana asked.

Could be any of them.

"Jeremiah Clark," Randy said, remaining quiet and letting the name sink in.

"Damn."

"Yeah, I figured you'd remember him. Your first fifteen minutes of fame in the legal world," Randy said. "Getting that kid's murder conviction tossed—that was one hell of a win."

Clark's case was the first serious felony appeal Liana had handled after joining the New York City Public Defender's Office. He was sixteen years old and got caught up with the wrong group of friends. One day they forced him to prove himself by shoplifting some expensive gaming equipment from a Best Buy in Queens. Clark had managed to stuff over $1,000 worth of merchandise into a backpack when a shot rang out. One of the other boys had brought a gun, and when the cashier resisted, the boy pulled the trigger. The jury convicted the whole crew of murder, and the judge threw the book at them all.

Liana had successfully argued that because Clark hadn't known the other boy had a gun, the jury's verdict couldn't stand. He wasn't exactly innocent but close enough, and the judge had reduced his sentence from twenty years for murder to a year for the larceny.

"What'd he get arrested for, Randy?" Liana asked.

"Murder. Again. After he did his time on your case, he tried to get his act together—went back to high school, got a job bagging groceries. Didn't last long. A few months ago, he started selling drugs. This time, he was the one with the gun. He fired at a rival dealer, but he hit some old lady getting off a bus instead."

Liana sensed that Randy was enjoying taking her down a peg—like she had gotten Clark off with some fancy legal footwork, and now look.

And who can blame him for reaching that conclusion? Isn't that exactly what happened?

The color drained from Liana's face, and her hands were shaking slightly. She could hear Deb to her left typing away furiously on her computer, not pausing to see what was happening. Liana swiveled in her chair to look out the window. Her office was just two short blocks from where the Twin Towers had stood. Liana had left home for college a few days after the attack in 2001. Now, a little over a decade later, she had a view of the nearly completed Freedom Tower at Ground Zero, a symbol that, somehow, good would prevail over evil. Sometimes, it didn't seem likely.

"Liana, you still there?" Randy asked.

"Yes."

"Well, it can't be a revelation that there are victims of the crimes these guys commit, right? I mean, this is a rough crowd for a nice girl like you to be mixing with." Liana could hear Randy cracking his knuckles, and she pictured him looking out at the newsroom, grateful to be surrounded by reporters and editors and not her clientele.

"Thanks for letting me know, Randy," she said, putting the receiver down. Liana closed her eyes and practiced her yoga breathing. Deb had still not looked up from her screen. *This day is not starting out well.*

When the cold shoulder became unbearable, Liana gave up. "Are you still mad at me for not babysitting Max on Saturday night?"

Liana's polite but firm refusal to watch two-year-old Max while Deb went on a blind date had not gone over well. When Deb finally relented and turned to Liana, her eyes were bleary and she looked exhausted.

"What happened to you?" Liana asked, a little afraid of what the answer would be.

"I'm trying to transition Max from his crib," she said. "I was up all night—the little bugger kept getting out of the new bed every hour and running into my room. I finally just locked his bedroom door so he couldn't come out," Deb confessed. "Could I be reported to Child Protective Services for that?"

Liana was stunned. Having no children herself, she didn't understand the sleep-deprived desperation that might drive such behavior. She had a vision of a raging fire and Max trapped in his bedroom.

"I'm not sure. Is that safe?" But Deb had pulled up Facebook on her computer and was busy perusing photographs from a high school friend's bachelorette party—she was a whirling dervish of energy, and the niceties of a conversation never held her long.

"What was that phone call about?" Deb asked. Her maternal instincts, such as they were, had kicked in when she'd seen Liana wilt. Before Liana could explain, Tony poked his head in their doorway, his eyeglasses sliding down his nose.

"Office meeting, ladies!" he rang out. "Don't be late! You know how the Boss hates tardiness!"

Gerry, "the Boss," was legendary in the criminal defense bar. He had been fighting the good fight for over thirty years, and he ran a tight ship. Liana could hear Tony as he stopped at each office in turn, cajoling the staff attorneys into the conference room.

"Damn. I totally forgot we have that meeting today," Deb groaned. "How does Gerry expect us to crank out these briefs and also sit through these ridiculous office meetings for hours?"

There was a brief filing quota—nicknamed "the brief of the month" club—which ran from July 1 to June 30. Many of the attorneys found the requirement onerous, but Liana worked at a steady pace, and she had met her quota with the brief she had filed the previous week. She was indulging in a silent moment of self-congratulation when Gerry interrupted her thoughts. He had a total disdain for exercise, and even this short journey down the corridor had him breathing just a bit too hard and trying to cover it up by speaking a bit too loudly in the enclosed space of Liana and Deb's office.

"Good morning, ladies! Liana, started working on your next case yet?" he said in his fingernails-on-a-chalkboard cheery voice.

"Not yet, Gerry," Liana lied. In fact, she had flipped through the file, discovering that her new client had a rap sheet a mile long and had now been convicted of selling crack cocaine to an undercover cop. Within five hundred feet of an elementary school. A dead loser.

"I just filed brief number twelve. Is there some reason you ask?" Liana ventured.

"No, not really. I just get so jazzed at the beginning of a new fiscal year—it's hard to contain myself!" If his enthusiasm hadn't been so undeniably genuine, it would have been comical.

Liana suppressed an eye-roll. "Gerry, I'll turn to the new case ASAP, and I'll have a real jumpstart on the quota for next year," she deadpanned. Deb sniggered quietly, facing her computer with her back to Gerry and clearly hoping that he would leave her alone.

"What a Goody Two-shoes," Liana said when Gerry was out of earshot.

"Only you still use expressions like 'Goody Two-shoes' when you're trying to hurl an insult," Deb said. "You're so feeble."

"I'll try to work harder on my epithets so they meet your approval," Liana said, relieved that she seemed to be back in Deb's good graces. "Let's go. We'll grab seats by the door so we can leave as soon as it's over."

The Public Defender's Office had been an obvious career path for an idealist like Liana. She'd fervently believed that most of the time the criminal justice system worked—the guilty would be punished, and the innocent would be set free. Nor had there been any question in Liana's mind which role she would occupy in the drama—that of Atticus Finch, fighting the uphill battle for the accused, losing most of the time but still feeling good about herself and her choices. It had all seemed so simple.

The two women made their way down the long, cheaply carpeted hallway, chatting with their colleagues as they joined the procession to the sterile and utilitarian conference room, where they took their places in thirty or so uncomfortable plastic chairs that surrounded a large rectangular table. No artwork adorned the stark white walls, only a few framed posters of the Twin Towers that no one had the heart to remove.

Liana felt immediately cheered as she looked around the room. The staff attorneys had a "we're in the trenches together" mentality that still spoke to her. As easy as the camaraderie was among the rank and file, Liana was increasingly out of sync with Gerry and the other supervisors. She looked at them now, sitting stiffly side by side on the far end of the conference table, and was reminded, albeit oddly for a Jewish girl, of Matthew, Mark, Luke, and John. Each had a slightly different way of spreading the Word, but they preached essentially the same gospel to the choir of staff attorneys: "Remember, we are entrusted with the task of doing God's work, representing the downtrodden, the disadvantaged, the wronged."

Initially, Liana had enthusiastically drunk the Kool-Aid that Gerry dispensed, driven by the belief that the next client could be the innocent one she alone was destined to save from a life behind bars. But now, with several years of practice under her belt, something had changed. After representing repeat offenders and defendants found guilty at trial of crimes too ghastly to imagine, she was having a crisis of faith.

When the staff attorneys had settled into their seats, Gerry stood and began to speak, his voice reverberating in the crowded space.

"Thank you, everyone, for coming and for being punctual. I know that the end of the fiscal year is tomorrow, and some of you are scrambling to finish up your briefs for quota. I didn't want to cancel today's meeting, but we'll try to keep it short. Who has a case they'd like to discuss?"

It was always the same. Gerry would invite participation, and the attorneys would sit stonily, some staring down at the table, others doodling on their legal pads, all looking anywhere but at the front of the room where the supervisors sat. For a group of articulate, opinionated people, they acted like small children; no one wanted to go first or be called upon by the teacher. Eventually, someone would clear his or her throat and break the awkward silence.

"I have a case I could use some guidance on," Franny volunteered. She was younger than Liana—had just passed her one-year probationary period in the office and graduated to representing clients convicted of the most serious crimes. Liana had taken a shine to her; she was a sweet girl, round-faced and rosy-cheeked, earnest and serious.

She reminds me of myself when I was a newbie.

"My client's name is Derwin Jackson. He was convicted of second-degree manslaughter for recklessly killing his infant son, Tyrone—the medical examiner testified that the cause of death was shaken baby syndrome. At trial, Jackson tried to shift the blame, saying that the mother had been the one caring for the child at the time he was killed, but the jury didn't buy it." Franny was now speaking in such hushed tones that Liana could barely hear her from just a few seats away, and her eyes had welled up with tears.

Maybe she isn't cut out for this.

But Franny soldiered on. "I'm trying to find a sympathetic angle—a way to humanize Mr. Jackson in the brief for the court, and for myself. I guess I'm just having a little trouble, given the circumstances." She took a deep breath and looked beseechingly around the room.

"Okay, we can help with that," Gerry said in a soothing tone. "It's important for your effectiveness as Mr. Jackson's attorney to dig a little deeper—stand in the shoes of the defendant and try to understand him—and to look for the good in him." Liana noticed a number of the attorneys nodding vigorously in agreement, and she let out an involuntary but audible sigh.

Gerry shot Liana a warning look from across the room and then continued.

"First of all, is Mr. Jackson the child's natural father?" he asked.

"No, actually, he's the mother's boyfriend," Franny said. "Does that matter?"

"Well, yes," Gerry said. "I mean, no, it doesn't matter in a strictly legal sense, but it's just different—less viscerally horrifying—if this isn't his biological child. Taking care of someone else's child—that's a big responsibility to saddle someone with." Liana kicked Deb under the table, as if to say, "See? You don't want me taking care of Max," but Deb refused to take the bait and kept her focus on Franny.

Gerry stood up and paced back and forth as he thought out loud about ways to explain away the defendant's heinous behavior. "Maybe Mr. Jackson had conflicting feelings about watching this child—I mean, if he isn't the baby's father, then his girlfriend pretty recently had been having sex with some other man. Maybe there's a way to explore that aspect of the story—the jealousy angle."

Liana shifted in her seat, staring at Gerry and trying to figure out if there could be any validity to what he was saying. She could discern none.

Gerry continued. "What's Mr. Jackson's educational level? Perhaps you could argue that he was like a child himself and lacked the understanding to appreciate that he could hurt the baby, or thought that he was comforting the baby with the physical contact." As he picked up speed, Gerry's face turned a shade of pink and small beads of sweat broke out on his forehead.

If he doesn't explode, it will be a miracle.

Then, to Liana's dismay, Deb got in on the act. "As a mother who never gets frustrated by the behavior of her small child"—there were a few knowing chuckles, and Deb winked at Liana, who tried to smile but found that she couldn't—"maybe you could paint Mr. Jackson as a caring stepfather who was trying to teach the boy good behavior, when something went terribly awry?"

Liana couldn't stand it anymore. She passed her legal pad to Deb. This is nonsense! Why is Gerry trying to dress this guy up as the maligned babysitter instead of finding something Franny can raise in her brief? she scrawled across the top of the page. Deb passed the pad back after scribbling, cool down. But Liana felt as if her head would burst. Before she knew it, she had turned her whole body toward Franny. She took a moment to modulate her voice, but her frustration was apparent nonetheless.

"I'm sorry, but can we stop this love fest for Mr. Jackson for just a moment? Franny, do you have an actual legal issue to argue on Mr. Jackson's behalf on his appeal?"

After a moment, Franny answered.

"Well, yes, I think I do. In the middle of the trial, a juror disclosed that a number of years earlier her daughter had died of SIDS—sudden infant death syndrome—a purely accidental death. The juror said she still suffered from that trauma, and she felt she might be biased against the defendant even though she understood he had nothing to do with her daughter's death. Despite this showing of potential prejudice, the court denied defense counsel's motion to remove that juror from the panel and substitute an alternate juror."

Liana was triumphant. "That's a great issue, Franny—a slam dunk winning issue! All this other stuff about believing in your client and trying to find his inner worth is—pardon my French—bullshit!"

"I think what Liana is trying to say," Deb interrupted, putting a calming hand on Liana's arm as if Deb were afraid Liana might quite literally self-destruct, "is that the most critical part of every appeal is identifying the legal issue that stands the best chance of helping our client, whether you believe your client is innocent or guilty. But we also have to remember that the defendant is a human being. It helps you do a better job if you can emotionally invest in the defendant and relate to his situation."

Liana could feel the pressure of Deb's touch, silently urging her to let the matter drop. But she was too far gone.

"Actually, that's not at all what I meant. What I mean is that in this job, ninety-nine point nine percent of the time, your client is guilty. That's why he lost at trial, and that's why he's your client now on appeal. Forget about compassion. It doesn't matter if you feel bad for your client or if you understand your client or if you believe in your client's underlying goodness or even in his innocence—you're not your client's girlfriend or his mother or his shrink or his priest. Just do your job—be his lawyer and try to figure out a way to win his case."

Deb frantically shoved the legal pad in front of her: Shut up, Liana, right now. You are totally out of line!

Liana looked at Deb, and seeing the concern on her friend's face brought her back to reality. She sat down slowly and carefully—*when did I stand up?*—concentrating on her breathing and looking at her folded hands on the table. The entire room was engulfed by a shocked silence. Supervisors and staff attorneys alike sat motionless, as if wondering how they would go on after such an outburst. After what seemed like an eternity, Gerry rose from his seat.

"Well, Franny, I agree with Liana that your legal issue is excellent," he crooned. "But your impulse to seek the good in your client—that willingness to empathize and give of yourself emotionally, to open yourself to the possibility that your client does not belong behind bars—that's what separates a great public defender from a merely competent one. It's very hard to do this job if you don't have the feeling, on some level, that there, but for the grace of God, go I. You would all do well to remember that."

After a moment of respectful quiet in recognition of the mayhem they had just witnessed, the attorneys started up their usual chatter, pushing back their chairs from the table and heading back to their offices. As Franny passed her, Liana reached out and touched her gently on the elbow.

"I'm so sorry, Franny. I didn't mean that as a personal attack. You're doing great, and you're going to win this case for Mr. Jackson. I'm just kind of out of sorts," Liana said, feeling how desperately inadequate those words were to describe her state of mind.

"It's okay." Franny took a couple of steps toward the door, then turned back. "The thing is . . ." Franny hesitated but met Liana's eyes, which pleaded for a kind word, and went on. "The lawyers, especially the younger ones, we look up to you. You're smart and generous with your time. If someone like you doesn't believe in the mission of this place, and in these clients, it's kind of like we're all lost." Franny hurried from the room, leaving Deb and Liana looking after her silently.

"Come on, let's get out of here. I think you've inflicted enough wounds on yourself for one day." Deb held out her hand and practically lifted Liana out of the chair, and the two women walked solemnly back to their office.

After lunch, Liana was feeling calmer, the debacle of the office meeting already fading in her mind into old news. So when she saw the note at the front desk—Liana, please stop by when you get back. Gerry—she was more than a little irritated.

"Any idea what this is all about?" she asked.

"Nope," Tony replied.

"He's so . . ." Liana muttered under her breath.

"No question there," Tony said.

Liana walked to her office to get a legal pad and a pen, a holdover habit from her days as a summer associate at the big corporate law firm, when she would be called to a partner's office to take an assignment, not to get dressed down for some perceived offense. Deb wasn't at her desk, which was unusual.

She liked to drop Max at day care early, work her seven hours without a lunch break, and get back to the day care by four to pick him up. It was hectic, but the working mom thing, a necessity, was palatable to her only if she didn't feel like strangers were raising her kid. The ex-husband was helpful but had already moved on to wife number two. Deb was realistic about the situation. "Max is my priority and my responsibility," she'd said to Liana on more than one occasion.

Liana sat down, hoping Deb would arrive and give her a shot in the arm before she faced Gerry. When there was no sign of her after a few minutes, she ran to the Starbucks in the lobby to grab a double espresso macchiato to calm her nerves; she was not about to let Gerry see her flustered. When she returned, she knocked lightly on his office door, and Gerry swiveled around from the computer so fast that Liana almost jumped backward.

What's he so eager to talk to me about?

"Please, come in and sit down," he said. Liana sat in one of the chairs opposite Gerry's desk; the other chair was piled high with client files. His office was always a complete mess, his desk laden with paperwork in total disarray. Every inch of floor space was covered in cardboard boxes holding reams of legal research. Liana couldn't fathom how he functioned in this clutter; her own office was always neat and organized.

"How was your weekend?" Gerry asked her, as if this were a social call.

"Fine." Liana had once thought that she and Gerry might be friends. But nothing much had developed, and he took his role as her superior way too seriously for anything genuine to take root.

"Liana," Gerry began, sounding revved up, relishing the moment, "that was quite a performance you put on in the office meeting today."

"Excuse me?"

"Well," Gerry said, "I don't want to belabor this unnecessarily, but there's been a perception of late that you don't have the same positive attitude about our clients and about your role as their attorney as you did when you started working here. Perhaps ennui has set in or you've had a change of heart about the cases we handle. Your outburst at the meeting did nothing to dispel these concerns."

Liana was speechless. She had enough self-awareness to know she was having motivational difficulties, but she didn't think it was terribly serious, and she didn't think it was that obvious. Besides, she had done consistently excellent work, winning a number of reversals in high-profile cases—Jeremiah Clark's included—that had made the front page of the *New York Law Journal*. How could she be chided if, with more experience, she was more realistic about the kind of people her clients were?

When she was finally able to speak, she said, "I'm sorry. I have no idea what you're talking about."

Gerry was more than happy to elaborate. He sat back in his chair and stretched out his legs, looking up at the ceiling.

"Perhaps I can explain it this way. You sometimes speak disparagingly about the clients, as though you believe the world would be a safer place if they remained in prison." He paused dramatically. "This kind of work requires more of an attorney than just good research skills and persuasive writing and a competitive desire to win; it requires heart. We're public interest lawyers—we need to believe in the guiding principles of the trusted position we hold. And the number one rule must be that we treat each client as an individual, with hopes and dreams, deserving of our energy and skill and passion, no matter what he may or may not have done to land himself in our care. Sometimes, Liana, it seems as though you don't like our clients."

In a nanosecond, Liana went from stupefied to furious, but she managed to keep her expression and her tone of voice neutral.

"You know, Gerry, I don't consider liking my clients part of my job. I'm here to represent these people to the best of my ability, in a wholly professional manner. I raise the best legal issues I can find, and then I let the appellate court do its job in deciding who wins."

Gerry sat silently through Liana's retort, looking only mildly perturbed. He had run the office for years, and no challenge from an upstart like Liana was going to rattle him.

"No one is suggesting that you aren't performing your duties. You're an excellent attorney. I just wanted to let you know, as your friend, that it would be in your best interests to recommit wholeheartedly to the undertaking of the Public Defender's Office if you want to keep working here. Cynicism is a disease, Liana, and it's contagious. If your attitude about our clients starts to have a negative effect on the other attorneys, especially the younger ones, we'll cut you out. It's as simple as that."

Liana mulled over what Gerry had said. Her heart was racing, and when she spoke, she sounded as if she were underwater.

"Well, I'll get back to work. Thanks for the heads-up."

Liana got up from the chair and not-so-accidentally knocked a few of Gerry's papers from the desk onto the floor, leaving them there as she walked out of his office. She felt totally drained, as if she had been hit over the head with a big supervisory frying pan. She walked unsteadily down the hall to her office, where Deb was now sitting in front of her computer, and shut the door.

"What the hell happened to you?" Deb said.

Liana turned away from Deb and shuffled a few papers on her desk, trying to regroup and process what Gerry had said. Replaying the conversation in her mind, she put her head in her hands in a futile attempt to hide her emotions from Deb, who was sitting just inches away.

"Hey, what's eating you, Cohen? What'd I miss?" Deb

respected resilience, so Liana sat up tall and turned to her with her best game face.

"So apparently there's a perception, quote unquote, that I'm jaded and I don't like my clients," Liana said.

"No shit, Sherlock—that's not exactly breaking news."

"What? How can you say that? I bust my butt every day for these guys!"

"You're careening toward burnout."

Liana looked at Deb as if she were speaking in another language.

Deb rolled her chair even closer and put her hand reassuringly on Liana's knee.

"Look, we're required to represent every impoverished Tom, Dick, or Harry that walks in the door, innocent or guilty. That's our job. But you've stopped trying to find anything redeeming about the clients. You don't even entertain in your mind the possibility of innocence anymore. It's the negativity, the resignation, that Gerry can't stomach."

Liana started to object and then decided there was no point. She hung her head and waited for Deb to dispense some wisdom that might help her salvage the situation.

"And you talk too much. Everyone knows you think that virtually all of these guys are not only guilty but just plain bad. If you can't be enthusiastic, at least be savvy. There are attorneys here—Gerry chief among them—who would swear that they'd bring every single one of these guys home to Mama. You have to remember who your audience is."

Can the Boss tell me how to feel about the clients? Am I really supposed to operate as though I "like" my murderers and pimps and drug dealers?

"Do you want to keep this job, Liana?" Deb asked.

"You know I do. But I can't pretend these guys are saints when they're . . ." Her voice was defiant but a single tear slipped down her cheek.

Deb sat back in her chair and studied Liana.

"You know what I think? I think you're jealous of the other attorneys, especially the younger ones, and that's why you lashed out at that meeting today."

"Jealous? You're crazy. Why would I be jealous?" Liana said.

"Because they're hopeful. Someone like Franny comes to work believing that her next client could be someone really worth fighting for, maybe even someone innocent. You used to be that way—open to the possibility. You aren't anymore, and you wish you still were."

"That's not hopeful," Liana said. "That's delusional."

Deb shrugged. "Suit yourself. But listen to me, because I'm the only one here who'll give it to you straight. What would really turn you around is a client you could believe in. But that's not under your control. So put your nose in the law books, and go through the motions. Think what you want, but keep your mouth shut. Try it with your next defendant." She wheeled her chair over to her filing cabinet and gave it a death stare. "Speaking of which, I'm going to give you a second chance to do me a favor since you failed so miserably on Saturday night."

Liana sighed. "Shoot."

"I need to transfer my next guy to you," Deb said. "I'll fix it up with Gerry." She handed Liana a file marked "Daniel Shea."

"Why?" Liana asked. "What's wrong with him?"

"Nothing, as far as I know," Deb said. "I'm just way behind on my caseload. His file has been sitting in my cabinet for almost seven months—soon he's going to get hostile. If he waits for me, it will be another month before I get to him."

"You're not trying to pawn off some disaster on me are you?" Liana asked. "Because that'd fit in with the kind of day I'm having."

"I swear I don't know anything about him—I haven't even written to introduce myself. He's all yours. He'll be the test case for your 'all business, no empathy' methodology."

As if to announce, "Case closed," Deb turned back to her computer, her hands pressing on her lower back. Liana knew that Deb had her best interests at heart, even if her brutal honesty was hard to swallow. She made up her mind to follow Deb's advice. She'd show Gerry that she could play the game her way—that she could be true to herself and still get the job done.

But it would wait for tomorrow. She was late to meet Jakob.

CHAPTER 2

"I'll have a Macallan, straight up, please." Liana didn't usually drink—at five feet four inches tall and barely 105 pounds, alcohol went straight to her head. But she knew that she wouldn't get through the evening after the day she'd had without taking the edge off. Socializing with Jakob's corporate colleagues, who wouldn't know the Fourteenth Amendment from a Diet Coke commercial, was trying at the best of times. And these were not the best of times.

The young bartender slid the glass across the mahogany bar, and Liana closed her eyes and threw back the shot. She could feel his eyes on her, taking in her rowdy blond curls, the pink lace tank top and snug blue jeans. She was pushing thirty, but she still turned heads.

"Not your scene?" he asked.

She looked around at the sea of suits. "Not exactly, no."

"Another one? I'm buying," he said, smiling hopefully at her.

"Nope. My boyfriend likes me mostly sober," she said, turning her back to the bar and scanning the room for Jakob.

It was the annual summer associates' welcome get-together for the new crop of law students working at Jakob's firm, Wilcox & Finney, and one of the very few social obligations connected to his job that Liana grudgingly attended. Jakob had sweet-talked her into coming. "These things are so tedious without you," he had pleaded. "Won't you be my arm candy?" He had sealed the deal with a promise to take her to the all-you-can-eat buffet at their favorite Indian restaurant on Twenty-Third Street as soon as they could make a decent escape.

The event was always held in a space without much personality on the East Side, close to the office, so the partners and associates would have no excuse not to make an appearance and pretend to look interested in the chatter of the second and third year law students. Many of them had never worked or lived in New York City before and were still getting used to the outsized salary they were being paid for the gig, sometimes overdoing it in their after-hours escapades. Liana found the whole scenario disturbing.

Another woman might have been self-conscious about her casual attire but not Liana. She appreciated the couture of the more senior women partners, who were decked out in Chanel and Carolina Herrera, but they were leading such different lives that it didn't faze her. One of the upsides of her low-wage job was that she only had to put on a suit when she went to court. Liana owned one black lightweight wool number that she had bought during law school, and she hauled it out every month or two when she faced the judges. Otherwise, she was free to dress like the underpaid and underappreciated public servant she was.

Jakob spotted her and waved none too subtly from across the room, where he stood tall in a clump of youngish partners, midlevel associates like him, and three fawning summer associates. Jakob was nice looking, in a very preppy, clean-cut sort of way. He had what her mother called "an honest face"—dirty blond hair, warm green eyes, and an engaging smile. He was the type of guy who looked as if he worked out more than he actually did; his broad shoulders, especially, were solid and sexy—Liana still got a little breathless when he went shirtless. She meandered over, and he put his arm around her waist, squeezing her close. The place was getting crowded and noisy, and he practically had to shout to be heard over the din, even though he was speaking right into her ear.

"Thanks for coming, Li; I know you don't love these things. It means a lot to me."

Liana looked up at him and saw how genuinely pleased he was to have her with him, and she felt a pang of guilt. She couldn't control it—she had what felt like an allergic reaction to the law firm every time she got close, making it nearly impossible for her to share in Jakob's professional life. Although she knew she shouldn't take it out on him, it only got worse the more Wilcox & Finney wrapped its tentacles around him. But that was a problem for another day. For now, she just smiled.

"I'm happy to be here," she said.

Jakob introduced the summer associates. "This is Tameka from Chicago Law School, and Max from Stanford, and Tiffany from Fordham"—the firm's blatant attempt to show that it could be broad-minded about the pedigree of its summer associates, at least in very limited quantities. And to the attorneys from the firm, Jakob gave his usual intro: "You all know Liana. She pulled the old bait and switch on me. She could have been an associate here at Wilcox, raking in a hefty salary and keeping me in style, but instead she went to work at the Public Defender's!" This never failed to get a laugh or a condescending smile from the attorneys. And, although it was technically accurate, it wasn't quite true.

They had, indeed, met when they were summer associates together at Wilcox four years earlier, after their second year in law school. Jakob had made a hugely positive impression on everyone he worked with, both with regard to his legal assignments and in his navigation of the social niceties. At the summer outing at Glen River Country Club, he played golf with the head of the hiring committee and conversed easily with the most senior partners at the five-star-restaurant lunches the firm sponsored to woo the top law students. Jakob was determined—Wilcox & Finney was the pinnacle of New York law firms, and he wanted in.

Liana, in contrast, was a fish out of water. She aced her assignments—outperforming the other summer associates, even Jakob—but she was a mess. That one summer convinced her that she didn't have the stomach for the work, the lifestyle, and virtually all the attorneys who chose that path. She was reduced to tears on more than one occasion when suddenly called into the office of a partner late in the day to be given an assignment on which she was expected to work into the night. The lack of control wreaked havoc on Liana's body and soul, leaving her feeling agitated and empty. And the necessity of pretending to enjoy the company of the hyper-driven attorneys, during the workday and after hours, was just too much for her. So Liana was sure she would get a polite kiss-off when she was called into the hiring partner's office at the end of the summer.

"Ah, come in, Liana, please sit down," he said. She sat in the big leather chair across the desk from him, feeling small and fully expecting him to tell her that the firm had decided not to extend an offer to her. It would be a black mark on her otherwise pristine law school record. Instead, he handed her an envelope.

"Liana, this letter is an offer of employment with Wilcox & Finney upon your successful completion of law school and contingent on your passing the bar exam."

The astonishment must have registered on her face, because the partner laughed.

"Liana, you did excellent work here, and if you'd like to come back as a permanent associate, the door is open. You're intelligent and diligent and well-liked. But may I offer you some words of wisdom from an old goat?"

"Of course," Liana said.

"Find a job you're passionate about—a job that when you get up every morning, you say to yourself, 'Damn, I can't believe they pay me to do this!' I'm not certain that this kind of firm will be that for you."

Liana had taken his advice and accepted an offer from the appeals bureau of the Public Defender's Office, fully believing that representing indigent defendants was her passion. His "bait and switch" joke aside, Jakob said he was proud of her decision, and she believed him.

Did I make a mistake?

Liana was pulled out of her reverie by Tameka attempting, as a good summer associate should, to keep the conversation going. "What exactly do you do as an appellate public defender?"

"I'm appointed as the attorney for people who can't afford counsel to represent them on appeal. What that means is that these men—and women, but mostly men—have already lost at trial. Every defendant is entitled under New York law to one appeal—to have the legal issues of his case reviewed by a panel of judges." Jakob grinned, satisfied that bringing Liana to the event had relieved him of the need to be entertaining.

"What kinds of crimes have these people committed?" Max asked.

"Felonies. Everything from drug selling to burglary to robbery to assault to rape to murder," Liana rattled off.

"Oh my God!" shrieked Tiffany. "And you have to hang out with these guys?" For a split second, Liana saw the situation through sweet Tiffany's eyes.

Does she really think I sit around on a couch with convicts, maybe share some Chinese food, talk about their plans for the weekend?

"No, Tiffany. These defendants are in prison, usually way upstate near the Canadian border, many of them for twenty years or more. We communicate by mail; sometimes we talk on the telephone. But I almost never meet any of my clients. Everything I need to know for the appeal is in the transcript from the trial. It would just be a waste of time and money, although certainly most of the guys do ask me to visit."

"Well, I'm sure they do," piped in Frank, the partner for whom Jakob did most of his work, a big smirk on his face. Frank—in his late forties, twice divorced, with a full head of salt-and-pepper hair—had a reputation as a bit of a letch. But he was on the money with this one. Although Liana was scrupulously careful to keep all her contacts with her clients professional and never to reveal even the smallest personal detail about herself, the guys with half a brain could figure out from her name that she was a woman. And, in the context of being locked up without any contact with the opposite sex, that was really all they needed to know to have quite a flourishing fantasy life about their assigned counsel. Liana frequently received frilly cards and letters from her clients, mostly very polite, replete with their protestations of love. She tended to ignore these missives entirely, and 99 percent of the time, the client gave up and resumed a normal exchange.

Slightly annoyed but not wanting to appear without a sense of humor, Liana retorted, "Frank, these men are not my type."

"Whoa," Frank said, in pretend shock, his palms out as if fending off a truly offensive parry. "I wasn't accusing you of anything, Liana. I know you are hooked on young Jakob here. Certainly no criminal could hold a candle to him!" Everyone laughed, Jakob perhaps the loudest—laughing at your boss's jokes was key to law firm success.

Then Brian, a third-year associate and a friend of Jakob's, asked the question that Liana constantly fielded at cocktail parties but which irritated her when asked by an attorney who should know better.

"Don't you ever feel bad about representing these guys who you know are guilty, trying to get them off on some technicality?" Normally, Liana would have just sighed and given her canned response about the Constitution entitling everyone to a defense. But with Gerry's warning still fresh in her mind, and in the presence of the summer associates, she suddenly felt defensive and obligated to give a more substantive answer. Jakob put his arm around Liana's waist and pulled her close, speaking quietly but firmly in her ear.

"Hold your fire, Tammy; these people are not the enemy." In private, Jakob called her his "little hot tamale," or sometimes just "Tammy" for short. Liana's temper had gotten her into trouble on more than one occasion, and she had, at Jakob's urging, been making a concerted, albeit sometimes unsuccessful effort of late to hold herself in check.

"I'm not sure that's true," Liana whispered back. But she figured this was as good a time as any to try out Deb's advice. No selling the defendant down the river, but no fabricated devotion either. She would play it straight.

"Well, I take issue with your premise. As the defense attorney, I don't actually know whether my client is guilty or innocent. I wasn't on the street corner when the drug exchange was made or in the bar when the gun was brandished. And no client admits to his attorney that he's guilty; every person I've ever represented claimed to be 'falsely accused.'"

This sort of "true crime" shoptalk always enthralled people; she had them in the palm of her hand. Liana continued, "But it's completely irrelevant if I think my client is guilty or innocent. My job is to look damn hard for something that went wrong—whether it's a technicality or something that goes to the fundamental fairness of the trial—so that my client can get a do-over and due process of law. My feelings don't have anything to do with it." Liana glanced at Jakob, who gave her an almost imperceptible nod of approval.

Brian took a long swig of his beer without taking his eyes off Liana. He wasn't a bad guy, but he held the standard corporate law firm attorney view of criminal defense attorneys—thinly veiled disgust.

"I get all that, Liana. I respect that defense attorneys are a big part of what keeps the system honest, and that certainly justifies doing this sort of work. I guess what I'm really asking is more personal, about what keeps you—Liana Cohen— going, day after day, because it has to be tough representing these people. I mean, a lot of them are just scum, aren't they? Is it just about doing your job, or do you hold on to a belief that the next guy who walks through your door might be someone who really deserves you?"

It was a version of the question Liana had been asking herself subconsciously for some time now and that Gerry had posed so starkly after the office meeting—did she still have the proverbial fire in the belly for this work? She had no good answer. Liana momentarily envisioned Jeremiah Clark firing the gun, and she watched as someone's grandmother fell to the ground, the city bus continuing along its route, unaware of the tragedy unfolding.

Liana accepted that she wasn't the eternally optimistic poster child for the Public Defender's Office she'd once been, but she resented that her inability to answer Brian's question had revealed her as a fraud. She was suddenly overwhelmingly exhausted and wished she had let the cute bartender buy her a second Scotch. When she caught Jakob's eye, she pointed to her stomach and looked longingly at the door.

Get me out of here, she pleaded silently.

"Well, this has been fun, but I have a hot date with my feisty public defender for some chicken tikka masala and naan. See you folks tomorrow," Jakob said, steering Liana toward the exit, one hand protectively on her back.

They stepped outside into the warm night, and Liana turned to Jakob. "Sometimes I think your corporate buddies are onto something," she said, her voice a little shaky. "Maybe representing these guys is just so vile that there's no way to rationalize it."

Jakob stopped and took her hands in his. "Hey, don't say that and don't put yourself down. These big firm lawyers are smart and capable, but they wouldn't last five minutes in your job. You're fighting for justice for the underdog; they're fighting only for themselves and the next paycheck."

Jakob pulled her into a big hug and then hailed a cab. "Come on," he said. "Our Indian food is calling."

CHAPTER 3

Liana came into work early the next day, ready to do battle. Although the conversation with Brian at the Wilcox event had cost her a good night's sleep, she felt liberated. She was all business from now on.

She cleared the surface of her desk and took the folder Deb had given her out of the file cabinet, placing a pristine blank legal pad in front of her. Liana was one of the few attorneys who still took notes by hand; everyone else worked directly on the computer. But she was old school, and she felt that the act of handwriting somehow allowed the information to go from the transcript into her brain.

It was this moment that Liana still found inspiring, when the file was before her and she was poised to open it and see what awaited her, despite the unsavory clientele, the low pay, and the lack of respect in the larger legal world. If her faith in the underlying decency of her clients was flagging, there was still the possibility of a great story, a winning legal issue, or, if not a winning issue, an argument she could throw herself into with total abandon.

Liana scanned the front of the file, which the paralegal had filled in with the basic information about the case. She knew the client's name—Daniel Shea. His date of birth was noted as October 18, 1986, making him almost twenty-four years old at the time of the crime two years earlier on July 4, 2010, five years younger than Liana was now. She always calculated the client's age first. Liana hated when the clients were really young, sixteen or seventeen—old enough to be held accountable as an adult for their criminal actions but too young to have impulse control or any idea of the consequences of their stupid behavior.

This guy was a reasonable age—a person should have his head on straight by twenty-four. And his name intrigued her. Daniel Shea—*could he be Irish?* Liana had never had an Irish client as far as she knew.

Then she looked to see what Shea stood convicted of, how much time he was doing, and where he was serving it: rape in the first degree, fifteen years, Dannemora Correctional Facility. Shea had faced twenty-five years for the crime, which was classified as a class B violent felony. The judge had given him fifteen.

Probably a first offender. Nothing like starting big.

Liana had handled a couple of sex offense cases before, and she found them difficult. She wondered again whether Deb had intentionally unloaded Shea on her, but it seemed petty to give him back. It was hard to dredge up much compassion for rapists, and she found herself overly relating to the victims. But, Liana reminded herself, this was no longer of concern to her—she needed no empathy for Shea; she needed only the law on her side.

Liana flipped through the papers clipped in on the right-hand side, which were copies of the official court documents: the indictment, various ministerial and scheduling orders, and the sentencing papers. She would go through all these materials later, more carefully, to see if there were any errors lurking there. In the indictment she learned the complainant's name and age, eighteen-year-old Jennifer Nash.

Well, at least she's over the age of consent.

There would be no issue of statutory rape here, which was almost impossible to defend against once it was established that the victim was underage. She read through the barebones allegations listed in the different counts—"vaginal penetration by forcible compulsion"—and noted that there was no weapon involved. Not that you needed a gun or a knife to rape someone, but use of a weapon upped the ante and made her job even harder.

Then Liana looked at the left-hand side of the folder, where correspondence from the client would be attached. The case had come out of Brooklyn Supreme Court, and the conviction was dated December 3, 2011. Deb was right; soon the defendant would be getting antsy about the delay. Some of the clients were downright nasty, taking the attitude that "you get what you pay for," and therefore their assigned counsel—who, they usually believed, worked for free—must be totally incompetent. Occasionally, Liana came awfully close to screaming into the telephone at a client who challenged her abilities, "I went to *Yale Law School!*" But she knew it would fall on deaf ears and likely only make things worse.

In the file there was only one letter, and it had just arrived. It was written out by hand in black ink in exceptionally neat block letters. Shea had been told of the change in his counsel, and he had written to Liana directly.

July 2, 2012

Dear Ms. Cohen,

I've been informed by your paralegal that you are now assigned to handle my appeal. I've done a little research on you in the law library. I'm impressed by your qualifications, and I see that you have won reversals on a number of very serious felony convictions. I'm pleased to have you on board.

Ms. Cohen, we don't know each other personally. I don't know why you chose this particular career path in the law. I can imagine that, coming out of a top school, you had your pick of well-paying positions where you didn't have to dirty your hands, so to speak.

If I were a betting man, and I'm not, I would wager that you became a public defender because you believe that every person deserves a fair shot under the law. I have complete confidence that, as my assigned counsel on appeal, you'll fight for my legal rights.

That being said, I hope you'll indulge me for a moment while I explain something important about my background that you won't learn from reading the transcripts of my trial.

I didn't have the privilege of a lot of parental attention growing up, for a number of reasons that I won't trouble you with right now. But I did have a grandmother who lived with us intermittently during my formative years. She was an Irish immigrant, and she was hardworking, stern, and demanded the best from me and my siblings. She was also a source of great warmth and kindness. My grandmother taught me many things, but one value she instilled with great ferocity was respect for women. My grandmother made sure that I grew up to be a gentleman.

Ms. Cohen, I'm no angel. Life has been too complicated for that. But I didn't rape Jennifer Nash. Hurting a woman goes against everything I was taught. I'm quite sure that every client you represent protests his innocence, and you must view this with a huge dose of skepticism. However, in this case, I'm telling you the truth. I swear it on my grandmother's life.

I understand that there may be fruitful avenues of appeal that have nothing to do with my guilt or innocence in this matter. However, as my attorney, it's very important for me to have you understand and believe in your heart that I didn't commit this crime. You will, of course, glean my defense from my testimony at trial. I just wanted to give you a heads-up.

I pray that you will have the courage to stand by me.

And then it was signed, "Sincerely, Danny Shea."

"Who is this guy?" Liana said. She'd never received a letter remotely like this one—the vocabulary, the pointed articulation, the subtlety of the legal understanding, and the seeming sincerity. She had the unsettling thought that this defendant might be better off representing himself. Liana read the letter to Deb.

"Maybe he's the one," Deb said, chewing noisily on a wad of grape-flavored bubble gum.

"Excuse me?" Liana looked up from the letter, which had drawn her in for a third read.

"Your innocent guy. The one you were meant to represent who restores your hope. You never know," Deb said, casually throwing the thought out as she checked her manicure to see if she needed a fresh coat.

"I do know," Liana said, peeved. "First of all, you were supposed to represent him, not me. So he's really your guy, not mine. Don't go giving me any of that 'meant to be' crap. And just because he has a crossword-worthy vocabulary and dredges up Grandma doesn't make him innocent. Remember, I'm not playing that game anymore."

"Okay, whatever you say," Deb said. "Still, that letter is intriguing. Look for his picture." Sometimes the file included the Prisoner Movement Sheet, which was just that—a piece of paper with the defendant's photograph on it that allowed the security personnel to relocate the prisoner, either within the facility or from one facility to another, and keep track of who they were moving. It took her a few minutes, but Liana came up with the document.

Although the photo was in black and white, there was no

mistaking it—Mr. Shea was strikingly handsome, even in his mug shot, with long wavy hair falling over his eyes, high cheek bones, and a strong jaw. Not in a fake, movie-star way either, although he bore more than a passing resemblance to a young Brad Pitt—before Jen and Angelina and all those kids took a toll on him. Liana passed the photo to Deb.

"Damn," said Deb. "Can't say I have ever wanted to sleep with a client before, but for him, I would make an exception."

"How does a guy with that kind of intelligence and those looks turn out to be so evil?" Liana mused.

"You didn't just ask that, did you?" Deb said with mock incredulity. "Remember, you no longer have to pretend to look for the good in your client, but you can't trash talk him either. Stay neutral, Counselor, if that's the best you can do. Now get to work, before Gerry does another patrol."

Before she cracked the binding on the two-thousand-page transcript, Liana stole another glance at the photograph of Danny Shea in the file. His eyes bore into her from the page, and she giggled, wondering at her own bad timing that she had sworn off "liking" her clients just as Shea landed on her desk. But she followed Deb's advice and kept the thought to her herself.

She settled down in her chair and ran her thumb through a big chunk of pages at the beginning of the transcript. The first four hundred or so were the record of the jury selection, the judge's instructions to the jury before the trial started, and the opening statements of both the prosecutor and defense counsel. She'd pore through these later, dissecting each word as she looked for the legal errors that often could be found in what appeared to be the more mundane parts of the trial.

For now, Liana decided that she'd treat herself by starting with the actual story of what happened. This was the best part—like reading a dime-store crime novel where you could root for the bad guy, the defendant, without feeling guilty, because you knew in advance that he ended up in prison where he belonged. She flipped to the page with the heading "Direct Examination of the Complainant" and let the movie play out in her head. Jennifer Nash stated her name and address for the record and swore to tell the truth:

The Prosecutor: Ms. Nash, how old are you?

Ms. Nash: I'm 19.

The Prosecutor: And how old were you on July 4, 2010?

Ms. Nash: I was 18.

The Prosecutor: I want to direct your attention to July 4, 2010. Were you a student at that time, or were you working? What were you doing that day?

Ms. Nash: I graduated from high school in the spring. I was working in the McDonald's near my parents' apartment so I could make some extra cash for school in the fall. I was planning to go to Kingsborough Community College in September.

The Prosecutor: Okay. I want to focus on the night. What were your hours at the McDonald's?

Ms. Nash: I was working a 6 p.m. to 11 p.m. shift.

The Prosecutor: And did you finish at 11 p.m.? Where did you go after work?

Ms. Nash: Well, I was supposed to meet my boyfriend, Daryl, after work. But he texted me he wasn't coming. I was pissed off, because I thought he might be cheating on me with this girl who he knew from his summer job. I guess I was kind of crying when I came out of the McDonald's, and then I saw him.

[Witness points at the defendant].

Defense Counsel: Objection, Your Honor. We had no notice that an in-court identification would be made today.

The Court: Well, I think that was pretty spontaneous, Counselor. I don't think the prosecutor knew either. Anyway, you have indicated in the pretrial proceedings, and I don't want to get specific in front of the jury, but that identity will not be contested, so the objection is overruled.

The Prosecutor: Okay, Ms. Nash. So you saw the defendant. Where did you see him and what happened?

Ms. Nash: I saw him outside of the McDonald's. He was in that little playground, just sitting on one of the benches. I guess I looked upset. He came up to me and asked me if I was okay.

The Prosecutor: Ms. Nash, do you need to take a break? Would you like a tissue?

Give me a break. We know she's emotional; do you really have to rub it in the jurors' faces? Get on with it.

Ms. Nash: No, I'm okay.

The Prosecutor: So what happed after the defendant asked you if you were okay?

Ms. Nash: Well, it was July 4th, and he asked me if I wanted to watch the fireworks and whether my building had a rooftop we could access. He said he had some weed, and we could smoke and just relax up there. I guess I sort of wanted to get back at Daryl, and I didn't want to go home, so I said yes.

The Prosecutor: And then what happened, Ms. Nash?

Ms. Nash: Well, we started to go to the door that went up to the roof, and I realized this was probably stupid—I mean, I didn't even really know this guy, and he was kind of old. So I told him I'd changed my mind.

Liana could hear her mother's voice in her head: *A girl is always entitled to change her mind.*

The Prosecutor: So what happened after you told the defendant you had changed your mind?

Ms. Nash: Well, he sort of was, like, pulling me up the stairs, but the whole time he was also telling me it would be fun, and he had some weed, and he had a six-pack of Budweiser. I mean, he kind of convinced me to go up there, and he was sort of forcing me at the same time.

Defense Counsel: Objection, Your Honor. I mean, what is the jury supposed to make of that?

The Court: Well, I guess the jury will make of it what it will. Please continue.

The Prosecutor: Okay, Ms. Nash. So you went up the stairs with the defendant. Did you reach the roof? I know this will be difficult, but you need to tell the members of this jury what happened to you when you got up to the roof.

Ms. Nash: So we got up to the roof. First we smoked a joint, and then we drank some beer. I was feeling a lot more relaxed, and I was kind of forgetting about Daryl a little, which was good. We saw some of the fireworks going on out over the water. I guess it was nice for a little bit. Then he asked me, did I want to dance? I said, "What? There ain't no music up here, how are we going to dance?" And he said he had some music on his iPhone and he would turn it on. So he did, and we kind of slow danced a little.

Liana found herself drifting, trying to remember the last time she and Jakob had slow danced. She loved that feeling of holding him close and swaying to the music; no dancing lessons were required, but Jakob still felt self-conscious. When she looked up, Deb was staring at her. "Girlfriend, you were far away there for a minute."

"Yeah," said Liana. "My rape case took a suddenly romantic turn, and it kind of got me thinking. Am I still allowed to say stuff like that?"

"Honey," Deb said, "in the confines of our little office, you can say whatever the fuck you want." Liana had never been more grateful for Deb.

The Prosecutor: What happened after you slow danced with the defendant?

Ms. Nash: Well, we were dancing, and then all of a sudden, he had my back up against the wall, and he was kissing me and rubbing his hands up and down my body. I guess the weed and the beer had kind of made my brain mushy, because at first I was like, "Okay, this is cool," but then he unzipped my jeans and pulled them down, and before I knew it, he was pushing himself in me. I was screaming and crying and trying to get out from under him, but he had one hand over my mouth and the rest of his body pinning me against the wall. He was ripped, like a weight lifter or something—he was so strong. Maybe I could have that tissue now?

The Prosecutor: Of course. You take your time. This is very traumatic.

Defense Counsel: Objection, Your Honor. If the prosecutor could please refrain from commentary.

The Court: Yes. I think the testimony will speak for itself.

The Prosecutor: I'm sorry, Your Honor. Okay, Ms. Nash, if you could go on and just finish telling the jury what happened.

Ms. Nash: Okay. Well, he kept going at it for a while; I don't think he really finished, but he got pretty close, and then I noticed my younger brother and one of his friends had came up on the rooftop, I guess to watch the fireworks. I yelled, "Jimmy!" and this guy froze, and I was able to get free and run—I left my purse on the roof, but I ran down the stairs with my brother and into my parents' apartment on the fourth floor. I told them what had just happened, and they called the police.

The Prosecutor: And where was the defendant during this time, if you know?

Ms. Nash: Well, when I saw him, he had zipped up his jeans, and he was waiting in the lobby of the building. He was just standing there when the police came. He didn't try to run or nothing.

The Prosecutor: Okay, Ms. Nash. Now, you had not given the defendant permission to have sex with you that night, had you?

Ms. Nash: No, I didn't.

The Prosecutor: And did the police take you to the hospital and have the doctors collect a rape kit?

Ms. Nash: Yes.

The Prosecutor: That's all I have for the complainant at this time.

The Court: Very well. We will take a short recess before the cross-examination, if anyone needs to use the facilities, now would be a good time.

Liana realized that, having downed several cups of coffee before and after she'd come to work that morning, she needed to use the facilities herself, and this seemed like as good a time as any. When she opened the door to the ladies room, Deb was standing at the sink, splashing water on her face.

"Hey," Liana said. "I was so lost in the testimony that I didn't even see you leave the room." She looked more closely at Deb. "You know, your color doesn't look too good."

"I'm not feeling great. I'm sure it's just the stress of getting that final brief in. No biggie," Deb said.

Liana was instantly flooded with the memory of the first time she'd ever heard Deb's name. She'd been hired for the job but not yet started when Gerry asked her to the barbeque he hosted at his brownstone in the Village each summer. Gerry loved to entertain, and he'd invited the attorneys and the staff over for sliders and shwarma chicken and cedar-planked salmon. As Liana chatted with her soon-to-be colleagues, someone mentioned that Deb was not there because she wasn't feeling well.

"I heard she thinks she might have toxic shock syndrome," one of the attorneys announced.

"Oh my God. That could only happen to Deb," the paralegal sighed.

"What's toxic shock syndrome?" one of the men asked.

"It's a bacterial infection caused by leaving a tampon in too long."

Liana, always on the squeamish side when it came to bodily functions, was horrified that something so personal would be bandied about so casually, especially in front of her, a total stranger. She quickly crossed the small backyard to escape the conversation. Deb hadn't had TSS, but it was an incident Liana had trouble erasing from her mind.

"Have you thought about seeing a doctor? I could go with you, if you want."

It was not an offer lightly made. Liana had a fear of all things medical that bordered on a clinical phobia, the source of which any amateur shrink or good hairdresser could have diagnosed. Liana's father had suffered his first heart attack when she was eleven, an event that would be traumatic for any preteen girl but was worse for an only child. As things panned out, Liana had been a twenty-six-year-old woman when her father passed away. But those intervening fifteen years had been suffused with subconscious dread and filled with medical close calls—she had been summoned from school to her father's bedside on numerous occasions. The experience of growing up that way had robbed her of a casual serenity that she admired in others who'd had more placid childhoods. It also meant that she almost never saw a doctor.

"You have no idea what it's like having a two-year-old and no husband and no help. When would I possibly go see a doctor?" Deb sounded upset, and Liana backed off. Of course she had no idea what it was like to have a two-year-old. When Deb turned to go into the stall, Liana left her in the bathroom and returned to her desk, not wanting to intrude further.

She opened the transcript to the cross-examination of the complainant. This was where the defense attorney, if he was worth his salt, could make the most sympathetic victim look like an outright liar. But it was a delicate affair when the charge was rape—you had to be very careful not to make it look like you were blaming the victim while simultaneously demonstrating to the jury that there were two sides to the story. Liana always got excited at this point, irrationally anticipating that the complaining witness would suddenly cave and admit that, in fact, the defendant had done nothing wrong at all. Despite Gerry's accusation that she wasn't pro-defendant enough, Liana knew that she engaged in this fantasy, even though she knew that the defendant ultimately had been convicted by the jury and that's why she now had the case. At this moment, she was entirely in Danny Shea's corner.

Defense Counsel: Ms. Nash, did you say that Mr. Shea—that's the defendant, but I prefer to call him Mr. Shea—did you say that he was a total stranger to you on July 4, 2010?

Ms. Nash: Yes, he was a stranger to me.

Defense Counsel: But you had seen him around before, right? In the McDonald's, or maybe in the neighborhood?

Ms. Nash: Well, yeah, I guess so. I had seen him a few times.

Defense Counsel: In fact, he had eaten in the McDonalds that very evening? Ordered a Big Mac and fries from you, about 9:00?

Ms. Nash: Yes.

Defense Counsel: In fact, he often ate at the McDonald's, and he would sort of engineer the line so that he could place his order with you, isn't that right?

Ms. Nash: I guess. I didn't really pay much attention to him.

Defense Counsel: Well, Ms. Nash, Mr. Shea was always pleasant; he would say hello and goodbye and thank you, right? He kind of stood out that way from some of the other customers that came in, didn't he?

Ms. Nash: You could say that. He was polite.

Defense Counsel: And he stood out in another way, didn't he, Ms. Nash? He was very handsome, wasn't he? I mean the kind of looks that most women would notice, wouldn't you say?

Ms. Nash: I don't really know. He wasn't my type.

Defense Counsel: No? Yet you agreed to meet him when you got out of work that night to go have a date on the roof?

Man, this attorney is good.

She wasn't often impressed with defense counsel at trial, especially those who were appointed for indigent defendants. She knew from her own experience doing appeals that, while there could be some very highly qualified and talented attorneys who worked for public interest organizations like hers, a lot of the attorneys who took these jobs were scrubs. So far, this guy was one to write home about. He had already succeeded in suggesting that Nash was hiding something—specifically, that she had at least a passing acquaintance with the defendant and maybe more.

Ms. Nash: Well, I agreed to go up there at first, but I didn't know what he was going to do to me.

Defense Counsel: Okay. But you were sort of friendly with Mr. Shea; he always said hello, and he was polite, and he had taken a certain interest in you, night after night in the McDonald's. And then he noticed when you were upset about Daryl, and he seemed genuinely concerned about you, right?

Ms. Nash: I guess you could say that.

Defense Counsel: Well, Ms. Nash, I don't want to put words in your mouth. I'm just trying to get an understanding of what happened here. So here's this guy. He's a little older than you; he's kind of hot. He's made a point of trying to talk to you over the last few weeks at your job. Then you get off work on July 4 and he's waiting for you outside—just sitting in the playground, right? Nothing threatening there, right?

Ms. Nash: No, not then.

Defense Counsel: Okay. So you go up to the roof— you testified that you shared a joint; you each had a beer. You are feeling better than you did earlier in the evening?

Ms. Nash: Yes.

Defense Counsel: Then Mr. Shea takes it to the next level. He asks you to dance. You dance. So far, so good, right?

Ms. Nash: Yeah. The dancing was weird, but it was okay.

Defense Counsel: Okay. So you dance for a while, and then Mr. Shea makes his move. He kisses you.

Liana was embarrassed to admit it to herself, but her palms were sweaty. She didn't realize how mesmerized she had become by the rhythm of defense counsel's cross-examination, and she was totally immersed in the slow dance and the kissing that followed. Sometimes, the transcripts dragged, and it was hard for her to become engaged in the action. This one was a page-turner. Liana wondered if the women on the jury had been similarly carried away, especially with Danny Shea right there in the room with them. But she knew that the verdict of guilt had been unanimous, so clearly the female jurors had been able to focus better than she.

Ms. Nash: Yes. He kissed me, and then he raped me.

Defense Counsel: Objection, Your Honor. That's the ultimate question for the jury. It is improper for Ms. Nash to testify to that.

The Court: Okay. Let's everyone cool off. Continue your cross-examination.

Defense Counsel: Okay, Ms. Nash. Now, you were living with your parents at this point, is that correct?

Ms. Nash: Yes.

Defense Counsel: And they were cool with you hanging out with Daryl—they knew Daryl. But you knew they wouldn't be too happy if they knew you had gone up to the roof with a guy you just knew casually from the McDonald's, right?

Ms. Nash: No. They definitely would have been angry about that.

Defense Counsel: So when your younger brother came up to the roof and saw you messing around with Mr. Shea, you were afraid he would tell your parents, weren't you?

Ms. Nash: No, that's not how it was. Jimmy saw that he was hurting me.

Defense Counsel: Well, didn't you think Jimmy would go down to the apartment and rat you out to your parents, and that's why you took off so fast—even leaving your purse there on the roof?

Ms. Nash: No, you're twisting what happened.

Defense Counsel: Am I? Didn't you just testify that Mr. Shea waited around in the lobby for the police to arrive? Why would he do that if he had just raped you?

The Prosecutor: Objection, Your Honor. He's badgering the witness.

Defense Counsel: Withdrawn, Your Honor. I am done with this witness.

Liana had been so absorbed in the drama she hadn't noticed that Deb had not come back from the bathroom. She half walked, half ran down the hall to the ladies' room. She checked the stalls, but no Deb, so she went to Tony's desk to see if Deb had signed out for the day. She had. "Did Deb look okay when she left?"

Tony said, "She looked all right. She said she'd be in first thing on Monday."

"Okay," Liana said. It was after five and time to go. She gathered up her things, turned off her computer, and straightened her desk chair. As much as she wanted to read Danny Shea's version of the events of July Fourth, it would keep.

It's not like he's going anywhere anyway.

CHAPTER 4

Liana glanced at her watch. It was after seven o'clock, and soon the sun would set, and it would be too late to go to Friday night services. She looked out the window of her apartment, hoping to catch sight of Jakob so they could walk together down the block to Darchei Tikva, "Paths of Hope," one of the myriad Jewish synagogues of every stripe in her Upper West Side neighborhood. Although traditional, DT was an eclectic Manhattan institution through and through. The attendees were young, hip, and diverse; most of all, DT prided itself on its tolerance. The members were welcoming, and no one asked anything about Liana's and Jakob's religious background or practice, which was next to nil. They had wandered in one Friday night several months earlier, following a group of well-dressed young professionals, and liked the atmosphere. What began as a lark had become something more for Liana.

The rabbi, Jordan Nacht, noticed Liana and Jakob when they first started coming to services and was always solicitous, bonding with her over their mutual love of the New York Mets, chatting about their work, or asking after Liana's mom. He was ten years older than Liana, married with a bunch of kids, a transplant from Louisville with Southern style and a drawl to match. Liana appreciated that, as marginal a part of the synagogue community as she was, the rabbi knew her; it made the big city feel a little smaller. Like most of the other women congregants, Liana was not impervious to the rabbi's charms. His singing voice was so sweet that sometimes Liana blushed.

Jakob is running late, as usual.

Jakob was often the last attorney on his team to call it a night, putting in that extra time that made him one of Wilcox's highest billing and most prized associates. Just as she was contemplating calling to tell him she'd meet him at DT, Jakob buzzed. Liana hit the button, unlocking the outer door to the building, and locked her apartment door behind her. The security in her building was almost nonexistent; Jakob would have had to wait only another minute before someone let him in, even though he wasn't a tenant. Liana was all too familiar with the modus operandi of burglars, robbers, and other nefarious characters; she made a practice of locking her door and using the chain whenever she was home.

She stepped out of the elevator in the lobby and crashed straight into Jakob. She was enveloped in the familiar scent of his Armani Code aftershave and immediately forgot her earlier impatience in an overwhelming wave of comfort and longing, the sort of Proustian moment only smell can evoke. He put his arms around her and lifted her in the air.

"Put me down!" she giggled. "You look handsome."

"I went home after work to shower and shave," Jakob said. He was wearing her favorite pink oxford button-down and tan linen trousers. He dressed straight out of an L.L. Bean catalog, but it was a look she loved.

"And you look much too beautiful to be going to synagogue," he added, stepping back and admiring Liana's new ribbed jersey dress, which clung to her curves in all the right places. "We should be going out dancing or something."

"Maybe another time," Liana said. "I'm in the mood for this."

"Whatever floats your boat," Jakob said amiably.

They walked slowly down Seventy-Sixth Street, hand in hand. After a few minutes, Liana stopped in the middle of the sidewalk, just steps from the synagogue, and turned to Jakob.

"Can I ask you a question?"

"Of course."

"Why do you come to services on Friday night? What do you like about the experience?" She knew what appealed to her—how when the people arrived, each with his or her individual work problems and family issues, they were transformed into something greater than themselves. She felt herself drawn to that sense of community, waiting subconsciously for the moment when she would transition from watching to belonging. But she worried that Jakob was not on board with her forays into religious observance, however tentative.

"Truth?" Jakob asked.

"Of course. Don't we always tell each other the truth?"

"I come because it's meaningful to you, and I want to be with you, wherever you are." Jakob squeezed Liana's hand and started to walk again.

Liana stopped in her tracks. "Jakob! That's terrible! I'm guilty of religious coercion!"

He laughed and walked back to where she was standing.

"Don't be silly, Li. There are plenty of things I like about the service," he said patiently. "I like the way it's a little oasis in my otherwise frenetic week. I like the music, and I appreciate the poetry of the prayers. But it's not so terrible to do something just because it makes the other person happy. That's called love." Jakob wrapped his big comforting arm around Liana's shoulders, and they walked the last few steps to the building.

When they reached the synagogue, they parted ways—in accordance with tradition, women were seated on one side of a large circular sanctuary, men on the other. The Friday night service was brief but moving, filled with beautiful melodies welcoming the Sabbath Queen. There was the feeling that the day of rest had finally arrived and that some peace could be attained for the next twenty-five hours. No phones would ring, no email would be checked, no money would be spent. Liana was only a spectator, but she envied the discipline of unplugging and the rewards it offered. At least from her vantage point, these people seemed to know where and to whom they belonged.

At the end of the service, the president of the congregation—a young guy with a waxed handlebar mustache—and an adorable little dark-haired girl in a fuchsia dress hanging off his left leg rose to make announcements.

"I regret to inform the congregation of the passing of our longtime member Harry Rosen. The family will be sitting shiva at their apartment on Seventieth Street until Wednesday morning. May the family know no further sorrow."

"Amen!"

"On a happy note, I want to announce the engagement of Gideon Marks to Eva Sussman!"

"Mazel tov!"

"And I also have the pleasure of announcing the birth of a baby boy to David and Michelle Barkan. The bris will follow morning services on Thursday."

"Mazel tov!"

Liana always felt like a bit of an imposter chiming in with the congregation's hearty "amens!" and "mazel tovs!" but the goodwill was infectious. "Finally," the president intoned, "we would like to announce that we are starting a program for newly marrieds—by which we mean anyone married two years or less. There will be a rotating Shabbat dinner on Friday nights so you can get to know one another. Please contact the rabbi's wife if you are interested in participating."

Liana felt a catch in her throat. Every now and again, and with increasing frequency, Jakob brought up the topic of marriage. He was ready. She wasn't sure.

Liana left the sanctuary and looked around for Jakob in the lobby. It was Rabbi Nacht's custom to greet the congregants as they left the building, wishing them "Shabbat Shalom" and exchanging a few pleasantries before going home to have dinner with his family. Usually Liana looked forward to those few moments of connection with the rabbi—in accord with his religious practice, he didn't shake hands with women, but he always made eye contact in a way that was almost more satisfying than a touch would have been. But tonight she couldn't face the rabbi with the "newly marrieds" echoing in her head. Jakob didn't care about the meet and greet, and she easily led him out the side door without anyone noticing.

After dinner at their local Italian place, they walked back to her apartment. Before she knew it, Jakob had pulled her close to him on the sidewalk in a goodnight embrace. He was almost eight inches taller than she, and her lips pressed into the warmth of his neck as she breathed him in.

"Stay," she whispered.

"Li, I would do anything to stay and chase you around your apartment all night long," he said, playfully pulling at her dress. "But I have to go back to work. We have an electronic filing due in the Circuit on Monday. I'm going to be in the office the whole weekend."

She pressed herself against him, as if perhaps the warmth of her body would melt away his work deadline, but he eased himself away from her.

"I hate your job," Liana pouted.

"I love my job," Jakob said, "but I hate it when it keeps me away from you."

Do the married men also go back to the firm at night and leave their wives standing outside on the sidewalk? Is that what's in store for me?

She was well aware that big New York City law firms were pressure cookers and that the young associates especially worked insane hours. It was one of the reasons she hadn't taken a job at Wilcox herself. But Jakob seemed to volunteer to take on the extra burden, as though she didn't exist.

Liana looked down at her feet. "I miss you, Jay; that's all," she said quietly.

"I miss you too. It won't always be this way; I promise. Go get some sleep, babe." Jakob lifted Liana's face tenderly in his hands and gave her a quick kiss before he walked away toward the subway.

Sometimes Liana wondered if she would feel more settled in their relationship if she and Jakob were living together. When they'd graduated from law school and both accepted jobs in Manhattan, they had talked about it, even looked at some rentals. But partly out of deference to Liana's mother, who claimed she was old-fashioned and would be embarrassed to tell her friends that her unmarried daughter was "living in sin," and partly out of their own concerns that they weren't quite ready after just a year of long-distance dating, they'd settled on separate places. Now, three years later, the arrangement felt artificial.

She stepped into the tiny bathroom, stripped off her clothes, and turned on the shower full blast, high heat. The shower was what Liana liked best about her place, which, apart from its prime location, was a fairly nondescript one-bedroom that she'd rented from a friend who had moved on to better digs when she'd gotten married several years earlier. There was no doorman, and the apartment was boxy and small, with barely a kitchen, and looked out on an ugly white brick building across Seventy-Sixth Street. On the corner of Amsterdam Avenue was the Riverside Funeral Home. At first Liana was disturbed by the proximity of the dead, but Riverside had turned out to be quite a good neighbor. The doors were always open, and there were security guys and other employees working and visible round the clock. If, returning home late at night, Liana were ever spooked by someone threatening walking down the block, she knew that she could take shelter with the poor souls awaiting a proper Jewish burial.

But the shower was Liana's preferred refuge. She could stand in the scalding water for fifteen minutes and let her mind run over anything that was troubling her. Sometimes she ruminated over a legal issue she was trying to work to a client's advantage, and a clear, elegant solution would come to her as the bathroom's mirror steamed over. More often than not, she contemplated Jakob and their relationship, but so far, no matter how long she'd stayed under the punishing water, no clarity had come. There was no doubt in her mind that they loved each other. But things had been so much more straightforward in the beginning, when they were students with none of the pressures of the adult working world and all that mattered was being together, preferably wearing as little clothing as possible. Now he wanted her to commit to their future together at the same time his career ambitions were pulling him away from her.

Liana put a glob of shampoo in her hand and furiously attacked her hair. Her coiffure was a source of constant worry and required focused maintenance. On a good day, she looked sassy and cute, with a plethora of messy but chic blond curls setting off her blue eyes. On a bad day, the frizz was unbearable, and no amount of gel or mousse could contain the damage. She poured half a bottle of high-octane conditioner on her hair and let it do its work.

As the hot water beat down on her back, Liana played the highlight reel of meeting Jakob that summer four years earlier. She could pinpoint the exact moment she had first been aware of him. She had just arrived at the Wilcox & Finney annual Sail Around the City event—the firm had rented the Circle Line, and the summer associates and the attorneys were treated to hors d'oeuvres, an open bar, a jazz quartet, and spectacular views of Lower Manhattan. Liana had been at the firm for two weeks, and she didn't know many people. After getting herself a Corona, she was leaning on the railing of the boat, lost in thought, looking out over New York Harbor at the Statue of Liberty, when she sensed someone near her.

"Think she's going to sail the ship?" A very deep but lilting voice came from somewhere to her right, so close the man speaking might have been touching her.

"What?" Liana turned toward the sound, and she saw Jakob, six feet tall and athletically built, looking scrubbed and wholesome, his curly hair neatly cropped in stark contrast to her unruly mop. He lifted his chin over his left shoulder, and Liana followed his gaze. There, in the middle of the deck, stood a fifty-or-so-year-old woman in full blue-and-white sailor suit regalia fashioned into a pseudotrendy, "way too short for a woman her age" dress, gold epaulettes on the shoulders, and white sailor cap perched absurdly on her head.

"Oh my God!" Liana gasped. "Who is she, and why is she wearing that costume?"

Jakob smiled. "That's Irene McDonald; her husband's the managing partner of the firm. And she's wearing that *costume*, as you so aptly put it, because she's playing a role—best supporting spouse."

"I don't get it," Liana said, but she would have said anything to keep Jakob talking. His voice was gripping, and the fact that he knew who was who and what was going on was very sexy.

"Well," Jakob continued, "he is the rainmaker, and she's the one standing by his side, keeping the whole operation afloat."

"Wow. That's quite an analysis based on so little evidence. I don't think I could ever play that part," Liana mused.

"You won't have to," Jakob said. "You'll be the rainmaker partner, and your husband will have to wear the sailor's suit."

Liana laughed. "I don't think so," she said. "I doubt very

much I'm going to have that kind of career. And I'm not that attracted to nautical."

"Let me guess," Jakob said. "Do-gooder?"

"Guilty as charged," Liana said, smiling. "And you? You fancy yourself a big partner at Wilcox & Finney someday?"

"I do," Jakob said, turning serious. "It's one of the top firms in the city, and it has the best antitrust department—that's my beat. And I have to get a job where I can pay off my law school loans in some reasonable amount of time—my father has plenty of money, but he felt it was a good lesson in responsibility for me to pay my own way."

"Well then, you better start recruiting some cute sailors to audition for supporting actress," Liana said.

"How about we just begin with some sushi, before these hungry hordes demolish all the food?" They spent the rest of the event side by side, Jakob clueing Liana in to all the office politics and personalities, Liana hanging on his every word but pretending not to. When they had filled their plates, they sat on a bench on the upper deck of the boat, the lights of lower Manhattan just beginning to show off as the sun set.

"So what do you think of the whole summer associate thing so far?" Jakob asked, popping a spicy tuna roll into his mouth.

Liana sighed. "They have me on this case—we represent an accounting firm charged in this big fraud. I sit all day in a small conference room on the sixteenth floor with no windows, looking at computer runs—hundreds of pages of printouts of bank account ledgers—as if I'm going to suddenly notice some random numerical entry and say, 'Aha!' Honestly, I'm out of my depth."

"Sounds to me like you're doing just fine," Jakob said. They sat listening to a reggae band play some Marley, watching the skyline come ablaze. After a few minutes, the musicians went on break, and Jakob asked the keyboard player if he would mind him fooling around a bit. When he got the okay, he took Liana's hand.

"Come sit next to me; I want to play you something. It's an old show tune from *The Music Man* that the Beatles covered." He sat on the piano bench, leaving enough space for her to be close at his side.

As Liana sat, transfixed, he started to play, humming quietly but unselfconsciously, as though he truly had been expecting this moment.

"That's lovely," Liana murmured.

"Wait, here's the bridge—it's my favorite part. Listen. Can you hear the chord progression?" Jakob asked. "B flat, B flat minor, F . . ." Liana had no idea what he was talking about, and it didn't matter.

He kissed her then, somehow magically managing to keep playing for a moment while he did, ensuring that "Till There Was You" would always be the soundtrack of their romance.

By summer's end they were inseparable, until forced to part in September to go back to their respective law schools— Liana making the trek north to New Haven and Jakob taking the subway back uptown to Columbia. The year they'd spent apart had been simultaneously excruciating and unspeakably sweet; they'd appreciated each other in a way that they might not have if it had all been easy. And now, these years that they were together and in the same place were sometimes harder than Liana thought they should be. She and Jakob often battled their stress alone instead of together.

Would it be better if we were married?

She rinsed the conditioner out and pulled a brush through her hair, all with the shower still running. She thought for the thousandth time that she was lucky that she didn't have to pay for hot water. The prospect of not seeing Jakob for the rest of the weekend saddened her. She tossed and turned in bed, the rollercoaster of a week leaving her anxious, waiting for the other shoe to drop.

CHAPTER 5

"I'll have a tall coffee, room for milk, please."

Liana had resisted calling a small coffee a "tall" coffee for years, finding it just utterly absurd corporate manipulation, but lately she'd decided that she better learn to pick her battles. After last week's encounter with Gerry, she felt like she had an actual fight on her hands. She hoped against hope that there was a killer good legal issue in Shea's case so she could whale on his brief and make Gerry eat his words. Liana wasn't ordinarily a violent person, but when she got offended, the litigator in her came out.

"Sometimes I wonder what your insides must look like from consuming all that caffeine," Deb said by way of greeting as they got into the elevator.

"My insides are just fine; they thrive on corrosive materials," Liana replied. "But that reminds me, are you feeling better?"

"I'm not sure. My stomach hurts sometimes, and I have to pee a lot. And no, don't ask if I'm pregnant—definitely not."

"Don't you have a doctor you could go see?" Liana asked again when they reached their office. She herself didn't believe in routine medical care; she went to the doctor only in dire emergencies. "I'm offering to go with you—take me up on it before I wimp out."

"I really only have my obstetrician from when Max was born," she said.

"Well, maybe that's an okay place to start."

"Okay, okay, little Miss Pain-in-the-Ass. I'll give her a call. And I don't need you to hold my hand, although I do appreciate your asking." Deb put on her earphones, tuning out Liana and everyone else, and went to work.

Liana eagerly turned her attention back to Shea's case. She felt as if she had been holding her breath all weekend, waiting to get back to that rooftop. His direct testimony was not very long; Liana supposed that defense counsel felt he had done enough damage when he'd cross-examined Ms. Nash that he didn't need to drag out Shea's side of the story, which would, in turn, expose him to an extensive cross-examination by the prosecutor. After Shea was sworn in and gave his name and address, the following testimony was taken:

Defense Counsel: Mr. Shea, how old were you on July 4, 2010?

The Defendant: I was 24.

Defense Counsel: And were you working or in school or what?

The Defendant: I was working in construction for my Uncle Liam. I worked whatever jobs he had—it wasn't really regular hours, but it was enough work to pay the rent. At night I took classes at Brooklyn College toward my BA. I was taking the summer session. I would get out of class most nights at around 9.

Defense Counsel: Okay. And what would you do after you got out of class? Would you head straight back to your apartment?

The Defendant: No. After class, I would head over to the McDonald's on Flatbush Avenue and grab some dinner. I knew it wasn't very healthy, but the first time I went in there, around the middle of June when classes started, I saw a cute girl behind the counter, and I had to come back.

Every night for a few weeks, I made sure to order just from her—to let other people in line go ahead of me even. And as the weeks went on, we became friends. She would ask me about the classes I was taking and the projects I was working on for Liam, and I would ask her about her family and her plans for the future. Nothing heavy, just friendly repartee. I didn't really think it would go anywhere; I was just killing time with a pretty woman.

Defense Counsel: And how old did you believe Ms. Nash to be?

The Defendant: Old enough to know she was flirting.

The Prosecutor: Objection.

The Defendant: I mean, I knew she had graduated from high school. She wasn't jailbait.

Defense Counsel: Okay. So let's talk about July 4, 2010. Tell us what you remember about that night.

The Defendant: Well, first of all, I didn't have work or class that evening, because it was July 4th. But I had gotten so accustomed to my interaction with Jennifer that I figured I would go to the McDonald's anyway, in case she was working the holiday. I got there around 9. Even though the sun had already set, the heat and humidity were relentless.

"Repartee," "relentless." Who the hell is this guy?
Liana was reminded of his letter to her in the file, where he had used the words "remiss" and "propensity" and "glean." This was no ordinary defendant. Half of her clients would write the word "trail" instead of "trial" in their letters. She wasn't making fun of anyone; most of these men had never had a real opportunity to go to school and make something of themselves. But Shea's accurate usage of high-wattage SAT-quality words was both startling and somewhat unnerving.

Defense Counsel: So, you got there at 9, and did you go into the McDonald's?

The Defendant: I went in, and I immediately spotted Jennifer behind the counter. There was a bit of a line—it seemed like people were trying to get their food sorted out before the fireworks display at 11. I waited until I could be next in line for Jennifer to take my order, and I asked for a Big Mac and fries. I could see right away that she looked distracted. I asked her what was up, and she said her boyfriend had broken their date for later. I admit that my heart skipped a beat—I thought, well, now she's free tonight, maybe she'd be willing to hang out with me.

Defense Counsel: So did you make a plan with her?

The Defendant: Yes. I told her I would wait for her out in the playground until her shift ended, and then maybe we could go up on the roof and watch the fireworks and chill out. I had brought some weed with me, and while she finished working, I went to the bodega on the corner and got a six-pack. I didn't have any thought that I would really get anywhere with her; I just figured we could have some fun.

Defense Counsel: Okay. So her shift ends. Then what happens?

The Defendant: Well, she came out to find me in the playground like we had arranged. I guess over the two hours since I had seen her she had gotten kind of worked up over the boyfriend, and she was crying. Now, I'm not saying I am any kind of Prince Charming, but I can't help being gallant with a damsel in distress.

The Prosecutor: Objection, Your Honor. This defendant is trying to make a mockery out of this trial.

Defense Counsel: Your Honor, he is entitled to testify on his own behalf and to tell the story from his point of view. It will be the jury's province to decide whose version to believe.

The Court: Well, I agree that the defendant's presentation has been more colorful than we usually hear, but let's carry on, Counselor.

Defense Counsel: Okay, cut the fancy language, Mr. Shea. Just tell us what happened next.

The Defendant: So I gave her a clean tissue I had in my pocket, and she mopped up her face a little—her eyeliner was running, and she looked pretty bummed out. I suggested again that we go up on the roof, and she said okay. We went up there, and we relaxed. We shared a J, and we each had a beer. The beer was really cold because I had just bought it, and it was incredibly refreshing in that heat. I think she was feeling better, and I was just happy to be there with her. Jennifer was a sweet girl. I liked the way she always wore her long brown hair pulled back. I'm not saying I had any big designs on her. I'm just saying it was a nice way to spend some time.

Defense Counsel: Now, you heard Ms. Nash say that you sort of half forced her, half cajoled her up onto that rooftop. Can you explain that?

The Defendant: Yes. She was flirting. She wasn't a child; she was a woman who had a boyfriend, maybe others in the past. She knew how to play the game.

The Prosecutor: Objection, Your Honor. This was not a game that night, and this is not a game that the defendant is playing here.

Defense Counsel: Your Honor, I asked the defendant a question about his perspective on testimony that the prosecution's witness gave here on the stand under oath. He is entitled to give his version of events and to express himself in his own words.

The Court: Okay. No one is going to abridge Mr. Shea's right to testify and invite a reversal on appeal. Go ahead, Mr. Shea.

Too bad.

This judge was awfully evenhanded, going above and beyond to protect the defendant's constitutional rights. If he'd been a bit more rash—told the defendant to wrap it up or something—Liana might have had something to work with. As it stood, this was a classic "she said, he said" case, and the jury had accepted what "she" said, even though "he" was more eloquent. Appeals that relied on trying to show that "he" was actually the more believable one rarely went anywhere, as the jury's decision was given deference by the reviewing court.

The Defendant: I wasn't trying to give offense. All I am saying is that she came up to the roof with me of her own free will, even if she was kind of a tease along the way. After we had smoked and drank a little, it was like she said—I asked her to dance. And after we danced under the stars for a while, we started to mess around.

Defense Counsel: Okay. So far, except for the minor details, you and Ms. Nash are largely in accord. From your standpoint, what happened next?

The Defendant: What happened next is that Jennifer was in a good mood. She had a buzz going, and she was angry with Daryl for ditching her. She said she was on the pill, and I took that as a green light. I'm not denying that I took the lead—that's the guy's prerogative.

Jeez. Maybe this jury just didn't understand this guy. He might've done better if he'd left his five-dollar words at home.

But she had to admit that his way of expressing himself was compelling to her; she could listen to him talk all night long. It was more than his vocabulary—although his use of language said something profound about him—he was a dramatic storyteller. Shea's narrative captivated Liana in a way no defendant's had before. He practically demanded that she believe his story.

The Defendant: So I undid her jeans and pulled down her underwear, and did the same for myself, and we made love standing up against the brick wall on the roof landing with the fireworks going off overhead.

The Prosecutor: Objection, Your Honor, to the term "made love"—that's a gross mischaracterization of the evidence.

The Defendant: What do you want me to say? We had sex? We fucked? I mean, yes, we did that too, but that isn't the way I talk. And I'm sorry if my understanding of what went on that night doesn't match Jennifer's, but I am happy to leave that decision in the capable hands of a jury of my peers.

Defense Counsel: Okay, Mr. Shea. No speeches. Just tell us what happened while you were having sex with Ms. Nash.

The Defendant: Well, things were going along fine. I was almost ready to climax, and I believe, based on my experience, that Ms. Nash was as well, and all of a sudden her younger brother and his friend appeared on the rooftop. Jennifer freaked. She was still living at home, and I think she panicked that her brother had seen what she was doing and would tell her parents. She ran out of there so fast she left her purse on the roof, which I picked up and took down to the lobby. I wasn't waiting for the police to come; I'm not an idiot. I had no idea anyone was calling the police because I knew I hadn't done anything wrong. I was waiting to see if Jennifer would come out so I could give her the purse and see if she wanted me to meet her parents and allay their fears if Jimmy had said anything.

Instead, I found myself surrounded by officers and hauled down to the precinct.

Defense Counsel: And do you have any prior criminal convictions, Mr. Shea?

The Defendant: No, sir, I do not.

Liana quickly read through the prosecutor's cross-examination of Shea. Although the assistant district attorney was combative, she didn't gain a lot of ground—the defendant was cleverer than she was, and she ended up looking a little prissy. Defense counsel then made the ballsy and unusual move of calling to the stand as a defense witness the first police officer to respond to the scene. The cops were almost always witnesses for the prosecution, not the defense, for obvious reasons. Although the officer testified that Ms. Nash appeared shaken—she was crying and being comforted by her parents—he also confirmed that he found Mr. Shea sitting in the lobby, holding Ms. Nash's hot-pink Gucci knock-off purse, a little wasted but plainly surprised when the police rushed into the building.

After the officer testified, the prosecutor and defense counsel entered into a stipulation that was read to the jury. In it, the parties represented that an expert in DNA testing and analysis from the Office of the Chief Medical Examiner would have testified that the vaginal swab in the rape kit collected from Ms. Nash was tested and semen was found. Two profiles were obtained from the vaginal swab; one female DNA, which belonged to Ms. Nash, and one male DNA. The male DNA profile matched a sample taken from Mr. Shea.

"You know what I hate most about sex crimes?" Liana asked, rolling her chair so close to Deb that their legs almost touched. "Hey, take out those earphones—I'm talking to you!"

"I heard you. Anyway, that's a pretty vague question, Counselor," Deb said. "And could you give me a little space here?"

Liana moved her chair back over to her desk. "I hate DNA!" She pounded her fist into her desk. "Once you have DNA evidence, you're totally fucked!"

"Literally," Deb said and then laughed at her own joke.

"I'm serious," Liana protested. "I don't know what I'm going to do with this case."

"Well, DNA does present the ultimate 'deny what you can't admit, and admit what you can't deny' scenario," Deb said, more reasonably. "I mean, once your guy's DNA was found in that girl's vagina, he couldn't say that the sex didn't happen or that he wasn't the one. The only defense left is that they were two consenting adults."

"And that defense almost never works," Liana said. The jury hadn't bought it here. But Liana wasn't so sure. Maybe Liana was swayed by Shea's good looks or the gripping way he expressed himself and his obvious intelligence. Or maybe it was the weeks of courting and the slow dancing that preceded the first kiss. More than anything, it was the fact that Shea had sat in that lobby with Jennifer Nash's purse in his hands. Although it was impossible to tell without seeing his demeanor on the stand, Liana thought that if she had been a juror, she almost certainly would have bought Shea's story, hook, line, and sinker.

"Deb, do you think there's any chance he could be telling the truth?" She couldn't believe she was even entertaining the question in her head, and now she had said it out loud.

"Does that matter to you?" Deb asked, not unkindly.

"No, I guess it doesn't," Liana answered.

Just going to do my job.

"Get some rest, Cohen—this case is messing with your head," Deb said, checking her watch and then heading for the door.

With the office to herself, Liana spun her chair around slowly, eyes on the ceiling, until she felt as physically disoriented as she did mentally. She had a lot of work to do. No way was she raising some lame generic issue that the prosecutor hadn't proved her case "beyond a reasonable doubt." Now that she knew the story and had been introduced to the cast of characters, she would read all of the sections of the record carefully—the pretrial hearings; the closing arguments; the judge's instructions to the jury on how to evaluate the evidence; and the notes sent out by the jury during the deliberations, asking the judge for clarifications on the law or asking to see exhibits. Liana knew there'd be something she could sink her teeth into; she could feel it in her bones.

As she got her things together and straightened up the surface of her desk, she noticed the message light flashing on her office phone. She'd barely moved from her chair since her midafternoon coffee run, but somehow she'd missed a call. Liana hit play and heard a recording of Tony accepting a collect call from Dannemora Correctional Facility, then transferring it to Liana's line. Danny Shea's voice was smooth and steady, with only the slightest tinge of fear.

"Hello, Ms. Cohen. This is Danny Shea. I hesitated before reaching out to you. I don't want to take you away from your work." Shea paused, either composing himself or deciding what to say next, Liana couldn't tell. "I really just wanted to make contact with you so you hear my voice in your head and aren't just reading my words on a typed page. Maybe it doesn't matter—" And now his voice broke slightly. "I just want to be real to you, Ms. Cohen. I want you to picture me, to hear me, to understand that there's a man in that trial transcript. I want you to feel how much is at stake here for me." She heard him inhale deeply before continuing. "That's all I wanted to say. Get home safely." And then the line went dead.

Liana stood staring at the telephone for a minute, as though she expected Shea to materialize in her office. She played the message again; Shea's voice was deep and soothing, a trace of pleading just below the surface of strength and confidence. He had no idea how real he was becoming for her, despite her best efforts to keep him at arm's length. She picked up her backpack and turned off the lights, standing in the darkened room, momentarily forgetting her own resolution to excise all emotion and sentimentality from her representation of Danny Shea. She felt wired—ablaze with professional lawyerly excitement and a pure hormonal rush that coursed through her in a volatile combination.

That night, after sleep eluded her for several hours, she took an Ambien and drifted off, visions of Jakob and Rabbi Nacht, Brad Pitt, and Danny Shea merging uncomfortably in her confused mind.

CHAPTER 6

Breakfast? Liana texted Jakob on a Sunday morning in late July.

Awesome, he texted back a few minutes later.

Office lobby in forty-five. Liana rolled out of bed, still sleepy. She had stayed up until two in the morning reading *Eclipse*, the third volume of the Twilight series, where Bella must choose between pledging her love to the gallant but undead Edward and becoming a vampire herself, or giving herself to Jacob, who appears to love her with fewer strings attached, although things are not always as they seem. Liana was Team Jacob all the way, but she was as drained by the struggle as Bella. She'd woken in the morning feeling that she would probably skip reading the final installment, unsure she could handle the drama.

Her Jakob had pulled another all-nighter at the firm, his third in as many months. Liana figured at least she could steal a few minutes with him before she headed out to Long Island to see her mom. Often, Jakob would make the trek with her; today he had to work on some hideous document production in the office all day. Liana wasn't sorry to be going by herself. Her mom had sounded somewhat wistful on the telephone lately. As an only child, Liana was accustomed to being the main support of her parents. After her father, Artie, passed away from a cardiac arrhythmia three years earlier at the age of sixty-seven, the electric current in his heart running amok, Phyllis had turned out to be much more independent than Liana had expected, and she was grateful. Still, it had to be terribly sad to be in the house by herself, surrounded by reminders of their life together and with so many years alone looming ahead of her.

Liana pulled on a pair of jeans and a decent T-shirt just out of the laundry and mostly unwrinkled. Her mother hated when she looked like a slob—how many times growing up had Liana heard the declaration, "Your appearance is a reflection on me!" Even as an adult, she would often put on an outfit and judge how she looked through her mother's somewhat critical eyes. She grabbed her backpack and headed over to the local bagel store. She bought Jakob two everything bagels with cream cheese, lox, and onion and then wondered if he kept a toothbrush in the office.

Good thing he's not kissing anyone at work.

When she got to his building, Jakob was nowhere to be seen. Liana sat down on a chair in the lobby. She couldn't go up to the firm; just being in the vicinity brought on the stomachache she had lived with the entire summer she had worked there. Jakob finally emerged from one of the elevator banks about ten minutes later and wrapped his arms tightly around her.

"Hey, stop—you're smooshing my bagels!" she said.

"Is that what they call them these days?" he said, raising his eyebrows in a good Groucho Marx imitation and making a furtive move toward her breasts.

"That's not part of this breakfast delivery," she said, slapping his hand away and attempting to sound offended through her smile.

"Thanks for doing this," Jakob said. "It's been a rough couple of days." He looked pasty and possibly unshowered, and Liana secretly hoped he could go home soon and freshen up.

"Let's sit outside in the sun; you could use an airing," Liana suggested. They went out the big revolving doors and sat side by side on the low wall that surrounded the building—Liana was always reminded of a moat, keeping her from reaching her beloved who was locked up inside the castle.

They ate in silence for a while, Jakob savoring his bagels as though he had not eaten in some time and Liana picking the chocolate chips out of her muffin and barely touching the rest. Although she knew it was irrational, she always lost her appetite when she was around the law firm.

"Come up and say hi to the team, okay?" Jakob said.

"No way!" Liana answered so quickly that it was clear she hadn't given the suggestion a moment's thought. "I'm not dressed," she added, lamely.

"It's Sunday morning, Li—you don't have to be dressed. Please, it's helpful to me. Frank likes you, and the associates enjoy hearing about your job." Jakob's attempt at reasonable was coming across as utterly exasperated.

"Be real, Jay—Frank likes anyone with two X chromosomes. And your coworkers don't enjoy hearing about my job because they are interested in criminal defense work—I'm entertainment. Like a freak show. They think what I do is totally off the grid. Lower than low."

"Look, Li, there's probably some truth to that. But do you think that's what I think too? Sometimes I feel as if you've labeled me "law firm asshole" and lumped me in with everyone else. It's not fair." Jakob sounded more hurt than angry, and Liana wished she hadn't gone down this road.

Before she could respond, her cell rang.

"Yeah, hi, Mom. Yes, I'm going to the train right now—yes, I got to see Jakob for a little bit. Sure, I'll take a taxi from the station; don't worry. Okay—see you soon."

Jakob shook his head slowly, fatigue and disappointment written all over his face. He looked at his watch and then at the doors before turning back to Liana. "I've got to go back in," he said. "Thanks for the bagels. I'll see you tonight, whenever I get out of here."

"I'll come up next time; I promise," Liana said but so quietly she didn't know if Jakob had heard. She watched him go back inside the building and across the floor to the elevator bank. Then she headed for the subway to Penn Station.

When Liana got to her mother's house, she found the front door unlocked and her mother in the shower.

Good thing she lives in a safe neighborhood.

Liana's mind filled involuntarily with the scenes of carnage that leapt off her transcript pages at work. She opened the unlocked bathroom door and yelled in, "Ma, I'm here."

"Good," her mother replied. "I'll be out in a little bit. There's coffee in the pot." Liana went into the kitchen and poured herself a cup in her favorite mug. She sat down at the round kitchen table, the same one that had been there since her parents moved in when her mother was pregnant with Liana some thirty years before. The legs were black wrought iron, all curlicues, promising a fancy eating surface but delivering only a smooth dark brown wood veneer. Its surface unmarked, it bore no evidence of the years it had served as the central gathering place of Liana's childhood for meals and arts and crafts projects, the rendezvous point of her teenaged friends at two in the morning when they'd had the munchies, and now as the last holdout of her aging mother's campaign to stay in her home, alone, against her daughter's wishes.

In the three years since Liana's father's death, the kitchen table had increasingly become her mother's anchor. Every inch of its surface was perpetually covered with various documents, which were merely pushed aside when she ate a meal. The projects were narrowly focused—telephone bills and scraps of paper would attest to an argument she'd had with AT&T over a surcharge; recipes or book reviews were cut out for Liana but not for herself. As her knees had started to stiffen, Phyllis would use the sturdy table to help get herself out of her chair, propelling herself toward the kettle on the stove and a cup of mango tea. Now Liana sat at the table, sipping her coffee, wondering if there was any specific reason her mother had been so melancholy the last few times she'd spoken with her.

Phyllis finally emerged, dressed in a pink terry robe and with her wet hair combed back from her forehead. "What can I get you to eat?" she said, without even the preamble of a "good morning."

"Nothing, Ma. I just got here. I brought Jakob breakfast at work; I had a muffin. Sit down with me."

"How is Jakob? I feel like I haven't seen him in ages," her mother said.

"You and me both," Liana answered. When her mother looked at her expectantly for more details, Liana continued, "He's okay. He's working like a dog, but he likes it. I wish we had more time for each other."

"And how's work going for you?" Phyllis asked.

Liana considered her mother's question for a moment. "I'm not sure. My boss and I have a difference of opinion on the best way to approach the clients. We'll see who's right, I guess." There didn't seem much point in worrying her mother by getting into specifics.

Besides, exactly how would I explain Danny Shea to her? I find my rapist intriguing? Sometimes I dream about him?

Liana finished the last few sips of coffee left in her mug and looked up at her mother, who had her elbows on the table, head tilted to one side, lips pursed, and brow furrowed. It was an expression Liana called her mother's "thinking face," and it was often followed by sage maternal advice. Liana hoped this was one of those occasions.

"Well, Liana, I'm your mother, and by me you are perfect and can do no wrong. But if you don't mind me saying so, the real question is not whether your boyfriend is happy with you or your boss is happy with you but whether you are happy with yourself. I'm not pretending it's easy, but if you are in a good place, everything else will follow."

How does she do that? I never said word one about being unhappy.

Her mother reached for a bowl of roasted almonds that had been hidden behind a stack of mail on the table, popped a few in her mouth, crunching them noisily, and pushed the bowl toward Liana. When it became apparent to both of them that Liana wasn't going to attempt either to answer her mother's question or eat the almonds, Phyllis got up from her chair.

"Come here; I want to show you something." Liana assumed it was a new leak or a running toilet that needed fixing; now that her father was gone, everything in the house seemed to be slowly falling apart. After some problem was pointed out to Liana, she would get Jakob to come over and try to address it. He wasn't much handier than she was, although he generally had a better sense of when you needed a professional to take over. So Liana was more than a little shocked when her mother sat down at the foot of her bed and pulled open the drawer of the mahogany dresser on the opposite wall, revealing a manila packet of about twenty loose eight-by-ten black-and-white photographs of Liana's father and herself, impossibly young and painfully beautiful, on their wedding day. It was as though the photographs had magically appeared from another era; Liana could barely catch her breath.

She had never seen the photographs of her parents' small wedding in 1972. There was her mother, achingly lovely and hopeful, in a pale pink sleeveless dress with what she termed a "petal" neckline but which looked to Liana like a charming banana being peeled. Artie was dashing and confident, with a full head of thick wavy black hair that Liana had never seen in person. While he was on leave from his service in the finance corps of the army during the Vietnam War, they were wed in the rabbi's study at Temple Emanuel on Fifth Avenue in Manhattan, surrounded only by their parents and siblings and a stubborn aunt who refused to be kept away.

"These are amazing, Ma. But why are you showing them to me?" Liana asked. "Why didn't you ever show them to me before?" Her parents' marriage had not always been smooth sailing. They'd argued, and there had been mornings when Liana found her father sleeping on the couch in the den. Nonetheless, they'd stayed together. Liana hadn't known the details, and she didn't want to know now.

Her mother looked up from the photographs, the young faces so simple in the purity of the love at that moment.

"I wasn't hiding them. I just have a lot of conflicting emotions, and these photographs only tell a part of the story." She pulled out one photograph from the pile in which she and Artie were gazing into each other's eyes, totally immersed in one another as though they were the only two people on the planet. "A marriage is made up of millions of moments, good and bad, and a photograph only captures one slice of time. Wedding photographs are the worst kind of skewed representation—a fantasy we indulge in that marriage is easy and beautiful and unchanging. Of course there are those idyllic moments, but marriage can also be wrenching and turbulent. You have to be ready for it all."

"And what if one of us is ready and the other isn't sure?" Liana asked.

Phyllis took off her glasses and wiped them on her bathrobe. "They say you shouldn't have children to try to save a marriage. I say you shouldn't get married to save a relationship. Your father and I had issues, but we loved each other. We were married for thirty-seven relatively happy years, and I would do it all again tomorrow. But for a relationship to be successful, you have to give it everything you've got. A good marriage, in my opinion, is not based on grand romantic gestures, or even great sex, although that helps."

"Ma, please stop!" Liana squealed, her hands jumping up to cover her ears.

"Oh, grow up, sweetheart," Phyllis said. "For a marriage to work, you have to reach the moment when Jakob's happiness is more important to you than your own, and vice versa."

Her mother's words brought Liana back to Jakob's definition of love—"to do something just because it makes the other person happy"—and then she pictured herself stubbornly refusing to go up to his office that morning.

Maybe Jakob understands love better than I do.

She felt like crying. But Liana hated being that vulnerable, even in front of her mother. She took a deep breath and managed, "I'm sure that's good advice, Ma. Don't worry—I'll give you plenty of time to find a dress."

CHAPTER 7

She had just dumped the fake orange powder that posed as cheese into her knock-off Kraft macaroni dinner when the telephone rang. Seeing Jakob's office telephone number on the caller ID, Liana answered, "Best Little Whorehouse in Texas. Can I help you?"

"Hi, babe." Jakob sounded slightly harried, as he always did these days, whether he was at work or not. Still, she felt her heart flutter just hearing his voice.

"Want to hang out? I'm making boxed macaroni and cheese like I'm in third grade. It's one of my signature dishes," Liana said. She was in a good mood, relaxing in her sweats and a slightly ratty Yale sweatshirt, and she could think of nothing in the world she wanted more than to have Jakob come over.

"I wish I could. I'm stuck here for a few more hours. I'm just going to grab a sandwich downstairs in the cafeteria. Listen, Li, you never let me know whether you're coming this weekend," Jakob said.

For a few seconds, Liana's mind went completely blank. She had been so focused for the past few weeks on Danny Shea's case that almost everything else had dropped out of the picture. She looked at the calendar on the wall in her kitchen and saw written under the date for Friday, August 3, Atlanta? and it all came rushing back to her. Jakob's cousin Zach was getting married, and Jakob's entire family was going—his parents, his younger brother and sister, and his grandmother. Jakob's aunt and uncle had taken pains to make sure that Liana knew she was invited too—the envelope for the gaudy invitation had read, in purple calligraphy, "The Weiss Family and Liana Cohen." Liana had delayed making a decision, and now the weekend was upon her.

"Oh, Jakob. I'm so sorry. Your parents must think I'm such a doofus. I meant to let them know; I just got so wrapped up in stuff that I completely forgot," Liana said.

"Does that mean you'll come? Please say yes."

"Well," Liana said, "who am I to say no to an all-expense-paid romantic weekend in a fancy hotel—it's in a fancy hotel, right?" she teased.

"Yes," Jakob answered, "the hotel will be very nice—it's the five-star Mandarin Oriental." He paused. "The romance I can't guarantee. This is going to sound incredibly retro, I know, but since Rebecca is still at an 'impressionable age,' we're doing it dormitory style, girls in one room and boys in the other. You'll be with my mom and my sister and my grandma, and I'll be with my dad and my brother." Liana could sense Jakob holding his breath on the other end of the telephone as he waited for her reaction.

She laughed out loud. "That sounds like a hoot. I'm in. Besides, you know I love a good wedding."

"Oh, this one should be a doozy. The girl Zach is marrying is a Southern belle gone traditional Jew. And I'm told they are pulling out all the stops in both regards. Weirdly, her family has some Louisville connection; I'm pretty sure they are flying your Rabbi Nacht down to perform the ceremony."

"Wow," Liana said, "another good reason to go. Listen, although I don't think it's possible to overcook this mac and cheese, I'm getting hungry. Love you; I'll talk to you later."

"I love you too," Jakob said. Sometimes, things were simple like that.

Liana was amazed at how incredibly gigantic and spread out the Atlanta airport was. She was glad she didn't have to navigate it herself and could just stick with Jakob and his family, following them from baggage claim to the taxi stand and then into the Mandarin Oriental, which was by far the nicest hotel she had ever stayed in. Jakob's parents had splurged and taken two interconnecting two-bedroom suites so that they could all sleep comfortably. Liana entered the girls' room and lay down on one of the beds.

"I think I'm going to stay here for the rest of my life," she told Jakob's grandmother. "I might actually die here."

"I think you'd get tired of living like this," Grandma answered.

"Have you seen the way I live now?" Liana asked her.

Liana went in to inspect the bathroom and check out the "free" toiletries and saw that there was a telephone installed in the frosted glass stall that separated the toilet from the rest of the facilities. She immediately called Jakob's room, planning to say "pizza delivery" and hang up like a ten-year-old if Jakob's brother or father answered. But Jakob picked up on the second ring. "Hey, where are you?" Liana asked.

"What do you mean? You just called my room."

"No, I mean are you in the toilet stall?"

"How could I be talking to you if I was in the toilet stall?"

"Go in there; you'll see."

A few seconds later, Jakob said, "Okay. I'm on the phone with you while I'm in the toilet stall. Are you happy now? Should I take a leak?"

"No!" Liana shrieked. "I've always thought when I strike it rich, I'll have a phone installed next to the toilet," Liana said dreamily.

"Are you planning on striking it rich at the Public Defender's Office?" Jakob retorted. "Shut up," Liana said with fake annoyance, then hung up the phone.

Liana and "the girls" unpacked their garment bags, putting their finery in the closet so that the wrinkles would hang out of their dresses. "Let me see what you are going to wear to the wedding, Rebecca," Liana said to Jakob's seventeen-year-old sister.

"I found the prettiest dress," Rebecca crooned, pulling a Betsey Johnson number out of the closet, black and fuchsia, with blinding sparkly stuff scattered all over.

"I love it—you're going to look awesome! The bride will be jealous. I wish I'd brought something half that stylish!" Truthfully, Liana loved her own dress too and couldn't wait to wear it the next night.

They had a quiet dinner on Friday evening in the hotel restaurant, strangely exhausted from the short, two-and-a-half-hour flight from New York. After polishing off her molten chocolate cake and wondering whether she'd still be able to zip up her dress, Liana was scanning the adjacent lobby when she spotted Rabbi Nacht, sitting at a small table in the corner. He was dressed in neat slacks and a buttoned-down shirt, his beard closely trimmed and his head covered with a yarmulke. Even at a distance, she could see that he was quietly chanting the traditional grace after meals, his lips moving and his head nodding very slightly with the intonation. Liana waited for him to finish. "I'll be right back," she said, squeezing Jakob's shoulder. As she approached the rabbi's table, she wondered if, out of context, he'd know who she was.

"Shabbat Shalom, Rabbi. Would you like some company for a few minutes?" Liana asked. "I'm sorry if I startled you," she added.

"Shabbat Shalom, Liana! What a nice surprise. What're you doing here in Atlanta? Please." He motioned to a large upholstered chair adjacent to his, and Liana sat down.

An empty plastic plate and cutlery remained on the table, and Liana realized that the rabbi had not eaten the nonkosher food in the hotel, that other arrangements must have been made. "Are you okay eating here in the lobby?" she asked.

"Yes. I enjoy watching the people coming and going," he

said. "All different sorts of lives, some intersecting and some not. Sometimes I invent stories about them, what they're thinking, the next conversation they'll have. I find it fascinating, even if it's just my imagination run wild. Want to play?"

"Seriously?" Liana asked.

"You have something better to do?" the rabbi challenged, eyebrows raised. "So this is how it works. We'll do one from your world so you can relate." He looked around the lobby until his eyes settled on a man in a grey wool pinstripe suit, standing against a wall with his arms crossed over his chest, about thirty feet away. He discreetly pointed him out to Liana with a nod of his head.

"That gentleman escaped from the Fulton County Jail this morning. He's not violent; he's more of a swindler, petty thief. He stole those clothes from a cheap department store because it was all he could find—who voluntarily wears that in this weather? It's hot as blazes down here. He's not sure where his next meal is coming from or where he's sleeping tonight. He came to the lobby of this swanky hotel, looking for an easy mark. Okay, your turn." The rabbi looked away from his subject and back to Liana.

She stared at him with her mouth wide open. "Didn't I learn in one of your sermons that it's a big no-no to speak badly of other people?"

The rabbi smiled. "It's just pretend, Liana. We're not hurting anyone."

Mollified, Liana sat forward in her chair and perused the possibilities.

"See that woman over there? The striking brunette wearing the too-tight red top. Ooh—should I not have pointed her out to you?" Liana cringed.

"I'm a rabbi and I'm getting old, Liana, but I'm not blind. So, what's her story? Is she the target?"

"Yes, and she's vulnerable, because she's feeling lonely."

"Why is she lonely?" the rabbi asked.

Amazing how concerned he sounds when it's only pretend.

"I'm not sure, honestly—she looks like she has a lot going for her. She came into the hotel to get out of the heat for a few minutes. But she's also an undercover cop, and she's not beyond using her feminine wiles to catch her quarry. This isn't going to end well for your guy."

"Excellent! I knew you'd be good at this. You need to figure out why she's lonely though." The rabbi shifted in his seat and focused back on Liana. "You still haven't answered my first question. What're you doing here?" the rabbi asked.

"The groom is Jakob's cousin—I'm here with his family for the wedding. Hey, what're you drinking?" she said, surprised at the glass she hadn't noticed in the rabbi's hand. "I don't think of rabbis as kicking back with a nightcap," she said, blushing at her own directness.

The rabbi laughed. "Well, I won't speak for the entire profession, but I like a good bourbon, especially when I'm back in the South and away from my family on Shabbat."

"That must be hard," Liana said, picturing how happy the rabbi's wife and kids always looked when the congregants were leaving synagogue on a Friday night and the family finally was able to go home.

"It comes with the territory," the rabbi said, a note of resignation in his voice. "I'm often thrust into the middle of critical moments in people's lives, whether joyous or sad, and that's both meaningful and humbling. Sometimes it comes at the expense of my own family. But you're a public defender; I don't have to tell you about sacrifice, do I? I admire you, Liana. I imagine it must be a very fulfilling job."

Liana's first impulse was to laugh, but she thought the rabbi might view it as disrespectful, which was not at all what she wanted to be. She took a deep cleansing breath. "I don't know, Rabbi. It all seems a lot murkier than it did when I took this job. At the beginning, I was totally stoked about playing my part in ensuring that justice, with a capital *J*, was done for every individual, even those who seemed to deserve it the least."

"The Bible makes that an imperative, Liana: 'Justice, justice you shall pursue.'" He took another sip of his drink and waited for her to continue.

"Yes, intellectually that still works, but . . . there are times when I would give anything to believe that if I work hard enough and I look hard enough, I'll encounter someone who really needs me, Liana Cohen, to fix a terrible wrong that has been done. And I don't mean someone who didn't get a fair shake from the system—that's easy, it happens all the time." Liana's eyes had filled with tears, and the rabbi was getting blurrier by the moment. Surprised by the assault of emotion, she squeezed her eyes shut and continued.

"I can't seem to muster that hope or faith or whatever you want to call it that someone like that is out there for me. And each day I represent another defendant who has done something unspeakable, I lose a little more of the dream that I'm making the world a better place." Liana opened her eyes. "Doesn't sound so admirable anymore, does it, Rabbi?"

The rabbi tilted his head back onto the plush chair and looked up at the lobby ceiling, where ultramodern crystal chandeliers hung, illuminating the hall with a soft, flattering light. Liana was worried she had tired the rabbi out with her ramblings or, worse, that she had disappointed him. But then he leaned forward and started to speak, his cadences soft and musical, the remnant of his Louisville youth.

"Should I tell you why I enjoy that game we played earlier, Liana? It's because it allows me to break a number of critical rules without any consequences. I can make all sorts of judgments about people and draw conclusions about situations based on nothing, and it doesn't matter. When I play, I indulge in the fantasy that I understand what's going on in people's heads and in their lives, when, in reality, I understand very little. In my line of work, and I would think in yours, what's most important is to keep an open mind and let things unfold. If I do that, I trust that God will grant me the insight I need to help when I can." He looked back over at the people milling about the lobby, and Liana thought he might start another round of the game, leaving her hanging. But after a moment, he caught her eye.

"Have you ever seen that Cher movie from the eighties called *Suspect*? She starred opposite Dennis Quaid and Liam Neeson?"

"Great cast, but I don't watch TV or movies about the law—same old, same old for me," Liana said.

"I think you'd like this one. Cher plays an overworked public defender in Washington, DC, and one day when she's feeling particularly burdened, she asks her colleague why he keeps doing this sort of work when it's so difficult. And the old guy answers—and I've always loved this line—'For the one poor bastard who didn't do it.'"

Liana followed the rabbi's eyes as he watched the beautiful woman in the red top walk past the man in the pinstripe suit and embrace a woman who had just arrived, kissing her on the lips and holding her close.

"Huh!" he said, with a quick nod of his head, and then he turned back to Liana.

"The Talmud teaches us, Liana, that whoever saves a single life, it's as if she's saved an entire world. So, if, over the course of your long and storied career, you chance upon one person, just one, whom you can save from a wrongful conviction, then you will have achieved something truly extraordinary." The rabbi finished off his drink, and Liana was afraid their conversation was over.

"And what if I don't ever find that one person?" she asked, her voice barely audible under her rising panic.

"Our sages have something to say about that too. The rabbis teach us that 'It's not your responsibility to finish the work of perfecting the world, but you're not free to desist from it either.' Everybody has a part to play in trying to make the world a fairer, kinder, more just with a capital *J* place, Liana. If it turns out that the Public Defender's Office is not right for you, you'll find another way to have an impact. But I wonder if your job isn't just a job for you. I wouldn't throw in the towel just yet. That poor bastard, if you'll excuse my language, could be just around the corner. Keep an open mind and let things unfold—people may surprise you. And remember—we're Mets fans. We gotta believe, long after all the evidence says we should quit."

Liana thought about the rabbi's words as he rose from his chair. "Do you always know the right thing to say?" she asked him.

The rabbi shrugged. "My children think I'm insufferable, always quoting something."

"Your children undoubtedly wish you were home now. Sleep well, Rabbi," Liana said, getting up and starting back toward the dining room, where she could see Jakob trying to catch sight of her.

"Good night, Liana. Please give my regards to Jakob and his family." With that, he made his way to the staircase to head up to his room.

Liana walked slowly back to the table in the dining room. *Could Danny Shea be that one person?*

As she entered the restaurant, Jakob pushed his chair back from the table. When Liana was within his reach, he wrapped his arms around her and pulled her onto his lap.

"Where did you go? I was getting lonely without you," he said, his breath warm near her ear.

Liana smiled up at him. "I needed to stretch my legs after sitting on that plane. But I'm back now." She glanced over her shoulder to make sure she was safely out of the rabbi's sight and then planted a kiss, soulful and sweet, on Jakob's lips.

"I can't believe we are in this gorgeous hotel and you are making me sleep with Grandma."

"Hey," Jakob said, "don't count Grandma out. She could probably teach you a thing or two."

The "girls" stayed up talking for a little while; it felt like Liana's apartment at Yale, when she and her graduate school room-mates, Charlotte and Katie, all had their single beds crammed into one room so they could keep the adjacent room empty to hang out in with friends. How many times during that third year of law school after she had started dating Jakob did Liana awake, wondering which new boyfriend she would find stowed away in one of her roommate's beds, while she and Jakob had to settle for long distance telephone calls between their visits? Liana had to admit that she was enjoying the vibe this week-end. There had been stretches of time she had been jealous of Jakob and his family. She longed for siblings, a grandmother to dote on—all of her grandparents were long gone—and par-ents who were still relatively young and, most importantly, alive. She no longer thought the Weiss family was perfect—she could see their strengths and weaknesses. Phyllis always said that when you married, you married the whole family.

I could do worse.

The wedding was scheduled for Saturday night, after the conclusion of the Sabbath, in accordance with Jewish tra-dition. When they arrived in the reception area outside the main ballroom, the smorgasbord was going at full throttle, the waiters and waitresses passing hors d'oeuvres and handing out fruity cocktails.

"Oh my God, Jakob, did we miss the ceremony?" Liana whispered.

Jakob laughed. "No. Apparently in more traditional Jewish weddings, the cocktail hour comes first, then the ceremony, and then the dinner and dancing. My grandmother gave me a primer on the flight down. If you're nice, I'll enlighten you as we go along," he said. Liana had been planning to stick close to Jakob anyway. She could barely walk in her high-heeled strappy sandals, but it was worth it for the effect of the shoes with her pale pink shift with silver sequins. She stood out from all the women in their little black dresses, and she felt sexy and good. She was glad she'd decided to come.

They walked the perimeter of the room, following her late father's oft-repeated advice to check out all the options before piling your plate with food. The bride's parents had chosen Atlanta's finest kosher caterer, and there were so many dishes featuring mock crab and mock shrimp and mock lobster that Liana thought she might be in a mock aquarium. Everything they tried was delicious, and Liana was especially impressed by the Southern offerings: panfried chicken, hushpuppies, and baby back barbequed ribs. She wished that she'd worked out with Jakob at the gym before the wedding so she could eat with more abandon, but she soon retreated to her usual stance—you only live once—and sampled everything that wasn't nailed down.

"Look, here's the next part of your lesson," Jakob said, steering her on her unbalanced feet toward the front of the room, where a large dais had been set up. A rail-thin but pretty young woman wearing a huge amount of florid makeup and a big white satin dress was sitting on a large wicker chair in the center. On either side of "Maggie May," according to the invitation, sat her mother and her soon-to-be mother-in-law, Jakob's Aunt Ellen. Stretching out on either side were the bridesmaids: Liana counted ten in total. The young women were wearing taffeta gowns in Pepto-Bismol pink, with modest scooped necklines, formfitting bodices, and floor-length hoop skirts straight out of *Gone with the Wind*. The bridesmaid code of honor prohibited Liana from mockery or laughing out loud. She remembered the getup she and Katie had been required to wear to Charlotte's wedding two years earlier. Although aesthetically head and shoulders above these, the gowns had been made of some ultrasynthetic material covered with tiny fake pearls that had left both Liana and Katie with a painful rash over 90 percent of their bodies for close to a week.

"Well, don't they all look festive!" Liana exclaimed. "But why are they sitting there like that? Are they for sale?"

Jakob was taking his role as wedding tour guide very seriously, which made Liana slightly anxious. But she would certainly want Rabbi Nacht to officiate at her and Jakob's wedding if that day ever came, and he would undoubtedly insist on these rituals. This would be an excellent dry run, if she could manage to tune out the bride's frightening fashion taste.

"This is called the *bedeken*," Jakob said. "The women sit here, and the guests greet the bride and *ooh* and *aah* over the bridesmaids and the flower girls. Then, in about twenty minutes, the groom, his father, his future father-in-law, and the other male relatives and groomsmen will come in from a second room, where they are currently eating more manly food and drinking a lot of very expensive bourbon. Zach will approach Maggie and make sure she's the woman he wants to marry."

"What? Shouldn't he have decided that by now?"

"It comes from the biblical story of Jacob. He was all set to marry Rachel—had the whole deal in place with Rachel's dad, who was kind of a jerk. Then at the last minute, the dad stuck Rachel's older sister, Leah, under the wedding canopy instead. Jacob had to work another seven years for Rachel. So from that time on, the custom is that the groom comes in and makes sure it's the right girl, then he puts the veil on the bride and retreats back to the bourbon room until the ceremony starts."

Liana could tell that her Jakob was impressed by his own knowledge of the story of his patriarchal namesake, especially because he knew something Jewish that Liana did not. But she also had a thing or two up her sleeve. "You know what else is very cool about this ceremony?" Liana asked.

"What?" Jakob said, surprised.

"Maggie and Zach haven't seen each other in a week. And they're fasting today. So by the time Zach comes in here from the other room, they're famished and faint and absolutely dying to see each other. Isn't that romantic?" she said.

"I guess," Jakob replied. "It sounds kind of like overkill to me. Well, I'm going to go to where the guys are hanging out. I'll be back when they come in here. Can you manage by yourself?" Jakob asked.

"Of course," Liana said.

After Jakob left, Liana wandered slowly and carefully up to the dais. She hadn't noticed Grandma up there before, but she looked so thrilled sitting with Maggie and Aunt Ellen. Liana had the fleeting thought that she and Jakob should get married in time for Grandma, who was no spring chicken anymore, to sit on her dais too. She hugged Grandma and Aunt Ellen and introduced herself to Maggie, kissing the air next to her face so she wouldn't smudge lipstick on her and gushing over how stunning she looked and how gorgeous her bridesmaids were. A few minutes later, over the restrained din of the women, Liana heard the sound of trumpet blasts coming from down the hallway.

The sound grew louder and louder and resolved into a familiar Jewish celebratory tune, and she saw Zach enter the room, supported at either elbow by his father—Jakob's Uncle Hal—and Maggie's father. Zach was beaming, if pallid, and all his young friends and even Rabbi Nacht were marching in behind him, singing and clapping. She spotted Jakob in the clump of men, looking bewildered but caught up in the joyous throng. Zach reached Maggie and bent toward her. He whispered something in her ear that Liana couldn't hear and looked adoringly into her eyes before kissing her tenderly on the top of her head and lowering her veil. All of the parents gave quick hugs and kisses to Maggie and Zach, and then one of Zach's friends hoisted him up on his shoulders and carried him out of the room, the rest of the men singing at the top of their lungs as the trumpets blared, clapping and hooting as if they were at a college basketball game. Liana hadn't realized it, but tears were streaming down her face. She had never seen anything so beautiful before in her life.

After the drama of the *bedeken*, the actual wedding ceremony was almost anticlimactic. Maggie and Zach stood under the chuppah, the wedding canopy, surrounded by their immediate family and the hordes of bridesmaids and groomsmen. Rabbi Nacht read the lengthy marriage contract in Aramaic, and distinguished male guests were invited up to recite the seven blessings of the wedding ceremony. The rabbi spoke a little bit about the couple, but it sounded stilted, as though he didn't really know them.

If this were my wedding, at least Rabbi Nacht would have something to say about us.

Then the rabbi began to sing a traditional Hebrew wedding ballad, "Night of the Roses." He sang about myrrh and roses and doves, the words incomprehensible to Liana, but the passion and longing palpable.

At the end of the ceremony, Zach smashed a glass, which turned out to be a light bulb wrapped in a napkin, with his foot, in commemoration of the destruction of the Temple in Jerusalem by the Romans in the year 70 CE and to remind the young couple that in life there is also sadness amidst great joy.

"Is that allowed, the whole light bulb substitution thing?" Liana whispered to Jakob.

"I think so," he said. "But I agree with you, it's kind of cheesy." The shouts of "Mazel tov!" were deafening, especially combined with the now earsplitting trumpets. The rest of the night was a whirlwind of traditional hora circle dancing, gorging on too-rare prime rib, and winding up, at nearly two in the morning, with slow dancing. Jakob held Liana close as they swayed, and she felt as though she could stay in the moment for all time, protected and safe and loved.

"Hey, Jay, listen to what they're playing!"

"Mmm," he murmured in her ear, "I had a little word with the bandleader. . . ."

The tones of "Till There Was You" filled the ballroom.

This is so perfect. Why am I so scared?

CHAPTER 8

"Well, look who the cat dragged in," Deb exclaimed in mock horror when Liana showed up to work close to ten thirty the morning after the weekend sojourn to Atlanta.

"Not that I owe you any explanations," Liana grumped, "but I had a showdown with a three-inch long water bug in my bathroom this morning. It was either going to be me or that big boy if I was getting into the shower, and in the end, I had to just close the bathroom door and run out of the apartment."

"*Ew!*" Deb squealed. Deb was the kind of woman who'd never leave home without being totally groomed, top to bottom. The thought of not showering wouldn't cross her mind, no matter the circumstances. "Well, you just stay on your side of the office," she warned, which was laughable—the office was so small that when both women sat at their desks, which were positioned on opposite sides of the room, the backs of their chairs touched. The guys in the mailroom had tried rearranging the furniture, such as it was, a dozen times—their desks, a couple of file cabinets, two low bookcases, two computer stands—but nothing they did made the office feel any more spacious. The room was meant as a single and was being used as a double, but Liana and Deb had stayed together even when they had been offered their own offices.

"Anyway," said Liana, settling into her chair, "I've been here a hell of a lot more than you have lately. How are you feeling? What did your doctor say?" August was always the slowest time in the office, with the attorneys taking vacations and days off here and there, a pattern of near work-stoppage that Gerry railed against every year but which persisted nonetheless. Liana had chalked up Deb's occasional absences to time spent with Max. She realized with a pang of guilt that this was the first she'd asked after Deb's health in a while. Deb sighed and looked up at the ceiling.

Was she trying not to cry?

"She said she doesn't know what's wrong with me yet but that she believes me that I'm not feeling right. She's going to run some more tests, and then I guess we'll make a plan. But at least she took me seriously; she didn't treat me like some drama queen."

"That's because she doesn't know you well enough," Liana said.

"Screw you," Deb said. Their dynamic intact, they both turned back to their work.

Liana had almost finished going through the entire record of Danny Shea's trial with a fine-toothed comb, and she still didn't have much she could raise on his behalf. It was now August, and she had worked all through July on his case—devoting more time than she should have allotted if she was going to stick to the schedule that made quota.

"So what do you have so far?" Deb asked.

"Nothing that doesn't suck," Liana responded. "I could cobble together an argument that he was denied a fair trial. At one point, the judge cut defense counsel off when he started questioning the girl about her prior sexual relationship with her boyfriend Daryl."

"Okay—but that's standard. The rape shield law protects the victim from having to give irrelevant and embarrassing details of her personal life on the stand," Deb said.

"I know, I know. What about this? At another point the prosecutor commented that Danny Shea had sat through the whole trial before he was called to the stand to testify—and that he 'tailored his testimony' as much as possible to match what the other witnesses had said, especially the victim, to make himself look more credible," Liana offered.

"All of which is probably true—although the DA's not supposed to say it because the defendant has a constitutional right to be present at his own trial. I don't know, Liana; you'd need a lot more egregious prosecutorial misconduct than that to do this guy any good on appeal," Deb said, shaking her head.

"You don't say?" Liana buried her head in her hands for a moment and then resumed reading the transcript.

Right before noon, Gerry strode into their office. "Deb, darling, how are you feeling, my dear?" As much as Gerry liked to needle Liana whenever possible, he loved Deb with a devotion beyond measure. She was just the sort of woman Gerry admired—she was beautiful but could curse like a sailor, and she was irreverent about everything from religion to relationships and all topics in between. Deb also knew how to play the game in a way Liana didn't; she harbored many of the same doubts about her clients, but she had learned long ago to keep those thoughts under wraps.

"I'm doing okay, Ger. Thanks for asking," Deb said, revealing nothing.

"And you, Liana? How are you coming with that brief? It seems like you may be falling behind. When can I expect to see it?"

"Slow but steady wins the race, Gerry. It'll be worth the wait."

When Gerry left, Deb turned to Liana.

"Cohen, you need a break. You're beginning to lose it. Come on, we're going out," Deb said, grabbing Liana by the arm and marching her down the hallway.

"Tony, we'll be back in hour," Deb announced at the front desk.

"Where are we going? I have work to do. I haven't found an issue yet," Liana protested, knowing full well she would follow Deb wherever she led.

"You're never going to find an issue in this case by banging your head against the wall. You need to look at it with fresh eyes. Right now, we're going shopping," Deb announced.

"Oh, no! I'm not going shopping with you!" Deb had a sense of style and a brash quality that telegraphed self-confidence and evoked Manhattan in a way that Liana's Long Island origins would never allow. Liana was utterly intimidated by her. Shopping was out of the question.

"Don't be stupid," Deb said. "We're not going to do a whole makeover. We'll start with something simple," she said, looking Liana up and down as they waited for the elevator. When it arrived, it was packed with people going out for lunch, and Liana and Deb just squeezed in as the doors closed.

"It's your shoes," Deb announced to the assembled riders. "Look at those clunkers—they'll put us over the weight limit."

Liana, along with everyone else, turned her attention to her feet, where she was sporting an ancient pair of thick rubber-soled sandals with wide faux-leather straps.

"Hey, my favorite weatherman on *Good Morning, New York* said there were going to be thunderstorms and flash floods today. These are perfect! I can go hiking in them through streams and jungles and during monsoons," Liana said.

"This isn't an episode of *Survivor*, Liana. You're at work. And there isn't a cloud in the sky," Deb said, the other elevator occupants all nodding and murmuring their agreement.

When the doors opened, Liana and Deb spilled out into the lobby, and Deb took off down the street, Liana in hot pursuit. They quickly reached the shoe department of Century 21. Within minutes of perusing the displays, Deb approached

Liana, holding a red leather gladiator sandal, straps lacing all the way up to the knee.

"What about these? They're fabulous!" Deb cooed.

"Now where would I possibly be going in those?" Liana said. She picked up a pair of black patent-leather ballet flats. "These are pretty and very sensible."

"I'm sorry, I got distracted. I thought I heard your mother talking. Kill me now," Deb said. "You're hopeless. This is going to be more frustrating than fun. I have another idea. Follow me," she said, leading the way to the escalator to the first floor as Liana, disappointed, rushed to put down the shoes.

Before Liana could get her bearings, Deb had honed in on an exquisite silk scarf, all purples and blues with flecks of gold.

"Everyone needs a great scarf," Deb said. "Put this on." She handed it to Liana, who looked at it adoringly.

"It's gorgeous, Deb. I love it. But I don't have any idea how to wear a scarf—I don't really accessorize, if you know what I mean."

"Really? I hadn't noticed," Deb teased. "Anyone, even you, Cohen, can learn to tie a scarf." Deb gently folded the material and tied it loosely around Liana's neck, turning her toward the mirror on the counter. "It's stunning. Get your credit card out," Deb ordered.

Liana carried her purchase all wrapped up like a present to herself that she wasn't sure she deserved. As they walked the few blocks back to the office, she felt her stomach begin to rumble. "Let's stop for a quick bite, okay? We still have time on our hour," she said.

"I'm not hungry, but I'll sit with you," Deb said.

They stepped into a Middle Eastern place a couple of doors down from their building. "I'll have a falafel with every-thing—salad, tahini, pickles, eggplant, cabbage, hot sauce . . ." Liana pointed to each component as the man behind the counter stuffed more and more into the pita bread. Deb looked queasy and retreated to a seat by an open window.

"Thanks for getting me out of the office," Liana said. "I do feel better. I can't explain why I feel so desperate to find something really great to argue in this case, but I do."

"Well, I can come up with two reasons. First, your job is on the line. And second, you believe in Danny Shea. You think he didn't do it." Deb brushed some crumbs left by the last diner onto the floor and tried not to look at Liana, who had tahini dripping down her chin.

"I don't know," Liana said between messy bites. "I think my job is safe as long as I keep my mouth shut. And as for believing in Danny Shea, I will admit only that my interest is piqued."

"Okay. And we'll just pretend that Mr. Innocent isn't so hot that his mug shot burns a hole in your file," Deb said, making unseemly kissing noises in Liana's direction.

"Stop it! Don't be crazy." Liana swallowed the last bite of her sandwich and took a swig of her Diet Coke. "Hey, can I ask you a serious question?" Liana said.

"If you must," Deb answered.

"Why did you and Steven break up? I mean, I know it didn't work out, but when you got married, were you both one-hundred-percent confident that it would last forever? Like, did you start out really happy, and then things just disintegrated?" Liana wiped at her mouth with the little square napkin.

"Wow. Are you and Jakob talking about tying the knot?" Deb asked.

"Not exactly. Jakob's talking about it, and I'm mostly avoiding the conversation," Liana said, gathering up the detritus of her sandwich in an effort not to meet Deb's gaze. She was relieved when Deb had mercy and didn't press her for details.

"Well, of course we went into the marriage confident and in love—why else would we have gotten married? And it was good for a couple of years. We had a really fun New York lifestyle—we went to clubs at all hours of the night and drank to excess in bars with beautiful and interesting people and got last minute tickets to indie rock band concerts."

"That sounds awesome; we don't really go anywhere. So what happened?" Liana hoped she wasn't overstepping her bounds.

"What happened is that I got pregnant with Max, and Steven thought all the fun would continue straight through until the delivery and then afterward. And I wasn't feeling it anymore." Deb's face went sour with the memory, and Liana wished she hadn't brought the topic up. They had been having such a good time.

"Wow. I didn't know," Liana said.

"You want to hear something ironic? Before the ink was dry on our divorce, he married some cute young thing from his firm, undoubtedly thinking he had found the ticket to a good time again. And guess what happened? She's pregnant!" Deb looked absolutely gleeful.

"No! How do you know?" Liana asked.

"Women's intuition," Deb said. When Liana blanched, Deb said, "Oh, don't be silly. Max told me. Although he thought she just had a basketball under her shirt. Come on, we better get you back to the office; you have a handsome young man to vindicate."

Liana was about to call it a day when she found it—the issue that she knew immediately would force the appellate court to reverse Danny Shea's conviction and order a new trial.

Bingo!

A reversal could be big for Shea. One of three things could happen: he could go to trial again with a new jury and be acquitted the second time around (unlikely); the district attorney could offer him a deal—plead guilty in exchange for less prison time than he was currently serving (possible); or he could go to trial again, be convicted again, and get the same exact sentence, arguably a huge waste of time and taxpayer money but, in some ways, validating that the system works (virtually certain). But for Liana, as his attorney, no matter what, a reversal of Shea's existing conviction would count as a huge win.

As if magically drawn by Liana's moment of legal inspiration, Gerry sidled into the office and leaned against Deb's desk, his arms crossed over her his chest and an expectant look on his face.

"What've you got, Liana?" he said. She stared at him in disbelief. Gerry continued, "You yelled 'Bingo!' so loudly that I thought I was back in my grandmother's nursing home in Miami Beach. You must've found something."

Liana looked to Deb for confirmation that she had, in fact, spoken out loud.

"I was planning on ignoring you, as usual," Deb said.

"Come on, Liana, don't hold out on us," Gerry said, his unique blend of animated and annoying on full display.

"Yeah, Liana, don't hold out on us," Deb mimicked.

Amazing how she gets away with that.

"Well—this is all very preliminary," Liana said. But she knew. The issue was so deceptively simple but so very powerful. "The jury had been deliberating for three days, meaning that at least one of the jurors believed Shea's story that the sex was consensual over Jennifer Nash's that she was forced. On the fourth day, the jury sent a note requesting to see the lab report that said that Shea's DNA was a match to the sample in the rape kit collected from Nash. Shortly after the jury was given the report, it sent out a follow-up that read, Who is Alba Velez?"

Liana paused to let Gerry and Deb envision the scene before continuing.

"The judge called the attorneys into the courtroom, and they examined the lab report. In addition to stating that

Shea's DNA matched the sample taken from Ms. Nash, it also indicated that there was a second match between Shea and a sample taken at some prior time, from some other woman named Alba Velez."

Gerry looked as though he wanted to pace, but the confines of the room wouldn't allow for it. He settled for wringing his hands.

"Well, Liana, was your client previously convicted of sexually assaulting this Alba Velez? Because if he was, under certain limited circumstances, that prior conviction could have been admissible against him in this trial, although it clearly was very prejudicial."

"Like if maybe this was his modus operandi," Deb suggested. "He takes women to rooftops, gets them a little high, slow dances with them, and then rapes them." Deb surreptitiously lifted up the copy of *Entertainment This Week* she had bought on the way back from lunch, revealing the cover photo of Brad Pitt. She mouthed "I love you" at Liana, quickly putting it down again before Gerry could turn to see.

"No, Shea had never been convicted of anything before," Liana said, trying to ignore Deb. "And the way this unfolded—it's like damnation by rumor. There are all sorts of innocent explanations for why Velez's name appeared on the lab report as being a hit to Shea's DNA—it could have been a clerical error or a false accusation or a mix-up of the rape kits. But once the jury saw this report, his ability to get a fair trial on this case was shot to hell. It was almost inevitable that the jurors would conclude that Shea had raped a woman named Alba Velez and that he was therefore guilty of raping Jennifer Nash as well. And that's what happened. An hour later, the jury convicted Danny Shea of first-degree rape."

"So who dropped the ball?" Gerry asked.

"Everyone! The prosecutor knew all along that Ms. Velez's name was on the lab report, but the judge accepted her claim that it was an oversight and she hadn't submitted it to the jury on purpose to prejudice Shea," Liana said.

"Fat chance," Deb said, looking up momentarily from the crossword puzzle she had started doing while Gerry had his back to her.

"But defense counsel bore the bulk of the responsibility. He didn't notice Ms. Velez's name on the DNA report, although he had the document long in advance of trial and was responsible for reviewing everything that would be submitted into evidence."

"And the judge?" Gerry asked.

"His so-called cure was to tell the jurors the whole thing was just a big mistake and they should pretend they hadn't seen Velez's name at all."

There was plenty of blame to go around, and Liana intended to lay it on them all.

"This is certainly a good start," Gerry said. "Now it's time to go do your legal research."

"Yes, Gerry—that's what I was planning to do. That's my job," Liana said.

When Gerry left the room, a wave of nausea washed over Liana. It was one of those rare moments when she could hear her late father's voice whispering in her ear, "This is why I sent you to law school? To put all your God-given talents into helping rapists and murderers?"

"Oh, hush up, Daddy," she muttered.

"Are you talking to yourself again?" Deb asked.

"Hey, sometimes I am the only one who will listen to me," Liana answered.

Over the next week, Liana worked furiously, researching the law of ineffective assistance of counsel. It was a legal issue she had pursued infrequently in the past, as it sometimes entailed, as it did here, accusing trial counsel of one error in an otherwise well-prepared and presented case. This attorney, who had done such a masterful job of cross-examining Ms. Nash and suggesting that she was a willing participant in the sexual encounter, and who had skillfully questioned Danny Shea in a way that humanized him in the eyes of the jury and engendered sympathy, had completely screwed up on this single issue of critical importance. It was an argument that pitted appellate attorney against trial attorney, with the former having the great advantage of twenty-twenty hindsight.

If I had been trial counsel, would I have insisted that Ms. Velez's name be removed from that lab report? Jumped up and down and demanded a mistrial?

There was no way of knowing how "effective" Liana would have been in the heat of the moment. Appellate attorneys didn't like to think on their feet; that's why they practiced a type of law that allowed deliberate, quiet consideration and extensive advance preparation.

Liana considered every facet of the case and crafted her brief as if she were creating a work of art. She threw herself into her work with an enthusiasm she hadn't felt in a long while, putting in long hours, acutely aware that she would be judged not just for her legal acumen but also for her zeal. She believed in the legal issue one-hundred-percent, and—although the shadowy presence of the mysterious Alba Velez did give Liana pause—Liana had committed herself to Danny Shea, no holds barred. She didn't have a legal basis to argue he was innocent of raping Jennifer Nash, but she had found a damn good way to win him a second chance at beating the charges. When she was done writing, she marched into Gerry's office, head held high, and handed him the draft.

"Here you go," she said. "This one's going to knock your socks off!" Gerry looked at her a little warily, narrowing his eyes and sitting back in his chair.

"Are you feeling okay, Liana?" he asked, feigning concern.

"Better than ever!" Liana chirped. It was taxing—all this pretending to be the model public defender—but she felt good about this brief and, despite herself, about this client.

When she returned to her desk, there was an email from Randy Napoli in her inbox:

Slow news day. What's cooking over there?

Nothing concrete yet, but here's a tip. Watch out for People vs. Daniel Shea. Should be a big win, down the line.

Thanks, Liana, will do. I owe you one, Randy responded.

I won't forget, Liana typed. It was a totally rash and outrageous thing to do, but she didn't regret it. She knew she had this one in the bag.

Deb swept into their office, and Liana was taken aback. *When did she get so thin?*

"Hey," Liana exclaimed. "Have you lost weight? Your clothes are falling off you!"

"I know," Deb responded, clearly pleased that Liana had noticed. "Isn't it great? I've gone down a dress size—and I haven't even been trying!"

"Well, whatever your secret is, that miniskirt looks fantastic," Liana said.

Now that she had handed in her draft of the brief, Liana had time to deal with the letter she had received from Danny Shea a few days ago but hadn't opened. He hadn't called her again, and, so far, the correspondence on both sides had been very straightforward. Shea was infallibly polite and respectful. He asked all the standard questions about the appeals process, and she had given all the standard answers: How long would it take for her to write the brief? (About five weeks because of quota pressure, but she told him a couple of months—clients didn't like it if they thought you were rushing.) How long would the district attorney have to file a brief in opposition? (About eight weeks; she would send it to him as soon as it arrived.) When would the Appellate Division, Second Department, hear oral argument, and would he be able to attend? (Several months after all the briefs were in, and no, he had no right to be present in court for the argument. If he had relatives who wished to attend, she would meet with them afterward.) When would he get the court's decision? (March or April at the earliest.)

It was a long process, but the wheels of justice did indeed turn slowly. When she got the draft brief back from Gerry and made any revisions, Liana would send Shea the final version that she was filing with the court for his review, and she would remind him that he could request permission to file his own brief. Unlike almost all of her previous clients, Liana was quite confident in Shea's ability to represent his own interests. He had demonstrated a more sophisticated understanding of the nuances of her legal arguments than several of her colleagues, and he had suggested amplification of certain angles to the argument at which she had only hinted. He was focused and meticulous in his legal research, spending any time he was allowed in the correctional facility's law library and sending her case law that was on point. In another life, Danny Shea would have been the attorney here; as it was, Liana felt that she had done him proud, which was oddly meaningful to her.

In fact, Liana was a little nervous that Shea might find something she had missed, which was why she had left the letter unopened. But she couldn't avoid reading it any longer. This one was a different kettle of fish.

Dear Ms. Cohen,

I hope you are well. I received your last letter, where you carefully and patiently explained the legal issue that you are planning to present to the Appellate Court on my behalf. I agree with you that this is a very promising avenue on appeal.

Ms. Cohen, I'm an intelligent man. Intellectually, I understand full well that this issue—the ineffectiveness of my attorney in failing to redact prejudicial evidence suggesting a prior sexual assault—is a "fair trial" point and one that does not require you to have an opinion as to my actual guilt or innocence. I also accept that your professionalism requires you to advocate on my behalf regardless of whether you think I raped Ms. Nash.

But here's the thing, Ms. Cohen. I feel in my heart that if I could sit with you, in person, and look into your eyes, I would be able to convince you that I am not the kind of man who could ever hurt a woman in that way. If you had a loved one who needed to plead for your understanding in a matter of dire importance involving his liberty and his life, I know you wouldn't tell him to "do it in a letter." Some things can only properly be broached and the truth revealed when two people sit in a quiet place, face to face.

I am sure you receive requests from most of your clients asking you to visit. Many of them likely are just aching to be near a woman, even separated by a glass divider and surrounded by prison guards. I'm not claiming to be above making such a request; I am, after all, still a man. But I'm asking to be able to see you out of a genuine need to have you 100% in my corner.

I have been moved from Dannemora to Green Haven, which, if I'm keeping my bearings straight—and that's hard to do in here—is much closer to New York City.
Please, come.
Sincerely,

He had signed simply, "Danny."

Liana read it through three times. It was the most romantic letter she had received in a long time. Jakob used to write letters to her during the year they were dating long distance, each in their third year of law school in different cities. Liana would go to her mailbox, and every other day or so there would be a long letter waiting for her. His letters had been funny and poetic, full of emotional and carnal yearning. She loved that he wrote to her by hand, on whatever paper he found lying around his apartment—while her roommates, Charlotte and Katie, would get the occasional email or text from a boyfriend, she had something solid to hang on to, a written record of their early courtship.

Now that they were both in Manhattan, she and Jakob would telephone when they couldn't find time to see each other, but the calls were often rushed or overheard by Deb or by Jakob's secretary. The urgency and simmering heat underlying Danny Shea's words, although hitting their target, had the additional unintended consequence of filling Liana with a fierce longing for Jakob. She was glad to be close to filing the brief so she could reclaim the rest of her life, Jakob first and foremost. Liana wasn't ready to share with Jakob the epiphany she'd had while looking at the photographs of her parents' long-ago wedding—that she might not be ready to get married and embrace his vision of what a supportive spouse should be—but she loved him and yearned to be with him.

But right at this moment, Danny Shea was the man who demanded her attention. Liana turned to her computer and dashed off her response to Shea's letter.

Dear Mr. Shea,
I'm glad that you received my last letter and that you understand and support the legal issue that I'm planning to raise on your behalf. I hope to file the brief shortly, after it's been through the supervisory process. I'll send you a copy of the final version when I file it with the court.

As I've explained before, on direct appeal I can only raise issues that appear in the minutes from your trial. Because of that limitation, I don't make client visits to the correctional facilities—I wouldn't be able to use any information that you could provide to me that is outside of the record. Also, although Green Haven is closer than where you were at Dannemora, we don't have the budget or the time to make such trips. Moreover, I don't have any opinion whatsoever regarding your guilt or innocence; I care only to ensure that you received a fair trial and due process of law.

Liana printed out her letter and read it over a couple of times. Strictly professional, formal, with no hint of the "heart" Gerry insisted that the job as a public defender required. It was factual and clear-cut. Although Liana's head told her this was the only way to go, whatever part of her was inexplicably drawn to Danny Shea told her otherwise.

She tore up the letter and started over.

Dear Mr. Shea,

I've received your recent letter. I was going to write you to tell you that I'm planning to visit you shortly in Green Haven. It has come to my attention that if we pursue your appeal and are successful in obtaining a new trial, you face the risk that certain charges that were dropped by the prosecutor at your original trial could be revived in a retrial. Because this is a technical matter that is difficult to explain in a letter, I'll come to the facility so that I can advise you of your legal rights and you can make an informed decision about how to proceed.

It wasn't exactly a lie, but it wasn't the truth either. The prosecutor had not bothered to pursue a couple of counts that charged Shea with marijuana possession and drinking out of an open container in public. The narcotics count was a misdemeanor, and the beer was just a violation. There was no way in the world that Shea would be prosecuted for those more minor charges if Liana won a reversal and the case went to trial a second time. And even if the prosecutor brought the counts again out of spite, they carried sentences of a year or less—nothing compared to the time Shea faced for the rape. But it would be a plausible enough reason to go visit if Gerry questioned her. He wouldn't delve deeper—Gerry was one of the few attorneys in the office who met with clients all the time, even though it was totally unnecessary, because he thought it showed how committed he was to the cause.

Liana had managed to avoid virtually all client contact for three years. Now, she was determined to meet Danny Shea to try figure out who he really was. And Shea was right—she had to do it in person.

Besides, it's safe enough to indulge a harmless fantasy with a man securely behind bars.

CHAPTER 9

"You stink, Mejia! You stink!" The Mets closer had blown the save, yet again, and Liana, a second glass of chardonnay in one hand, threw a handful of popcorn at the TV screen with the other as she yelled at the pitcher from her living room couch. Sometimes when the Mets had a particularly abysmal loss, she had the fleeting thought that she was glad that her father, from whom she had inherited this often painful allegiance, was no longer alive to see it.

Not really, Daddy.

She was still in a funk a few minutes later when her cell rang.

"Hi, Jay," Liana said, all doom and gloom.

"What's wrong?" Jakob didn't follow sports and was always perplexed that Liana's mood could rise and fall on the outcome of a baseball game.

"Nothing. Everything's fine," she sighed. "Should we make a plan for Friday night? Can you pick me up at seven to walk to services?" The Mets' lousy season notwithstanding, Liana was still on a high from unearthing a great issue in Danny Shea's case. Although she wouldn't swear he was that innocent guy that Rabbi Nacht had said might be around the corner, she planned to tell him that she was in a better place.

"That's why I'm calling. We have a conflict—Frank invited us to go out to dinner with him and his new girlfriend, Marissa. It's a big deal for me, Li. Partners don't ordinarily fraternize with associates on the weekends."

In response to Liana's silence, Jakob explained for the hundredth time why it was important that she come to Wilcox & Finney events.

"I have to socialize, Liana. When the firm considers me for partnership, it isn't just the work I do that they look at, or even whose son I am. It's also do I fit in, do they like me?"

Jakob's father was a major player in the New York legal scene. An expert on the First Amendment and past president of the New York Bar Association, all the partners at W&F, including Frank, fawned over Jakob on his father's account. The fact that Jakob was saddled with paying off law school student loans was a peculiar derivative of his father's wealth and prominence. "The boy should learn the value of money," Jakob's father would say, Liana thought somewhat pompously. And yet, Jakob idolized his father and wanted nothing more than to follow in his footsteps.

"But what does your popularity have to do with me?" Liana asked. She could feel Jakob valiantly trying not to lose his cool.

"Liana, we're a team. If you're part of me, you're part of this too. If I'm going to succeed, you have to help."

Liana was pretty sure that Jakob would succeed in the law firm world with or without her. He wasn't a run-of-the-mill associate. He was extremely intelligent and articulate and enjoyed his work. Even the long hours, although burdensome, didn't disturb him. He was considered an asset to have on whatever case came into the office, because he made such a good impression on the clients.

Frank, on the other hand, was simply an arrogant bore, and Marissa, if she fit Frank's usual playmate mold, would be very young, blond, buxom, and a total ditz. Still, Liana knew that Jakob felt she'd been remiss in her "girlfriend" duties.

Lord only knows how I would do as "wife."

"Okay, Jakob. You're on. Now let me go wallow in the misery of my pathetic Mets in peace before I hit the hay."

"Sure. But, Li? It scares me when you drink alone, babe."

"What the—? How did you—?" she stammered.

"Get some sleep, sweetheart. I'll see you tomorrow night"

The next evening, Liana put on a pair of dressy black pants, a not overly chaste silk tee, and a pair of Deb-approved sling-back heels. She focused a bit more on her makeup and gelled the hell out of her hair. The results were good.

"You look awesome," Jakob said when she came into the vestibule of the restaurant, where he was waiting for her. "You can be my date anytime." He surreptitiously ran his hand up the back of her leg and pinched her on the rear.

"I'll give you twenty dollars to skip this dinner and go back to my place now," Liana offered. "Fifty?" But she was happy; she had missed Jakob. And he clearly appreciated that she was making the effort.

They spotted Frank and Marissa at a table in the back. The restaurant, high-end but otherwise authentic Ethiopian, was dimly lit and fairly crowded, the tables set close together. After the obligatory kiss-on-the-cheek greeting all around—including Marissa, whom they had never laid eyes on before—they sat down at the small round table.

Frank looked Liana up and down, not even bothering to disguise the leer. "Great to see you, Liana. Jakob likes to hide you away—keep you all for himself. I don't think that's very generous—at Wilcox & Finney, we believe in sharing!"

Frank laughed at his own remark, while Jakob forced a smile and took Liana's hand, holding it protectively. "I'm sorry, Frank;

I have an exclusive on Liana." If she had forgotten for a moment, Liana now remembered why she avoided these social events. Not only did she dislike the attorneys at the firm, she sometimes didn't even much like Jakob when he was around them.

The waiter miraculously appeared, and they ordered the special—a huge platter of injira, the sour bread that serves as both plate and utensil, covered with various meat and vegetable stews. Frank had taken the liberty of getting each of them a carafe of tej, a deceptively alcoholic honey wine. When it arrived, Liana poured herself a glass and drank half of it in three large gulps.

Before things became awkward, Jakob got the conversation going. "Frank, I've been meaning to tell you, in my spare time I've been working up a new algorithm that I think could be extremely useful in our marketing efforts."

Liana was simultaneously impressed with Jakob's drive and shocked at his contention that he had free time. She was about to comment on the latter when Frank chimed in, saving her.

"What's your angle, Jakob?"

"Well, the computer program would allow us to compare prices across an industry for a particular product or service—for example, tickets for air travel—but then also factor in prices over a realm of related products, like, in this example, for fuel or airline food. We'd be able to get a fuller picture of antitrust issues that might not be evident just looking at the primary product. I think we could market it to our current and potential clients as a more holistic evaluation that would reveal more subtle trends." Jakob sat back with a hopeful look on his face, awaiting Frank's reaction.

Frank did not disappoint. "That's brilliant, Jakob. You know, Liana, your boy here is a rock star. You should be very proud of him."

"I am very proud of him, Frank." And she was. Liana pressed her knee against Jakob's under the table.

Well, this is going better than I anticipated.

"So what great wrong are you righting these days, Liana?" Frank leaned closer to Liana across the table, his hand casually playing with Marissa's wavy locks as he stared into Liana's eyes in a misguided attempt at pseudoseductive.

"Actually, I have an exciting case right now," Liana said, taken off guard and her enthusiasm bubbling over. Jakob smiled and gave her an encouraging nod. "I'm representing this guy who's convicted of raping a woman on the Fourth of July. It's not black and white, though—they knew each other, and they went up to the rooftop of her building together. They were getting high and drinking and watching the fireworks, even dancing—anyway, they had sex, but it isn't clear whether he forced her or she regretted having consensual sex with him so she cried rape."

"So you're saying you think this guy's innocent?" Marissa asked, her eyes wide.

Yes. No. Maybe.

"Well, for his appeal it doesn't matter whether I think he's innocent or not—what I'm saying is that he didn't get a fair trial," Liana said, speaking slowly to get better control of the exchange. "What happened was that the jury got exposed to information that the defendant's DNA was a match with a sample taken from another woman some time before. Once the jurors heard that, even though there was no further information about who this other woman was or what the circumstances were, there was no way Danny stood a chance. That's what I'm arguing," Liana said.

"So basically, because the jury found out that this lowlife is a serial rapist, you're going to get him off? How can that be justice? And are you on a first name basis with this bastard?" Frank looked positively appalled, shaking his head from side to side.

Watch it, Frank. That's my poor bastard you're talking about.

Liana was about to rip into Frank when she felt Jakob's arm around her shoulders, physically holding her in her place.

"Well, I think it is more complex than that," Liana said, teeth gritted. "I won't bore you with the constitutional issues."

At that moment, the food mercifully arrived. The others attacked it all at once, stuffing their mouths with the delicate flavors to keep the need for conversation at bay. When they had demolished everything, Marissa started in again.

"What kind of vibe do you get from this guy? Is he sexy?" She leaned across the table as if to draw Liana into some girlish conspiracy, her ample breasts now resting dangerously close to the remains of their meal.

Innocent and sexy is a dangerous combination, Marissa.

Liana could feel the heat rising in her face. She risked a sideways glance at Jakob and saw him studying her. Although only she knew how she'd allowed Danny Shea to worm his way into her consciousness, she thought she saw some vague understanding dawn on Jakob's face—as though the single-mindedness with which she had been working on the case now made a modicum of sense to him.

Liana looked at Marissa sharply and cut her down to size. "Most people don't find rape sexy, Marissa," she said. "Besides, I don't get a 'vibe' from my client; he's just a name on a transcript page." She hoped the lie would convince them; she hoped she'd convince herself. Forgetting that she had not told Jakob her plans, she continued, "But when I go to visit him in prison, I'll be able to make a better assessment of his credibility."

"You're going to visit him? You never meet your clients," Jakob said.

"Well, this guy must be something special, Jakob." Frank sneered. Marissa allowed herself a giggle.

Recovering, Liana said, "He has a complicated legal issue that I need to explain to him. He's a client, just like you have clients, Frank, and as his attorney, I have a responsibility to inform him of his rights. I know you don't approve of the type of law I practice, but you do still recognize that I have to do my job, right?"

Jakob, still looking confused by Liana's revelation, cleared his throat and suggested that they order dessert. They picked at the cheesecake and seven-layer cake, so incongruously American after what they had just eaten. Although a coffee might have helped Liana regroup, no one wanted to prolong the evening, and none had been ordered.

Liana knew she should just stay silent and let the rest of the dinner peter out, but she was riled up, and the honey wine had loosened her tongue. In her sweetest voice she turned to Frank and asked, "So which billionaire industry's monopoly are you currently protecting to the detriment of the average consumer, Frank? Bank? Airline? Oil company?"

Frank laughed half-heartedly; Jakob looked at Liana in dismay. She plowed on, as though some evil twin had inhabited her body, like in one of those horror movies she used to love to watch as a kid.

"I'm serious," Liana said. "I mean, everyone always criticizes me for representing criminals, but when you represent, for example, some huge pharmaceutical company trying to corner the market on a drug so that it can't be made into a generic that sick people can afford—isn't that just as morally reprehensible?"

Before Frank could respond, Jakob jumped in. "Please excuse Liana. She's been having a rough time at work lately—questioning whether this is truly the right place for her to use her talents. She's working through some issues right now, and it has her a little off her game."

Liana stared at Jakob incredulously but managed to nod slightly and look suitably abashed. When she reached for another glass of wine, Jakob gently took hold of her hand. "It's enough, Li," he said, so only she could hear.

Frank took care of the check. "Well, that was certainly an entertaining evening!" he said as they made their way to the door. "I do hope things work out for you, Liana. I always thought those criminals were lucky to have you." Frank put his arm around Marissa's waist and guided her out the door to a car waiting for them on the street. "Give my regards to Danny!" he called out over his shoulder as he closed the car door.

Jakob hailed a cab and gave Liana's address, and she let out the breath she hadn't realized she had been holding.

He's still coming home with me.

Deflated, Jakob sat with his chin resting in his hand and his forehead leaning against his window. It had started to rain. Liana wished desperately that she had played the part of supportive girlfriend that Jakob wanted and deserved, and she regretted the wine, which had definitely contributed to her bad behavior. Jakob said nothing for the entire ride, looking out at the soggy streets.

When they got into her apartment, Jakob paced the length of the living room like a caged animal, his frustration mounting. He rarely lost his temper and he didn't raise his voice, but the tension was palpable.

"Why would you sabotage me like that, Li? Frank's a piece of work, but he's my boss. One minute you're supportive and proud of me, and the next you're ripping him a new one. How am I supposed to react to that? All I'm trying to do is get my career set up, get us set up. Isn't that what you want too?"

Liana ignored his question about their future, too distraught over how the evening had gone.

"Can't you see how superficial these people are, Jay? Do you want to give the best years of your life kissing up to a guy like Frank? Do you want to end up like him, a new Marissa every month? Treating women like objects and attacking people for the work they do? I know your job pays well, but can the money really make up for the rest of it?" Liana could feel herself boiling over, a tea kettle overflowing with frustration and uncertainty.

"Is that what you think of me? That this job will turn me into a greedy, sycophantic womanizer? Is that who you think I am?" Jakob asked.

"I think Wilcox & Finney is swallowing you whole. I'm frightened that soon there'll be nothing left of the man I fell in love with," Liana said, sitting down shakily on the couch. "And how could you tell Frank that I was having doubts about my role as a defense attorney? That was private, and maybe it isn't even true anymore," she said.

"Wow," Jakob said, shaking his head. "Is that what this is all about? This Shea has really done a number on you."

Unable to deny or admit, Liana said nothing, retreating to the bathroom and giving Jakob a graceful way to leave if he wanted to take it.

She turned on the shower and stepped in, raising the heat as high as it would go. She let the blistering water pelt her face, mixing with the tears coursing down her cheeks.

How did this happen?

When she felt that the near scalding had cleared her head a little, Liana got out of the shower and put on her pajamas. She came out of the bathroom, peering around the corner into the living room to see if Jakob was there. When she didn't see him, she walked slowly into the bedroom, where she found him lying on his side of the bed, on his back with his eyes closed. He had folded down a corner of the quilt for her, and she crept in silently, even though she knew he wasn't asleep.

After a few minutes, she turned on her side and put her hand tentatively on his chest, feeling the warmth of his body and his heart beating under her fingers. "I'm so sorry, Jay—I didn't mean for this to happen tonight."

"I know. I'm sorry too. Frank pushed your buttons; that's what he does," Jakob said, his eyes still closed and his body taut under the covers.

"I felt like I was under attack," Liana said.

"So did I," Jakob said. "Let's put it behind us."

"I love you."

"I know. I love you too." Jakob turned onto his side, his back to Liana. A few minutes later, she could hear him breathing evenly, either sleeping or making a pretty good show of it. She stayed awake for what seemed like an eternity, until she finally drifted off in the early hours of the morning.

Liana awoke to her radio alarm set to the oldies station, Frankie Valli and the Four Seasons screeching "Big Girls Don't Cry" at an unbearable decibel level. She swatted at her bedside table violently, sending the crooners crashing to the floor. An almost sickening silence followed, allowing the memories of the dinner with Frank and Marissa to flood her. Liana pulled the duvet over her head, breathing in the sad warmth of her body. Jakob had gotten up at dawn to go into work, and she was alone.

She forced herself to get up and throw on her workout clothes, her head still throbbing. *How do the Ethiopians drink that stuff?*

There were some Saturday mornings when Liana walked from her cramped apartment on Seventy-Sixth and Amsterdam, with its occasional vermin and lousy security system, to Charlotte and Howard's breezy two-bedroom in the Bromley on Eighty-Fourth and Broadway, with its uniformed doorman and party room and gym and laundry facilities, and she couldn't help but see it as a blueprint for the trajectory of her life with Jakob. And then there were other Saturday mornings, like this one, where Liana was so preoccupied with the vicissitudes of her daily existence that she barely noticed anything as she strolled past Zabar's, Barnes & Noble, and the movie theatre on Eighty-Third, finally forcing herself to approach the entrance of the building—her weekend workout with

Charlotte, Katie, and their beautiful Czech personal trainer, Marta, awaiting.

"Good morning, Rico," she said to the elderly doorman. "Why do I subject myself to this torture every week?" she asked.

"I don't know, miss. I think you like to be around that sexy trainer—I would like that."

"I bet you would."

Her roommates from graduate school, Charlotte and Katie, had been complicated and substantive women when she met them at age twenty-two, and they were only more so now, some seven years later. Charlotte was soft spoken and innocent; she had grown up sheltered by overprotective parents in Savannah, Georgia. She was pretty in an unaffected, natural sort of way—straight, thick black hair setting off clear, soulful blue eyes. Her forays into romance when she was younger had had a naive feel to them: "Oh, that's what he meant when he said . . ." and "Can you believe he thought we would do *that*?"

Katie was savvier. In addition to her smarts, her looks had always been her ticket up and out of a midwestern, ordinary life, and she put them to good use. She had strawberry blond hair and was tall and thin, but curvy in all the right places, and her features were set exactly so that you had to stop and stare a little when she turned her gaze on you. Her time in business school had been a means to an end, and her dalliances had a similar feel. Katie always had the best looking boyfriend, until there was some snag in the relationship, and then she'd move on to the next.

The three women had spent an inordinate amount of time together during their graduate school years, studying, lying on each other's beds, eating cookie dough ice cream, and laughing—always laughing. That they had all ended up in New York seemed like nothing less than a miracle to Liana. They were the sisters she had never had.

Stepping into Charlotte's apartment, Liana saw that the session had already started, which was fine by her. Katie was running on the treadmill, and Charlotte was stepping up and down on the Bosu ball. "Get in here, Liana!" Marta barked. "You are missing the warm-up!" Marta, who never broke a sweat when the girls were all perspiring to beat the band, ordered Liana to jog in place, which only exacerbated her hangover, and her drill sergeant directives weren't helping either.

"You look like crap," Katie said to Liana.

"Thanks. You look fresh as a daisy. You must've slept alone last night," Liana responded.

"As a matter of fact, I did," said Katie. "And I'm not ashamed to say it."

"Why would you be?" Charlotte asked. Charlotte had married Howard two years earlier, and although she'd been known to have a good time in her single days, as a newly married woman, she took a much narrower view of what was appropriate for Katie and Liana.

"You know, Katie, you need to be choosy. Liana has Jakob; that's different. But you have to go slowly and make sure the guy is serious about you as a person before you have sex, if you want to get married. Remember what my mother always says: 'Why buy the cow when you can get the milk for free?'" Charlotte said solemnly.

"Charlotte, if my mother spoke that way, I think I'd throw myself out a window," Katie replied. Liana agreed with Katie, but she couldn't help thinking that Charlotte and her mom had a point on some level. She had been together with Jakob too long to think that wearing a virginal white dress was the only way to go down the aisle, but she did think that Katie could be a bit more discerning.

"Okay, girlies. Face each other in a triangle because I know you're going to talk. We're going to do squats. Stick your booties out and bend those knees, up and down, and one and two—lower!—and three . . ." They grunted and grimaced as five foot ten and 125 pounds of beautiful auburn-haired Marta put them through their paces.

Their weekly workout served as part exercise and part therapy session, Marta acting as the benevolent facilitator of both sit-ups and soul-baring. She knew everything about Charlotte's, Katie's, and Liana's lives—from their romantic ups and downs to their issues with their parents to their work problems. Between the push-ups and the rows and the crunches, Marta had heard it all, and they always valued the advice she dispensed. She hadn't had an easy life herself, but she didn't judge, and she could usually see the solution that the girls had missed even when it was right before their eyes.

"I barely see Jakob unless it is in the context of some firm-related command performance. And I don't do very well at those; last night I had too much to drink, and when Jakob's boss questioned my commitment to my clients, I lost it. Do you think if Jakob and I were married, it would be different?"

"Are you asking if you were Jakob's wife, would you act more like an adult?" Katie said. "I doubt it," she said, answering her own question.

"No—I mean, would I be more important to Jakob than his career?" Liana asked plaintively.

"Maybe, but maybe not," Charlotte said. Liana, Katie, and Marta all looked up—*is Charlotte going to say something critical about Howard?* They had barely heard a negative comment since the wedding, and it was beginning to irk them all. No one could be that perfect.

"Lie down, ladies—full sit-ups, forty of them," Marta said, trying not to get in the way of the conversation but still keep the exercise going.

"Howard is just as ambitious as Jakob. He gets up before I do and goes to work, and he often has to eat dinner with clients or go for drinks. He's usually way too stressed-out or drunk by the time we get into bed to do anyone any good. We spent a lot more quality time together in every arena before we were married." The women were all silenced by this revelation, even Marta, who was never at a loss for words.

"Well," Liana said, trying to think of a positive spin she could put on Charlotte's situation, "the bottom line is that you're tied to each other eternally, in the eyes of God and man, and he loves you, and he pays the rent on this nice apartment." Her remarks hadn't quite come out the way she intended, but Charlotte seemed to take some solace in what she said anyway.

"Anyway, has Jakob proposed to you? Why are you worrying so much about getting married?" Katie asked between push-ups.

"No, he's too good a lawyer for that. Never ask a question if you don't know the answer beforehand. But he's been feeling me out," Liana said. "Maybe I'm just overly romantic, but I'm looking for unconditional, all-encompassing love and total devotion. Isn't that what we all deserve?"

"Maybe you need a dog, not a man," Marta suggested. "Come on, less gabbing, more sweating!"

Marta ran through all the major muscle groups, doling out handheld ten-pound weights and resistance bands, marching the women around the room in painful lunges. "Lie down, girlies. We are going to do leg lifts—both legs straight in the air, and up and down and up and down . . ."

"Listen," Katie said, "marriage may not be all it's cracked up to be, but the dating scene out there is brutal—you guys have no idea. The other night I went out with this guy Tom—I met him on Match.com. He looked like a normal guy. He told me he was going to pick me up on his motorcycle, which I thought sounded kind of whimsical—he said I should wait outside my building because it was hard to park. So I waited out there in the ninety-degree heat, and he was forty-five minutes late."

"Oh, no!" Charlotte interjected.

"Oh, yes!" said Katie. "Then he took me to this trendy new restaurant in the meat-packing district, but the gimmick was that all the waiters and waitresses wore only their underwear. It was amusing for a couple of minutes, and then I started to think about the sweat and the hair and the chafing thighs, and I lost my appetite." Liana was laughing so hard she thought she would pee in her pants.

"Stop, stop!" she yelled.

"Oh, no. I won't stop because I'm not done. When we left the restaurant, he brought me home. He went to put his arm around me—prelude to a kiss, I guess—and I saw he had this gross, scaly rash on the inside of his arm—his bicep, right, Marta?"

"His bicep, yes, dear," Marta said.

"Yeah, his bicep. I didn't want any part of him coming anywhere near any part of me!" Katie looked as if the disgust still hadn't worn off some seventy-two hours later.

With the specter of Tom still hanging over them, Marta chirped, "Okay, my pretties, lie down on your backs, knees bent. We are going to lift our hips in the air and *squeeeeze* our buttocks, and little pulses up, one and two and three and . . ." The women continued their pelvic thrusts as the doom of Katie's situation settled on them all.

"You know, Marta, this exercise is the best sex I have had in a month," said Katie.

"Me too," said Charlotte.

"Me too," said Liana.

"Me too," said Marta. "Well, not really me too. You know what you girls need?" she asked.

They knew what was coming. Marta had become intrigued by pole dancing, and she was now a certified instructor and taught in a studio in the Village. "I'm telling you, there is nothing skanky about it! The women who take the classes are just like you girls. They are not hookers! They just feel sexier than you do!" Marta protested. Liana knew Marta was probably right, but she just couldn't get the picture out of her head of Marta in the four-inch stiletto heels and purple spandex that she had seen on the studio website. But they all held their tongues; they loved Marta and never wanted to appear disapproving of her.

"Seriously, Li—here's what you should do," Katie said. "You need to go away with Jakob—go somewhere for a romantic weekend."

"Ooh—good idea, Katie," Charlotte joined in. "Remember in New Haven when Jakob would come to visit you, and all three of us would stand out on the front porch waiting for him to arrive? And then he would be there, with flowers that he bought on the corner from those cult guys with the sign 'We are not Moonies'—it was so dreamy, and he wasn't even coming to see the two of us!" Charlotte looked absolutely misty remembering the scene.

"You need to tap back into that," Katie advised. "It's still there; it has just been buried in an avalanche of law-firm crap. And remember, Jakob is a great guy—smart and funny and devoted to you. Don't get scared off because he works too much—he wants to take care of you."

"I'm sure you're right," Liana said with a sigh, red-faced and slightly out of breath. She didn't tell them that Jakob might not be her number one fan after the scene she had made with Frank.

"Pole dancing," Marta said.

"You don't give up, Marta," Liana said, giving her beautiful young friend a hug.

Liana said goodbye and walked down Eighty-Fourth Street two blocks to Riverside Park. She sat on a bench and looked out at the Hudson while joggers and bicyclists streamed by on the path in front of her.

Everyone has somewhere to go, and I'm spinning out of control.

Danny Shea had somehow managed to infiltrate her defenses, haunting her waking and sleeping thoughts. And the more intensely she yearned to be the center of Jakob's world, the more she found herself pushing him away with antics like she had pulled with Frank. In both realms of her life, personal and professional, she was adrift in a way she had never been before, and it was downright frightening.

She pressed the button on her iPhone. "Does Jakob love me, Siri?" she asked pathetically.

Siri answered, in her computerized lilt, "Love is the flower you've got to let grow."

"John Lennon. Nice, Siri." Liana thought for a minute and tried another tack. "Siri, should I marry Jakob and live happily ever after?"

"You know, Li-an-a, happily ever after is for fairy tales. Real life is much more complicated."

"Siri, you sound just like my mother," Liana answered, despondent.

"Your mother is a wise woman, Li-an-a."

Liana sat, lost in thought, until a pigeon flew overhead and pooped on her. "Well, doesn't that just about sum it all up," she said, to no one in particular. She stood and hurried home to throw herself in the shower.

CHAPTER 10

When the buzzer rang on that hot Sunday morning in mid-August, Liana was still sleeping. Mistaking the sound for her alarm clock, she cursed a blue streak that would have made many of her clients proud, pressing every button she could find in her stupor. When the din continued, she realized someone was at the front door of the building, and she pulled herself out of bed and stumbled to the intercom on the hallway wall.

Probably some moron with a hangover locked himself out when he went to get the Sunday Times, *and now he is ringing every buzzer hoping someone half-asleep will let him back in.*

She pressed the intercom button. "Yes?" she said, hoping to sound as annoyed as she felt.

"Liana, it's Gerry."

"Gerry who?" she asked, still unable to process much of anything.

"Gerry Greenstein. Your boss."

"Oh my God," she said. "What are you doing at my apartment on a Sunday morning?" Gerry's partner Lars lived on the Upper West Side, somewhere up in the 90s closer to Deb's apartment. Liana ran into Gerry and Lars on the weekend once in a while, usually at Fairway, where they would be buying all sorts of exotic organic vegetables that Liana couldn't identify and where she went solely for coffee beans. Coming to her apartment was definitely against any number of unwritten rules of office etiquette.

"Liana," he said, "I need to speak with you. Could you please come down? I have Delancey with me." Delancey was Gerry's dachshund. Liana was not a dog person—she had no intention of ever having a plastic bag be the only barrier between her hand and steaming dog poop. But she liked Delancey, who struck her as a real gentleman of a dog.

"Okay, give me a minute to get dressed," Liana said into the intercom. "Not everyone is out and about at this hour of the morning, you know." She threw on a pair of sweats and an Elton John T-shirt she found in a pile on her bedroom floor. Her hair was going in eighty different directions, so she pulled on a Mets cap to lend an air of control and went downstairs.

Gerry and Delancey were standing on the sidewalk in front of her building. As soon as she saw them, Liana's pent up anxiety took over, and she burst out, "You haven't come here to tell me that I'm not a gung-ho public defender, have you? Because it's a false accusation, and anyway, I shouldn't have to deal with that on a Sunday morning outside my own home!" She gestured wildly to her faded-brick, doormanless building, which looked somewhat shabby in the early morning light.

When she came up for air, Liana looked at Gerry, and she saw immediately that his eyes were red.

High?

Unlikely at this hour of the day, although otherwise not a bad guess. Public defenders of a certain vintage were just as likely as some of their clients to partake in the occasional recreational drug—it was a remnant of the 1960s culture that the younger crew of attorneys "didn't know from," as her mother would have said. No, crying seemed much more likely.

"Did you have a fight with Lars?" Liana asked, with as much sympathy as she could muster.

"Liana," Gerry said. "I wanted to tell you in person. Deb is very ill." Liana felt a quick rush of light-headedness, and her hands and forehead were immediately cold and clammy while the rest of her seemed to be radiating heat. She was familiar with these symptoms—when she had long ago asked a doctor, he called it "vasovagal"—sometimes her fingers turned blue too, and she had fainted a number of times: once on the subway, once on an airplane. If she didn't sit down immediately, she'd soon be flat out on the sidewalk. She quickly scanned the vicinity for stray fecal matter, human or canine, and, finding none, crouched down and put her head between her knees.

"Liana, Liana, are you all right?" Gerry was standing over her, and he was getting frantic.

"I'm okay, Gerry. Just leave me be for a minute," Liana said, her eyes closed. She was vaguely aware of people stepping past, but Delancey was doing a marvelous job marking out an inviolable zone, marching around her and barking. When she felt like she wouldn't keel over, Liana stood up slowly and looked warily at Gerry, waiting for the bad news about her only real friend in the office.

"Deb has stage-four ovarian cancer," Gerry blurted out, no preamble.

"Oh, God," Liana managed before bursting into tears.

"She hasn't been feeling well—I guess you must've known that, sitting in such close quarters with her. It's a hard illness to diagnose early because the symptoms are kind of vague. Apparently a lot of women don't know they have ovarian cancer until it's pretty far along."

Please, Gerry. Please stop talking.

"She had emergency surgery on Friday. They took out so much . . . the tumors, her ovaries, her uterus, fallopian tubes, who knows what else," he stammered.

"Okay, Gerry," Liana said. She knew how much Gerry cared about Deb, but she just couldn't handle this strangely intimate situation any longer. "I appreciate you coming to tell me, I really do. Where is she? Can I see her?" Liana tried to stay calm, but she wasn't sure it was working. The noises of the street had all faded; she could only hear her own heart beating.

"She's at Sloan Kettering. Do you want me to go with you? I saw her yesterday." Liana had an unbidden pang of jealousy; how had Gerry known before she did that Deb was in the hospital? But she suppressed the petty thought as best she could.

"No, thanks. I'll go clean myself up and go over there," Liana heard herself say, although how she managed even that level of conversation amazed her. She was jolted by a vision of Max, and she wanted to ask Gerry what would become of him if something terrible happened to Deb. Instead, she waved inanely at Gerry, stroked Delancey on the head, said, "Thanks, pal," and went inside.

Liana thought a shower might calm her nerves, although she knew she was stalling. Her phobia of all things medical meant she definitely never voluntarily entered a hospital to visit anyone, except when absolutely necessary. She let the hot water batter her just long enough to clear her head.

How did she get so sick so fast? And how did I miss that it was happening?

She took a cab, afraid that if she went with public transportation, she would subconsciously reroute herself and not end up at the correct destination. She entered at the entrance on York Avenue, between Sixty-Seventh and Sixty-Eighth Street, and took the elevator to the eleventh floor ICU. She marveled at how hospitals always smelled the same to her—a scent that was impossible to recreate anywhere else—some combination of cheap but potent disinfectant, unnamed but incurable illness, and sheer terror. If Liana could have held her nose the entire time she was in the hospital, she would have, but she knew she risked that vasovagal thing if she tried a stunt like that.

She approached the nurses' station and croaked out, "I'm looking for Deborah Levine." The woman manning the desk unceremoniously pointed her to a room in the corner and said, "No more than ten minutes please, and don't excite the patient—she's been through a rough surgery." Liana couldn't imagine how she might possibly excite anyone at this point, but she nodded and willed her feet forward toward Deb's room. She peered in and saw that there was no roommate, for which she was wildly grateful—it was hard enough having to see Deb here, she knew she couldn't have handled having to "visit" with some stranger that just happened to be lying in the next bed. When she went into the room, Deb, who was perched up slightly on her pillows, looked straight at her. Well aware of Liana's failings when it came to being around illness, she normally teased her mercilessly.

"Wow, you must really love me," Deb said.

It was shocking to see her in a hospital gown, without any makeup and with her hair pulled back in a simple ponytail. She looked even younger than she was, washed out but still beautiful. Liana was relieved that Deb wasn't in obvious pain, even as she noted the morphine drip that was keeping it at bay.

"Oh, Deb," Liana whispered, choking back tears, and she went to hug her, but there were tubes coming out of her arms and leads attached to her chest, and as soon as Liana touched her, machines began to beep and wail. Liana jumped back. "I'm not supposed to excite you!" she blurted. Deb started to laugh, and the nurse came charging into the room.

"What did I just tell you?" she chastised as she reset the monitors.

"It's fine, Joanie. This is my very good friend Liana. She wasn't exciting, I promise. She's just a little klutzy." The nurse looked appeased but still gave Liana a withering glance as she left the room.

"You have nine minutes left," Joanie said.

"Wow, she's tough," Liana said when Joanie was out of earshot.

"She's an excellent nurse," Deb said. Liana knew from her many stints of hanging out in the hospital with her dad that, just as with the support staff at work, it was critically important to befriend the nurses. They were the ones that really held your life in their hands; the doctors barely made an appearance most of the time. Liana was impressed that Deb had intuited this and that she was already best buddies with Joanie, even though she hadn't been in the ICU long.

"What happened?" Liana asked. It was kind of a dumb question, but she felt as if she needed to know.

"Nothing all that mysterious," Deb said, slipping immediately into her "lawyer" voice, giving Liana a factual recount of the situation as if she were talking about someone else—someone she didn't particularly care for—as opposed to herself.

"I haven't been feeling well for about six weeks—symptoms that could be anything, but a lot of discomfort, lack of appetite, and then the weight loss. I guess that should have tipped me off. My gynecologist had me go for a CT scan and then an MRI; they saw something on my ovary, and then they did the biopsy." Deb wiped away a stray tear that had slipped down her cheek with the back of her hand, nearly knocking into the IV and coming dangerously close to summoning nurse Joanie again. Liana looked on the bedside table and saw the strategically placed box of tissues. She handed one Kleenex to Deb and kept one for herself.

"When it came back malignant, I had a PET scan, which showed the cancer had spread around in there; no need to get into all the specifics—I don't want you to lose your breakfast." Liana was glad that Deb wasn't outwardly falling apart, but it made her own anguish all the more apparent in comparison. She blew her nose loudly into the tissue and hoped she wasn't making the situation worse for Deb by not being strong at that moment.

Maybe just being here now is enough.

"Where is your family?" Liana had been surprised to find Deb alone.

"My parents were here all day yesterday," Deb said, kindly overlooking Liana's somewhat accusatory question. "They are beyond distraught. I don't want them to spend a lot of time here. There'll be plenty of opportunity for them to see me when I'm recovering at home."

"And your brothers?" Liana asked, unable to refrain from the follow-up question.

"I'm sure they'll be in to see me; they live out of town, and it isn't that easy to just drop everything." Deb sounded disappointed, and Liana hoped that the brothers got their act together on the double.

"So you had to have this surgery right away? You didn't get a second opinion?" Liana regretted the question as soon as it left her mouth, but after years of living with a parent with a chronic illness, second opinions were just part of the landscape. She couldn't imagine doing anything serious to her body without at least two white coats telling her it was the only way to go.

"No," Deb said. She didn't sound offended, just controlled, as if she were a newscaster reading a tragic story from a teleprompter and trying to inspire confidence. "This is the best hospital in the city for this"—avoiding the word cancer—"I didn't see any point in prolonging things; I just wanted all of this stuff out," she said, motioning to the lower half of her body as though she were shooing away a pesky fly.

"How's Max? Where is he?" Everything Liana said was coming out wrong. Obviously Deb would have made plans for Max, and it would only make her feel worse to have Liana ask, as though maybe he had been left home, locked in his bedroom, until her return.

"He's with his father," Deb said simply. "I'm relieved that I don't have to worry about those logistics, for now." The implication that she would have to make arrangements for Max sometime in the future was too painful to bear, and Liana was grateful it was left unsaid. Deb was getting sleepy, her body rebelling against much more interaction. She put her head back and closed her eyes. Liana sat with her quietly, holding her hand lightly, wondering whether she should leave.

Liana had only a few more minutes to spend with Deb before Staff Sergeant Joanie returned, and she was trying to come up with something reassuring to say when Deb abruptly opened her eyes and asked, "So why are you going to see him?" Caught off guard, Liana had no idea what Deb was talking about.

"I'm sorry?" Liana said.

"Why are you going to Green Haven to see Danny Shea?" Deb asked. "Gerry was trying to distract me, and he told me something about a risk you need to discuss with Shea in person—what the hell kind of risk could there possibly be in that case?" Deb asked.

Liana was amazed at Deb's clarity after what she had been through, not to mention her interest in something as peripheral to her life as Liana's appeal. Liana thought if she were direly ill, about the last thing she would think about was her clients or anyone else's. But Deb was different—she had no instinct for self-pity, even when it was well deserved, and she did not suffer fools. If she had something on her mind, she would not be deterred, cancer or no cancer, and Liana couldn't bring herself to lie to her.

"There's no risk," she said quietly, unable to look Deb in the eye.

"Then why are you going?" Deb repeated, more insistently. When Liana didn't answer, Deb's eyes widened, and with a great effort, she hoisted herself up on her elbows so she could face Liana squarely.

"*Oh my God!*" she squealed, delighted. "You have a crush on your rapist!"

"Shh, Shh!" Liana motioned Deb to lie down before the nurse came running in. "I don't have a crush on him, and I would appreciate it if you didn't call him 'my rapist,'" she said, with as much indignation as she could marshal.

"Why shouldn't I call him that?" Deb asked, perplexed. "Isn't that who we are talking about—that guy I unloaded on you? I've had a lot of anesthesia. Am I mixing him up with another one of your clients?"

"No, you know exactly who we're talking about," Liana said. "I'm going to see him because I'm curious to see what he has to say, what he's like in person—whether he has an innocent air to him," she stammered. Liana thought Deb might burst a blood vessel she was laughing so hard.

"Oh, so all of a sudden you think one of our clients is wrongly convicted? And it just happens to be the best looking, most charming, most articulate guy anyone in the history of the Public Defender's Office has ever represented? You're pathetic, Liana. You know that, right?"

"Yes," Liana admitted, looking at her feet. "You're not going to tell Gerry, are you?"

"No, Liana. I'm not going to report you to the authorities. Just don't do anything stupid or beneath you." She motioned for Liana to pour some water into a little Dixie cup on her tray table, took a few sips, and continued.

"Look—I don't know—maybe he's as pure as the driven snow and this is your chance to play the hero. But he's got a motive here—he needs you to be on his side, whether he's innocent or guilty as hell. Just remember when you're there, you're his lawyer, not some floozy girlfriend going to visit to give him a peek at her boobies through the glass partition. And the overwhelming likelihood is that, no matter how smooth talking he is, if he didn't commit this crime, he probably did something else just as bad," Deb cautioned.

Liana knew Deb was right, but she still felt a thrill run

through her at the very mention of the visit. When Joanie stuck her head in the doorway to tell Liana her time was up, she was happy to go before she betrayed any more of her bizarre emotional state.

She kissed Deb on the forehead. "Remember, you gave me Danny Shea to restore my passion for the job," Liana said, only half kidding.

"Don't be ridiculous," Deb said. "And don't blame me for your poor judgment."

"Okay, I won't, I promise. See you back at the ranch. Please don't take too long to recuperate. Obviously, I can't be responsible for my actions without you in the office," she said. A glimmer of a smile passed over Deb's lips as she closed her eyes.

Liana made it out of Deb's room and down the hallway before she sank down on a wooden bench, waves of dread and panic passing over her. She didn't know how long she'd sat there before a volunteer noticed her, asking her kindly if she would like a cup of tea. When the agitation finally subsided, Liana walked back down the hallway past Deb's room, sneaking another glance at her friend, asleep now, having overexerted herself with Liana.

At least I made her laugh. That has to be worth something.

CHAPTER 11

Liana tossed and turned most of the night before getting up at dawn to make the 6:45 Metro-North out of Grand Central Station to Beacon, New York, where she would catch a cab the rest of the way to Stormville. There were several prisons right in the area, about an hour and a half north of New York City—Green Haven, where Danny Shea was currently housed, was maximum security, men only. There had been famous inmates there over the years, most recently John Gotti—better known in legal and mafia circles as the Teflon Don for the many times he had evaded conviction before the law finally caught up with him. But Shea was one of the faceless legions of men serving out some portion of their sentences there now, in a town that was way down on its luck—so much so, that the prison industry was the mainstay of the economy.

In preparation for the visit, the first she had ever made to a correctional facility, Liana had spent the previous evening on the Internet, glancing at the rules regarding visitor conduct and scrolling through extensive advice offered by family members on various websites serving the extended prison community. There were caveats about what you could or could not bring to the inmate, as well as a long list of dos and mostly don'ts regarding what to wear and how to behave.

"Don't bring home-baked cookies." "Don't wear see-through clothing." "Don't make out in the visiting room."

The posts were written by, and aimed almost exclusively at, women visiting their husbands or boyfriends or baby daddies. Liana tried to extrapolate what she could about attorneys visiting clients, but most of it wasn't very relevant. She did, however, take some time to pick out an outfit that would be professional and radiate authority, neither alluring nor too off-putting. She settled on a pair of plain navy trousers that did not hug her rear in a particularly flattering way and a yellow, slightly loose-fitting short-sleeve crew-neck knit top. If it hadn't been August, she might have opted for some getup that showed no skin at all, like a burka, but she didn't want to sweat in there. For all she knew, perspiration might contain sex pheromones. In the morning, she corralled her curls into a severe knot at the back of her neck and scrubbed her face clean. She put on no makeup, not even the swipe of eyeliner she usually wore to bring out her eyes.

"Beacon, next station stop is Beacon, in ten minutes," the conductor called out at eight o'clock. Liana had taken the train instead of renting a car, figuring she might be able to sleep a little and hopefully be refreshed when she arrived. Unfortunately, although the train was nearly empty, it made all the local stops, and Liana woke up at every station. She had finally fallen into a deeper sleep when the conductor gently touched her shoulder. "Miss," he said, "we're almost at your stop."

Liana opened her eyes, and for a moment she had no idea where she was. She'd been dreaming that Jakob had been falsely accused of insider trading and she'd been hired to defend him, but in the dream she'd also been the one who'd turned him in to the authorities. Liana wasn't much into the interpretation of dreams, but she was pretty sure this one meant she might be a double agent—appearing to be on Jakob's side but secretly stabbing him in the back. She felt the oatmeal she had eaten for breakfast churning in her stomach, and she tried to push the dream out of her mind.

"Do you know where I can get a taxi to Green Haven?" she asked the conductor.

"Yes, you'll see the taxi stand right where you get out. There will be other women also waiting to go see their husbands who are up here—first time visiting?" he asked, looking at her sympathetically.

"Yes," she said, "but I'm an attorney. I'm going to visit a client."

"Oh, sorry, miss. I didn't mean anything by it. We don't get that many attorneys coming up by train—this crowd is usually the wives and girlfriends, sometimes a mom. I always feel the worst for the mothers—I mean, no one thinks their little boy will end up here, right? Anyway, you'll probably have to share a taxi with someone, so you might as well know the scoop," he said.

"Yes, thanks. I appreciate the information," Liana said. She made sure everything was in order in her briefcase and rummaged around in her purse for the cab fare. When the train stopped in Beacon, she was the first one off.

What am I doing here? Better to get this over as quickly as possible.

She walked over to the taxi stand, and the driver sitting in the first car rolled down his window. "Where you headed?" he said.

"Green Haven."

"Hop in."

Liana sat in the back seat. She looked at his license, and after a couple of minutes of idling, Liana asked, "Can we get going soon, Boris?"

"Yeah," he said. "There's another train that comes in from Albany in a few. We're waiting to see who else needs to go to Green Haven. You're not the only Juliet coming here to see her Romeo today." Liana was going to give him the "I'm an attorney" speech and then decided it wasn't worth it. Besides, she thought the doomed lovers was a pretty apt metaphor for what was going on for most of these visitors, and she didn't want to discourage Boris's literary streak.

Liana looked out the window at the women coming off the train that had just pulled in, anxious to see which desperate loser would be her companion for the ride. Liana assumed that the women would all be unattractive, overweight, or old—or some combination of the three.

Who else besides someone with very low self-esteem would voluntarily get involved with or stick around for a guy serving time for a violent crime?

Liana saw Boris motion to someone, and then a young girl slid into the backseat next to her. She could not have been more than nineteen or twenty. She was tall and willowy, with brown legs that went on for miles; she was wearing a fashionably tight and short pink skirt that Liana was not sure would pass muster with the prison guards in terms of the dress code, although she was certain that they would give the girl an A for effort. Her black hair hung down straight and thick to her waist, and her eyes were a crystal blue.

She must be part Native American, part Norwegian princess.

In short, she was a knockout, and Liana could not for the life of her imagine why she was sharing a cab to Green Haven with her at a quarter past eight on a Tuesday morning in late August.

"Rosa," the girl said and extended her hand to Liana.

"I'm Liana," she replied, taken aback by friendliness that simply didn't exist in New York City, where you would sooner run across four lanes of speeding traffic than engage in conversation with a total stranger.

"I'm going to Green Haven," Rosa said. "It's my first time."

"Yes, I'm going there too," said Liana, "and I'm a virgin too."

"Oh, wow!" Rosa exclaimed. "But I'm not a virgin," she said quietly, looking down demurely at her lap. Boris looked at the women in the rearview mirror and raised his eyebrows. They were all silent for a few moments as Boris whisked them toward their destination. Rosa was very nervous, tapping her foot rapidly on the floor and twisting her hands together.

"I'm going to see my boyfriend," she confided.

"Your boyfriend is at Green Haven?" Liana wanted to add, "How could that be?" but stifled the impulse.

"Are you going to see your husband?" Rosa asked.

"No. I'm an attorney. I'm going to visit a client to explain some legal issues to him," Liana answered. Boris nodded knowingly in the front seat, as if he had figured that out long before.

"What did he do?" Rosa asked.

"Well, they say he raped someone." Liana knew she had to be careful, even with people she would never see again, not to divulge any confidential information about her client—she prided herself on scrupulously following the rules.

"But you don't believe it," Rosa conjectured.

"It doesn't matter what I believe. I'm just doing my job," Liana answered. She looked out the window to avoid looking at Rosa.

Changing the subject, Liana asked, "How did you meet your boyfriend?"

"I haven't met him yet," Rosa said. "We're pen pals—it's a program run through an online church." Liana had heard about such things before from her colleagues. The inmates were always looking for someone to write to—they had time on their hands, and often their own family members didn't want much to do with them. So they would hook up with these outfits that gave them women who were willing—the letters on both sides often bordered on pornographic, and the women would sometimes send suggestive pictures of themselves to make it more real for these guys. They were all using each other, and perhaps no one was the worse for wear, but it still had an awfully sad feel to it.

Could lovely Rosa really be part of that?

Registering that Liana was familiar with the pen pal scenario, Rosa explained, "It's not what you think. We've written to each other for about six months. Joe is a nice man. There's nothing dirty about it. And he asked me to come visit, so I decided I would meet him and see what kind of person he is. Maybe he won't even like me," Rosa said.

"Ha!" Liana blurted out while Boris shook his head from side to side. "And what did Joe do to land himself in Green Haven?" Liana asked.

"Yeah, what did he do?" Boris chimed in.

"Well, they say he killed someone—another crack dealer who owed him money. But I don't believe it. He writes really sweet letters, and he told me he didn't do it," Rosa said. Liana thought again of the letters that Danny Shea had written and wondered how much his good penmanship and grammatically correct sentence structure had influenced what she thought about him.

Was Joe also a gifted correspondent?

Liana's thoughts were interrupted by Rosa's question, "Are you married?"

"No, but I have a boyfriend," Liana responded.

"Are you going to get married?" Rosa persisted.

"I hope so, yes," Liana said. She thought about Jakob and how strained things had been of late. And now, here she was, going to meet Danny Shea out of a dangerous mix of neediness and attraction she could barely admit she felt.

Deb was right. I am pathetic.

"I'm thinking about marrying Joe," Rosa said.

"What?" Boris yelled and slammed on the brakes.

"Rosa." Liana tried to reach a calm internal place before she continued, "How much time is Joe doing for this murder you think he didn't commit?"

"Twenty-five years," Rosa said.

"So how old will you be before you can really be together? And I'm not talking about the occasional conjugal visit—I'm talking on the outside," Liana prodded.

"I'll be forty-four," Rosa answered, doing the math as the horror of that advanced age sank in a bit.

"I know it isn't any of my business, Rosa, but why on earth would you marry this man?" Liana said.

"Because I love him. Isn't that what people who love each other do?" Rosa asked. Liana was taken aback momentarily by the sincerity of the question.

"I guess so, Rosa," Liana said. "I guess that's right."

As huge brick walls loomed above them, they pulled into the facility. Liana took care of the taxi fare for both of them. "Thanks so much," Rosa said. "Wish me luck!"

"I wish you all the luck in the world," Liana said. She arranged with Boris to pick her up in two hours. She let Rosa get a head start on the long line to enter the facility, hanging back until she could no longer see the girl's pink skirt ahead of her. She was glad to feel frumpy in her outfit and gladder still that hormones and pipe dreams were not propelling her to the front of the line. This trip was both completely unnecessary and ill-advised, but the cab ride had put things in perspective. Liana felt calmer than she had in a while.

When she stepped through the metal detector, the alarms went off. The guard pulled her aside. "Anything in your pockets, Counselor? Cell phone? Coins? Pickaxe? That was a joke, Counselor."

"No, sir," Liana said, not amused. She had emptied everything she had into the little basket.

"Okay—please step over to Officer Nunez. She just needs to go over you with the wand."

"Sure," Liana said. She was all for tight security. She didn't even mind in airports when she had to take off her shoes and her jacket and her belt—although she never understood how the Department of Homeland Security's having Liana Cohen undress in the terminal protected against some radical fundamentalist terrorist blowing up the plane.

Officer Nunez, who was long past retirement age but apparently no one was brave enough to tell her, passed the wand over Liana's arms and legs and then over her chest, where it made a high-pitched wailing sound. "Aha!" said the guard. "Did you carefully read the rules about visiting?" Nunez asked Liana.

"Yes, in fact I did," Liana lied.

"Well, you obviously missed the one about no underwire bras."

"What? You're telling me that you've let some of these women pass through in microminis that barely cover their butts, and you're going to stop me for a bra that supports my modest bosom and ensures that I won't sag in twenty years?"

"Exactly," said Nunez, enjoying Liana's discomfort.

"So what's supposed to happen now? I go all the way back to New York City without seeing my client?" Liana asked, starting to lose it.

"Not unless that's what you want to do, honey. If you want to see your client, you go behind that screen and take off your bra. Then you're good to go!" Nunez announced triumphantly. Liana made a face as if she'd just been told to parade naked in front of the entire prison population, male and female guards included.

When she'd regrouped sufficiently to speak, Liana politely thanked Nunez and went behind the screen. Certainly, visiting with Shea braless would not have been her first choice. But she was here, and it wasn't as though she was wearing a tube top or anything terribly revealing. Still, she was self-conscious, and she feared Shea might now enjoy the visit a bit more than she had intended. She decided to try to forget about her state of undress and forge ahead. "Okay," she called out from behind the screen, "I'm ready."

"Hallelujah," Nunez said and handed her a chit to redeem her bra after her visit.

Another guard—Officer Franks, according to his badge—came to escort Liana to where the attorneys met with their clients. The facility smelled like a men's locker room that hadn't been cleaned in six months; the stench in the hallways was so strong that Liana thought her oatmeal might make a reappearance. She half expected to see the inmates standing in their cells, like in the movies, big unshaven men with their hands clenched around the bars, yelling obscenities at her as she passed by. But if there were cellblocks where such a scene might have played out, Franks led her a different way. As they wended their way toward the visiting area, Franks waited to hear the deafening clanging shut of the door they had just passed through before he unlocked the next. Finally, he opened the last door and showed her into a small room with a table in the center and a chair on either side. "Isn't there supposed to be a glass partition separating me from him?" Liana asked.

"Nah, some rooms are outfitted with that if the parties are not allowed to have any physical contact—but that's not usually an issue with attorney-client visits," Franks said. "I'll bring in the inmate in a few minutes and uncuff him, in case he needs to read something, turn the pages, whatever."

"Okay, great," Liana said. She had brought the brief that she'd filed on Shea's behalf—once she was coming all the way here, she figured she'd make a personal delivery rather than mailing it. "And do you stay in the room, Officer Franks?" Liana asked.

"Now, how could I do that?" he asked. "Wouldn't that destroy confidentiality, kind of wreck the attorney-client privilege?"

Liana thought Franks might have winked at her. "Good point, Officer Franks. I guess I was actually thinking more about my own safety. What happens if I need you?"

"I'll be watching through the window in the door, Counselor. Don't worry. You just wave; I'll see if you're in trouble," Franks said.

"Okay," Liana said. Her mind returned involuntarily to the photograph of Shea, and she was glad that there wasn't too much trouble she could get into with Franks looking through the window.

She sat down at the table and was going through the papers she'd brought when the door opened. Shea walked in but kept his eyes averted and his back to her while Franks removed the handcuffs. Only when the guard was finished and had closed the door did Shea turn toward Liana. For a person living in a hellhole and wearing a prison jumpsuit, he remained remarkably easy on the eyes. Liana stood up and extended her hand to shake his; it was the professional way to start the meeting. But when he looked at her, a tiny sound escaped his mouth—something between a gasp and a sob, of surprise or yearning Liana couldn't tell. Shea stared at her, and she looked away, withdrawing her hand and sitting down to break the intensity of the moment.

"I'm sorry, Ms. Cohen," he said softly. "I just wasn't expecting you."

"What do you mean? We had a confirmed appointment for today," she said, frantically searching her mind to see if she could have made a mistake on the date.

"Yes, I knew you were coming. What I meant was that I wasn't expecting you to be . . . as you are," Shea said.

He sat down and leaned back in the chair, tipping it slightly like a teenage boy in history class. Shea was even more compelling in person than he had been in the photograph, fit and tan from working outside in the yard, and Liana was having trouble concentrating on the task at hand—especially since she didn't really have a task at hand. She had never found any other client even remotely intriguing in either a physical or emotional way. She knew she shouldn't blame herself for being attracted to Shea—it wasn't the sort of thing you could control. She hoped to God that her breasts, unbounded, were not betraying her thoughts, but she dared not look down.

Liana opened her briefcase on the table, pulled out the papers she had prepared for Shea. "I've brought the brief that I filed with the court to show you. As I explained in my last letter, you have thirty days to ask for permission to file a *pro se* supplemental brief—that means you write it yourself—"

"Yes, I know what it means, Ms. Cohen," Shea interrupted.

"If you have other issues you want to raise . . . Maybe you want to look the brief over and see if you have any questions?" Liana suggested.

"I don't really want to waste the time I have with you reading the brief," Shea said. "I have a lot of time to read here." He was confident and smooth, and Liana knew that, in combination with the nature of his conviction, she should feel disgusted. Instead she was feeling a heat all over her body that was difficult to ignore.

Liana followed Shea's gaze, which had thankfully moved away from her, his eyes alighting on the newspaper in her open briefcase.

"Would you like to look at the *Daily News*, Mr. Shea?" The inmates didn't have much access to newspapers, at least not on a very current basis. He nodded once, and she handed him the paper, which he took and flipped quickly to the Sports section.

"Maybe you could let the court know that it's cruel and inhuman punishment to make a man miss the entire baseball season," Shea said as he skimmed the pages.

"Which team do you follow?" Liana asked. But she didn't need to wait for an answer as she saw a pained expression momentarily mar his handsome face. The Mets were having a horrible season, the jubilation over Johan Santana's no-hitter having faded fast.

"Lifelong Mets fan," Shea responded. "Would have to be with a name like Shea, but, unfortunately, no relation." He handed Liana the paper, neatly folded, and she put it back into her briefcase. She had a fleeting urge to tell him of their shared passion and then thought better of it.

When she was silent for a moment, Shea said, "Wasn't there something you came to explain about a risk I run if I pursue the appeal?" He looked at Liana so directly that she understood without him saying so that he knew there was no risk, that it had been a ruse. She didn't try to pretend.

"No," Liana said.

"Then why did you come, Liana?"

"Because you asked me to," she said.

Why is he calling me by my first name, and why don't I stop him?

Shea nodded, then rose slowly from his chair so as not to alarm her or inadvertently summon Officer Franks. He paced the length of the small room several times before stopping within two feet of Liana and fixing his attention on her.

"I asked you to come because I wanted to tell you in person that I didn't hurt Jennifer Nash. I need to explain to you more of what went on that night." His tone was challenging and not menacing, but she knew she needed to shut him down.

Liana held up her hand. "Please, Mr. Shea, this isn't necessary. I've explained to you that it makes no difference to me whether you are guilty or not. I have a job to do, and I'm doing it." She felt a surge of strength from hearing her own words, putting her back in control.

It didn't last long.

"I hear what you're saying, Liana. I don't buy it. You can't tell me that you don't get more fired up about a guy who is innocent. That would be the only normal human reaction— to get your juices flowing over a man you thought actually deserved you." His voice was deep and throaty and had lost most of its con-man tenor. He stared at her intensely for a beat too long, and Liana felt a simultaneous rush of panic and excitement.

"Okay. I'm listening."

Shea turned the chair around backward and straddled the seat, leaning forward and speaking quietly, never taking his eyes from Liana's.

"I got to know Jennifer pretty well over those weeks of seeing her every night at her job. There were a lot of things I didn't say on the stand because I didn't want to embarrass her."

Liana interrupted. "If you didn't testify about it, I can't use it, Mr. Shea. We've been over this."

"I know that. But what you can use on my appeal isn't the only thing that matters to me. I need you to understand the truth."

Liana felt a shiver go up her spine, although she couldn't pinpoint why she was afraid. It was just talk; it made no difference.

"Go on," she said.

"We were friends; that's what I'm trying to explain. I would be there eating, and Jennifer would take her break and sit with me and talk. She had a lot going on in her life, and she confided in me. Should I have told that jury full of strangers that she almost didn't graduate from high school because she was failing a bunch of her classes? Or that her mother had fat-shamed her so harshly for the couple of pounds she'd gained working at Mickey D's that she had pretty much stopped eating altogether? Should I have exposed that Jennifer was heartsick over her little brother—that kid who supposedly saved her from me—because he had joined a gang?"

Shea stood up from the chair and walked to the opposite side of the small room. Liana noticed his excellent posture and his proud gait—he didn't look like a man weighed down by guilt. Then he paused for a moment and rested his forehead on the cool wall. When he turned around and spoke, his voice was strong and sure.

"She went up to that rooftop because she trusted me; we were friends. And what happened between us was two adults enjoying each other on a hot summer night."

And then you betrayed that trust.

Or she betrayed you.

"Do you believe me, Liana? Do you believe me when I tell you that I'm innocent of this crime?"

"I'm trying to keep an open mind, Mr. Shea. Don't push it," she said.

"Fair enough," he said, sitting down across from her again. A shadow of a smile played on his lips and something like hope flickered in his eyes.

"Listen," Liana said, breaking the spell, "I brought you something." She pulled out a new marble composition notebook from her briefcase and several Uniball pens she had swiped from the office supply closet. "You write very well. I brought you a blank notebook—I thought you might use it as a journal. It could help pass the time. You can write down things that happen or your feelings or thoughts. Sometimes I keep a journal, and I find it very therapeutic—it helps to sort things out when you see things in writing." She was babbling. He made her nervous.

"Thanks, Liana," Shea said. "Thing is, not much really happens around here that is worth recording, and it's hard to differentiate one day from the next—except, of course, a day like today." It was the worst kind of flattery, yet Shea executed it so sincerely Liana was almost taken in. He reached for the notebook, touched the back of her hand with his fingertips, and lingered there. It couldn't have been more than a second or two—so fleeting yet so intimate—and a charge ran from the soles of her feet to the top of her curl-covered head. She jumped up from the table and waved at Franks, who opened the door immediately.

"Everything okay in here, Counselor?"

"Yes, Officer," she responded. "I just think it'd be best if I left now." She turned and walked out of the room without so much as a glance at Danny Shea, who remained seated at the table. Liana could feel him surveying every inch of her as she walked out of the room, and she heard him sigh, long and low.

She followed Officer Franks down the hallway, through the many heavy metal doors, stopping to douse herself liberally with Purell from the dispenser outside the reception room. Her hands were shaking.

"Did something happen in there? You weren't here very long," Franks asked.

"No, Officer. Everything was fine. We just ran out of things to talk about."

Liana thanked him again for guarding her so well and left the building. She walked back and forth in front of the facility, waiting for Boris to arrive, and then got into the back seat of his cab.

"How'd it go?" he asked.

"It was good, Boris. But I'm reminded of some wisdom that my friend Deb gave me a couple of years ago, when I got aggravated about something a client had done. She said, 'Liana, always remember, the difference between you and the client is that you get to sleep in your own bed tonight.'"

Boris looked puzzled, but he good-naturedly responded, "All right then, let's make sure you catch that train," and he stepped on the gas. Only when she got home and undressed to shower did Liana realize she had left her bra behind.

A few days after meeting with Danny Shea, Liana arrived at work to find a letter from him on her desk. She realized that, subconsciously, she had been waiting to hear from him like a teenage girl waits for a boy to telephone for a second date.

I'm really losing it.

Dear Liana,

I just wanted to take a moment to thank you for coming to see me. I hope things didn't end on a bad note; I wasn't quite sure why you left so abruptly. In any event, it was great to finally meet you, and I very much appreciated the opportunity to give you a fuller picture of my relationship with Jennifer. I hope that knowing what you know now, you have a more nuanced understanding of what went on that night.

I hope I can take the liberty of also telling you that your visit meant a lot to me personally. You were a beautiful breath of fresh air in an otherwise totally dismal reality. I know that my reputation precedes me, but I hope that, having met me, you now have even more reason to doubt that I'm the person the prosecutor claims I am. I think we have a certain connection, and I pray it will grow stronger.

Please keep me updated on any developments in my case. I won't write to you unnecessarily but will wait for your correspondence.

Sincerely,

Danny

Liana sat at her desk, stunned.

How did I possibly let things get to the point where a client would suggest we have some sort of bond?

It was a more charming version of a letter she would normally laugh off, showing it around to her friends in the office and commiserating about these sex-starved clients. But she knew she had encouraged his attention, and the letter was so sweet she couldn't bear to ridicule him. When she remembered the way he had looked at her, her first impulse was to take the letter home and put it in her dresser drawer for a rainy day. Instead, trembling, she ripped it up into tiny pieces and threw it in the trash. She took out a sheet of blank paper and wrote him by hand so there would be no trace on her computer.

Dear Mr. Shea,

Thank you for your letter. I enjoyed meeting you as well. I have to insist that you please keep all your correspondence strictly impersonal and refrain from any improper remarks or innuendo. If your behavior becomes at all troubling to me, I will have your case reassigned to another (male) attorney in the office.

I'm sure you understand the position that I am in. I have many clients, and I try to treat each one with the respect he or she deserves. I do not have the time or inclination to become friendly with my clients, as that would detract from the representation that I can provide.

I will keep you up to date on all aspects of the case.

Sincerely,

Liana Cohen, Esq.

Liana hoped her response was stern without being unduly hurtful. She folded the letter and put it into a blank envelope, writing out Shea's address and inmate number on the envelope and, rattled, putting her own apartment as the return address. She dropped the envelope in the mailroom in the middle of some letters to other clients and went home, feeling relieved. This had gone too far already, but she would get herself back on track.

CHAPTER 12

The autumn months after Liana filed Danny Shea's brief dragged. Now that the district attorney's opposing brief was in, there was nothing to do but wait for a date for oral argument of the appeal before a panel of judges in the Second Department. Liana hadn't had any more contact with Shea; he'd promised he wouldn't write to her without a legitimate purpose, and he understood that they were in a holding pattern. Still, she hadn't been able to put him or her visit to the prison completely out of her mind. Sometimes Liana pictured Shea in the Green Haven interview room patiently waiting for her to come back, Jennifer Nash's pink purse in his hands.

Deb had finally returned to work a couple of weeks before Thanksgiving, but she was weak from the chemo, and she only stayed in the office for a few hours a day before going home to rest and be with Max. She never mentioned her prognosis, but she was brave beyond words and utterly determined. If anyone had a chance to push the limits of this disease, it was Deb. Despite what she had been through, she was still herself: sharp and funny and challenging. She was also occasionally melancholy and needed constant reassurance that she looked well and was thinking clearly, neither of which was always the case.

Jakob had been working like a dog. He kept erratic hours and was traveling to such scintillating locales as Boise, Buffalo, and Duluth for his various cases. Somehow, although it confounded Liana, he managed to enjoy not only the intellectual aspects of his work but also the cutthroat politics of the firm, which inspired him on some level. When he wasn't up to his elbows in document review or deposition prep, he was looking for ways to impress the partners who would soon determine whether he had a long-term future at the firm or whether he'd be searching for another position and almost starting over again from the lowest rung. Following Charlotte's suggestion, Liana had persuaded Jakob to take a couple of days in Newport over Thanksgiving weekend; they were both frazzled, and Liana was convinced that some fall foliage and the romance of a B&B were just what they both needed to recharge and get back on track.

They'd rented a car on the Saturday morning of Thanksgiving weekend, still feeling stuffed from the extravagant dinner Jakob's mother had prepared on Thursday. It had been lovely. Liana was always grateful that the Weiss family included her mother; she couldn't imagine spending the holiday apart from her, and Thanksgiving for two at her mother's house sounded overwhelmingly depressing. They had overeaten as required—pumpkin soup, turkey with stuffing on the side (conforming to Jakob's mother Arlene's mandate, "Never cook the stuffing inside the turkey—you could get terribly sick from the bacteria"), corn fritters, sweet potatoes with pecans, and way too much dessert. Afterward, they had played a round-robin ping-pong tournament that Rebecca had orchestrated. It was Liana versus Jakob in the finals—they were very evenly matched, and Liana beat him twenty-five to twenty-three in overtime.

"You only won because you distracted me with that low-cut shirt," Jakob teased. "I could see your purple bra."

"Shut up," Liana answered. "It's not my fault if you can't keep your eyes on the prize."

"I was hoping you were the prize," Jakob retorted.

"Shh, not in front of Rebecca," she scolded.

Liana helped Jakob's mother and Rebecca clear up the table, rinsing off Jakob's grandmother's lovely white china with the tiny blue cornflower pattern and putting away the crystal glasses. "You don't have to do the work, Liana," Arlene said. "You're supposed to be a guest."

"I hope I'm not a guest," Liana said. Arlene put down the dishtowel she had been using to dry the silver and gave Liana a little squeeze around the waist. Liana figured that she meant it to be encouraging—a "you'll be part of the family soon enough" gesture—and a wave of confusion washed over her.

They woke up early on Saturday and left the city by eight o'clock so they would have as much of the day as possible in Rhode Island. For kicks, Jakob had rented a neon-yellow convertible, and they cruised up I-95 with the top down and Liana's hair flying, feeling like they had taken a break not only from Manhattan but also from their ordinary life. The drive took a little over three hours, and they crossed into Newport over the Jamestown–Newport bridges singing "My Sweet Lord" at the top of their lungs.

Liana had made a reservation at the Puritan Inn on Spring Street, a Victorian-style bed and breakfast that had originally been a private home in the nineteenth century. She hoped the place would appeal to Jakob's love of history, and she thought that the room, with its antique oak bed and lace curtains, might be a good setting to rekindle—between her work and his, they had both been so tense. She was encouraged when Jakob's face lit up seeing the wide front porch—before they even checked in, he grabbed her hand, and they commandeered two of the big white Adirondack rocking chairs.

"I love a front porch. Did you notice the ceiling?" he asked. She looked up and was surprised to see that the wood panels overhead were painted a beautiful robin's egg blue. "That's called haint blue," Jakob explained. "In South Carolina in the early nineteenth century, people believed that the blue would ward off evil spirits. Now painting porch ceilings blue has become popular all over the country."

"Well, I guess that's a good omen for our weekend!" Liana said.

After they brought their bags up to the room, they decided not to squander any of their limited time, and they walked to Bellevue Avenue, where they signed up for a tour of the Breakers, the most famous of Newport's grand summer "cottages."

"Wouldn't it be great to have a house like this someday?" Jakob said, surveying the mansion as they waited for the group to assemble.

"A house like this? Earth to Jakob, Earth to Jakob! Is that why you are working like such a lunatic? Is this what you aspire to?"

"I was kidding, Liana. I didn't really mean 'like this.' I just meant a house like we grew up in, with some space, a yard. Kids." Mercifully, Jakob didn't wait for a response but took Liana's hand and led her to where the group of tourists had gathered in the front hall.

Bree, their impossibly chipper young docent, led them through a fraction of the seventy gigantic and ornately decorated rooms, pointing out the architectural quirks and telling mildly amusing anecdotes about the Vanderbilts, the family that had built the house in 1893. Compared to her cramped apartment, Liana felt as if she had landed in outer space as they drifted from dining room to sitting room to parlor to library to great hall.

"Don't touch anything!" Bree belted out intermittently, and the adults looked just as fearful as the few children who had been forced to tag along. When they entered the music room, Jakob zoned in on the French mahogany piano standing in the corner of the room near the marble fireplace. As Bree ushered the group into the billiard room, he pulled Liana over to the piano bench with him and started to play a jazzy version of "Somewhere over the Rainbow." The acoustics in the room were, unsurprisingly, magnificent. Jakob sang to Liana, and for a moment, she was back on the booze cruise the summer they had met, utterly astonished at the strength of her feelings for this boy. They were lost in the music and in each other when Bree sprinted into the room and screeched, "I told you not to touch anything!" Still laughing and having had enough of Bree and the others, Liana and Jakob snuck out a side door as the tourists made their way into the kitchen.

They found themselves in the gardens, secluded and peaceful. The trees were exuberantly parading their colors while simultaneously beginning to lose their leaves—one phase of life transitioning into another. Liana and Jakob sat down on a bench, and he put his arm around her shoulders, pulling her in close to his side. When the laughter finally subsided, Jakob said, "That was the most fun we've had in a long time."

"I know," Liana agreed. "Why do you think that is?"

"Oh, Li." He sighed. Although Jakob had not taken his arm from around her, he shifted just enough so she felt his withdrawal. "You just have no idea what my life is like these days, and when I try to talk to you about it, you don't really listen."

Stung, Liana wasn't sure what to say. She fought the urge to be defensive, to shut out his words. But she knew he was right. When he tried to talk to her about the substance of his work, which he found engaging, her brain reflexively turned off. And when he talked about the partners and the intrigue and the backbiting, it was all so repulsive to her she couldn't engage enough to be helpful to him

"Can you try me again?" Liana asked, her voice, barely audible, catching in her throat. "I'm listening now."

"Okay, so here it is." Jakob's tone was affectionate, but Liana detected the underlying frustration. "I spend all of each and every day trying to figure out how I'm going to succeed in this job. It isn't a passing thought—it's a constant, all-consuming strategizing about how to make myself indispensable to the egomaniacs who run the firm, how to ingratiate myself with the demanding clients, how to squeeze in the most billable hours, how to make sure I'm included in the right meetings and on the right committees and copied on the right emails. You have no idea of the pressure I'm under. Maybe I'm not as good as I should be at managing my priorities, but for me this job is all-consuming right now."

Liana was grateful that Jakob had given her another chance to understand what he was going through, but she still wasn't sure where that left them.

Do stressed-out midlevel associates with no free time marry their girlfriends and then continue on as stressed-out midlevel married associates? Will I end up like Charlotte?

"Okay," she said. "I'm listening, and I understand that your job is outrageously demanding and it's taking pretty much everything you've got to make a go of it. I'll try to be less high maintenance. Let's at least make the most of this weekend." Jakob took Liana's hands in his and pulled her gently to her feet, then wrapped his arms around her.

"It'll all be good, Li—let's just let things play out. I need you by my side."

After lunch, they strolled along the Cliff Walk, looking out at the Atlantic Ocean, Liana stumbling every now and then and Jakob there to catch her before she fell. When they got tired of maneuvering among the Thanksgiving weekend crowds, they walked along the cobblestone streets of colonial Newport, stopping every thirty feet or so to read the plaques affixed to the old houses that explained who had once lived there. They didn't talk much, but Liana was just glad to be near

Jakob—he had always had a calming effect on her. Nothing had really changed about that.

They were meandering down Spring Street toward their hotel at close to five in the afternoon, and it was beginning to get dark, when Liana noticed people strolling in through the front doors of a stately building, some dressed nicely, some in jeans and sweatshirts.

"Oh, look!" she said. "That's the Touro Synagogue—it's the oldest congregation in America. I read all about it on the Internet. It was founded by Spanish and Portuguese Jews in the mid-seventeenth century—it's the sister congregation of the Spanish-Portuguese synagogue on West Seventieth Street, near my apartment. After the Revolutionary War, George Washington visited and wrote a famous letter to the congregation affirming the country's commitment to the right to freely practice one's religion.'"

"Check you out—you did your homework," Jakob said, impressed.

"Let's go have a look," she said. But Liana's interest was more than academic. Just as she envied the Darchei Tikvah regulars their faith and sense of belonging, she felt the pull again here as she watched the congregants making their way into the sanctuary. Something about the rituals and the sense of community suggested both a stability and balance that Liana felt were just out of her reach.

"Why is everyone coming at this hour?" Jakob asked. Liana looked at her watch and then up at the sky, where she could see some stars on the verge of poking out.

"Shabbat is almost over," she said. "We can catch Havdalah. Come, I bet it will be beautiful."

"We're not exactly dressed," Jakob said, gesturing toward their beat-up sneakers.

"It's okay; there are plenty of people gathering near the doors. They're used to tourists here." They made their way quickly, so as not to miss the short ceremony that marked the conclusion of the Sabbath.

They stood at the very back. The interior of the synagogue was starkly beautiful. White walls accented in a pale bluish-green set off brown wooden benches, while silver chandeliers with real flickering candles hung from the ceiling. Arched windows lined the walls, both on the ground floor and in the women's gallery above. As they took it all in, a young rabbi made his way to the middle of the sanctuary. He held a silver cup filled with wine, and he handed an elaborately braided six-wick candle to a little girl of about seven with a full head of red curls. The rabbi lit the candle and leaned toward the girl.

"Hold the candle as high as the man you dream you will marry is tall," he said in a stage whisper. The little girl looked around the room, locked her eyes on Jakob, and reached her arm up as high as it could go. The rabbi said the blessings over the wine and the flame and the spices as the men and women passed around small mesh bags filled with cloves and cinnamon sticks and everyone breathed in the sweet scent, prolonging the joy of the Sabbath for a few seconds more. Then the congregants and tourists ambled out of the building, back to homes or hotels, returning to the workweek.

When the room had emptied out, Liana and Jakob wandered up to the front of the sanctuary and sat down on a wooden bench near the ark that held the Torah scrolls. He held her hand, and she settled her head on his chest. "Wouldn't this be a great place for a destination wedding? It's so historical," he mused.

"Oh, Jake," she said. Liana felt him struggling with himself, deciding whether to tell her what he was thinking or just let the awkward moment pass.

"Penny for your thoughts?" she said.

"Liana, I'm not oblivious to your feelings, and I know you're unsettled about a lot of stuff right now. But I need us to be committed and supportive of each other in every aspect of our lives. Part of that is your understanding that my career is important to me and you wanting to help me succeed. Maybe I'm crazy, but sometimes I feel like you're not all in, not a hundred percent."

He put his hands gently on both of her shoulders and looked at her for a minute tenderly before continuing. "I'm in love with you, Liana, and I want you to be with me, by my side, forever. Is that a crime?"

She forced a smile but could not stop the tears which were now freely flowing down her cheeks.

"I don't know," she said. "I'm no expert on crime."

That night, they made love in the big antique oak bed, urgently yet tentatively, as though they were afraid to hurt each other further.

In the morning when Liana awoke, she found Jakob dressed and sitting in the upholstered chair next to the bed, intently typing on his iPad. She came and stood next to him, looking over his shoulder. "It's a shit show at work," he said. "I know we were supposed to have today to relax, but I'm going to be uptight because I know I should be in the office," he said.

"It's okay, Jay," she said. "Let's just have breakfast, and then we can go back."

He got up and held her close to him, whispering in her ear, "It's all for you, babe. I swear."

"I know," she said. But she wasn't sure what she knew anymore.

CHAPTER 13

Bam! Bam! Bam! The sound of the gavel reverberated throughout the courtroom.

"Ladies and Gentlemen: The Justices of the Court. Hear ye, hear ye, hear ye: All persons having business before this Appellate Division of the Supreme Court, held in and for the Second Judicial Department of the State of New York, let them draw near, give their attention, and they shall be heard."

Liana loved the formality of the opening of the court session. Sometimes, during the arguments, the proceedings more closely resembled a nursery school classroom, with the judges and the attorneys bullying, cajoling, whining; but the day always started off with a promise of grandeur. The court had scheduled oral argument in Danny Shea's case for December 20, 2012, the last day before the Christmas–New Year's break. There was an air of restlessness among both bench and bar, and Liana hoped that the judges would give her case the hearing it deserved. She had been disappointed when she saw the makeup of the panel—Justices Brady, Lincoln, Aubrey, and Simon. Three out of four women judges for a rape case did not bode well. On the other hand, all of them were pretty middle of the road—none were former prosecutors or former legal aid attorneys but had instead been in private practice before they were appointed to the bench. And none of them were rookies—they wouldn't be afraid to take a tough stand.

She had been anticipating this day for months. Despite her self-imposed vow to represent Danny Shea free of any emotional investment, Liana had strayed from the purely professional to the somewhat personal. He had grown on her. On the plus side, Gerry had noticed Liana's positive attitude, the long hours she put in, the diligent research, and the polished brief she produced. Liana's less than strictly aboveboard interest in Shea was well hidden, apparent only to herself in sporadic moments of honest reflection and occasionally to Deb, when Liana let down her guard. But today, in court, she was all business. She had prepared thoroughly for her argument, and she was ready to fight.

Shea's case was second on the court's calendar, and the room was crowded with attorneys awaiting their arguments. Liana didn't mind having an audience; it kept her on her toes. And she liked being second—she would watch the judges carefully during the initial argument to see what sort of mood they were in and how familiar they were with the details of the case. The presiding judge always made the same claim during the introductory remarks: "Counselors, we are a 'hot bench.' We know the facts of your case. Please proceed directly to the argument of your legal claims." But the truth was there was always one judge who had slept through the fact section of the brief or who was willfully misconstruing some fact to work to the detriment of the defendant. Liana knew she had to be vigilant, because if the judges got the facts wrong, it made no difference how strong you were on the law.

She turned to look around the rest of the courtroom, trying to pick out anyone who could be Shea's mother or girlfriend—he hadn't told her anyone would be coming to the argument, but sometimes relatives showed up anyway. She didn't see anyone that fit the bill. She nodded at Deb and Gerry, who were seated a few rows in back of her. Deb motioned to her, and Liana made her way over to where they were sitting.

"Are you ready?" Gerry asked.

"Of course," Liana said.

"Not quite," Deb said, standing up with some difficulty and carefully retying Liana's scarf. "I have such good taste. Now you look fabulous, and now you're ready. Go get 'em." She gave Liana a little push back toward the front of the courtroom.

Liana had seen Deb only sporadically over the last few weeks—she was holding her own, but between appointments with her oncologists and her chemo treatments, she was coming in to the office less and less. Still, Deb had kept track of Danny's case—or more accurately, had kept protective tabs on Liana's involvement in Danny's case—and she had come to lend moral support. Gerry had come to be a pain in the ass, although officially he was there to make sure Liana gave it her all, which amounted to the same thing. If she weren't so focused on her argument, she would have been disgusted.

Why do I feel like a probationary attorney all over again, when I've proved my worth so many times?

The first argument was lively, the judges actively engaged in questioning the attorneys. When the litigants had left the lecterns, the clerk announced, "The People of the State of New York versus Daniel Shea." As Liana rose to take her spot, she saw Jakob enter the courtroom through the back doors and quietly take a seat in the last row. Liana's heart raced a bit, as it always did when she saw him—but she also had the uncomfortable sensation that somehow he had caught her, in flagrante delicto, with Danny Shea. Jakob didn't normally take time out of his schedule to watch Liana argue but he knew this case might determine her future in the office. Besides—he was no fool. Liana suspected that he knew that Shea had gotten under her skin in a way that was different from her other clients. She pushed the image of Shea out of her mind and turned to face the court.

The prosecutor, sitting at the table to Liana's right, waiting her turn, was like a seething volcano. Liana could feel that venomous fervor that the assistant district attorneys exuded, especially the women, wafting over her. The rivalry between the Public Defender's Office and the State almost always remained civil, but when it did bubble over, it was usually here, in the majestic room on Monroe Place, with its oak-paneled walls and gold-leaf ceiling. This particular ADA, Ms. Ava Wellington, looked like she could eat Liana and the judges for breakfast.

Liana waited for the presiding justice to give her a nod, indicating she should begin.

"May it please the Court, my name is Liana Cohen of the Public Defender's Office, and I represent the appellant-defendant, Daniel Shea," she began, her voice as authoritative as she could make it.

"Trial counsel in this case made one mistake that completely vanquished Mr. Shea's ability to get a fair trial. These jurors were diligently doing their job, taking their oath seriously, and deliberating conscientiously for three full days, when they were suddenly faced with a startling revelation. At least according to the plain words on the piece of paper that had been entered into evidence by the prosecutor, this defendant's DNA had been found in the rape kit of a second woman, not Jennifer Nash, the alleged victim here, but some other woman the jury knew nothing about." Liana paused for effect. "And once the jury was exposed to that fact, true or false, this case was over."

The judges jumped in.

"What is the legal standard for finding trial counsel ineffective?"

"Was the judge's proposed curative instruction sufficient to fix defense counsel's blunder?"

"How competent was defense counsel during the other parts of the trial?"

Most of the questions were softballs—the court already knew the answers, allowing Liana to argue even more forcefully the merits of her case. She was feeling confident and very well prepared when Justice Simon leaned over the bench and asked, softly but deliberately, "But, Counselor, who is Alba Velez?"

At first, Liana was dumbfounded. *Does the judge really not know that Alba Velez was the second woman on the DNA report that set this whole legal error in motion?*

Then it dawned on her. The judge knew full well that Alba Velez was the name on the report. The judge wanted to know *who she was*—how did she have Danny Shea's DNA in her rape kit? Liana was appalled, and her tone reflected it.

"Your Honor," she began, as respectfully as she could, "as you know, that would be a fact totally outside the record. It makes no difference whatsoever to the legal issue here who Alba Velez is or why her name appeared on that report. The only pertinent issue is that her name was, in fact, on the report, defense counsel failed miserably in not noticing it, and this error caused this jury to convict my client within an hour of being privy to that information. Who Alba Velez actually is is completely irrelevant here."

Justice Simon tilted back in her plush leather chair behind the bench, keeping her eyes fixed on Liana, a small frown hovering around her mouth.

"That may be so, Counselor, in our ivory tower, and I'm just thinking out loud here, but in the real world, who Alba Velez is, and whether she was indeed another woman victimized by your client, may be the only question that makes any difference," she mused. "I'm not asking you to tell us, Counselor," she continued, "but do you know who Alba Velez is?"

Liana felt totally dejected. In a tiny voice, she answered, "No, Your Honor. I don't know who Alba Velez is. If the court has no further questions, I will rest on my brief." Liana sat down, feeling as if she had let herself and her client down. She knew that the judge's question had no legal significance to the issue on appeal. But stripped of all the official niceties, what the judge wanted to know was, Should we feel badly for Danny Shea, that he got a raw deal here, or is he a serial rapist? It was the question she had been fighting against asking herself for months.

She was so distracted that she did not hear any of the prosecutor's argument, and only the clerk's calling the next case woke her from her trance and sent her walking out to the antechamber.

Deb and Gerry were waiting right outside the doors to the courtroom. "Liana, you were great!" Deb gushed. "You totally had the better side of every legal argument; the prosecutor barely made a dent. Although, as usual, she killed in that pantsuit; we might have to take you shopping again . . . ." Deb looked Ms. Wellington up and down admiringly as she exited the courtroom. Gerry was more muted.

"You did a fine job, Liana. You might have come up with something a little stronger with Justice Simon—she was totally out of bounds, asking you those questions about a fact not in evidence. Of course, she's right, in a certain sense. The question of who Alba Velez really is goes to the heart of why this was reversible error. You should have argued that the jurors were left to their own devices to make up whatever they wanted after seeing that name—they could have decided that Alba Velez was the nun that taught the defendant in fourth grade and whom he stalked all these years later and brutally raped. The fact that the jury was free to invent an identity for Alba Velez is why defense counsel's lapse was so prejudicial to his client. But it's hard to think that fast on your feet," Gerry said.

Thanks, Gerry.

"I still think you are going to win," Deb said, putting her arm around Liana. Deb had gotten so frail that her touch barely registered, and Liana realized what an effort it must have been for her to make it to court.

"Thanks again for being here," she said, giving Deb a quick hug and ignoring Gerry. She knew he was right, and she hoped the judges were smart enough to draw that same conclusion, even though she hadn't fed it to them.

Jakob was waiting near the front doors, checking his watch and looking antsy when Liana approached him. They had seen each other only a handful of times since the Thanksgiving trip to Newport three weeks before; Liana had decided that she would back off, let him focus on work, and try to be there for him when he surfaced. Not having to manage her expectations left them both less stressed-out, but she missed him.

"Hey," she said. She hadn't yet recovered from the oral argument, but seeing Jakob there helped.

"Hey, yourself. I brought you these," he said, handing her a small bouquet of lilacs, her favorite.

"Where did you find these in the middle of winter? They're beautiful, Jay," Liana said. "What are you doing here?"

"You've been pretty obsessed with this case—I thought I should come down and get some tips on the kind of guy that really turns you on," he teased. Liana looked away, trying not to let Jakob see her squirm.

"Seriously, Li, you were great in there. So passionate. I love to watch you. If I didn't know better, I would think you really believed in this guy," he said. He poked her lightly in the ribs. Liana blushed. She hoped Jakob would think it was because he was messing with her and not because he had, inadvertently or by design, revealed that she had some feeling for Danny Shea, whether it was a belief in his innocence or something less lofty. "I've got to go back to work," he said. "Are we still on for New Year's Eve?"

"Of course," Liana said. "Although now that Dick Clark is dead, I'm not sure exactly what we'll do."

"I think we can figure out something," Jakob said, giving her his best lascivious smile. He kissed her on the cheek and walked out into the cold.

Gerry and Deb, who had kept a respectful distance while Liana was talking to Jakob, walked over to her. "We're going to stop at Starbucks on the way back to the office," Deb said.

"But we think that gentleman there is waiting for you; he was in court for your argument. Must be a relative," Gerry said, gesturing toward a solid looking white guy wearing a leather jacket and dark jeans, standing outside the attorney room near the coat racks. Deb and Gerry got their coats.

"We'll meet you on Montague," Deb said.

"Okay. Can you get me an iced skim latte?" Liana said, but they were out the door, chatting animatedly to one another. Sometimes she envied their closeness—it seemed so much less complicated than the relationships she had with each of them.

"Hi. Were you waiting to speak with me?" Liana said.

"Yes," the man said. He was tall—around Jakob's height—but older, maybe close to fifty. His hair was attractively grey around the temples, and he had small wrinkles around his deep-set light eyes. Liana could see he was in good shape, even with his winter clothes on. She could envision him tending bar in some classy pub downtown, then remembered that this was only coming to mind because she thought he was one of Danny Shea's Irish relations.

"I'm Liam O'Flaherty," he said. Liana's mind was still a bit addled from the argument, but she knew she recognized the name from somewhere. As she tried to remember, O'Flaherty added, "I'm Danny's uncle."

"Oh, yes!" Liana said. "He testified that he worked construction for you. I wasn't sure if that was something he just made up on the stand to make himself look like he had a responsible job or if he was telling the truth," she said, forgetting herself for a moment. O'Flaherty laughed.

"No, it was the truth. He's worked for me on and off since he was in high school—I've always tried to help him out if I could," O'Flaherty said. Liana was embarrassed; she'd just inadvertently suggested that she thought her client had been lying on the stand.

Sometimes I really worry about myself in this job.

But O'Flaherty was undeterred.

"I don't know if Danny mentioned it, but I sat through his trial. Now, mind you, I wasn't up on that rooftop. But Danny is basically a good kid who has had a rough time of it. I think a lot of what he said when he testified was probably the truth—not just about working for me or going to school but about that girl too. Anyway, I just wanted to thank you for putting so much effort into Danny's case. I know you people must not get paid much; I think it's a real service you do, dedicating yourself to those less fortunate." Liana tried to see herself as Liam O'Flaherty did—a bright, articulate attorney, attractive even in a conservative five-year-old black suit, fighting the good fight for the disenfranchised and disadvantaged. It was a pretty picture, but she wasn't sure she fit the bill.

"Thanks, Mr. O'Flaherty," she said. "I really hope we win. As I explained to Mr. Shea, though, even if this court reverses his conviction, he won't get out of prison. He'll just get a second shot at a fair trial," Liana said.

"I know, Ms. Cohen. Danny told me when I went to see him. By the way, he was very touched that you had come to visit," he said. Something in the way O'Flaherty looked at Liana gave her to understand that Danny Shea had said more than that, and she decided it was time to wrap up this little conversation. She wasn't proud of the fact that by visiting him in prison when it hadn't been necessary, she had led Danny Shea on; it had been a severe lapse in judgment on her part. And Liana knew that the excuses she had made to herself for her behavior did nothing to change the reality. She had stepped just marginally out of the bounds of the attorney-client relationship, and it had been simultaneously foolish and undeniably exciting. This wasn't what Gerry meant by "feeling for the client." Liana knew it must never happen again.

"Well, we'll know more in a couple months. Have a Merry Christmas and a Happy New Year, Mr. O'Flaherty."

"To you as well, miss," he responded. Liana started to walk toward the exit and then turned back.

"Mr. O'Flaherty—do you know who Alba Velez is?"

"I do, miss," he said, looking down at his hands, in which he held a grey woolen winter hat.

"And?" Liana wasn't sure she wanted to know, but she had gone this far.

He looked at her intently, holding her gaze much as Danny Shea had weeks earlier. "And that's Danny's story to tell, miss, not mine. But I hope you won't rush to judgment like that jury did," O'Flaherty said.

Liana nodded and quickly left the building, racing toward the caffeine fix she so desperately needed.

CHAPTER 14

When she awoke on New Year's Day, it was almost noon. Liana instinctively reached out to Jakob's side of her bed, patting the emptiness but hoping he might still be there. Although in her attempt to be convivial she'd had a few too many when they had gone out with Jakob's work friends the evening before, she had kept herself in check, and she distinctly remembered him sleeping over and making the night worth her while. She felt around on his pillow, even though she knew for certain now he was gone, and her hand landed on a folded-over piece of paper.

> Dear Li, Sorry to leave so early. Believe me, you wore me out—I could have slept all day. My mom texted me this morning—Kyle and Rebecca are both home. She asked me to come and spend the day. Maybe you want to call your mom? I can meet you back at your place tonight. Love, J.

For a moment, she was overwhelmed with hope—the easy intimacy of the note made her think that maybe 2013 would be the year they would really figure things out.

Liana felt around on the floor among her discarded bra and jeans for her phone and called her mother. After chatting for a few minutes about the G-rated portion of her New Year's Eve, she asked her mom if she would like a visit, explaining that Jakob was already gone for the day with his family.

"Thanks, sweetheart," her mother said, "but I have other plans."

The words "What other plans could you possibly have?" were halfway from her brain to her lips when Liana swallowed them back. Her mother was nearly seventy years old, an accomplished, intelligent, and independent woman. Wasn't she entitled to have a life without justifying it to her daughter? Liana could be the mature one here and just leave it alone. She told her mother to have a good day and quickly hung up the phone.

Left to her own devices, Liana poured herself a bowl of Froot Loops, dragged a quilt to the couch in the living room, and ordered her favorite movie, *The Notebook*, on Netflix. It had come out in 2004, when she was a junior in college, but she had first seen it a few years later with Charlotte and Katie in their apartment in New Haven, the three women swooning with abandon over Ryan Gosling. Since then, she had probably watched it ten times. Liana was always transported by Allie and Noah—the improbable romance between the poor but ridiculously sexy country boy and the beautiful, spoiled little rich girl. So mismatched on every level yet such chemistry between them. She had just gotten to her favorite part—where Noah, begging Allie to stay with him instead of going back to her far more appropriate fiancé, says, "I want all of you, forever, everyday. You and me . . . everyday"—when she noticed, with a start, that in her mind's eye she had cast Danny Shea as the leading man opposite herself. She marched into a cold shower, forcing herself to stay there as long as she could stand it and until she could return Jakob to his rightful place.

She was still in a towel and dripping wet when the buzzer rang at three o'clock. "Who is it?" she said into the intercom.

"It's us; let us up. It's freezing out here," Katie said.

"What are you doing here?" Liana said.

"We brought Chinese. Open the door!" Charlotte yelled.

When the girls barreled into her apartment, Liana said, "Don't you people have better things to do on New Year's Day?"

"Well, clearly not," Katie said matter-of-factly.

"Go put some clothes on," Charlotte ordered, always the sensible one. Before she knew it, Charlotte had set paper plates and chopsticks on the small table in the vestibule that doubled as Liana's dining room, and Katie had unveiled vegetarian dumplings, moo shu chicken, beef with black bean sauce, and Liana's favorite, chow fun. They ate ravenously, barely speaking, until they had demolished everything. Then they sat, stomachs gurgling, in an uncomfortable food coma, wishing they had been more restrained.

"I don't even like Chinese," Katie declared.

The three women collapsed on Liana's couch, spreading the quilt over their legs, reveling in the familiarity and safety of their long friendship. Liana had a flashback to the first time Deb had seen the gleaming new white couch in her apartment. She had looked at it and remarked, "You obviously don't have children." As if on cue, little Max, then just over a year old and learning how to walk, made a beeline for the sofa, sticky hands reaching out in front of him, ready to leave a lasting impression. But Deb's reflexes were quick back then, and she had scooped him up before any damage could be done.

The roommates gabbed as effortlessly as they had in graduate school, even though their circumstances had changed since their days in New Haven. Charlotte was now what she euphemistically called "between jobs." After finishing her degree at the Yale Child Study Center, she had been a teacher when she met Howard, working in a pretty dicey neighborhood in the South Bronx and learning to reach students who had very little support at home. But after they got married, it just didn't seem worth it to keep it up—Howard made a lot of money as a banker, and he didn't really want her working.

"I know my life must look good from the outside," Charlotte said unselfconsciously, "but it's actually really hard not working. I'm anxious all the time. And the errands and stuff that I used to get done on the weekends—now I have all week to get them done. I find myself putting off things—like I could go to the dry cleaner and pick up Howard's shirts on Tuesday, but I'll save that to have something to do on Thursday. It's kind of a disaster," she said, crestfallen. But then Charlotte's face lit up. "But all of that will change soon!" she announced.

"You have a new job?" Liana asked.

"What will you be doing, Charlie?" Katie said.

"Well, it is a new job, of sorts," Charlotte said slowly, clearly enjoying the suspense. "I'm pregnant!" There was a moment during which all three of the women silently considered the announcement, trying to comprehend what this baby would mean for each of them and for their friendship. And then Katie and Liana shrieked simultaneously, boisterously but carefully wrapping their arms around Charlotte and baby girl-boy Simpson.

"Oh my God! I can't believe it!" Liana said.

"That's crazy!" Katie marveled.

"Well, is it really that surprising?" Charlotte said. "Am I missing something? We've been married for over two years, and I'll be thirty in a few months. It just seemed like the reasonable thing to do, especially since I'm not working. I mean, doesn't it seem like the right next step?" She looked beseechingly at her two best friends, a hormonal rush of emotion descending on her.

"Of course it is, sweetheart," Katie responded. "It's the most wonderful news. It just seems kind of like a far-off reality for your two bachelorette friends here." She wrapped an arm around Liana's waist in a show of solidarity. Liana pulled away slightly and almost told Katie to speak for herself—and then she remembered that while she was theoretically closer to marriage and children than Katie, she was still some distance away.

"Well, you guys aren't upset, are you?" Charlotte asked, as if maybe she would call the whole thing off if they said they were.

"Of course not!" Liana said. "Big news just takes a little getting used to."

"Since we're having true confessions here . . ." Katie said, and Liana's heart sank. How many more life-affirming announcements could she take when she was so bewildered about her own situation? But Katie was not to be outdone, even if her reveal was not quite as momentous as Charlotte's.

"I think I met a man who's up to the task," Katie said. She had been the most financially successful of the three friends, and she viewed the dating scene as one long and, thus far, futile attempt to find the man who would be equal to her earning potential and unafraid of a relationship with a strong, smart, well-educated woman. Liana never had those worries—she and Jakob were very evenly matched, although they had chosen drastically different career paths.

"You just don't understand," Katie would always say to Liana when the travails of dating came up. "Most men out there want a ditzy woman with a big chest who wears tight clothes and spends all her time telling them how great they are." According to Katie, there were not a lot of single, quality guys like Jakob. Liana knew it was true, although she figured Jakob probably wanted those things too sometimes.

"His name is Rob," Katie continued, "and I met him at an equity research conference in Las Vegas a couple of weeks ago. He was married before, but he's divorced now, and no kids, thank God." When she saw the expression on Charlotte's face, she added quickly, "I mean, it would be different if they were our kids, Charlie—I just don't really want to start off with someone else's kids."

"Are you already talking about getting married and having kids?" Liana asked. She thought that the chow fun might not be as "fun" on the way up as it had been going down.

"My God, no, we haven't talked about it—I mean, it's only been a few weeks. And I think he got pretty burned the last time he tied the knot. I'm just saying, he's the first guy in a long time that I could actually see myself with on a long-term basis," she said reasonably.

"Well, I have some news too," Liana announced, surprising herself as much as her friends. Seeing their faces immediately transformed with joy and anticipation, Liana quickly interjected, "No, no, it's not what you think." She hoisted herself up from the squishy couch with some difficulty and planted herself in front of her friends, throwing back her shoulders in an attempt to imbue herself with strength and purpose. "I've made a New Year's resolution. I'm going to decide by my thirtieth birthday in May whether I will marry Jakob or we should both move on."

Both women gasped in unison.

"Yes," Liana said, not actually having made any such resolution or even known her own mind until she'd started speaking, "as my father used to say, 'Fish or cut bait, Liana Cohen!'" She didn't have the heart to tell delicate Charlotte that her father had used a more colorful expression—"Shit or get off the pot"—but the message was the same. And now that she had put it out there, it seemed like the only fair thing to do.

How long can I make Jakob wait for me?

After the girls left, Liana went down to the bodega on the corner to buy some Tums and diet ginger ale. Between the greasy Chinese food and the discussion, she felt more than a little queasy. As she crossed Amsterdam Avenue to get to the store, she saw someone who looked remarkably like her mother come out of the Jewish Community Center on the corner of Seventy-Sixth Street and hail a cab. When she got over her initial shock and determined it was indeed her mother, Liana leapt in front of the taxi, which was very slowly moving away from the curb, throwing herself on the hood so that the driver had to stop. He yelled through the front windshield, "What the fuck are you doing, crazy lady?" There was no good answer, so Liana simply slid down the front of the car as gracefully as she could and walked to the left passenger side door, opened it, and directed her mother out of the cab.

"Sorry about that," Liana said to the driver. Without looking back, she led Phyllis across the street and up to her apartment. Her mother, neatly coifed and wearing a trim wool pantsuit in rose pink, didn't say a word.

"What was that all about?" Liana demanded when they got upstairs. "You come into the city after mysteriously telling me you had 'other plans' so you couldn't see me, and then you sneak out of the JCC across the street from my apartment without so much as a hello to your only child?" Liana was incensed, although she couldn't have articulated why.

"Liana, I appreciate that show of filial devotion, although it was a bit extreme. I wasn't trying to hide anything, but I didn't know I had to report my every move to you," her mother answered. "I'm an adult, you know—I have a life."

"Well what was your adult life doing at the JCC today, if I may be so bold as to ask?" Liana said, unable to give it up.

"I joined a seniors' discussion group," her mother said. "Today was the first meeting. We talk about current events, the Middle East, politics, Judaism in America—whatever topics are of interest to the group."

"But you're not even interested in current events and politics!" Liana exclaimed, feeling as if she had caught her mother in a lie.

"No, not particularly," her mother readily admitted.

"What I like is that the group attracts quality, intelligent, older Jewish men who are looking for like-minded mature women and not girls in their forties. Just today I met three or four men around my age I thought I might like to get to know. There was this one fellow in particular—Irv, I think was his name. He had the most well-kept fingernails—not manicured, just neat and clean. And he still wears his gold wedding band but on his right hand, although he said his wife had died more than ten years ago. 'I'm ready to go on but not to let go of the love,' he said. I thought that was very touching."

Liana desperately wished she had not been distracted from her expedition for the Tums and ginger ale—she was surely going to need them now.

"You're trying to meet men, Mom?" she said weakly.

"Well, would that be so bad? I've been a widow for three years; I don't think your father is coming back. And I'm a young seventy. Would you want me to be alone for the next ten, fifteen, twenty years?"

"Of course not. I don't want you to be lonely." Liana tasted the salt in her mouth before she realized she was crying. "I just miss him." They sat on the couch, and her mother held her in her arms, stroking her head in the same soothing way she had when her first boyfriend had broken up with her in the eighth grade and Liana thought the world had ended.

"I miss him too, sweetheart. I always thought we'd grow old together. But that wasn't meant to be."

She looked at her mother, really looked at her, for the first time in months. Her mom and Charlotte and Katie—the important women in her life—had all come to the same realization. It was time to move on.

Maybe it's time for me too.

CHAPTER 15

After the holidays, Deb had taken a turn for the worse. New tumors had appeared in unexpected places, and the chemo was barely keeping them at bay. Still, she remained positive, mostly for Max's sake, and she pushed herself to come into the office on occasion. She wasn't really doing any work to speak of, but her cameo appearances allowed Gerry to keep her on the health insurance plan, and Deb's visits to the office gave her a destination to break up the week between doctors' appointments.

"Hey, so glad you're here!" Liana said as she walked into the office and saw steam rising from a cup of coffee on Deb's desk. Still in her usual morning fog, she hadn't registered that the body in the chair was not Deb's now waiflike figure but a rather dough-boyish young man with round gold-rimmed glasses and a mop top of chestnut waves.

"Hi," he said cheerily, assuming that Liana's nice greeting had been meant for him.

Liana jumped back, spilling her small-tall coffee down the front of her white sweater. "Damn, that's hot!" she yelled, wiping uselessly at her chest with the Starbucks napkins. Later, she'd reflect on the poor impression she had made on Bobby; for now, she was just confused and upset. "Where's Deb?" she demanded.

"I'm sorry—I don't think I've met Deb yet," he said, smiling affably.

"Okay. Don't move," she ordered, although she wasn't sure why.

Liana raced down the hall to Gerry's office, where she found him with his feet up on his desk, placidly reading *The New York Times*. She began to breathe again, knowing that no one besides Gerry would be as upset as she if something had happened to Deb.

"Who is that man sitting at Deb's desk?" Liana hissed, teeth clenched. Gerry slowly folded his paper and put it down on the desk. He loved nothing better than knowing news before someone else did, even bad news—or maybe especially bad news.

"I tried to figure out another solution, but I just couldn't," he began. "Deb is here so rarely these days, and Bobby, the new hire, needed a desk. I thought it'd be a good idea for him to sit with you, an experienced attorney, so you could show him the ropes."

What the hell is going on here? Has Gerry lost his mind?

Six months ago, Liana was persona non grata—the attorney without a heart, infecting the rest of the office with her negativity. Had she executed her ersatz transformation into model public defender so successfully that the Boss believed she was now emotionally committed to the cause, and would trust her with an impressionable neophyte? Or had Gerry sensed that Liana's commitment to Shea, even with its questionable genesis, had given her a genuine renewed enthusiasm for her job?

Liana had the sinking feeling that Bobby might be a spy, but she was too concerned about Deb to worry about that. "So where's Deb going to sit when she comes in?"

"There's a free desk in the room at the end of the hallway, where the mail room guys hang out when they're slow,"

Gerry said. Other attorneys would find that insulting, but she knew that Deb shared her view on this one. The "mail room guys"—Carlos and Sam and Piotr—were the nicest, most down-to-earth people in the office, and they adored Deb. She'd be just fine.

Having resigned herself to her new rooming situation, Liana was on her best behavior with Bobby over the next couple of weeks, dispensing advice and wisdom and filling him in on the office gossip on a need-to-know basis. She liked him well enough, although she noted that he had become a bit too bud-dy-buddy with Gerry. She toed the party line on all the rules and expectations, keeping to herself the indiscretions she had committed with regard to Danny Shea, both real and imagined.

And she threw herself behind her new client, Martin Johnson, a psychotic forty-something-year-old man convicted of murder, who had killed his aunt by throwing a Molotov cocktail at her, believing she was the phoenix who would rise from the ashes. Liana planned to base a large part of her pitch to the appellate court for a reversal on the journal Johnson kept—page after page of the incoherent ramblings of a madman, a person, she would argue, who couldn't have formed the intent to kill anyone. She was glad to find that her interest in Johnson was purely clinical and lawyerly—her personal attachment to Shea, however bizarre, would be the exception, not the rule.

One afternoon in the middle of January, Deb poked her head into Liana and Bobby's office. "Want to grab a slice?" she asked Liana, making sure to exclude Bobby.

"Sure," Liana answered, happy that Deb had an appetite for something—lately it looked like she had stopped eating altogether, or maybe she just couldn't hold much down. Something about Deb's tone of voice tipped Liana off that the lunch might be unpleasant, but she wasn't sure why. After a couple of bites and a few minutes of general office chitchat, Deb got down to business.

"You haven't been a very good friend lately, Liana," she said. Deb did not mince words.

"Excuse me?" Liana said, baffled.

"I've hardly seen you at all. When I'm here—which is seldom enough to impose on your busy schedule—you barely stop into my 'office,' such as it is, to say hello. You sit there with that new guy, like I'm already dead." There was no show of emotion, just a recitation of the facts as Deb saw them. And it was devastating.

If Deb had reached over and slapped Liana in the face, she would not have felt worse or more directly rebuked. Liana tried some feeble excuses, but they sounded lame even to her own ears. Unlike the petty slights that Deb had manufactured to keep Liana on her toes and to stir the pot before she got sick, Liana recognized that this time she had really screwed up. She was grateful that Deb had thrown down the gauntlet and given her the opportunity to repent. "I'll do better," she said, and she meant it.

As January dragged on, Deb put Liana to the test. Twice she commandeered Liana to accompany her to chemotherapy sessions at Sloan Kettering, the two women pretending to watch *The View* as the drugs dripped slowly into Deb's arm. Liana was thankful to be allowed to keep Deb company at such an intimate moment but still tormented by the very presence of the needle—an irrational, but nonetheless real, phobia. Another afternoon, Deb asked Liana to babysit for Max for a couple of hours while she napped. Liana didn't mind the children's television programming—she actually enjoyed *Clifford the Big Red Dog* and *Barney*—but Max was still in diapers, and she almost telephoned Charlotte to come over and get in a little practice. On the days that Deb made it into the office, Liana made a point of getting sandwiches for them to share for lunch and swinging by the room where Deb sat, surrounded by her loyal mailroom bodyguards, several times during the day to check on her. If at first Liana's attentions felt forced, both to Deb and to herself, eventually she won back Deb's trust. By the end of the month, Liana had redeemed herself, but it was also becoming clearer by the day that Deb was fading.

The first week in February, Deb turned thirty-three years old. Liana telephoned her from the office to wish her a happy birthday.

"I made it to the same age as Jesus," Deb said to Liana.

Purposefully ignoring Deb's use of the past tense, Liana responded, "And you should live until a hundred and twenty," invoking the traditional Jewish blessing for a long life. Liana continued, "Anyway, Deb, you're Jewish. Is Jesus meaningful to you for some reason?"

"Well, duh . . . Jesus was Jewish too, silly. But, no, that's pretty much where the similarities end, unless you count the fact that I like to eat olives and wear cool sandals. Listen, Steven is making me a little birthday brunch tomorrow, just my closest friends. Will you come?"

Liana was puzzled. "Steven, your ex-husband?"

"Yes. Don't worry, no earth shattering news there—we're still divorced. He's stepped up with Max, and who else was going to organize this thing?" Deb asked. Liana was touched to be included and assured Deb she would be there.

When she arrived at Deb's apartment, Liana surveyed the room, somehow still expecting to see her friend at the height of fashion, decked out in chunky silver jewelry and a trendy lipstick color, wearing tailored wool slacks, a cashmere sweater, and boots with heels. But Deb had not been into the office for about ten days, and Liana was shocked at how rapidly she had deteriorated in such a short span of time. She was extremely weak. She spent the entire party seated in her favorite comfortable chair in a corner of the living room, covered with an afghan, the slight remainder of her hair tucked up into a cozy wool cap instead of the wig she usually wore to the office. She seemed pleased to introduce her friends from different parts of her life to one another—Liana couldn't help but marvel at her attitude, given how sick she clearly was. But she was still Deb, holding court and tossing barbs around the room—"What, you couldn't put on some decent clothes to come to my party?"—though none of them seemed to stick anymore. Liana was inordinately moved when Deb chose her to make her a bagel with cream cheese and lox, knowing how minimal her appetite had been.

As she nibbled at her food, Deb turned to Liana, who was sitting on the ottoman at the foot of her chair, and said, "I have to ask you something. You can say no, but you should understand that it's very important to me." Looking at Deb, Liana knew she would refuse her nothing. Deb spoke very softly, pulling Liana in closer with her voice and shutting out the chatter around them. It was as though they were alone in the room, although Liana could see Steven hovering close by, protectively.

"When I die, will you help with the funeral arrangements and all that stuff?" Liana's eyes grew wide with terror, despite her best efforts to keep her face neutral.

Deb continued, undaunted, as usual, by Liana's discomfort. "My parents are so overwhelmed already; they're barely functioning as it is. I'd like to spare them having to deal with the logistics. And my brothers will come in, but nobody lives in New York. It would be hard for them to figure it all out long distance, and it'd just delay everything."

Liana had not responded, but her mind had gone to Steven, and she had unintentionally tilted her head in his direction. Picking up on Liana's nonverbal cue, Deb continued, "Honestly, I don't really want Steven and his new wife doing this—it's enough that they'll have Max to deal with." Deb started to cry, and Liana took her hand, which felt small and feverish, although she was touched to see that she had somehow managed to get a manicure before the brunch. "Look, I have other friends I guess I can ask if this is too much for you," Deb said, Liana's body language as she slumped slightly on the ottoman unwittingly revealing her hesitation.

Deb was giving her an out, but Liana wouldn't take it. The last few weeks after Deb had demanded that Liana step up as her friend had cemented their bond in a way that neither woman had anticipated. They had transformed their relationship into something deeper, and now Liana was being asked to commit herself to one final act of devotion.

"Of course, Deb. I'll do whatever you need me to do."

Deb had obviously thought a lot about this, and without missing a beat she said, "When the time comes, you'll call the rabbi of that synagogue you took me to—Rabbi Nacht. He can make sure everything is done right, and he'll walk my parents through the funeral and the burial and shiva."

Ah, that's why she is turning to me.

Liana had brought Deb to services on Friday night a couple of times—once before she was sick and once after. She had been impressed by Rabbi Nacht's kindness and erudition, but she, like Liana, wasn't particularly religious. Although Liana remembered Deb commenting on the rabbi's nice voice and good looks, she certainly hadn't been moved to become a regular attendee.

"Deb—you're not so observant; do you really want the whole Orthodox enchilada when it comes to this?" Liana asked, trying to lighten the moment.

"You know what, Liana? I've come to think that sometimes, not in every situation but in some, there's right and there's wrong. And I want to do this right," Deb said. As in so many moments in their friendship, Liana knew there was just no point in arguing with Deb.

"Okay, I'll do it, but no time soon, okay?"

"Okay," Deb said, squeezing Liana's hand. "Now, where's that birthday cake?"

CHAPTER 16

Liana had always thought of Valentine's Day as a Hallmark holiday at best. She had never held Jakob to any particular recognition of the day—she didn't expect red roses or chocolate or for him to serenade her or write her a sonnet. But with her self-imposed deadline to make a decision on their future looming, she intended to give their love, and its long-term prospects, every advantage. Spending so much time with Deb—and faced so starkly with the precariousness of everything—had strengthened Liana's resolve to make sure Jakob knew how she felt about him and how much she wanted them to be together through life's ups and downs.

And maybe focusing on Jakob and the prospect of marriage will help me stop daydreaming about Danny Shea.

The embarrassing frequency and intensity of the unbidden and absurd visions were making her anxious.

So she invited Jakob to her apartment for a romantic homemade dinner on the fourteenth—a curious choice, as Liana had never learned to cook. In college, she'd been on the full meal plan for all four years, happily lazing around the dining hall with her friends, refilling her plate with salad and French fries, and going out late at night for ice cream. Her eating habits hadn't changed—she was all about takeout of every ethnic variety, and when she was forced to make something at home, she stuck to whatever she could warm in the microwave. So when she woke up on February 14 with no idea what to whip up for Jakob for their repast, she called her mother in desperation.

"Well," Phyllis said, "your impulse is a good one. The fastest way to a man's heart is through his stomach. But you're asking the wrong person what you should make for Jakob."

Liana was dejected.

Is she going to abandon me at this crucial moment?

"You need to call Arlene," her mother instructed. "A man wants the food his mother cooks."

"Really?" Liana asked. "That sounds so Neanderthal or Oedipal or primal or something."

"Trust me on this, Li. A couple of his mother's old standards, and you will have Jakob eating out of your hand. Or whatever it is that you young people do these days for fun," her mother said.

"Ew, Mom! Please don't go there. Love you."

Liana hung up the phone and immediately called Arlene. After explaining her predicament and reminding Jakob's mother that her culinary skills were nonexistent, she convinced Arlene to work out a menu of his favorites, easily prepared in Liana's tiny kitchen and suitable for dining in the middle of winter in her overheated apartment. A few minutes later, Arlene emailed Liana her recipes for cold cucumber soup, asparagus pie, curried couscous salad, and apple cobbler with vanilla ice cream. Liana was elated, if a bit nervous. After a quick trip to Fairway, she began, wondering if she should have taken Arlene up on her offer to do the cooking and pass it off as her own.

By six thirty, everything was ready. Liana wasn't confident that she'd replicated each dish perfectly, but certainly the food was recognizable and sufficiently similar to Arlene's that, if Phyllis's theory was right, Jakob would be both comforted and seduced by Liana's efforts. She set the small table with a red-and-white checkered tablecloth—a bit picnic casual, but it was what she had—and she stuck some long, tapered red candles incongruously in the small silver-plated candlesticks she sometimes used on Shabbat. She took out her two best wineglasses and opened the expensive bottle she had bought to breathe. Liana had laughed out loud when Arlene had started to make suggestions for the wine; her inability to cook had resulted, long ago, in her becoming enough of an oenophile to make her welcome, bottle in hand, at anyone else's home-cooked meal.

When she was satisfied that the room looked lovely and enticing, she turned with the time that remained to preparing herself. A quick trip to Victoria's Secret after the grocery shopping had yielded a sexy new black silk bra and panty set—nothing that would make either of them blush but enough, at the right moment, to divert Jakob's attention from Liana's rendition of his mother's food and put the spotlight back on her. Over her new lingerie she put on jeans and a sweater; there was only so far she could go in pretending this wasn't a weeknight in her apartment, after all. She pumped up her curls, dabbed on a little perfume, and checked to make sure the food was ready to go—soup cold, asparagus pie and cobbler hot, couscous room temperature. Then she sat on the couch and waited for Jakob to arrive.

Seven o'clock came and went, but Liana was accustomed to Jakob being late, and she wasn't worried. When it got to seven thirty, she started to pace, and as it neared eight, she felt both hurt and a little foolish. She called Jakob's office, and a secretary working overtime answered. "Mr. Weiss's line, may I help you?"

"Yes," Liana said, without identifying herself. "Is he available?"

"No, I'm afraid he's not at his desk. He's in a conference; would you like me to try to pull him out?" she said agreeably.

"No, thank you. He must've forgotten," Liana said to herself, oblivious to the secretary on the line. She hung up, dazed, not sure whether to be angry at Jakob or at herself. Had she reminded him during the week of their date? She couldn't recall. But most guys, even those as clueless as Jakob, would know it was Valentine's Day. As she sat looking at the flickering candles and the shimmering wineglasses, she made a decision. She'd rise above her reflexive impulse to be furious with Jakob and his job. She'd be the compassionate and understanding woman that he needed.

In a few minutes Liana located the large wicker picnic basket she'd bought at Williams and Sonoma when she moved to Manhattan, imagining that she and Jakob would spend long, lazy Sundays in fine weather sprawled out in Central Park, sipping chilled Chablis and eating Camembert cheese and strawberries. The idyllic Sundays hadn't materialized, both she and Jakob recognizing that it was more important to use their free time to visit with their families, especially after Liana's father died. But the basket remained, stuffed onto a high shelf in the hall closet, and into its pristine interior Liana now placed paper plates, plastic cutlery, and Tupperware containers filled with cold cucumber soup, asparagus pie, couscous salad, and apple cobbler. The a la mode would have to wait for another day.

Hopping into a taxi, Liana felt better and more secure in her relationship with Jakob than she had since their weekend in Newport in November. She longed to see him—even if they just had a little while to have some dinner together—and then she'd go home, knowing that she hadn't been that pesky girlfriend, losing her temper and criticizing him for his work obligations that were out of his control.

"Thanks," she said to the taxi driver. "This is great. I'll get out here." She paid the fare, impulsively adding on a tip that was almost as much as the cost of the whole ride. The driver gave her an encouraging thumbs-up as she got out of the cab, picnic basket in hand, clearly a woman on a mission.

If only he could see these undies.

When she reached the sixteenth floor, she breezed past the receptionist and headed toward Jakob's office. The woman filling in for Jakob's regular secretary was sitting at the desk, looking bored, only the overtime pay making up for the fact that she was in the office at nine in the evening on Valentine's day.

"Hi. Do you know which conference room Jakob is using?" Liana asked.

"Yes, he's in 1630—is he expecting you? I can show you where the room is," she offered.

But Liana remembered the layout of the floor from her days as a summer associate, and she knew right away that Jakob was holed up in the same depressing place where she had spent most of that summer after her second year of law school. A wave of empathy washed over her.

How sad that Jakob is stuck in a bleak and lonely conference room when he is supposed to be at home with me eating asparagus pie.

She raced down the hallway, moved to be coming to his rescue.

They were sitting close, their backs to the door, their bodies inclined toward each other but not touching. The thin column of air between them sizzled with what Liana perceived, gratefully, as yet-unrealized possibilities. When she entered the room, they were absorbed in conversation, speaking quietly, and they didn't notice her. Jakob looked tired but relaxed, his legs stretched out in front of him and crossed at the ankle under the table. The sleeves of his no-longer-crisp white shirt were pushed up to his elbows, and he had unbuttoned the top button and loosened his tie. The papers on the table had been moved carefully to one side, and a now-empty medium pizza box rested in front of Jakob and the woman, who were each holding a small plastic cup half-filled with red wine.

"Drinking on the job? That could get you fired," Liana said, attempting a lighthearted reaction that could in no way counter the pathos of the picnic basket draped over her arm.

Jakob turned around, so surprised to see her that he didn't speak. But the woman, clueless and smiling, said, "Well, it's Valentine's Day, you know."

Liana looked searchingly at Jakob, willing him to recover and take control of the situation as she felt the strength flow out of her.

"Liana," he said, finally, "this is Michelle, the paralegal working on my case. We have to work late; we were just grabbing some pizza." When Liana didn't respond or move any farther into the room, Jakob continued. "Michelle, this is Liana, my girl-friend. Would you mind giving us a few minutes?"

Michelle got up slowly from the table, looking as though she did not want to leave and miss whatever scene might follow her departure. She was young—just out of college, Liana surmised—making decent money as a paralegal before deciding whether to go to law school, and sleeping with a few of the attorneys along the way for good measure. Liana had nothing against the standard paralegal strategic plan, as long as it didn't involve Jakob. This one, Michelle, was pretty in an unusual way—thick red hair and porcelain skin, big blue eyes and sub-stantial curves poured attractively into a tailored navy suit. If she didn't leave right away, Liana feared she might accidentally drench her in cold cucumber soup.

When she had finally sauntered out of the room, Jakob asked, "What're you doing here, Li? You refuse to come to the firm when I ask you to, and now you show up without even calling at nine at night. I don't get it."

"Honestly, Jakob, I think you have more to explain than I do. You were supposed to come over for dinner tonight, and when you didn't show up, I got worried." A cloud passed over his face, and Jakob looked chagrined, but he didn't interrupt

Liana. "Then I called, and the secretary said you were stuck here, so I thought I'd bring you dinner and salvage the night. And what do I find? You and the paralegal, all cozy. What's going on, Jay?" She felt sapped of all her energy and reluctantly sat down in the chair that Michelle had vacated.

"There's nothing going on, Liana—I swear," Jakob said. Liana waited patiently for him to continue. She knew what she had seen, and it may not have been much, but it was decidedly not nothing.

"Michelle's a kid. We're friends." Jakob was rarely at a loss for words, but he was flailing now. "She's easygoing. She gets this world—my world, Liana—and she doesn't give me a hard time about being a part of it."

Liana was wounded, but she was no fool. She sensed that a misstep here could send Jakob into Michelle's arms or someone else's, and no way was she going to let that happen. She would make the decision about a future with Jakob—no one would make it for her.

She reached down into the picnic basket. "Apple cobbler?" she asked.

"Let's get out of here," Jakob said, relieved both to have not strayed and to have been forgiven.

Liana pictured her apartment, the table sitting forlornly, set with her good wineglasses, the candles now burnt down low, the smell of the wax lingering in the air.

"Can we go to your place? My apartment's a mess," she said.

CHAPTER 17

```
Nice job, Liana!
    Great win!
    You rock, girl!
    Very good decision. Please see me at your
earliest convenience.
```

Liana had been checking the Appellate Division's website every Wednesday afternoon for the last month, looking for the court's ruling on Danny Shea's case. Today, she had gotten distracted and forgotten—but the emails from her colleagues told her she'd won. She hurried to pull up the decision on her computer. She read the majority opinion, which adopted almost verbatim her argument that Shea's trial counsel had been ineffective for failing to redact Alba Velez's name from the DNA lab report. Judge Simon had dissented, writing that she couldn't join the majority opinion because there was no way to determine whether Shea was prejudiced when the jury learned of Ms. Velez's existence or the error was harmless because the evidence was so overwhelming that Shea would have been convicted anyway. Liana wished, for the thousandth time, that she had answered Judge Simon's question at oral argument instead of punting, but, in the end, the dissent didn't matter. The court reversed Shea's conviction and ordered a new trial.

"Hey, Liana, you won that case!" Bobby squeaked, a little late to the party. Listening to his perky voice reminded Liana of how much she missed having Deb around—Bobby had been pretty good company for a while, but now that Deb was no longer coming into the office at all, his presence was a constant reminder of her absence. Liana was mostly successful in pushing the thought to the back recesses of her mind, but the notion of no longer working with Deb was oppressive. As mercurial as she could sometimes be, Deb was honest and direct, and Liana felt unmoored without her. She picked up the phone.

"Hey, you! Guess what? I won Danny Shea's case!" Liana looked forward to giving Deb some news, maybe a momentary lift.

"I know, silly," Deb said. "Gerry told me half an hour ago. Classic that the client I gave you turned out to be a winner." Deb was kidding, but Liana could feel her longing to return to her normal life.

"Oh, Deb. I would trade any win to have you here in the office doing your own work. You'll be back soon." It was a hard reassurance to pull off, but Liana tried.

The mention of Gerry's name reminded her that he had asked to see her.

"Listen, Gerry wanted to talk to me. I guess I better go. I'll talk to you soon. Kisses to Max." She reluctantly hung up on Deb.

Before heading to Gerry's office, she called Jakob.

"Hey," Liana said excitedly. "I won the Shea case!" When Jakob didn't respond, she added, "You know, the one you came to see me argue."

"Oh, that's great, babe," Jakob said. He sounded distracted; he'd put her on speaker, and she could hear him typing on his keyboard.

"This case is important to me, Jakob." She knew she should be glad he hadn't figured out how emotionally involved she had gotten with Shea, but her disappointment at his lack of interest took center stage.

Contrite, Jakob tried again. "I'm sorry, Li. I'm just in the middle of twenty things here. It's wonderful that you won your case; I'm really proud of you. I hope Gerry is appreciative." Jakob always got down to the bottom of things, and Liana realized she better deal with whatever Gerry had in store for her.

"Thanks. I'll let you get back to work," Liana said. It was a way of getting off the telephone that Liana had picked up from her mother and that she detested. Whenever Phyllis wanted to end a discussion, she would say, "Well, I'll let you go," as though Liana had been the one to suggest that the conversation had run its course. It never failed to irk her. Jakob, on the other hand, seemed only too happy to be released from the call.

Liana wasn't sure what to expect when she went to speak with Gerry. There wasn't much follow-up to do when the court reversed and ordered a new trial for a client. She'd have to write to Danny Shea and tell him the good news, being careful to manage his expectations. It wasn't as though the appeals court had dismissed his case and he'd be let out of prison "forthwith"; rather, he'd be brought back to the trial court in Brooklyn, and the proceedings would start all over again.

The fact that Liana believed in him—*Why would such an intelligent, seemingly decent man have sat holding Jennifer Nash's pink purse, "waiting to allay" her parents' fears, if he had just raped her? And weren't Shea and Nash friends, on their way to becoming friends with benefits?*—was irrelevant. In all likelihood, Shea would be found guilty at trial again in six months or a year, and she'd have to represent him again on his appeal from the retrial. But she'd make sure not to mention that to Gerry, who would definitely not appreciate that, in her mind, her victory was already relegated to the pyrrhic.

"Liana, come in," Gerry said, motioning her to the guest

chair. "Are you happy?" he oozed. Liana wasn't sure if it was a trick question.

"I'm pleased with the decision, Gerry. Is there something you wanted to discuss?" She'd warmed to Gerry slightly since Deb had become ill. He genuinely cared about her, and that did speak well for him. Besides, Liana had been invited to Deb's birthday brunch and Gerry hadn't, and she felt that proved something about their relative status in Deb's eyes. But she still didn't trust him as far as she could throw him.

"Liana, I'm proud of the way you handled this case. And not just because you won. You put your heart and soul into representing Mr. Shea, and it showed. That's a real achievement. That's what we are about in this office."

She wasn't sure she could pull off a neutral response, so she didn't try. Gerry didn't notice.

"I just wanted to remind you of a few things," he continued in his "I am your supervisor" voice. "First, if the press calls, we don't comment on ongoing cases." Liana knew the drill, but Gerry didn't know about Randy Napoli. Liana was sure to be featured on the front page of tomorrow's *New York Law Journal* on Danny Shea's case.

"Of course," she said.

"When is Mr. Shea due back in the trial court in Brooklyn?" Gerry asked.

"I haven't heard yet from the DA's office, but I'd assume it could be as early as next week," Liana said. "Why?"

"Well, you need to appear on that first date when Mr. Shea is brought back to Brooklyn Supreme," Gerry said.

So this is why he wanted to see me.

There was no reason for Liana, the appellate attorney, to represent the client in the trial court—the assigned public defender from the trial office would be much better suited to taking care of the preliminary matters than she would, as well as the retrial down the line. Besides, there was no way she was risking seeing Danny Shea again in person, much as some part of her longed to do just that.

Liana's distress was written all over her face; Gerry continued. "His trial attorney was found ineffective, Liana, so when Mr. Shea comes to court for the first appearance on his retrial, he won't have anyone representing him until the court appoints a new trial attorney. You need to go and stand up with Mr. Shea until you're relieved by new trial counsel."

"But, Gerry—"

"It's no big deal—you just stand there next to your client, remind the judge of the grounds of the appellate court's decision granting a new trial, and wait for the court to assign a new trial attorney. It'll be five minutes max—you barely have to say anything. You'll take the kid with you."

Liana snapped to attention. "What kid?" she asked.

"Bobby—you'll take Bobby with you. It'll be a good experience for him to see what it's like in trial court and how you interact with a client," Gerry said. Liana was sure that Gerry was smirking, although the expression was so close to the normal arrangement of his facial features it was hard to tell. "You did a great job with this case, Liana. I know that a number of months ago, you were feeling conflicted about our clients, but it seems like your experience representing Mr. Shea has reignited your fervor. I'm so glad to see that. We value your work here. It'll be good for you to see Mr. Shea in court; I'm sure he'd also like to express his appreciation."

Did Deb share with Gerry that Danny Shea affects me in a way that is not entirely professional?

The thought was humiliating, and Liana ordinarily would have been angry at Deb's betrayal, but under the circumstances, she didn't begrudge Deb the laugh she must have shared with Gerry at her expense.

When she returned to her desk, there was an email from Randy Napoli.

Awesome decision, Liana. You knew you had this one as soon as you filed it. Call me when you get a minute. Working on the article for tomorrow's paper. As Liana gave Randy the lowdown over the phone, her feelings about the testimony and about Shea came rushing back to her. She tried to remain as clinical as possible, but she knew it wasn't working; she could feel her breathing quickening.

"Hey, this guy really made an impression on you!" Randy said, sounding a little jealous. "I know you can't give a comment, right?" Randy tried. Liana felt the constraints slipping away from her. In her attempt to figure out Danny Shea, she had already broken more serious rules—destroying client correspondence, visiting a client on a total pretense, secretly lusting after a client—this one seemed like nothing.

"You can quote me as saying that I'm confident that, with competent trial counsel, Daniel Shea will be acquitted of all the charges at his retrial." She was so lost in her own fantasy world that she forgot Bobby was sitting there.

Bobby followed Liana into the criminal court building at 320 Jay Street like an obedient puppy. She had been leery of taking him along, but now she felt that maybe it hadn't been such a bad idea. He could act as a reality check—a reminder to her that Danny Shea was just like any other client, if conceivably innocent and on a totally different order of magnetic. Bobby would also be a buffer zone—a pudgy, obsequious one—between her and Shea. She realized she was being overly dramatic; how much damage could be done in a ten-minute appearance in open court with a man who was only momentarily out of handcuffs and surrounded by court officers?

They entered Justice Martin's courtroom and made their way over to the defense table. "You sit here," Liana directed

Bobby, placing him in the middle so that he would be between herself and Shea. Bobby, who had never seen the inside of a trial courtroom before, had no idea what was happening and dutifully sat down. Liana glanced over at the prosecutor's table and noticed that among the attorneys was Ms. Wellington, the assistant district attorney who had handled the appeal.

"What's she doing here?" Bobby asked. Just as it was unusual for Liana, the appellate defense attorney, to be present in the trial court, so too there was no obvious reason that the prosecutor who handled the case on appeal would be there.

"I have absolutely no idea," Liana answered, trying not to let Ms. Wellington's very being unnerve her.

"All rise!" the bailiff called out. The attorneys got to their feet as Justice Martin entered the courtroom.

"Good morning, everyone. We are here today to begin the proceedings on the retrial of Mr. Daniel Shea. I see that new counsel is here for Mr. Shea. Counselor, are you ready to proceed? If so, we will bring the defendant up from the holding pens."

Liana quickly addressed the court to correct the misimpression her presence had made.

"Your Honor, my name is Liana Cohen. I served as appellate counsel on this case. I'll be appearing for today's adjourned date only, until Your Honor can appoint new counsel for Mr. Shea, who was and remains unable to afford his own attorney. As Your Honor may recall, the Appellate Division found that Mr. Shea's trial counsel was ineffective, and therefore he must have a new attorney appointed for these proceedings."

"Ah, Ms. Cohen!" the judge said, his tone a mixture of false delight and masked annoyance. "I believe you also convinced my esteemed colleagues at the Appellate Division that I also didn't adequately protect your client's rights during the first trial. I'm surprised that you didn't ask for the retrial to proceed before a different judge. That was a remedy you could have pursued, was it not?"

Liana started to squirm. She wanted this to be over, and she was beginning to think that too much was happening without Shea in the courtroom—the last thing she wanted was for the defendant to be able to claim that she was ineffective because she hadn't protected his constitutional right to be present at all phases of his trial.

"Your Honor, we didn't request a new judge, nor are we asking you to recuse yourself now. We're very confident that you'll conduct the retrial in accord with all of the defendant's rights. At this time, I'd ask you to please have the defendant brought into the courtroom so that he may participate in the proceedings."

"Of course, Counselor," the judge said, directing his courtroom clerk to call for the defendant. "I see, Ms. Cohen, that you have a young colleague with you observing, and that's fine, although if you're going to be the one speaking to the Court, I would ask you to switch seats so that your client can have your ear," the judge instructed. Liana and Bobby swapped places, Bobby giving Liana a look that said, *Didn't you know that?* Then the judge turned to the prosecution.

"And Ms. Harrison, I see that you have another attorney with you. Can you state your appearance please?"

"Ava Wellington, Your Honor. I handled the appeal for the DA's office. I'm here in case the Court has any questions about the legal basis for these proceedings, especially regarding what we believe is going to transpire here today." Bobby shot Liana a questioning glance, but she had no idea what Wellington was talking about. Nothing at all was supposed to "transpire"; that's what Liana was prepared for—nothing. She'd kill Gerry if this got out of hand.

Liana heard the jangling of keys, and her heart plunged into her stomach. She reassured herself that Bobby would attribute the look of panic that crossed her face as courtroom jitters rather than nervous anticipation at the thought of seeing the man who, with just a glancing touch, had caused her to flee a maximum-security penitentiary without her undergarment. The court officer unlocked the side door and led Danny Shea in; another officer followed behind him. Someone, probably his Uncle Liam, had brought Shea civilian clothes for his court appearance, which Liana thought was both unusual and unnecessary, since he was going right back to the facility after this brief court appearance. Shea was wearing a crisp haint-blue button-down shirt that exactly matched the color of his eyes—*how did I miss those eyes when I saw him before?*—and a pair of pressed black trousers. He could have walked straight out of *GQ* magazine. Even Bobby unconsciously whistled under his breath.

The officer uncuffed Shea, and everyone sat down. Shea leaned in toward Liana and whispered in her ear, "Hey, what a relief. I didn't know you'd be here." His breath was warm and sweet. She put her hand reflexively up to check her hair.

"Please be quiet, Mr. Shea."

"I just wanted to say thank you for everything you've done," he persisted.

"You're welcome. But remember, you're not going anywhere but back to Green Haven today," she said quietly.

Ms. Wellington stood. "Your Honor, if I may, I'd like to update the court regarding what has happened with this case since the defendant's first trial." Ms. Wellington was dressed in another of her signature pantsuits, which lent her a certain military air, and her expression broadcast that if she could have spit on Mr. Shea, she would have. "This case was sent back to you for retrial because defense counsel failed to notice that the DNA report proved that Daniel Shea is a serial rapist."

"Objection, Your Honor!" Liana leapt to her feet.

"Counselor," the judge said, almost patiently, "we're not on trial here yet. You don't need to formally object. And I believe I understand what Ms. Wellington is doing—it's a bit out of line, but I'll let her say her piece. I have a feeling I see where this is going," the judge said, sounding a bit melancholy. Liana didn't see at all where this was going, and having Danny Shea six inches away from her was making it difficult to think clearly.

"May I continue, Your Honor?" Ms. Wellington asked.

"Please do, Counselor."

"This defendant was convicted on December 3, 2011, which is almost a year and a half ago. Since that time, the complainant in this case, Ms. Jennifer Nash, fortunately, has moved on with her life. She has worked extremely hard to begin to get past the trauma of the attack." Ms. Wellington paused for effect, and Liana started to get to her feet again, but the judge shot her a look that kept her in her seat. "And she's decided to pursue her education out of state. She's no longer within the jurisdiction of the court, and she has no interest in reliving the night of July 4, 2010, in court or anywhere else. Therefore, we're in the position of not being able to pursue the retrial." Ms. Wellington looked as if she would prefer to rip Danny Shea's head off, but instead she merely gazed beseechingly at the judge.

Liana felt the courtroom begin to spin, and she had no choice but to put her head down on her folded hands on the table. Ava Wellington was actually telling the judge that her office was going to let Danny Shea walk—not because he was not guilty but because the victim no longer wanted to testify. And although Liana had allowed herself to believe in Shea's actual innocence many times over the past six months, she had never remotely contemplated that he might exist in her world as a free man.

"Are you okay?" Shea's voice was so full of concern and his body was so close to hers, she almost swooned again. Liana managed to pick herself up in time to hear the judge admonishing the prosecutor.

"Ms. Wellington, I'm not about to tell the District Attorney of Kings County how to run his office. But there's a very obvious solution here. Ms. Nash gave sworn testimony at the first trial. At the retrial, you can simply read that testimony into the record, and it will stand as her testimony at this trial. It isn't ideal, but that's what happens when a witness has become unavailable. Certainly you would have to make more of a showing first that she really wouldn't come in and testify, but I think it would be a better way to proceed than ditching the whole case, don't you agree?" Justice Martin asked.

As Wellington consulted with the trial ADA, Bobby kicked Liana under the table. "Don't you think you should say something in favor of dismissal?" he whispered. Liana looked at him as if he were an alien from another planet and then rose to her feet.

"Your Honor, as you'll recall, this jury was out for three days before returning with a verdict an hour after they saw the prejudicial DNA report. That is an indication that they were weighing very seriously the competing accounts of the events of that night. In fact, the descriptions by Ms. Nash and Mr. Shea of a fully consensual encounter were almost identical, until they diverged in the final moments. So for those three days, the jury must have been considering the demeanor of the witnesses on the stand and their credibility. And until that moment when the reversible error occurred, the jury was unable to decide who was telling the truth. There's no way that Mr. Shea can receive a fair retrial if his accuser isn't in court for the jurors to evaluate, to hear her voice, to look into her eyes. Jennifer Nash can't be words read by court personnel from a piece of paper."

Liana realized with astonishment that Shea had himself fed her this very argument months before. Just as he had convinced her that to truly represent him she needed to know the man behind the transcript, Liana was now arguing that justice demanded that a jury assess Jennifer Nash in person as well. She sat down, praying it would work. Bobby gave her a thumbs-up. Shea looked at her proudly and nodded slightly.

Ms. Wellington's face sagged, and her nose began to twitch; she looked like someone had just run over her dog. "Your Honor," she said, "unfortunately, the district attorney has come to the same conclusion. My boss doesn't believe that a conviction won under those conditions would withstand appellate scrutiny, and he doesn't wish to risk a second reversal. Our office is declining to prosecute."

Silence followed. Even Justice Martin, who always had something to say, sat woodenly, staring at the attorneys. Then he turned to the court reporter—"Marci, we're off the record"— before focusing his attention on Mr. Shea. He leaned over the bench, the lights in the ceiling bouncing off his bald head.

"Well, Mr. Shea, it appears that in a few moments, you will walk out of my courtroom a free man. I severely regret the part that I played in making that come to pass. You may have almost fooled the jury, but you didn't fool me. You have your excellent appellate counsel, Ms. Cohen, to thank for your second chance—or maybe it is your third or fourth chance—at leading a law-abiding life. But listen to me, and listen to me good: if you so much as touch another woman without her express written consent, I'll lock you up for so long you won't even know what your wiener is for if you ever get out again. Do you hear me, Mr. Shea?"

"Loud and clear, Your Honor."

"Back on the record, Marci," the judge said. "Case dismissed." Panning the room with one final look of disgust, the judge left the courtroom.

Across the aisle, Ms. Wellington sat looking at her feet for a moment and then turned toward Liana. "I had the facility allow Mr. Shea to dress in his regular clothes, and they've also got his personal belongings—wallet, cell phone, keys, whatever. He can pick them up in the probation office downstairs on his way out," she said softly.

"Thanks," Liana said, still unable to believe what was happening.

"Are you happy now?" Ms. Wellington asked, her voice choking with emotion. Liana looked at her, marveling at the level of investment in her mission that would prompt her opponent to ask such a question with such intensity of feeling.

"Ms. Wellington, I'm doing my job. I'm not happy or unhappy. Trial counsel fucked up, and I took advantage of that for my client's benefit." Liana picked up her briefcase and walked to the back of the courtroom, where Bobby was chatting predictions for the upcoming baseball season with Shea.

"Can you speak with the court reporter about ordering a copy of today's minutes? I think we should have a record of what went on here. I'll meet you out front," she said to Bobby. When Bobby had walked to the front of the courtroom, Liana reached out to shake hands with Shea.

"Wow," he said, his handshake firm. "This is unbelievable. And you were unbelievable, Liana," he said.

"I'm glad things worked out," she said, using all her powers to maintain eye contact without revealing anything more. "Okay, well, I'm going to go back to the office with Bobby now. If you have any questions, you know how to reach me."

"Hang on. You just got me my life back. You aren't going to buy me a cup of coffee?" he asked. Liana was so startled at his nerve she laughed out loud. She looked at Danny Shea and noticed, for the first time, the utter joy on his face. It was irresistible. And why shouldn't she be happy for him? She wasn't a defense attorney automaton after all—his case had proved that to her, even if it wasn't always in a way the Boss would have advocated. She had just done something really good for someone.

I hope to God he deserved it.

"Don't you think you should be the one buying the coffee?" she said.

"You got it, Counselor. First I need to go down to probation and get my stuff," he said, clearly pleased that she had agreed to spend a little time with him.

"Do you know where the Starbucks on Montague is? I'll meet you there after I ditch Bobby," she said.

Liana made up something about needing to pick up an order at the Appellate Division across the street and told Bobby she'd meet him back at the office.

"Do you want me to tell Gerry what happened, or do you want to tell him yourself?" Bobby asked.

"You can tell him; I'll be back in an hour," she said. She had already moved on in her mind from the courtroom and was propelling herself toward a drama of a different sort.

Housed in the ground floor of a brownstone, with exposed brick walls and comfortable furniture, the Starbucks experience in Brooklyn Heights gave the illusion of drinking coffee in someone's living room. When Liana came in, she found Danny Shea sitting on a couch in the corner, sipping a chai tea latte, looking to all the world like a handsome hunk who happened to have a brisk March day off from his job as a male model. Only a nervous tic near his left eye and the way he occasionally looked over his shoulder toward the door, as though he expected to be hauled off to the slammer at any moment, gave away his anxiety at being cut loose.

"I think I'll buy my own coffee," Liana said, feeling that somehow that would restore the balance of power.

"Suit yourself, Counselor," he said.

When she got to the counter, Liana was overcome with nerves. She had never had any urge to fraternize with any of her clients before; she even preferred letters over telephone calls to keep the contact to a minimum.

What am I doing here? Am I crazy?

But really, Shea wasn't a client anymore—he was a former client. And she had something she still needed to ask him.

Agitated, Liana turned to the barista, a cute little blond

thing named Simone, and said, "I'll have a small coffee with room for milk, please."

"You know," Simone said, "here we call that a 'tall.' Using the right lingo makes you seem younger, more clued in."

"And you do realize how asinine that lingo is?" Liana said, her voice rising. "Why would you want to be a part of a corporate culture that forces you to substitute the word 'tall,' which would seem to indicate that the coffee was large, for 'small,' which in every other coffee establishment in the country gets you a twelve-ounce cup of coffee? Doesn't that strike you, a young, clued-in person, as bullshit?" She was close to hyperventilating now, clearly a deranged woman in an out-of-style black suit who had lost her marbles. Liana was trying to block out the gawkers as she waited for Simone to hand over her coffee when she felt the pressure of Shea's hand on her back, the heat of his touch burning through the fabric of her jacket.

"Okay, everyone, chill. There's no problem. My friend and I are just going to sit down now," he said smoothly and guided her to a large sofa chair opposite the couch where he had been sitting a moment before.

"Sorry," Liana said. "It's a pet peeve of mine, and I guess I'm on edge."

"It's okay," Shea said. "I'm a little freaked out myself. Didn't exactly expect to be getting out today. I need to call my uncle—I think I can crash there," he said, more to himself than to Liana. She was glad to hear he had somewhere to go, and she knew from her conversation in December that Liam O'Flaherty would do whatever he could for Shea.

"What will you do now?" she asked. The scene could not have been more surreal, but something about Shea's self-assuredness in the face of what must have been both an exhilarating and terrifying moment for him calmed her.

"I hope to pick up where I left off. Get back to school and work. I was only eight credits short of graduating when this all went down," Shea said. They were quiet for a few minutes, sipping their drinks, absorbed in their own thoughts. Liana envisioned the rooftop again, seeing in her mind's eye the dancing and the kissing; then she watched the divergent versions, like the old Japanese movie *Rashomon* from 1950 that her dad loved, playing out to the—almost —climax.

"Can I ask you something, Mr. Shea?" Liana said.

"You can ask me anything, Liana, if you call me Danny." He was challenging her, she knew, but her question was too important to get hung up on etiquette.

"Okay, Danny," she said, exaggerating his name. "Who is Alba Velez?"

Danny sat back on the couch and looked at Liana directly, his glance never wavering. When he spoke, his voice was steady and strong.

"Alba Velez was my first real girlfriend in high school. We started dating in the tenth grade, when we were both sixteen. She was a nice girl. I helped her with her English homework; she helped me with geometry." He paused, unhurriedly took a sip of his tea. "We were each other's first sexual experience. Once we got things figured out, we had a pretty good time together." Liana tried, in vain, to conjure up her first time to divert her from imagining the lithe body of a sixteen-year-old Shea, but the cadence of Danny's voice was too compelling to picture anything other than the story he was telling.

"We went out the whole school year, but as it got toward summer, I got restless. I figured it might be more fun to be free, play the field while school was out. We went to the beach in Far Rockaway one night in late May, and we had sex there. And then I told her it was over. It wasn't gallant, I admit, but it wasn't a crime either."

Except it was. It is sexual misconduct to have even consensual sex with someone under seventeen, an A misdemeanor. Not a very

*serious crime and rarely charged when the other party is also a teen,
but a crime nonetheless.*

"So what happened?" she asked. Liana realized that Judge
Simon was right; in the real world—if not the legal one—the
thing that mattered most in figuring out Danny Shea was
whether he had raped Alba Velez or not.

"Well, I should have known better than to be messing
around with a cop's daughter. Alba's dad is Charlie Velez—
maybe you've come across him. He was some kind of brass in
the Sixty-Eighth Precinct in Bay Ridge, where we grew up.
Alba came home upset that night because I had broken things
off—undoubtedly called me some terrible names, which I
probably deserved. And when Charlie found out that his little
girl wasn't a virgin, he went ballistic."

"You don't have to tell me all this," Liana said, feeling
guilty now that she had asked and not sure she really wanted
to know anymore.

*What does it matter now? This is the last time I will ever see
this man.*

"Yes, I do," Danny said. "I'm sorry if it's hard to listen to,
but I need you to know. So Charlie flipped out. He made Alba
go through the whole humiliating process as though I'd raped
her—made her talk to cops and the DA's office, have a rape kit
done at Downstate, the whole nine yards. He turned her into
a victim, even though she'd never claimed I'd done anything
wrong. I got arrested, and I had to give a DNA sample. I didn't
deny that I'd had sex with Alba that night—we both told the
police we had been having sex exclusively with each other for
a few months. I got charged, but my Uncle Liam had some
extra cash at the time, and he didn't want me to have a record at
sixteen; he hired a lawyer who worked out a youthful offender
adjudication—no criminal conviction, no time, sealed record,
you know the drill—but that DNA hit to Alba is still out there.
Well, you know that part."

Liana hadn't taken her eyes off Danny while he spoke. He didn't look in the least bit nervous—he didn't fidget or sweat or struggle for words. Just sober and sad, as if he had gone over all of this in his mind for a good long time and somehow come to terms with it.

This guy is either ridiculously unlucky in love or a pathological liar.

Somehow, she believed him.

"Well, I appreciate your sharing that with me, Mr. Shea."

"Please, don't go all formal on me and put that distance between us, like I'm just some client," he said. "You're my angel, Liana." He said it quietly, without any pretense.

"Danny, I was doing my job," she said. Liana found that each time she repeated that phrase, its meaning became more elusive.

"Can I explain something to you that I've thought a lot about? You know, I've had a lot of time to think lately," Danny asked, smiling sadly. When she didn't answer right away, he continued. "Are you a religious person?"

"That's a pretty personal question, Danny—I'm not sure that we should have that kind of conversation." She felt as if she was in way over her head already; a theological discussion seemed like a very bad idea.

"Fair enough," he said. "You don't need to answer that now. But here's what I believe." He put down his tea and sat forward on the couch so that their knees were almost touching.

"Sometimes in life you encounter an angel. You may not even know it at the time. It could be a person who says a kind word to you and lifts your spirits at an important moment. Or it could be someone who points you in the right direction at a crossroads. But sometimes there's no mistaking it. You're my angel, Liana. And I need you in my life."

He was mesmerizing, more so in person even than he had been on the printed page, but Liana managed to stammer out, "Don't you think I've done enough already?"

Danny chuckled. "I think you've done enough for today. I'll let you drink the rest of that coffee in peace. But I'll wait for you for as long as it takes, Liana. I'm not asking for anything in return. I just want to spend time with you." He touched her knee lightly as he got up from the couch, and then he bent down over her and softly kissed the top of her head. Before she could breathe again, he was out the door.

Simone, who had been wiping off tables nearby, approached Liana, still sitting in her chair, dazed. "He dumped you, huh?"

"Not exactly," Liana said. Then she not so accidentally knocked over her small coffee cup, which she had drained save for the last few drops at the bottom, spilling the dregs on the floor.

"Oops," Liana said, "I've made a tall mess." She got up and walked out without looking back.

CHAPTER 18

"Did you know that according to the new Pew survey, only sixty percent of American Jews attend a Passover seder, down from ninety percent only twenty years ago?" Irv asked. They were sitting in the dining room of Jakob's parents' house, about to start the evening's rituals. The table was set with fine white china and silver cutlery, and the wine goblets were filled with Manischewitz Extra Heavy Malaga. Liana's mom, Phyllis, had asked if she could bring Irv, the man with the nice fingernails whom she had met on the first day of her class at the JCC. Although he was undeniably well-groomed, Liana had yet to figure out what Phyllis saw in him. But they'd been spending more and more time together since January. They'd taken a film noir seminar at the New School, and sometimes after class they went out for dinner. Liana worried on the nights when her mother got home late.

"What do you make of that, Irv?" Jakob's father, Stan, asked.

"Well, I think young people today have no allegiance to anything greater than themselves. They think the world revolves around them, and there's no need for community or religion. It's sad really. This whole phenomenon of social media has made this generation feel that they're all connected and there are endless possibilities, but they're missing out on making the real bonds that last a lifetime." In an uncomfortable role reversal, Liana felt protective of her mother, as though she were a teenager making her first forays into the dating scene. Liana was skeptical of everything that came out of Irv's mouth, but she found herself nodding in agreement.

"Liana and Jakob go to an Orthodox synagogue," Arlene ventured, as if to counter Irv's attack on the youth of America.

"We go occasionally, Mom, but we aren't religious like the regulars there. We go because Liana likes the rabbi," Jakob said.

"You like the rabbi too!" Liana protested. To change the subject, she turned to Irv and asked, "Irv, do you follow baseball?"

"Sure. Who doesn't? I try to make it to a couple of Yankees games every year. That Jeter is really something else, isn't he? I don't like A-Rod much, though."

Liana glared at her mother, silently reprimanding her— *What gives, Ma? How could you bring a Yankees lover to the table?*—but her mother didn't seem to notice. The Cohen family had always been serious Mets fanatics, especially Liana's late father. They bled orange and blue. Now here was her mother, just a few years after Artie was gone and mere days away from the start of a new baseball season, canoodling with a Yankees fan. And not even a true fan, which Liana could at least respect, but a lame one. But Phyllis was oblivious. She patted Irv's knee and smiled at him. Liana was incredulous.

"Maybe we should get started," Stan said. He lifted up the seder plate and began to explain the different components— the matzo, the egg, the shank bone—and how each related to the holiday, reading from the worn yellow-and-red Maxwell House Haggadah that they had used for years. Irv suddenly reached for the raw horseradish, unquestionably phallic in appearance, and held it by the bulb, shaft pointing upwards.

"Well," he said, grinning like a schoolboy, "we certainly know what this represents! And it's happy to see us too!"

Phyllis tittered, almost girlishly; everyone else just stared. Liana turned away, wishing she were anywhere else.

When they got to the section of the "four questions," traditionally recited by the youngest person at the table, Rebecca protested. "I'm going to be eighteen in September. You can't make me say the four questions."

"Until there are grandchildren, you're it, Rebecca," Arlene said.

That could be a while.

At the juncture when the leader was supposed to explain the story of the exodus of the Jewish people from Egypt, Stan rose dramatically from his seat. He adopted his professorial attorney stance and addressed the assembled guests.

"Tonight we tell the story of how the Jews went from slavery to freedom, from bondage to redemption. Although it's a story rooted in history, and Egypt is certainly a physical place where the Jews were made to endure hard labor, it's also a story of how a people learned to leave behind a slave mentality that had held them back from achieving greatness. The Jewish people were trapped by their Egyptian slave masters but also by themselves—by their inability to take risks, to reach for the stars, to broaden their own horizons and take control of their own destinies. And we too, as modern-day American Jews and as individuals, must constantly ask ourselves if we're being self-limiting—if we're holding ourselves back out of fear and insecurity from the greatness we could achieve. We must all remember that Egypt is also a state of mind."

Stan had given the same "Egypt is a state of mind" speech, or some version of it, every year Liana had attended the Weiss family seder. This time, his words resonated with her. Perhaps she was stuck in this rut with Jakob not because of any external factors, not even because of Jakob, but because she herself was unable to push past the boundaries of her own fears and insecurities. Perhaps it was time to take control of her own destiny.

They got through the rest of the prescribed programming, skipping liberally, until they reached the festive meal. Arlene brought out all the traditional Passover foods: the gefilte fish, the matzo ball soup, the brisket, and the potato kugel. While they stuffed themselves silly, Stan turned the conversation to one of his favorite topics, Jakob's career, oblivious to the discomfort it caused his son to be dissected in front of the family.

"So, Jake, how is your progress at the firm in bringing in new business of your own?"

"You know, Dad, it doesn't really work that way anymore. Maybe it did when you were starting out, when the firms were smaller, and even someone junior could reel in a client. Now it's very hierarchical. I barely go to the bathroom without Frank's say-so, and it's the partners who bring in the business, get credit for it, and then dole out the work to the grunts below." Jakob didn't sound angry, but Liana knew that the pressure his father put on him got him down.

"I'm sure that's generally true, Jakob," Stan said, refusing to give up, like a cat playing with a half-dead mouse. "But your priority, as I see it, is to get out there and be your own man, make a name for yourself." Liana's heart sank.

Why does Stan take every opportunity to berate Jakob this way?

Jakob pushed back, to a point. "Maybe instead of making a name for myself, I should just rely on your good name, Dad? Wouldn't that be easier?" It was a low blow, delivered with an uncharacteristic caustic edge, but Stan was undeterred.

"If that's what it takes, Jakob, by all means."

"It's not the way I operate."

"Well, maybe you need to grow up a little, son. That's the way the world works." Stan often opined on "the way the world works," relying on his observations to shut down just about any opposition. "And does Liana help you climb the ladder of success at the firm? Arlene was with me every step of the way, from helping me strategize about how to deal with a difficult superior to picking out my power ties to being a beautiful and charming companion by my side at firm events."

Jakob was caught off guard, but Liana thought he must be wondering how to answer the question truthfully without betraying her inadequacies. Before he could pull himself together, Arlene said, "Stan, that was a very different time. Liana has her own career—she's not just Jakob's loyal sidekick."

"Well, it might be a bit of a stretch to call her job a career, dear. And a wife, if that's where this is headed, even in these times, should put her husband's aspirations above her own." Stan tried to mop up the last of the brisket gravy on his plate with a piece of matzo, which he then popped into his mouth and crunched noisily.

Liana had been so surprised by the turn in the conversation that she hadn't said a thing in her own defense. They were all quiet for a minute, until Arlene brought out several light and fluffy cakes, miraculous confections for a holiday that eliminated all use of leavening. There were "oohs" and "ahs" from Phyllis and Irv, and then everyone dug in, relieved that they could chew instead of talk.

When they finished dessert, Liana turned to Jakob and whispered, "I need to get out of here. Can we walk to the park?"

"Great idea," he said, and they practically ran out the door before anyone could think to ask to come along. The park was only about a block from his parents' house, and Liana and Jakob had spent many hours there the summer they met and fell in love. They had played Frisbee on the big green lawn, hung out at the pool, and knocked tennis balls around on the courts. On the last night they had together in Westchester that summer, when Liana was set to go back to New Haven the next morning, they had taken a half-full bottle of vodka from Stan's abundantly stocked liquor cabinet and sat on the grass. They had drunk and got maudlin and cried and vowed to stay together as they went their separate ways.

Now they walked through the gate holding hands and made their way to the playground, where she sat on a swing and he pushed her high into the air, until the matzo ball she had eaten resurfaced at the back of her throat and she told him to stop. Then they walked to the dock that reached out into the water and strolled all the way to the end. Jakob stood behind Liana with his arms around her waist and his head resting in her curls as she looked out at the Long Island Sound and the lights of the north shore of Long Island, where she had grown up, far across the water.

"What do you think of Irv?" Jakob asked.

"I prefer not to think about him much."

"Your mother's a lot less lonely. I think he seems nice," Jakob said.

"That's because he's not sleeping with *your* mother," she replied.

"You think they are?" Jakob asked, a note of admiration creeping into his voice.

"I told you, I try not to think about it." They stood quietly for a few more minutes, looking out at the view. "Honestly, I worry so much about my mom in that house alone. I'd give anything to see her with someone who'd look out for her. I don't know if Irv is the right guy, but I guess that's her call, right?"

"I guess so. He's harmless enough. You're a good daughter, Liana, but I don't think you need to worry so much." Jakob gently moved her hair to one side and kissed her on the back of her neck.

Distracted by his touch, Liana fought to keep her focus and tell Jakob what was on her mind. She pulled away so she could face him.

"I don't get why you never stand up to your father. Why don't you tell him that he's out of touch and doesn't know how things work now? He has no business putting you down or, for that matter, telling me that he thinks my career is a joke and that I should devote myself to helping you succeed." Liana felt like shaking Jakob, but she settled for putting her hands on his chest and looking up into his face.

"Jakob, I'm lonely. Sometimes I feel like we're in this weird love triangle—you, me, and Wilcox & Finney. Your father doesn't get it—I don't really care whether you're a rainmaker. I would rather you have some less demanding job so we could spend more time together."

Jakob didn't respond immediately. When he did, he sounded more like his father than himself.

"That's very sweet, Li, and I know you think you mean it. But my dad's right. I need to be realistic about how things work and what it means to succeed and support a family at some point. And I know he's old-fashioned, but I think he's right about husbands and wives believing in each other and helping each other."

Her thoughts were racing, but Liana was too frightened to speak. She longed to tell Jakob that her rapidly approaching thirtieth birthday felt like a big boulder that would crush her if she didn't somehow get moving with her life. And she was desperate to tell him that she loved him beyond measure but that when he talked about marriage and his vision of their future together, she felt confined, as if she couldn't breathe. Most of all, she yearned to tell him that she needed to know she was the center of his world. But, somehow, she couldn't say anything at all.

As they stood there, both immobilized, Liana's cell vibrated. She pulled it out of her pocket.

"Hello?" she said.

"Liana, it's Danny." His voice was warm and strong and confident. She felt an unexpected pleasure wash over her. She looked at Jakob to see if he had overheard, but he was looking at his feet, still processing Liana's silence.

"I can't talk now," she said quietly into the phone. She tried to sound stern, but she couldn't hide the combination of thrill and panic in her voice.

"Please, don't hang up," Danny pleaded. "I want to apologize for the other day at the Starbucks—I came on too strong. When I like someone, I push the envelope."

"It's okay," Liana whispered into the phone, turning slightly away from Jakob.

"Anyway, I recognize that I don't have anything to offer a woman like you except my friendship. No strings attached, Liana, I promise. I just want to get to know you. But I won't keep you now. Take care." And then the line went dead. Liana put the phone slowly into her pocket.

Somehow, Danny must have gotten her phone number when they were at the Starbucks, although she couldn't fathom how.

"Who was that?" Jakob asked, taking a couple of steps toward Liana.

"Just work," she said.

"Your office calls you at night, on Passover? Even Frank wouldn't have the nerve to do that, I don't think. I heard a man's voice. Was it Gerry?"

"No. It was a client." Liana was getting flustered, and she knew this was going to end badly. She took a few strides forward toward the house, and Jakob gently, but firmly, reached out and held her upper arm to restrain her.

"You give your clients your cell phone number? Is that wise?"

She shook her head no but couldn't find her voice.

"Who was on the phone, Liana?"

"Danny Shea," she answered.

After a minute that felt like much longer, Jakob spoke.

"I'm not sure what kind of game you're playing here, Li, with me or with him. But I can tell you it's dangerous. Remember who Danny Shea is, and remember who you are."

They walked back to the house in an uncomfortable silence.

CHAPTER 19

Growing up on Long Island in the 1980s and '90s, Liana's family considered themselves "culturally Jewish." Proud of their heritage, they supported the State of Israel, they counted each year how many Nobel Prize winners were Jews, and they celebrated the major Jewish holidays by briefly attending synagogue and eating the appropriate foods with the appropriate relatives. But the real religion in the Cohen household was New York Mets baseball.

Liana's father had become a fan when the franchise started in 1962 and he was a nineteen-year-old kid studying accounting at Baruch College. He'd suffered through the first seven terrible seasons, catching the occasional game at the Polo Grounds and then at Shea Stadium but mostly following on the radio at night. In 1969, the year that the "Miracle Mets" would beat the Baltimore Orioles in the World Series, Artie experienced his own miracle. On Saturday, September 13, playing hooky from synagogue on Rosh Hashana, he met Phyllis Stein in line at the hot dog concession stand on the third level of Shea Stadium. As they waited to order, they heard a deafening roar rise from the stands: Ron Swoboda had hit a grand slam in the eighth, breaking a one-to-one tie and extending the Mets winning streak to ten games as they marched toward glory. The story of how they missed the Mets moment but found each other would become the stuff of Cohen family legend.

Liana went to her first Mets game with her father during the magical 1986 season. It was June 10, and she was too young to understand the hoopla when Tim Teufel hit a walk-off grand slam homer in the eleventh to beat the Phillies, but the intensity and the excitement of the moment were seared into her soul. With no brothers or sisters to compete for their attention, Artie and Phyllis poured all their baseball knowledge and love into Liana, who soaked it up like a sponge. She had no athletic ability to speak of, and she was no tomboy, but she knew every archaic baseball rule and obscure stat better than any boy in her school. Her room was decorated with posters of her most handsome Mets players—Todd Hundley, Rey Ordonez, John Olerud, and a little later, Mike Piazza—clean-cut, wholesome young men who could hit a ball out of the park or make a diving catch look easy.

In 2009, when the Mets moved to Citi Field, Liana's parents were simultaneously wistful about the demolition of their beloved, if dilapidated, Shea Stadium and enthusiastic about the beautiful new ballpark, with its variety of eateries and good views from every seat. It was a horrible year for the Mets—the team was riddled with injuries and finished with an abysmal seventy wins and ninety-two losses—but it was a tragic one for the Cohens. Artie passed away during the off-season, disappointed in his team but ever hopeful for better things to come. Instead of some biblical phrase in Hebrew that Phyllis said would be meaningless to Artie, she and Liana engraved his headstone with "You Gotta Believe!"

Liana had vowed that she would never miss an opening day, as a lasting tribute to her father. Jakob understood how much the ritual meant to Liana and had gone with her to the home opener all three seasons since Artie passed away. This year, she bought her tickets for Monday, April 1, 2013, months in advance. She kept things economical, choosing seats in the nosebleed section. She preferred to pay for the tickets herself, since Jakob, who enjoyed a cold beer and hot dog but had no real interest in baseball, was only going for her sake.

As she sat at work on the Friday afternoon before the game, daydreaming of baseball and her dad, she realized she hadn't spoken with Jakob to arrange where they would meet. In fact, she had not spoken to him at length since their walk in the park the week before and the Danny Shea phone call fiasco. Liana hoped that opening day, that beacon of new beginnings, could be the way past this latest bump in the road. And she had no time to waste; her milestone birthday was rapidly approaching, even though the deadline for figuring out her future was self-imposed and Jakob did not know it existed.

She picked up the phone and dialed his number at the office. Jakob's secretary answered, "Jakob Weiss's line, may I help you?"

"Hi, Gloria. Is he around?"

"Yes, you just caught him, Liana. I'll put you right through."

"Hey, babe," Jakob answered. She was relieved that he seemed glad to hear from her. "I'm up to my ears here in computer printouts of banking records that I can't make heads or tails of. It is going to be another dreadful weekend in the office." He sounded exhausted but pumped at the same time.

"I know you're busy; I just wanted to check where we should meet on Monday," Liana said. She could almost hear the wheels turning as Jakob tried to figure out what he was supposed to be doing with her on Monday and how he was going to break it to her that he couldn't do it, whatever it was. After a few seconds, she took pity on him.

"Monday is opening day, Jay."

"Oh, wow," he said. "I totally forgot. I'm so sorry, Li, but I have to go to Frank's country club on Monday—we have a team off-site for my case." Several weeks earlier, Jakob had been asked to work on a new matter as the senior associate under Frank, a vote of confidence for someone fairly junior. "I can't miss it. Besides, Frank wants us all to meet his new girlfriend, Sofia. I think she may be a mail-order bride from Eastern Europe." His attempt at humor fell flat.

"Jakob, it's *opening day*!" Liana felt a rush of frenzied raw hysteria, and she could hear it creeping into her voice, but she couldn't help it. Bobby looked at her sympathetically, miming throwing a pitch and mouthing, "Let's Go Mets!"

"I know, and I know how much it means to you. Honestly, I don't have a choice," Jakob said. "I can't tell Frank that I'm skipping his off-site to watch the Mets."

She tried to see the situation from Jakob's point of view. She was only marginally successful, but she pretended. "Okay, Jay—I get it. It's only a game." She hung up the phone before she added anything she would regret.

Liana ticked through the possibilities in her mind. Deb would enjoy an outing, but she was way too frail to negotiate the stadium and the crowds, and the temperature on opening day could still be uncomfortably cool. Katie was traveling for work—she had called the night before from balmy San Diego, where Rob was meeting her to spend the weekend. Charlotte knew absolutely nothing about baseball and was so hugely pregnant that Liana would be afraid to cheer too wildly in case she induced early labor in her friend. And no way Rabbi Nacht could go to the game with an unmarried woman—Liana was sure that would violate some rule, although she didn't know exactly which one.

She picked up her cell phone and hit the speed dial.

"Hi, Mom," she said when Phyllis answered.

"Hi, sweetie. Aren't you supposed to be working?" Her mother was always worried that somehow Liana was shirking her responsibilities if she made even a five-minute phone call during the day.

"It's okay, Mom. Listen, it turns out that Jakob can't go to the game on Monday, and I was wondering—"

"Oh, Li, I can't." Phyllis had not been back to the ballpark since Artie's death, finding it just too painful.

"I know it's really hard to be there without Dad, believe me. But we'd be there together, and—"

"No, Li, that's not it," Phyllis said.

"What's wrong? Are you sick?" Liana's Jewish mother persona came out most strongly when interacting with her own Jewish mother.

"I'm fine. It's just that Irv got us tickets to opening day for the Yankees."

In an unprecedented scheduling quirk, the Yankees' home opener was being played across town at the same time on the same day as the Mets'. For a moment, Liana could find no words. When she was able to speak, she said, "Ma, how could you?"

"Oh, Liana, it's only—"

"—a game. I know, Mom, I know." Liana hung up the phone and the tears came.

"Liana," Bobby said, "I'm not really great around crying women. I'm going to step out for a little while and let you get yourself together. Will you be okay if I do that?" He sounded as if he were speaking to a three-year-old, but Liana figured she deserved that.

"Yes, Bobby. That would be very thoughtful of you," she said between sniffles. She blew her nose hard into a tissue, and Bobby fled. Not five minutes later, she was mostly recovered when Tony's voice came over the intercom.

"Liana, you have a call on one," he said.

"Who is it, Tony?" she asked.

"Daniel Shea."

"You've got to be kidding."

"Do you want me to tell him you're unavailable?" Tony asked.

She considered it but said, "No. Please put him through."

Liana checked her hair in the small mirror she and Deb had hung on the wall, inhaled and exhaled to the count of four, as her father had taught her to do before starting every important exam, and picked up the phone.

"Hello, Mr. Shea. What can I do for you?" She concentrated on keeping the tremor out of her voice. It had been three weeks since she had seen Shea at Starbucks, and she'd forced herself to push him out of her mind, when she wasn't replaying the scene over and over again to relive the kiss on her head. Nor had Liana forgiven him for the Passover evening phone call or for the fact that somehow, without her realizing it, he had gotten hold of her cell phone long enough to figure out her number. But Liana decided it was better to pretend none of that had happened than to get into some sort of back and forth with him. He was too smooth and she was too weak—she knew she would lose.

"Liana, it's Danny," he said. "I need to see you."

"Why? Have you been arrested? Where are you?" she asked, the concern too evident in her voice.

"Hey, hey—slow down, pretty lady," he said. "You don't have a lot of faith in me. No, I haven't been arrested, and no, I'm not in trouble. I told you I'd be patient, and I'm trying so hard, but it's difficult. I'm not asking for much, just to spend a little time with you."

The morning's rejections still ringing in her ears, Liana asked, without allowing herself to think, "Do you have plans for Monday?"

"My dance card is still pretty open," he retorted.

"I'll meet you at the Homerun Apple outside the Jackie Robinson Rotunda at twelve thirty. The tickets are my treat."

"You're joking, right? You're inviting me to opening day?" Danny asked. If he had been a twelve-year-old boy, he couldn't have sounded more excited. Liana wondered if he'd bring his mitt to try to catch foul balls.

"Don't say another word, or I'll come to my senses," she said and gently put down the receiver.

She was so involved in the phone call that she hadn't noticed when Bobby came back into the office. "You found someone else to take to the game?" he asked, clearly relieved that Liana had stopped crying.

"Yes," Liana said, "someone who'll appreciate what's happening on the field and will appreciate being with me."

The whole idea is nuts, but what is there to worry about?

There would be over forty-two thousand people in a sold-out stadium—she wouldn't have a moment alone with Danny Shea. Besides, she figured he might be better company in some ways than Jakob, who didn't care if the Mets won or lost. Liana knew she was being somewhat unfair—Jakob might be working harder than the other associates, but he was striving to be the best. But she was so damn tired of playing second fiddle to Wilcox & Finney. Maybe it would do her good to have a day out with a man whose sole desire was to be with her and who didn't want anything in return.

Even if he is an ex-client and an ex-con.

On Monday, Liana headed out to Citi Field, dressed in a form-fitting Johann Santana jersey over black leggings, her hair tucked up into her favorite well-worn Mets cap. Although the game didn't start until 1:10 p.m., she had treated herself to the whole day off from work, boarding the number 7 train to Flushing in plenty of time to meet Danny. She loved soaking in the high spirits of the fans on the subway, forgiving the unruly ones who had started to drink before getting anywhere close to the stadium.

Even among the growing crowd, she easily spotted Danny by the Apple. He was wearing faded blue jeans, ripped at the knees, and a tight black Mets T-shirt that showed off every muscle in his chest and arms—pecs and biceps and triceps undoubtedly sculpted over the year in the prison gym. Marta would be impressed. He had no cap on, and his longish, dirty-blond hair was hanging loose, falling in waves over his eyes in just the same way it had in the photograph Liana had first seen in the file. She sighed.

What a pity that this beautiful man is so absurdly inappropriate.

Still, it was opening day, and the world seemed filled with possibilities.

"Hey," she said.

"Hey to you," Danny replied, a big grin on his face. "This is awesome. I've never been to opening day."

"Huh. In my family, opening day—" She stopped abruptly, remembering to keep her personal life out of this. Danny didn't notice—he was so entranced by the hubbub of the fans, the electricity on the first day of the season. "Come on," Liana said. "I like to hear the National Anthem. It reminds me how great it is to be an American and have baseball as our national pastime." Danny looked at her, amused, and followed her through the gate and up the escalator. The seats were high up, and by the time they got to their row, a beautiful brunette was making her way to the microphone.

"Who's she?" Danny asked.

"That's Emmy Rossum. She's a singer, but she's also the star of a show that runs on Showtime called *Shameless*. It's really good. Have you ever seen it?" Only after she asked the question did Liana realize that the show had premiered while Danny was incarcerated.

"Nah," Danny said. "I don't have a lot of time for television, and I don't have any of those premium channels." He didn't sound bitter, which Liana would have been without HBO, just matter-of-fact. They stood up for "The Star Spangled Banner," and Liana removed her cap, reluctantly letting her curls fly free, much to Danny's obvious delight. He had a surprisingly pleasant voice—he wasn't Rabbi Nacht, and he wasn't Jakob, who had more music in his little finger than anyone else on the planet, but he could sing on key, and he sounded sweetly boyish for so manly a man.

When they sat down, to make conversation, Liana continued, "The plot of *Shameless* is interesting. It's about an alcoholic, drug-addicted dad who has, like, five or six kids—I can't remember what happened to the mom, but she's not around. Emmy Rossum plays Fiona, the oldest child—she's the most responsible, and she always ends up having to deal with the younger children because the father's such a screwup."

"I could star in that show; too bad no one asked me," Danny said quietly but without rancor.

Liana felt like a jerk. Here she had been talking nonsense, just to avoid any awkward silences, and she had touched a nerve. "I'm sorry, Danny. I didn't realize. The nature of my job—it's very circumscribed," Liana said, proud that she had used a Danny-type word that he'd appreciate. "I don't really know anything about life for the client before I represent him, and I don't know much about his life after either."

"That's okay," he responded. "It saved me having to get you up to speed. Besides, I'm not your client anymore, remember?" They sat in an awkward silence for a few minutes, until Rusty Staub ran out to the mound to throw out the ceremonial first pitch and everyone stood and started cheering like crazy. Before he sat back down, Danny pulled a scorecard and a pencil out of his back pocket.

"You score the game?" Liana asked.

"Yeah. Keeps my head in it," he said. Liana was impressed. They talked about the Mets roster—dissecting the familiar favorites: David Wright, Lucas Duda, Daniel Murphy, the pitcher Jonathon Niese.

"Who the hell is Collin Cowgill?" Liana said, seeing a new name playing in center field.

"He got traded in the off-season from the Oakland A's,"

Danny said, sounding pleased that he knew something that she didn't. "He's a relatively young guy—like my age." He winked at her, and Liana wondered if he knew she was pushing thirty. She couldn't believe how refreshing it was to be at a game with someone who knew what was going on, even if he was teasing her; it made her miss her dad even more.

"My father was crazy about the Mets," Liana said, apropos of nothing, suddenly feeling the need to share something personal.

"Was? It's hard sometimes to root for them—did he give up?" Danny asked.

"No. He passed away three years ago."

"I'm sorry, Liana."

"It's okay," she said.

He would have liked you.

In the bottom of the second, Danny bought them each a beer, a hot dog, and a pretzel. Liana tried to pay him back, but he was having none of it. "You bought these tickets," he said. "The least I can do is buy you something to eat." In between innings, they watched what Artie used to call "the shtick" on the big screen in center field—the trivia games, "This Day in Mets History," and a tribute to the first responders during Hurricane Sandy.

"Do you know why Jason Bay sucked at the plate last year?" Danny asked, referencing the player du jour that fans loved to hate.

"Because he was sluggish and lazy and couldn't stay off the disabled list?" Liana suggested.

Danny smiled. "Well, that was certainly part of it. But I have another theory."

"Hit me," Liana replied.

Danny gazed out over the fence in center field. "Bay's timing was all off. Timing is everything. Every at bat is another opportunity to get it right. If you're overanxious or impulsive,

you swing too soon and you miss. If you're unfocused or inde-
cisive, you swing too late and you also get nothing but air.
But if you're patient, you don't rush or stall but you seize the
moment at just the right time, the sky's the limit."

The hope in Danny's voice was so pure it was almost
painful. Liana wondered when his moment would come and
whether she would recognize her own moment when it arrived.
They sat in silence for a few minutes, each lost in contempla-
tion. Opening day could have that effect.

By the fourth, the Mets were beating the Padres seven to
one. Liana had bought them each a second beer, and she had a
pleasant buzz on. She was happy she had invited Danny to the
game. He had been totally considerate and gentlemanly, and he
knew the ins and outs of the game and the team. Not as well as
she did—but she didn't let on, keeping her more esoteric facts,
figures, and opinions to herself.

"Want to hear something funny?" Danny asked, turning
away from the game for a minute.

"Always," Liana answered. Jakob often said that he spent
90 percent of his free time trying to think of ways to make
Liana laugh. Lately, it hadn't been working too well.

"Do you know what I was studying before all of this
happened?" Danny turned back to the screen in center field,
where the Yankees score was being displayed—the fans were
avidly following both games. *Red Sox 4, Yankees 0* flashed on
the screen, and the crowd erupted.

When the sound died down, Liana said, "Nope. Tell me."

"Prelaw." Danny said. "Pretty ironic, right?" He stared
fixedly at the scoreboard, the color rising in his cheeks.

She watched him, carefully choosing her words before
speaking so he wouldn't doubt her sincerity.

"You'd make a fantastic attorney, Danny," she said. "I've
never had a client who intuitively understood the fine points of
the arguments the way you did and who could express himself

as persuasively as you can. You'd be a credit to the bar." For a moment she pictured Jakob—golden boy of Columbia Law School and rising star at Wilcox & Finney.

If things had been different, if Danny had enjoyed the advantages Jakob had, couldn't he have done just as well?

"Well, that's sweet of you to say, Counselor. But I think that ship has sailed." He turned his focus back to the game, immersing himself in every pitch, shutting down the conversation with his concentration.

After the inning was over, the fan-favorite kiss cam got rolling. Liana was transfixed. The gimmick was always the same: the cameraman would focus in on a man and a woman and wait for them to notice themselves on the jumbotron in center field; then the crowd would goad them into the smooch. Liana watched intently as the picture first zeroed in on a young, good-looking couple. After the initial shocked look, they went at it with a vengeance—too much tongue and groping—and the crowd groaned. Next was an older couple, probably in their late sixties, sweet but kind of unappealing; who wanted to see them kiss? They brought to mind her mom and Irv, and Liana felt sad and unsettled. The next couple turned out not to be a couple—both the woman and the man shook their heads vehemently and turned away from each other.

Liana was so absorbed she didn't realize what was happening when Danny gently took her face in his hands, turned her toward him, and kissed her, slowly, gently, but intensely and insistently, the taste of the salty pretzel still on his lips. Completely transported, Liana wrapped her arms around his neck and pulled him closer, his warmth and passion spreading through her whole body. Seconds passed before the sound of the crowd and the feel of Danny's unfamiliar hair between her fingers brought her back, forcing her to remember where she was and who was with her.

"You bastard!" she yelled, pushing her hands uselessly against his chest.

He held her wrists lightly and shrugged. "Kiss cam," he said, nodding his head toward center field. And there they were, forty feet tall on the big screen, a cute blond trying to shove away a gorgeous younger man's ripped torso. The fans, undoubtedly thinking that the protest was an act after seeing the all-consuming kiss, were cheering at the top of their lungs. Liana broke free and sat with her head in her hands, the cameraman soaking up the drama and continuing to broadcast it to the crowd's delight until play on the field resumed. For a moment, Liana thought she had been on television, forgetting that the big screen was internal to the stadium.

For the next two innings, Liana sat in stony silence, staring at her feet and refusing to say a word to Danny or even to cheer on the team. She wasn't sure if she was angrier with him for crossing the line or with herself for having, momentarily, given in to a magnetic attraction.

Liana knew she needed to put an end to this nondate, but the kiss lingering in the space between them and the questions it raised were like a paralyzing force keeping her in her seat. Danny continued to take in the action on the field and the whole scene, totally unruffled. He sat back in his seat, relaxed, drank another beer, and bought a bag of peanuts, which he cracked open and ate, filling the floor space around him with peanut shells.

"I'm really sorry," he tried. "The kiss cam was on us. What was I supposed to do?" he said, only half joking. When she looked at him but didn't answer, he continued, staring straight at the field and speaking deliberately, with a hint of hardness, just loud enough to be heard over the din. "Listen, Liana. I made it very clear from the day you got me sprung that I wanted to spend time with you. You invited me today—I'm sure there were plenty of people who would've been more than happy to take your free ticket to opening day."

"I did invite other people, but—"

Without turning his eyes toward her, Danny raised his hand in a signal for her to stop talking, and she fell silent.

"So I have to figure you want to be with me too. I intrigue you. You still can't believe that the guy who was just supposed to be another name in your transcript is flesh and blood now. And the kiss cam was convenient, but that kiss would have happened at some point, because we both wanted it. You let your curiosity run a little wild, and now you're scared. You're a bit of a tease, Liana, but it's okay; I don't mind. I told you I'd wait for you, and I'm a man of my word."

Moments later, when Danny got to his feet to sing "God Bless America" during the seventh inning stretch, Liana finally pulled herself together, stood up, and turned to him.

"I'm going. I was wrong to think we could be some kind of friends, and I'm sorry if I led you on—it wasn't my intention. Please, stay, enjoy the rest of the game and the rest of your life."

She walked to the aisle and down the steps to exit the section, a handful of fans booing her unpatriotic departure. She could feel Danny watching her every move. Out of the corner of her eye, Liana saw him mark something on his scorecard.

As she got down to the rotunda, there was a sudden roar from the crowd, as if the whole stadium had exploded. The sound was so deafening Liana barely heard the *ping* of her text notification.

Cowgill. Grand slam. Wish you were here. D.

CHAPTER 20

The next morning, Liana called in sick to work. "I've got a spring cold, Tony. I'm going to stay home and take it easy today," she said.

"Okeydokey, Liana," Tony responded. "How about those Amazins yesterday?" The Mets had beaten the Padres, eleven to two.

"Yeah, I had some stuff going on. I didn't see the last couple innings." If Tony was suspicious that something was up, he had enough tact not to say anything. Still creeped out that Danny had her cell phone number, Liana continued, "And, Tony, if Danny Shea comes to the office looking for me, please make sure not to tell him where I live."

"Jesus, Liana, what kind of receptionist do you think I am?" Tony asked. "Besides, you got him out of prison—I would think he'd be your biggest fan."

Good thinking, Tony.

When she got off the phone, Liana got back into bed and tried to sleep, but she was too agitated. She thought about Danny and the kiss cam, and her anger flared, and then she thought about the kiss itself. She recalled Jakob's warning: remember who Danny Shea is. But she couldn't cast Danny in the one-dimensional role of "criminal," as she had so easily before; she knew too much now. He had started as the object of Liana's experiment in totally arms-length lawyering, and she had ended up, albeit briefly, in his arms.

She must have dozed off, because when she heard her cell phone beep, it was already eleven. There was an email from RNacht@dt.org. Liana opened it, wondering what new synagogue social justice activity the rabbi was promoting today.

The email was brief. Hi, Liana. Was at the game. Saw you on the kiss cam. Not prying. If you'd like to talk, I'm in the synagogue office all day; just stop by. Rabbi N.

Of course.

Rabbi Nacht was one of the few people in Liana's life who had the same allegiance to the Mets as she did, especially now that her father was gone and Phyllis had crossed over to the dark side with Irv. She was momentarily surprised that the rabbi would have been watching the kiss cam closely enough to notice her and Danny, but she guessed that they'd made quite a spectacle of themselves.

Well, maybe it was a blessing in disguise.

Perhaps what she needed was some rabbinic guidance; Lord knows, nothing else was really working. Her New Year's resolution to figure out her future was suffering the fate of most such vows. Just like all those flabby people with good intentions who join the gym on January 1 with lofty goals of exercise and weight loss that inevitably peter out by February, Liana's goal was sputtering too. And it didn't help that her ability to think clearly about Jakob was being sabotaged by Danny.

She took a shorter shower than usual and dressed in a conservative skirt and top. She walked down the block to DT and went around the side of the building, where she pressed the button next to the door leading to the office and the rabbi's study. Rabbi Nacht's secretary buzzed her in. "Hi, Liana," she said, recognizing her from the clothing drive she had helped out with the month before. "Do you have an appointment?" Before Liana could answer, the rabbi poked his head out of his office.

"It's fine, Judy. I asked Liana to come by." He motioned for her to come in and sit down. Liana sat stiffly on the guest chair opposite the rabbi.

Why did I come?

They surveyed each other across his desk. He watched her, saying nothing, waiting patiently for her to begin. Liana crossed and uncrossed and recrossed her legs, fidgeting with her hands. She had no intention of starting this discussion; he was the one who had intruded on her day at the ballpark. The telephone on his desk rang.

"Excuse me," the rabbi said, peering at the caller ID screen. "I've been waiting for this call."

"Of course," Liana said, relieved at the reprieve. But as she looked at the rabbi for a signal that she should give him privacy, she saw his shoulders slump very slightly, his head bowed. He spoke so quietly she couldn't have heard what he said even if she'd tried. After a couple of minutes, he hung up the phone, pinching the bridge of his nose with his fingers.

"Do you know the Robinsons? Their son—he's twenty-one—was in an accident. He didn't make it." The rabbi spoke evenly; his tone was neutral. Not unfeeling, but tragedies were part of his training, and he'd been a rabbi for many years.

"No, I really don't know anyone," Liana answered. "Listen," she said. "I think I should come back another time." She started to get up.

"What makes you think I want to be alone? Please don't go," he said. The poker face of a few moments earlier had dissolved; the pain was obvious. Before long, the rabbi recovered himself. He looked at Liana and said, "May I ask you a direct question, Liana?"

"Okay," Liana responded.

"What on God's green earth was going on there yesterday?" he said. Liana was so shocked she was unable to utter a sound.

The rabbi continued, "I'm sorry to have put that so crudely, and you know from our conversation in Atlanta that I try not to jump to conclusions. But, to be honest, I was surprised and frankly curious to see you on the big screen just sitting next to that man who clearly wasn't Jakob, and then, the next second, that kiss . . . well . . ." He paused, appearing simultaneously entranced and repelled by the vision in his mind's eye.

The rabbi shook his head from left to right, as if clearing the scene away on the Etch A Sketch Liana used to play with as a child.

"I just . . . I guess, from what I've seen over this past year—I like you and Jakob so much as a couple. I thought things were moving in a good direction—that it was significant that you went all the way to Atlanta for Maggie and Zach's wedding with Jakob's family. You seem very committed to one another, and I love seeing you two in synagogue on Friday night. Of course, it isn't really any of my business."

Liana sat quietly through the rabbi's sermon, staring at her feet. She appreciated that he'd noticed how serious and loving a couple she and Jakob were, how they belonged together, but could he see how much strain there was too? How pressured she felt to live up to Jakob's expectations and how neglected she sometimes felt? She guessed that the kiss cam episode had given the rabbi some insight that everything was not as idyllic as it seemed, even if he had misinterpreted what he'd seen happen with Danny Shea.

When Liana failed to respond, the rabbi tried a new tack. "Do you have feelings for that young man on the jumbotron?"

"It's complicated," she answered.

"Life is complicated, Liana."

"That's what my mother says," Liana answered.

"Your mother is a wise woman," Rabbi Nacht replied.

"So I've been told."

They sat in silence for a moment. Rabbi Nacht tried again.

"You know, Liana, there is a midrash, a traditional story, that asks, 'If God created the world in six days, what has he been doing with himself since?' And the rabbis give the answer, 'Matching couples for marriage.' If you and Jakob are meant to be together, then it'll happen . . . when the time is right," he added.

"Rabbi," Liana said, "I love Jakob—we love each other. But we are in such different places. He's sure about what he wants in life, professionally and personally, and I'm still figuring things out. This isn't going to sound right, but . . . sometimes I feel like even though he has carved out a special place for me, I'm not the center of his world."

"And is he always the center of your world? It didn't look that way on the big screen yesterday," the rabbi said.

"Hey! I thought you weren't going to judge!"

"And I'm not. But what I hope you'll consider is that sometimes we get so focused on what we are getting out of a relationship that we fail to focus on what we are putting into the relationship. It's a give and take, Liana, and if you let the giving take precedence, in my experience, the rest will work itself out."

Liana pondered what the rabbi had said and decided to be more blunt.

"I've given myself a deadline to decide if I want to marry Jakob or if I should let him go. It's coming up pretty soon, and I don't know what to do."

There. I said it out loud.

The rabbi was so serious and studied Liana for so long that she thought she might have stumped him. But, as usual, that wasn't the case.

"Liana," he said, "I have a couple of thoughts for you."

She smiled sadly.

The rabbi leaned back in his chair, his fingers pressed together as if praying, and looked up at the ceiling—for inspiration or to avoid putting too much pressure on Liana, she wasn't sure.

"As you know, in the Genesis story, God created Adam first, and only later did God say 'It is not good for Adam to be alone,' so he created Eve. But in the Bible, Eve's role isn't described as 'wife' or 'soul mate' or 'life partner'—rather, she's described in Hebrew as Adam's *aizer kenegdo*, a helper opposing him. Our great sage, Rashi, explains that this describes the ideal relationship as one in which two people struggle to complement and complete each other—like two imperfectly cut pieces of a jigsaw puzzle that just barely, but beautifully, fit together as one."

Liana nodded. "Kind of like the yin and the yang?"

"I guess, yes. I suppose every philosophy has a similar concept, because it's true," the rabbi said, a smile playing on his lips. "But it isn't always pretty. If you and Jakob challenge one another and demand what you need from each other, but you do it in good faith and in a supportive way, you don't always have to be on exactly the same page. Sometimes you'll disappoint each other, and that's part of the relationship too, and it can make you stronger."

Would Jakob think that kissing Danny Shea was done in good faith? She shuddered.

Then the rabbi said quietly, "So that's Rashi. Do you know what Babe Ruth said?"

She shook her head.

"He said, 'It's hard to beat a person who never gives up.' Don't give up on yourself and Jakob yet, Liana. I wouldn't be so presumptuous as to tell you that he's the one God meant for you to marry. But I can tell you that I've seen you interact, and I see the love you share. And I'd hate for you to throw it away because you have set yourself some sort of artificial deadline. You're a young woman, with your whole life ahead of you. Be patient. Wait for your moment."

Liana thought about Deb, another young woman who should have had her whole life ahead of her and who, if Liana carried out her friend's wish, the rabbi would soon be burying.

"Rabbi, can I ask you something else?"

"Of course. I've got plenty of time; the Mets aren't playing tonight," he said.

When she went to speak, Liana found her voice had retreated to a safer place. She could barely whisper, "My friend is sick."

The rabbi nodded slowly, his concern evident. When she seemed unable to continue, he gently prodded her. "What's your question, Liana?"

She sat up a bit straighter and willed herself to speak. "I want to pray for her, and I don't know how."

The rabbi looked at her directly, waiting to catch her eye. When she finally looked up from her lap, there was such kindness in his gaze that she could have wept.

"Well," he said, "first of all, I take issue with your premise. Whenever you realize that you, Liana Cohen, aren't in control and you sincerely turn for help to a power greater than yourself, you're praying. There are no magic incantations, and there's no particular language that needs to be used. Your heart will seek mercy and healing for your friend, and that will be your prayer."

Although she recognized the validity of the rabbi's answer, Liana pressed on. "My friend isn't religious, but she has a notion about doing things 'right.'"

The rabbi nodded again, and it was a comfort just knowing that he'd heard so much from so many before. "If by 'right' your friend means 'in the traditional Jewish way,' then let me show you the words we say in our daily prayers." The rabbi pulled a prayer book off the bookshelf behind him, then came around his desk and sat in a chair next to Liana.

"Here, on page 118, there's a general prayer asking God to 'bring complete recovery for all our ailments,' and then you can insert a more specific prayer that God 'speedily send a complete recovery from heaven, healing of both soul and body, to the patient.'" The rabbi paused, looked at Liana, and pointed to the smaller print, adding, "And then you insert the person's Hebrew name."

Liana, who had been buoyed by the straightforwardness of the rabbi's answer and by the words of the prayer, suddenly deflated.

"I don't know my friend's Hebrew name or if she even has one," she said, her legal mindset assuming that this deficiency would preclude her.

The rabbi was unfazed. "That's okay. It happens to me all the time. When it does, I just close my eyes and envision the person, and I believe that God will know who I'm talking about."

Liana knew that she should get going; she had already taken far too much of the rabbi's time. But she felt weighed down, as though by asking him about the formal prayer, she'd committed herself to something she might not be able to carry through. The rabbi, as if reading her mind, offered an alternative.

"There's another traditional prayer, Liana, that's easy to remember—it has the feeling of a mantra almost, or a chant. Moses had a sister, Miriam, and God made her sick because she spoke harshly about Moses's wife. When Moses saw that Miriam was suffering, he uttered the shortest and most poignant prayer in our liturgy. It's just five words: 'El na, refah na la,' which means, 'Please, God, heal her.' It isn't flowery, but it gets to the point."

Liana tried it out a few times, to make sure she remembered it correctly. She thanked the rabbi for his time and for taking an interest in her and Jakob. She was halfway out the door when the rabbi called to her.

"Liana. I want you to remember something important."

"Yes, Rabbi?"

"If your friend doesn't get better, I don't want you to conclude that God is not listening to your prayers. God hears you. Sometimes the answer is 'No.'"

CHAPTER 21

"They say that April is the cruelest month, Bobby," Liana ruminated during one rainy afternoon in the office. She stared out the dirty window, watching the drops splash off the sill. It wasn't Bobby's fault, but as her mood plummeted, Liana found that his sitting just inches away from her was increasingly disturbing.

Deb was barely leaving her apartment now, as the doctors no longer had any more experimental chemo drugs to offer her. A couple of times a week, Liana went to visit her, bringing food that she used to love but could no longer eat and toting shiny hardcover books for Max about elephants that could fly or sheep that could dance. Liana would sit on the couch between Deb and Max and read the books over and over as Max laughed with delight, yelling, "Again, again!" as he pulled at her curls and Deb "rested her eyes." After an hour or so, Deb would be sound asleep and Max would need lunch, and Georgia, the private nurse that Steven had hired, would politely thank Liana for coming and escort her out the door.

In a strange turnaround, Liana felt more invested at work than she had in some time, although things were heating up as the last quarter of the fiscal year began. She was way behind, having spent much more time than she should have allotted on

Danny's case over the summer, and she knew that it would take a great push for her to make the quota this year. That being said, she was working diligently and with a renewed sense of purpose. One unexpected side effect of her encounters with Danny, however surreal and imprudent, was that she'd rediscovered the human beings behind the names on the transcript pages.

Her new client, Gillian Black, had been convicted of killing her boyfriend while they sat in the front seat of his parked car. Gillian had testified at trial that the gun discharged while the boyfriend was choking and punching her. Based on this testimony, Liana was arguing that the jury should have been told they could consider whether Gillian had acted in self-defense. Liana let herself imagine Gillian's terror as she sat in that car with someone whom she had once trusted.

What would I have done in that situation?

While her professional life had improved, the situation with Jakob had ground almost to a halt. She tried to follow the rabbi's advice, taking a step back before she reflexively complained about Jakob's work obligations and instead acknowledging the pressure he was under and giving him space. Without Liana penciling herself into the interstices of his schedule, Jakob threw himself into his work with no respite. He ate his meals either at the firm or on his way home and rarely returned to his apartment before eleven at night. Liana gave up on inviting him to Friday night services, preferring to go alone and glean what spiritual boost she could rather than feel as if she was taking him away from something more important. They were both grateful for the nights Jakob escaped earlier from the office and came straight to Liana's apartment, where they would fall into each other's arms and make love, hungrily but with a sense of impending sadness. There had been no knock-down-drag-out fight, no accusations or harsh words that couldn't be retracted, no ultimatums issued, and no formal breakup.

But we're in trouble.

Liana was depressed. Maybe not at a level warranting medication, but she was utterly and desperately miserable.

One Saturday evening in late April when her phone rang and she saw Katie's number on the caller ID, she almost let it go to voice mail but forced herself to answer.

"Oh! I'm glad you're home!" Katie said, putting on a cheerful voice.

"Where else would I be?" Liana droned.

"Okay, whatever. You need to come out with us tonight. We're going for rice and beans at your favorite hole-in-the-wall on Broadway. It's amazing we've never gotten violently ill from food poisoning there," Katie said.

"I don't think so. But thanks for asking." Liana marveled at the perseverance of her friends, even now, when being around her was such a drag.

"Come on, Liana. This is getting nuts. You have to get out of your apartment. Charlotte wants to see you; she's so gigantic, I swear to God she's having twins. She won't confirm or deny, just gives me this vague little smile when I bring it up. And I want you to get to know Rob better. You'd like him. I think he'd get along with Jakob. He also likes Bob Dylan and John Berryman and all those highbrow sorts of cultural figures." Katie was trying really hard, and Liana appreciated it, but she still couldn't muster the strength.

"I'd just be a fifth wheel, Katie. I'm not going to call Jakob and tell him he needs to come—I have to reserve those requests for when I need him on something really critical."

"What happened to your New Year's resolution?" asked Katie, who was never one to let a sleeping dog lie. "Are you really planning either to tell Jakob you'll marry him or break up with him by your thirtieth birthday? May I remind you that we are two weeks away and counting?"

Liana needed no reminding. But as the date crept closer,

she wondered whether she would have the courage to make any decision at all. Maybe she would just let things play out; surely some resolution would eventually come. And as much as he loved her, Liana didn't think Jakob would wait around for her forever.

"I don't know." Liana sighed. "I guess I don't always govern the timetable of everything," she said, picturing her mother, Deb, and Rabbi Nacht sharing a cappuccino and a chuckle over Liana's naïveté in believing that she was in control of anything.

After a few more half-hearted attempts at convincing Liana, Katie gave up. When her phone rang again a few minutes later, she assumed it was Katie calling back, having come up with a new angle. She let the call go through to her voicemail and then listened as it played in her living room.

"Liana," a man's voice said, "it's Steven. If you're there, can you pick up please?" Although she felt that she almost couldn't bear it, Liana reached for the phone.

"Hello?"

"Oh, hi, Liana. Great, I caught you. I wish I had something better to tell you. We took Deb to hospice today at Bellevue Hospital." Liana could hear Steven's new baby crying in the background of his apartment. She felt a pang of jealousy on Deb's behalf, and then she remembered how devoted Steven had been over these many months. Liana was glad that he'd go on with a new start and that Max would have a baby sister.

"Deb probably doesn't have long," he continued. "The doctors want her parents to consider taking her off nutrition, but it isn't happening right away. Anyway, she's on a lot of painkillers, but if you wanted to come see her, I think it'd be okay." He sounded fried but tranquil, as if he knew he'd done all he could. Certainly, he had.

"Thanks for calling, Steven. I'll definitely come this afternoon. Is there anything I can do for you?" she asked.

"No, I'm doing okay. I have Max with me, and he's the best medicine. Just come see Deb. You've been a good friend, Liana. It'll mean a lot to her." Liana would repeat those words to herself many times in the days to come, taking solace that she had managed to achieve something of what Deb had demanded and deserved.

Liana contemplated calling Gerry and giving him the heads-up but figured that if Deb wanted Gerry to visit, she'd let Steven know to contact him. She decided to spruce herself up—Deb hated a slob. She put on a cute dress she had bought the summer before at the flea market on Seventy-Sixth Street and a new pair of pink flats that wouldn't quite meet Deb's footwear standards but at least wouldn't upset her. Liana poured a ton of gel into her hair and mostly succeeded in making the curls manageable, if stiff; put on a little lip gloss; and spritzed herself with Chanel No. 5, her only cosmetic indulgence. Before she got on the subway at Seventy-Second Street to go downtown, she bought copies of *People* and *Vogue*. She knew she wasn't kidding anyone about Deb's condition or interest in reading silly magazines, but her mother had ingrained in her not to arrive anywhere empty-handed.

When she got to Bellevue, Deb looked worse than Liana had expected from Steven's relatively modulated telephone call. *How incredibly vibrant Deb had been, larger than life almost!* She had been the kind of Upper West Side woman who shopped only at Zabar's—even for regular groceries like yogurt and peanut butter—brunched on sable and whitefish at Barney Greengrass, and took salsa lessons, solo, in the basement apartment of "some guy named Carlos" on Columbus Avenue. Liana couldn't think of a word to describe how frail Deb was now.

Deb perked up as soon as Liana walked into the room. "Oh," she whispered, "you look nice. And you've taken the time off in the middle of a workday to come and visit me. I hope you won't miss quota because of this," she quipped. Liana didn't have the heart to tell her it was Saturday.

How could a person possibly keep track of the days of the week in a place like this?

"I might not make quota if I stayed at the office night and day for the next two months," Liana confessed.

"Why's that?" Deb wanted to know.

Liana wasn't sure how to start or how much her dying friend really needed to hear. But she had always relied on Deb's good counsel, and she didn't think that trying to pull the wool over her eyes at this point made a whole lot of sense. She thought for a moment and then said, "Work sucks without you there, and things are kind of a mess with Jakob too."

Deb's whole demeanor changed, although Liana had trouble deciphering whether it was anger or pain that transformed her features. She tried to sit up, but when she didn't have the strength, Liana moved her chair closer to the bed. Mercifully, the bells and whistles and wires had been almost entirely removed; Liana was glad not to have tangled again with the medical interventions, but it hit her like a punch to the gut that it was no longer necessary for the nurses to come running anymore if Deb began to fail.

"Please tell me that whatever's going on with Jakob has nothing to do with Danny Shea," Deb whispered.

"No, Deb, it has nothing to do with Danny Shea."

Well, that's not entirely true.

Her encounters with Danny—who believed Liana was sent from heaven and who was prepared to wait patiently to devote himself entirely to her, body and soul—had revealed how boxed in and distant from Jakob she often felt. Liana smiled at Deb and told her not to worry. Deb looked skeptical.

"Listen, you bequeathed me Danny Shea," Liana said, trying for a laugh. "You must have had your reasons." It was a notion that had come to her repeatedly, as though Danny were Deb's parting gift to her and that fighting for Danny was fighting for Deb too.

With great resolve, Deb reached out and took Liana's sleeve, pulling her closer. "Keep your wits about you, Cohen. Don't get so bamboozled by the bad guy that you forget who the good guy is here. Jakob is your good guy."

To change the topic, Liana filled Deb in on whatever petty gossip she could think of from the office—how Gerry had so intimidated a new attorney that he'd quit after filing his first brief; how the communal refrigerator had been taken over by a form of mold never before scientifically identified; how Bobby spent most of his days playing solitaire on his computer but had ingeniously programmed a button that he could press and a fake brief would appear instead of his hand of cards. It was all so incredibly stupid, but Deb was grateful.

When it was time to go, Liana gave Deb a quick and gentle squeeze. As the women separated, Deb said, "You'll remember about Rabbi Nacht, right? I'm sorry, Liana, but this time it will be soon."

"I'll remember," Liana said. "He's a good guy too. He'll come through." She looked at Deb lying helplessly in the bed. She wished she hadn't burdened her with her own problems— that she had told her, true or not, that she and Jakob were getting married and would live happily ever after. But Deb had no patience for dissembling, and she would have been the first to understand that life was complicated.

Liana walked over to Steven and gave him a hug. "You're the best," she said quietly. She turned back to Deb and tried for a casual wave, as though they'd see each other again soon. Deb blew her a kiss.

"El na, refah na la. El na, refah na la. El na, refah na la. . . ."

CHAPTER 22

To Jakob's credit, he'd cleared his calendar and suggested any number of expensive restaurants to celebrate Liana's thirtieth birthday, but she just couldn't get excited about anything. She walked through her days as if she were in some weird underwater attraction at a theme park she couldn't escape. Katie and Charlotte were appalled that their offer to throw her a party had been rebuffed, and even her mother had settled for buying her a lovely pair of earrings instead of spending some part of the day with her.

"It's a big birthday, Li. Don't just let it pass by—let's celebrate," Jakob had said on the telephone the night before.

"It's Cinco de Mayo. Let's go out for tacos and margaritas. That'd be enough for me. Maybe you could look into it and pick a good place," she suggested.

"Sure, if that's what you want, that's what we'll do," he said. For some reason that Liana couldn't quite fathom, Jakob was pretending everything was normal between them.

Is he so completely consumed by work that he hasn't noticed the strain, or is he in mega-denial that anything has changed?

In her lowest hours, when she had trouble seeing her way back to Jakob and to how things had been, she felt the temptation of Danny Shea abuzz in the air around her. She knew, for a certainty, that he'd be by her side at the slightest invitation, grateful to be close and ready to take care of her. It was frightening and exhilarating at the same time. Sometimes it was almost too hard to resist.

When Liana awoke on her birthday, instead of the clarity with which she'd hoped she'd greet the day, she was hit with a powerful malaise. It occurred to her, not for the first time, that this deadline had been self-imposed, that Jakob was unaware of it, and that she could let it pass with no one the wiser. Perhaps this wasn't the day for grand declarations.

Maybe I'll just let the moment go.

They met in Greenwich Village at an upscale Mexican place that Frank had recommended—he had met his latest young squeeze, Estrella, when she'd waited on his table there the week before. Jakob looked handsome but tired, and Liana almost wished she'd told him to take a nap instead of taking her out. "I'm thrilled to be here," he said, reacting to something Liana hadn't verbalized but obviously had communicated. "This is the first Sunday I've had off in weeks."

They ate quesadillas and drank tequila, listening to the mariachi band. The restaurant was dark and noisy, filled with Anglos appropriating someone else's holiday, and they hung out together without having to talk much, which suited them both. When they were finished eating, Jakob paid the bill, and they sat a few more minutes. It was almost eight but still light out.

"You know what I'd like to do?" Jakob asked.

"Tell me," Liana said.

"Let's walk across the Brooklyn Bridge. I never have, and it's supposed to be beautiful, especially at night."

Jakob liked to walk more than anyone Liana knew. Together they'd walk for miles, wherever they were—in the city on the weekends or on the beach on vacation—in the early morning or late at night. Sometimes they'd talk; more often now, they'd each be lost in thought, and they'd walk together, exchanging hardly a word but comfortable in the shared silence.

"That sounds lovely," Liana said. They took the number 4 train down to the foot of the bridge on the Manhattan side and started to stroll toward Brooklyn. Holding hands, they matched their pace and their breathing to each other's.

It's so easy to fall back into the comfort of him.

When they reached the center of the span, they stopped walking and leaned on the steel girders, looking out over the water at the Statue of Liberty, just like the night they met. The city seemed eerily quiet from this vantage point, and even the thrum of the cars driving below them was soothing. They stood that way for a few minutes, not wanting to break the spell and oblivious to the other pedestrians and bicyclists making their way to the Brooklyn side of the bridge. When Jakob gently removed his arm from around her shoulders, Liana turned to find him down on one knee, an open Tiffany's box with a beautiful diamond ring in his outstretched hand.

"Marry me, Liana," he said—not a question, but his voice was touched with apprehension.

"Oh, Jay," she said, her hand over her mouth as she took a couple of steps backward, away from him.

He stood up slowly and came close to her, as one would approach a fearful child, and took her hand. "That doesn't sound like the resounding 'yes' I was hoping for," he said, smiling tentatively.

How can I say no to the man I love? But can I accept if I'm not one-hundred-percent sure?

"I so wish I could say yes, Jakob. I'm just not certain of where I fit into your world, and I don't want us to make a terrible mistake," Liana said, tears beginning to run down her face.

Jakob pulled her close to him, wrapping his arms around her and speaking quietly into her ear. "I don't know where you got that notion, Li, but you *are* my world. Let me be certain enough for both of us," he said, his hand under her chin, tilting her face up to his. "Please."

She pulled away and wrapped her arms around herself in a protective hug. Jakob put his hands, Tiffany box and all, on top of his head, as if to physically hold himself together.

"Li, don't you understand? I'll be totally lost without you. I don't know what kind of proof of my love you need."

Proof beyond a reasonable doubt.

She didn't trust herself to speak, so she began to walk slowly away. Jakob followed her.

They reached the other side of the bridge, the warehouses and lampposts of Brooklyn Heights stretched out before them. Liana felt that going across had been much more than just a physical journey—she had crossed into another place in her life, and right now, that place didn't include Jakob. She had a gut feeling that she should not walk back across the bridge to Manhattan with him tonight—that it would set her back and destroy whatever progress she had made.

"I wish more than anything that I could say yes, Jay. But you have your life figured out, and I'm still a work in progress. I'm not sure that's a good combination."

She looked out over Brooklyn, to the courthouses and the streets she knew so well.

"I'm going to walk a bit more on this side of the bridge before I go home. Don't worry, its perfectly safe here." Liana kissed Jakob on the cheek and walked away. He hadn't said another word. When she looked back, he was still standing at the foot of the bridge, the small blue box in his hand, as if he didn't know what to do next. She had an almost irresistible urge to go back, to tell him she'd changed her mind, and to put the ring on her finger.

But sometimes you have to fish or cut bait.

Liana walked the blocks of Brooklyn Heights for half an hour, trying to steady herself and clear her head. When she found herself on Montague Street, she went into the Starbucks. Simone was behind the counter again.

"I'll have a children's small hot chocolate with whipped cream, please, Simone," she said. "And don't even think about telling me I'm too old." Simone looked past her, and Liana realized she was looking to see if the dashing Danny Shea was with her again.

"No, he's not here," she said. "I'm all alone."

She took the subway from Brooklyn, walking from the station on the Upper West Side, lost in thought as she rounded the corner from Amsterdam Avenue to Seventy-Sixth Street, heading to her apartment. Although she didn't see him, she could feel that Danny was near, like an electrical current sizzling in the air.

How did he find me?

A shiver of dread and desire ran up her back, and she quickened her step, opening the always unlocked door of the funeral home and stepping inside the lobby.

"Can I help you, miss?" the night security guard asked.

"Is it okay if I stay here for a few minutes? I thought someone might be following me," Liana said.

"Of course," he said. "Always glad for a little company. Gets mighty quiet in here sometimes."

When she was no longer shaking, Liana thanked the guard and quickly traversed the hundred feet to her building, glancing over her shoulder. She got into her apartment, a little before eleven, and saw the message light flashing on her landline. She had turned off the ringer on her cell, and there was a message waiting there as well. She half expected it to be Jakob asking for a do-over or at least checking that she had gotten home safely, which made Steven's voice especially jarring.

"Liana, Deb's very bad. She's holding on, but I think it'd be a good time for you to call your rabbi, if you're still willing to do that. Please let me know if I can help."

Liana picked up her cell. She wasn't sure of the etiquette of calling the rabbi at home at eleven o'clock on a Sunday night. She reasoned that he must be accustomed to emergencies, recalling his calm and strength when she had witnessed him receive the call in his study the day she'd gone to speak with him. She reached him right away. The rabbi remembered their recent conversation about Deb, and it took Liana just a few minutes to explain Deb's request that Liana involve him and ease the burden for her elderly parents. The rabbi was compassionate and patient and immediately took control of the situation in a way that Liana found overwhelmingly reassuring. She was out of her depth, playing a role in Deb's life and death that she never could have foreseen. And while she was honored to help in this way, it was also dreadfully frightening.

"Liana, you need to call Riverside Chapel tonight," the rabbi said.

"But she isn't dead yet," Liana protested. The thought of Deb reposing on the corner of her block, where she herself had just taken refuge, was almost too much for her.

"They'll wait. But it's good to give them the heads-up. And tell them you want the Orthodox preparation for Deb," he instructed.

"But she's not Orthodox," Liana stammered, suddenly confused and not at all sure of what she was doing.

"All it means is that everything will be done according to the tradition. That's what Deb wants, right?" he asked patiently.

"Yes," Liana said, grateful that the rabbi hadn't referred to Deb in the past tense. There'd be plenty of time for that. They discussed the logistics of the funeral—it would be graveside, as Deb had requested, her final attempt to keep the day more manageable for her parents—and the shiva, which would be held at their apartment.

"Do you think Deb's parents would want me to speak briefly at the service?" the rabbi asked.

Liana thought back to Zach and Maggie's wedding, remembering how the rabbi had done his best, but there was no covering for the fact that he didn't know the bride and groom.

"I will ask them, but I think her brothers will speak, and maybe some friends," she said, wondering if she too would eulogize her friend. She had been unable to speak at her father's funeral, too overcome with emotion, and she'd regretted it ever since.

"Do you think maybe you could sing at the cemetery?" Liana asked.

"That would be unusual," he paused, "but why not?"

Liana was glad her rabbi didn't always play by the rules.

Liana was thirty, and Deb was dying, and Jakob's rejected proposal was nearly an afterthought.

Two days later, early on Tuesday morning, Steven called to tell Liana that Deb had passed away during the night. She felt terribly empty, but the tears wouldn't come. Before she did anything else, Liana called Jakob. She called him at home and on his cell and in the office, but she didn't reach him. She left him messages all over. Each time, she said, simply, "Jakob, Deb is gone."

Liana called the rabbi and called Riverside for a second time, setting the funeral for noon on Wednesday at Sharon Gardens in Valhalla. After several more calls—to Steven, to Deb's parents, to her own mother—Liana called Tony and dictated an email to send around to the office, notifying her colleagues of Deb's death. "Before you send it out, please put me through to Gerry," Liana said. It seemed the least she could do, and she knew that Deb wouldn't want Gerry finding out through an email.

The funeral was simple and dignified. The casket was brought out of the hearse to the open grave, carried by Deb's three brothers plus Steven, Gerry, and his partner, Lars—an odd conglomeration, but Deb had some pretty wide-ranging friendships. Rabbi Nacht directed the pallbearers to stop seven times on the way to the grave. "We don't rush the journey to the final resting place," he said.

Liana looked around the cemetery, the open grave seeming to wait patiently for Deb's coffin to be lowered. She knew a few of the handful of people there. Deb's parents had respected her wishes, and only her closest family and friends had been asked to come to the burial—the other people who loved her, maybe hundreds, would show up at her parents' apartment to pay a shiva call over the next week. Deb's parents sat stiffly on two chairs that had been placed close to the grave, where soon the rabbi would say words meant to comfort.

Conspicuously absent were the attorneys from the office; only Liana and Gerry, now standing on opposite sides of the small clearing, represented that part of Deb's life. All the frustration Liana had felt over the past year threatened to bubble over. She swallowed, trying to get rid of the bile, as Gerry approached her.

"Liana," he said quietly. "I know this isn't the place to hash out our differences," he began.

"No, it isn't," she replied.

"I just want you to know that I loved Deb deeply as a friend. I wouldn't presume to compare our grief—I know how very close the two of you were. But this is a hard day for me too."

Liana looked at Gerry and saw the weariness and sadness in his eyes. She had known him to be arrogant and sometimes downright nasty—but his despair was raw.

She reached out and touched his arm, the crisp cotton cool on her fingertips. "I know, Gerry," Liana said. "I know." He turned away from her and walked slowly back to where Lars was standing on the opposite side of the grave.

When she looked up, she saw the rabbi looking at her, his kind question written in his slightly raised eyebrows. She nodded once.

Yes, I'm okay.

The rabbi said several prayers, and then Deb's brothers spoke about their little sister. Deb's parents held hands and cried while everyone else stood, grateful for the cool breeze on a warm May morning. When the rabbi asked if anyone else wished to speak, Liana stepped forward. She hadn't prepared anything because she wasn't sure she could get through it, but she was feeling surprisingly calm.

"Deb wasn't my closest friend, and she wasn't my easiest friend. But she taught me a lot about many different things. She taught me that it's good to have strong convictions but better to have enough discretion to know when they should be shared and when they should be kept to oneself. She taught me that to really live and really love, you have to let down your guard and let people in, even if it means that sometimes you get hurt or sometimes you lose the people you love. She taught me that friendship involves not the theoretical 'being there' that everyone talks about but the down and dirty—being there when it isn't pleasant or when it goes against every fiber in your body. She taught me that it isn't the length of your days that matters, although I so wish she'd had more time, but what you do with your days and whom you touch. And she taught me how to tie a scarf—well, at least she taught me how to tie this scarf," she said, touching the beautiful silk around her neck, "and she taught me that the only appropriate place to wear sensible mom shoes is to a graveside funeral."

After Liana finished speaking, Rabbi Nacht began to sing the twenty-third Psalm, his voice so ethereal and soothing that even Deb's parents stopped crying to listen. He sang in Hebrew and then translated: "Though I walk through the valley of the shadow of death, I will fear no evil, for You are with me; Your rod and Your staff, they comfort me. Surely goodness and mercy shall follow me all the days of my life, and I will dwell in the house of the Lord forever."

Afterward, the rabbi explained that in the Jewish tradition, the mourners, and not the cemetery workers, fill in the grave. He began himself, lifting several shovelfuls of the earth, which came crashing down on the wooden casket with a deafening thud. After Deb's brothers took turns, Liana shoveled, Marta flashing through her mind as she lifted the heavy earth. She passed the shovel to Gerry, who began to scoop from the opposite side of the grave, standing precariously on the mound of dirt and quickly, forcefully, digging and lifting and depositing the earth into the hole.

"Rabbi," Liana said, "he's going to fall in!"

"No one's falling in, Liana," the rabbi said.

And then Gerry fell into the grave. At first there was silence. And then everyone laughed.

They laughed in a rush of released tension, and they laughed in horror. They laughed as they watched the rabbi pull Gerry out of the hole, and they laughed as they pondered whether Deb would have been mortified or amused. They laughed because it was funny. And they laughed because there could not be enough tears.

CHAPTER 23

It was late afternoon on the day of the funeral by the time Liana paid a shiva call at Deb's parents' apartment on the East Side. It was very crowded—Deb's friends from Barnard and Fordham Law School and work, people she knew from the neighborhood, and relatives and friends of her parents and brothers were crammed into a smallish two-bedroom apartment. Liana could barely breathe. She looked around, unsuccessfully, for Max; among all the adults, he was hard to spot. She hoped he'd been whisked away by someone loving to somewhere quieter. She wondered how his three-year-old mind would begin to process his unfathomable loss and how much he would remember about Deb. A numbing exhaustion crept over her, and she stole away, taking the cross-town bus at Eighty-Sixth Street and then walking down to her apartment. The evening air revived her slightly.

Liana was grateful to be home. She felt depleted, physically and emotionally. It had been too warm at the funeral for her black wool court suit, but it was the only one she had, and she'd wanted to look respectable. She hadn't eaten much all day, afraid she would have trouble holding something down before going to the cemetery and repulsed by the platters of cold cuts and bowls of potato and macaroni salad that had covered the dining room table at the Levines' apartment.

Jakob still hadn't called. She marveled that he'd managed to turn off his feelings for her so completely over the last few days that he could ignore an SOS from her like this. He hadn't known Deb very well, so it wasn't that Liana expected Jakob to be sad. But she did expect him to be sad for her—he knew how close she and Deb had become during the course of her illness. It was the first time in nearly five years that she hadn't been able to rely on Jakob to support her, and the loneliness of that reality was piercing.

Liana had just kicked off her shoes and opened the fridge to look for leftovers when there was a knock on the door. No one had buzzed from outside, so she figured it was either one of her neighbors complaining about the Carly Simon song she'd been blasting over and over again since she came home or a Chinese food delivery guy who couldn't find the right apartment. She opened the door as far as the chain would allow and looked out. When she saw his blue eyes through the opening, she gasped.

"How did you find me?" she asked. She felt her throat constrict as her face flushed with heat.

"You wrote to me from this address, Liana. Are you going to let me in, or am I going to stand out here all night?" Danny teased.

"I'm not sure."

"My intentions are honorable, Counselor."

"Honorable, my ass," she said, giggling despite herself.

"Hey, you're the one who brought your ass into this," he answered. "Seriously, Liana, I need to talk to you. Just give me ten minutes." His voice was calm and reassuring. Liana knew from an appeal she had worked on a couple of years before that it took only eight minutes to strangle someone to death. But Jakob was gone and Deb was gone and Danny was here.

"Let me in, Liana, please," he said, his tone firm and encouraging. She unlatched the chain and opened the door.

Danny strode into the apartment. He surveyed the scene—Carly was belting out "Haven't Got Time for the Pain," one of Deb's favorite songs, on a continuous loop, and Liana looked tired and slightly disheveled in the black suit he had seen her in once before. Without any preamble, he put his arm around her waist, drawing her close, and kissed her long and hard, possessively, on the mouth. It was a very different kiss from the one at the baseball game. She didn't exactly kiss him back, but she didn't exactly resist either. Then he stepped away, as if to slow everything down and savor this moment of unexpected success. Danny looked around the room for a moment until he located Liana's phone, and he turned down the music.

He held out the bottle of wine he had brought, showing her the label, a pricey Australian Shiraz.

"Nice," she said. Then Danny walked into Liana's tiny kitchen and opened a couple of cabinets until he found her wineglasses. He took two down and set them on the counter.

"Corkscrew?"

"In the drawer to your left," she said.

Liana could feel Danny's eyes on her as she took off her suit jacket and threw it over the back of a chair, revealing the off-white camisole underneath. She carefully untied Deb's scarf and laid it on top of the jacket, drawing her fingers slowly over the silk. Danny handed her a glass of wine.

"Why are you all dressed up? Were you in court today?" he asked.

"Funeral," she said. And then the tears that had refused to come all day began to flow.

"Tell me," Danny said, steering Liana to the big white couch in the living room and sitting down with her, his arm around her shoulders, refilling her wineglass when she emptied it and passing her Kleenex from a box he found on the floor.

And she did. She told him about Deb and about their sometimes demanding friendship and her illness and how she couldn't face work without her and about Steven and Max and the rabbi, and then she told him about work and Gerry.

"You know, it was your case that helped me realize I still had the passion to do my job."

"I don't want to talk about my case."

When they'd finished off the Shiraz, Danny disappeared into Liana's kitchen again and found the bottle of merlot she had planned to drink with Jakob on Valentine's Day before that evening had gone awry. He returned to the couch with her glass refilled and the rest of the bottle at the ready. And then Liana told him about Jakob. She talked for half an hour, coming up for air only to drink her wine and not noticing that Danny had stopped keeping pace. As she spoke, Danny drew her closer and closer, incrementally, until she was lying in his arms as they reclined together against the soft cushions, her head on his chest as he stroked her hair.

"It's okay now, Liana. I'm here," he murmured. And then he lifted her chin toward him and kissed her lips, softly and languidly now, as though they had time to spare. The element of danger was more intoxicating than Liana would have predicted, and she felt her control slipping. Danny was strong and determined but gentle, and he smelled good, sweet and complex—something Liana couldn't quite place, but she thought it might be roasted almonds. He kissed her forehead and her eyelids and her throat, and his hands wandered the length of her body. She gave in to the pleasure, shutting out the notes of protest her clouded mind tried to send. She felt so out of it that she had the fleeting thought that maybe he had spiked her drink.

Danny deftly moved Liana onto her back, his hands underneath her cami. "Wearing a bra today, Counselor? What a shame," he said as he expertly removed it with one hand without taking off her top—a trick Liana remembered learning in sleepaway camp when she was thirteen—and tossed it on the floor.

He pulled off his own T-shirt, revealing a tiny, delicate lady-bug tattoo right above his heart. Liana absentmindedly traced its outline, marveling at the intricacy of the work. When she touched his skin, Danny moaned, his voice hoarse with desire.

"The ladybug is for luck in love. And now I have you."

She knew she should say something to make him understand this wasn't really happening, but she felt far away, and the words wouldn't come. Carly was still crooning quietly in the background, and she could feel Danny's weight on top of her as he caressed her breasts.

The shock of his cool hands on her warm thighs as he reached under her skirt and pressed himself against her propelled Liana into a moment of lucidity.

Liana whispered, "Stop."

"Hmm?" Danny said, his mouth on her neck.

"I said stop," Liana managed, her voice improbably gaining strength, some reservoir of self-preservation taking hold. "I don't know what I'm doing."

"You're doing just fine, Liana." His breath warm, his tongue in her ear.

The whole room was beginning to spin. Liana knew instinctively that she had to appeal to the romantic, the gentleman in Danny while there was still a possibility of saving herself.

"I'm begging you, Danny. You know I've always believed in you. Prove to me you are the man you say you are. Stop right now and walk out that door." The extra heavy feeling that had come over her was getting worse, but Liana put every ounce of her energy into her words.

Danny lifted himself onto his forearms and looked at Liana steadily. And then he slowly rolled off her and sat up on the couch, his elbows on his knees and his head resting in his hands.

"Oh, Liana." After a moment, he picked up his shirt, put on his shoes, and stood up. He walked to the door and opened it to let himself out.

"Come put the chain on, Liana," he said softly. She made her way painstakingly to the door and locked it behind him. She got back to the couch before she collapsed.

Liana was essentially unconscious for twelve hours. When she woke up the next day, it was after ten in the morning. She thought about showering and going in to the office, but she just didn't have the strength. And while she had a vague recollection that the couch she was lying on had been the scene of something scandalous involving Danny Shea, she couldn't remember any of the specifics. She was glad to find she was still mostly dressed, although more than a little alarmed to see her purple bra lying on the floor next to two wineglasses and two empty wine bottles.

She had been so out of it that she hadn't heard her telephone ring, and she was surprised to see the message light flashing. She pressed the playback button.

"Hi, Liana. It's Tony. Just checking on you to see if you're okay and if you're coming in today. Give a call when you have a chance." *Beep.*

"Good morning, Liana. It's Gerry. I see you're not here today, and I totally understand. It was a very difficult day yesterday, even though we all knew it was coming. I thought your rabbi did a lovely job with the service. I hope he wasn't too disturbed by what happened. I guess my balance isn't as good as it used to be. But I did provide some comic relief! Anyway, just wondering when you might have a draft of Gillian Black done. I'm hoping to take a few extra days of vacation around Memorial Day, and I think it would be good for you if you can get this filed soon—I know you're kind of behind on quota. So think about it, and maybe we can talk tomorrow." *Beep.*

"Liana, it's Jakob. I'm really sorry that I couldn't get back to you yesterday. I was out of town with Frank on the case, and I managed to leave my cell phone in the taxi we took from the airport—I guess I'm a little out of sorts. I didn't check my other voicemails until I got home this afternoon. I'm terribly sorry to hear about Deb. If you need me, please don't hesitate to call." *Beep.*

The formality of Jakob's message made Liana impossibly sad, and she saw no point in calling him. She wasn't sure when the last time was that she had eaten, and she was still feeling pretty woozy. Finding the leftover quesadilla from her birthday in the fridge, beans and cheese congealed in an unappealing mess, she ate it on the couch, cold. Then she got back into bed and collapsed again.

CHAPTER 24

When Liana came into the office on Friday morning, she was overcome with a sense of doom. The finality of Deb's absence was overwhelming, even though her friend hadn't physically been in the office for months. She was relieved to see that Bobby had taken the day off—at least she wouldn't have him to contend with while she tried to get her head together. Her draft on the Gillian Black case awaited her, but the thought of dealing with Gerry almost sent her home again.

She was distractedly flipping through her emails from the days she had been out of the office when a new one popped up on her screen.

Liana—call me ASAP. Randy.

She dialed his number as she thumbed through the client mail on her desk.

"Napoli," he answered on the third ring.

"Hi, Randy. It's Liana Cohen. What's up?"

"Liana. Thanks for getting back to me. I just wanted to give you a heads-up. Your guy got arrested again on Wednesday night. I'm doing a story for Monday's paper."

"Which one of my guys?" she asked. But this time, she already knew the answer.

"Daniel Shea."

"What did he get arrested for?" She tried to keep her voice as neutral as possible. Wednesday night meant that whatever Danny had done, it had been some time after he left her apartment.

"He tried to attack some young woman walking her dog in Prospect Park. It was a little dog—one of those wiener dogs, but I guess it had a ferocious bark and a mean bite, so Shea only got so far, and then he gave up and ran. But the cops caught up with him about a block away, and the girl identified him on the spot. She was pretty freaked out—her shirt was torn halfway off—and the dog went apeshit when he saw him."

Liana felt whatever remaining energy she had drain out of her.

How could I have been such a fool? And if this is really who Danny is, why did he let me go?

Randy was still talking, and she tried to focus on what he was saying.

"I spoke with Ava Wellington before I reached you, and she said she feels pretty good that the conviction will stick this time."

"Why's that?" Liana asked. She knew this kind of conversation was probably improper, not that she could possibly represent Danny again, but she couldn't resist getting the inside scoop. It was why she had befriended Randy, who had pretty loose lips, in the first place.

"Well, apparently this guy kept a journal."

Oh God, Danny. I gave you that journal as an escape, and you used it to hang yourself.

"He was quite prolific," Randy said, "and an introspective type. Ava said he wrote a lot about becoming obsessed with women and the internal struggle he feels between his chivalrous self, which loves women and wants to take care of them, and his impulsive self, which just can't take no for an answer."

Randy's voice was thick with sarcasm, but she recognized truth in Danny's painful revelations.

It's that yin and yang, but here it's just Danny vs. Danny. And nobody wins.

Liana felt dizzy and put her head down on her desk, cradling the phone in the crook of her arm.

"Anyway, Ava says she thinks a lot of his journal entries will come in under the hearsay exception for admissions against penal interest. She's confident she'll find a way for the jury to know about this stuff."

When Liana was silent for a minute, Randy asked, "Hey, Liana, you still there?"

"Yes."

Randy was quiet for a moment too, and Liana could feel that he was weighing what he would say next. Finally, he continued: "Turns out this Shea also had some imagination, Liana."

She tried not to panic. "Why do you say that, Randy?"

"Well, let's just say there was quite a lot about you in his journal, and some of it was downright racy. But I guess a lot of these guys must have a pretty active fantasy life about their female attorneys, right?"

"I think that's probably a safe bet," Liana said.

"Well, don't worry. Ava said none of that stuff about you would come in, because it isn't really relevant to the crime he's charged with. I just thought you'd want to know. So look out for the article on Monday; it should be on the front page of the *Journal*. I'll do my best to keep your name out of it. We're even now, Liana."

"Thanks so much, Randy. Yes, we're even now."

But I'm not playing this game anymore.

On Monday morning, Bobby was back in his chair, and the *Law Journal* was faceup on Liana's desk.

MAN ARRESTED IN PROSPECT PARK, CHARGED WITH ATTEMPTED SEXUAL ASSAULT

Suspect had recently been released after rape conviction was overturned on a technicality

By Randy Napoli

Liana skimmed through the article, her heart beating frantically. True to his word, Randy had not mentioned Liana by name, although anyone in the least bit interested could pull up on the Internet that she had been the attorney of record on appeal. The article was thorough and evenhanded; Randy was a good journalist, if a bit of a busybody.

"Tough break," Bobby said. He looked at Liana for so long that she felt forced to return his gaze, and then he spoke to her so quietly she could hardly hear him, even though his head was only inches from hers.

"Don't worry," he said. "I won't tell Gerry the things I heard and saw."

She knew immediately that Bobby already had ratted her out and that her fears about him had been founded from the start. She was pretty certain he hadn't been a fly on the wall in her apartment that night with Danny, and some of what Bobby probably thought he "knew" was pure conjecture. But he was familiar enough with the facts of the case to know that Liana's visit to Danny in prison had been unnecessary, and he had seen her with Danny in the courtroom in Brooklyn. The chemistry between them had been hard to miss. Unless Bobby was totally clueless, he likely had figured out that she had gone somewhere with Danny after court the day he was released when she didn't come straight back to the office. Had Bobby seen any of the ripped up letters or her handwritten correspondence to Danny? Had he worked out whom Liana had taken to the

Mets game or heard about the kiss cam appearance? She didn't know, but Bobby was snarky enough to have put two and two together, and he'd served her up on a silver platter to Gerry.

"You know what, Bobby, you go ahead," Liana said. "It will save me the trouble."

Once she had made the decision to leave, Liana saw no point in prolonging her departure. She spent the next several hours packing up the few personal items she kept at work. She wrapped in newspaper the framed picture of herself and Jakob at the farewell dinner for the summer associates the year they had met, the one of herself, Katie, and Charlotte at Charlotte's wedding, the picture of her parents in their season ticketholder seats at Shea Stadium, and the one of her and Deb at an office bowling party, when Deb was still healthy and strong. She put in a box her Yale Law School mug and the Mickey Mouse ears that Tony had brought back for her from Orlando two years before.

It's amazing how quickly you can dismantle what took so long to put together.

She took down the newspaper clippings from her bulletin board—articles Randy had written in the *New York Law Journal* about cases she had won: "Mental history of accuser admissible at trial," "New trial ordered where juror expressed racial bias," "Assault conviction overturned where People did not prove that teenager shared mental culpability of other perps," and others. Of course, many more cases had been lost, the clients serving out their long prison terms, but that was the nature of the beast. She wished now that she had lost Danny Shea's appeal and spared his new victim the trauma of being attacked in a place and at a time she undoubtedly thought was safe. But she had been doing her job. She felt a wave of relief that, in a few moments, it would no longer be her job to do.

She was taking in the view of the Freedom Tower one last time when Franny knocked lightly on her door.

"Wow, you're almost all packed up," she said. "May I come in?"

"Of course," Liana said. She motioned to Bobby's chair, but Franny remained standing.

"I'm too antsy to sit," she said, pacing a little, her hands in loose fists at her side. "It's so sad in here without Deb."

Liana perched on her desk, giving Franny time to put her thoughts together.

"I can't believe you're quitting," she blurted out. "None of us can. What kind of a message are you sending? About our work and our clients? What about the rest of us?"

Liana took her time to respond, understanding that Franny's question was heartfelt and that her answer mattered.

"I was wrong when I tried to convince myself that you can do this job with just the law on your side. I understand now that you have to believe that you're somehow helping to repair the world, one client at a time. It's a noble way to practice law, Franny. It just isn't right for me anymore."

Before Liana could register what was happening, Franny had wrapped her in a tight embrace. "I know you'll find another way soon, Liana. We're all rooting for you." Then she walked quickly out of the office.

When she was done cleaning up and writing short memos on each of her cases that would need to be reassigned, Liana headed down the long hallway to the Boss's corner office, past the mail room where Deb had spent her last hours at work hanging with "the guys." Liana rehearsed the various ways she might explain to Gerry why she had decided to quit. When she stepped into his office, Liana could tell that he was expecting her. At that moment, all her legal training and all her ability to make eloquent arguments failed her. Liana looked at Gerry and said, echoing her favorite Mets announcer, "I'm outta here."

CHAPTER 25

The first two weeks that Liana spent at home, unattached and unemployed, were brutal. She took long steaming hot showers, trying to cleanse herself of everything she'd been through and hoping for the insights that would let her move on. She stayed in her pajamas all day and barely ate. She didn't answer the phone, except to speak with her mother, who'd gathered that something was profoundly wrong but who hadn't grasped the extent of Liana's misery. She watched the clock and was amazed at how long a day could be. She slept at odd hours, sometimes like a rock and sometimes tossing and turning, unable to find comfort even in that escape.

Both Charlotte and Katie telephoned Liana repeatedly, but she didn't take their calls. They left lengthy messages on alternating days, monologues on her answering machine, keeping her in the loop. Charlotte had confirmed that she was, indeed, expecting twins. She and Howard had purchased the one-bedroom adjacent to theirs in the Bromley, and they were in the process of doing construction to join the two apartments into one fabulous one. And Katie and Rob were still going strong. They'd discussed moving in together but decided to wait until the fall, to make sure that it still seemed like a good idea after the summer vacation they were taking in Provence.

And, of course, Jakob was no longer a part of her life. She had told him flatly that his love was not enough.

I have made a terrible, terrible mistake.

When June inevitably arrived, Liana started to surface, slowly, taking baby steps toward getting a foothold on whatever awaited her. She was still moping around her apartment one afternoon—but was at least showered, dressed, and watching *General Hospital*—when the buzzer from the outside door sounded. Forgetting for a moment that she was unavailable, she pressed the intercom button.

"Fedex delivery. Please come down to the lobby to sign for a package." The slightly accented voice was familiar but somehow muffled. Liana rarely shopped online or had things sent to her building for precisely the reason that she had no doorman and no one to sign for anything, but she was curious. She put on some flip-flops and went downstairs. When the door of the elevator opened, she came face to face with Marta, decked out in her Lulu Lemon bright green workout gear, flanked on one side by an enormously pregnant and somewhat out of breath Charlotte and on the other by Katie, dressed to kill in a red Armani suit and tapping her foot, impatient to get back to work but happy to see her friend.

"It's so good to see you all. But what're you doing here?" Liana hugged each woman in turn, taking extra care with Charlotte.

If Liana was all dark rain clouds, Marta was blazing hot sunshine, and there was no way to avoid her exuberant warmth. "We're doing an intervention," Marta said, her Czech inflection now liberally poking through. "You've been in that stuffy apartment way too long. It isn't healthy. It's time to get moving."

Liana looked at her, aghast. "You guys, I couldn't possibly work out now. Every muscle in my body is atrophied. And I haven't eaten anything remotely healthy in weeks; I'm surviving on Double Stuf Oreos."

"Do I look capable of exercise?" Charlotte said, holding her stomach with her hands as though she were afraid the bottom might fall out at any moment. Or the babies.

"We weren't thinking about working out, Liana," Marta said with a mischievous smile.

Liana thought for a moment. "Oh, no, I'm not going pole dancing!"

Katie put an end to the guessing game, as the clock was ticking away on her lunch hour. "We were actually thinking something more on the order of ice cream sundaes. What do you say?"

"I say you're good friends," Liana sighed. They walked to the 16 Handles around the corner on Amsterdam, stopping every so often to let Charlotte regroup, and filled the largest cups with three flavors of frozen yogurt and five or six different toppings. They sat down in a booth, and, between spoonfuls, Liana poured out her heart to friends.

"I'm still not ready to get married," Liana said, "but I love Jakob. I screwed up. And I learned from Deb's death that you don't always have all the time in the world to make things right."

They all nodded sympathetically, and then Katie let loose.

"Liana, you threw away the kind of love that most people are never lucky enough to experience in their whole lifetime, a love that you stumbled upon when you weren't mature enough to recognize it." When Liana opened her mouth to protest, Katie waved her off. "And why? Because Jakob didn't follow you around like an obsessed, lovesick puppy. He adores you, but he also has a life and goals and a career he finds rewarding, even if it isn't the sort of law you think highly of or a corporate culture you can handle. He's not some hopeless romantic like you are—you need to appreciate him for who he is."

When Liana's eyes welled up with tears, Charlotte's followed, her hormones running wild in a prematernal onslaught.

She took Liana's hand in hers. "Liana, we're not saying Jakob is perfect. Nobody is. But you took him for granted."

Then Marta addressed the elephant in the frozen yogurt store. "And it doesn't matter what happened or what could have happened or what you wished had happened with that Shea person. You lost your mind for a little while. That's over now. If you regret your decision, you need to get Jakob back. It might be too late, but you won't know if you don't try."

Liana knew that her friends were right, and she wanted nothing more in the world than to fix things with Jakob. But a debilitating weariness had overtaken her, and she couldn't imagine how it would ever happen.

"How will I do it? I need to show him that I'm not the same woman who left him standing on that bridge," Liana said, pain washing over her as she pictured Jakob that night.

"Something will present itself to you as a way to prove your love. Keep your eyes open. Promise you will be patient. When it happens, you'll know." Marta's voice had gotten that faraway foggy sound she sometimes adopted; she had a mystical bent that surfaced occasionally and that Liana found hard to tolerate. Katie rolled her eyes. But Liana had nothing to lose.

"I promise," she said.

Later, sitting on her couch in her silent apartment, the rabbi's words came back to her. *When you give up believing you are in control and ask for help sincerely, God will hear your prayers.* Liana closed her eyes and prayed, hoping this time the answer wasn't "no."

Days passed. Liana looked for signs everywhere—anything that might give her a clue about how to make her way back to Jakob. She left her apartment more often to roam the neighborhood, in case her inspiration didn't know how to find her on her couch in front of the television. But no epiphany came.

She was beginning to think Marta's approach was faulty. She was beginning to lose hope.

Then something happened. Just as Liana was contemplating throwing in the towel, she discovered that when she stopped looking for the grand revelation—that ah-ha! moment that would change everything—other smaller gestures seeped in through the crevices of her armor.

One afternoon, Steven emailed Liana: `Max has started a summer program for three-year-olds at the JCC across the street from you; if you want to visit with him, I'll put your name on the list so security will know it's okay.`

She immediately emailed back. `Meet you both at pickup tomorrow.`

At half past noon the next day, Liana walked slowly through the sliding glass doors into the facility—the noise of the children was deafening, and she was nearly run over by the parents, mostly moms, in their trendy workout clothes, pushing their Maclaren strollers toward the exit. Steven waved at her from across the room, where he was standing with another dad, laughing over some mutual observation about the women around them. Liana was happy to see Steven smiling—it had been a long time.

"Hi," she said, giving him a quick hug and shaking hands with Gus, Steven's new comrade in arms. "Where's Max?"

Before she knew it, Max had his arms around her legs, squeezing so hard she thought she might fall over.

"Hey, buddy!" Liana said. "I brought you something." She handed him a hastily wrapped package, flat and hard. "It's a basketball," she said, straight-faced.

"It's not a basketball!" Max yelled and began to wail.

"Oh, no! No, I'm sorry!" Liana said, trying not to laugh. She'd forgotten how literal Max was and how difficult it could sometimes be to get the interaction just right. "Open it, cutie," she said.

Max ripped the paper off, revealing a shiny new hard-cover book, *Everyone Poops*. Liana sank down onto the sticky linoleum floor, sat "criss-cross applesauce," and scooped Max into her lap. They flipped the pages, ignoring the din, Max laughing uproariously at the large elephant pooping large poop and the tiny mouse pooping tiny poop and everything in between.

"We were doing great on the toilet training for a little while," Steven commented, a little defensively. "Then it kind of took a back seat, if you know what I mean. And the stress the little guy has been under certainly hasn't helped."

"I didn't even know that's what the book was about!" Liana admitted. "I just liked the title!" She gave Max another squeeze. She thought back to when Deb was transitioning him out of his crib and wished with all her heart that she could have dealt with the parental milestone of toilet training too. But Max was lucky to have Steven.

When the atrium was almost empty, Liana said to Steven, "Can we do this again? Maybe sometime you could come to my apartment after camp? I make a mean mac and cheese." She lifted Max up as high as her biceps would allow after her hiatus from Marta and handed him over to his father.

One Friday, about a week later, Liana's cell phone rang while she was running in Central Park, her attempt to get some endorphins on board and trim the couple of pounds she had added during her weeks of lethargy and depression. She was happy to see the rabbi's name on the caller ID. Although she'd been attending Friday night services more regularly, she hadn't spoken with the rabbi since Deb's shiva. But she knew it hadn't escaped his notice that Jakob hadn't been with her in synagogue for quite some time.

"I've been meaning to call you and talk to you about something," the rabbi said, after asking how she was doing in a roundabout, nonbadgering sort of way. Liana was brought back momentarily to her discussion with the rabbi about Danny and Jakob after the kiss cam.

What's coming next?

The rabbi continued, "DT has a *Bikur Cholim* committee, a group of about six or eight people who walk on Saturday afternoon from the West Side across Central Park to New York Hospital. We visit with patients—Jewish and non-Jewish—who are hospitalized and who are alone." Familiar with Liana's usual reluctance to commit, the rabbi hedged, adding, "It's a good deed mostly devoid of religious ritual but high on human compassion. It'd be a very meaningful way to honor Deb's memory, Liana. And I think it would do you some good too."

A year earlier, Liana would have said no before the rabbi even finished asking the question, a result of her own medical phobias. Now, with Deb's journey having come to an end and Liana no longer able to help ease her way in whatever marginal way she could, she welcomed the opportunity to perform this particular good deed. "Thank you, Rabbi. That sounds like just what the doctor ordered," she answered.

In many ways, Liana's road forward was becoming clearer. But the path back to Jakob was still uncertain.

CHAPTER 26

Liana woke on July 4, 2013, with a level of melancholy that she thought she'd successfully banished. As she brooded over what might be significant about this day in particular, she was transported back to that Brooklyn rooftop three years earlier, Danny and Jennifer dancing as fireworks lit the sky.

What really happened that night?

Liana believed now that Jennifer had been attracted to the good in Danny—his good heart in addition to his good looks—as she herself had been. Having earned Jennifer's trust, had he then gone on to do the unspeakable, to force himself on her? If so, had there been something different about Danny's feelings for Liana? What had given him the strength to change course and leave her, so vulnerable, essentially unharmed? And afterward, why had Danny kept silent about what had happened between them, protecting Liana from the consequences of her behavior rather than exposing her? Liana would never know, and it haunted her still.

Wallowing in these thoughts, Liana was relieved when her telephone rang.

"Come meet me and Irv for brunch at the Jewish Museum after the first session of our new book group," her mother said. Irv had turned out to be a good egg. Although Liana had been wary of anyone trying to fill her father's shoes, her own loneliness had given her a new understanding of her mother. She was happy that Phyllis had found someone determined to get out there and give things a whirl, who was smart and thoughtful and enjoyed being with her. Liana still did her best to pretend they were "friends without benefits," and she was enormously thankful that they were too discreet for public displays of affection.

She found them in a corner of the café, seated at a small table, heatedly discussing whether the character of Bruno in the novel they'd read was supposed to be imaginary or real.

"I don't know, Phyllis—I got the feeling that Bruno never existed at all. He was one of those imaginary friends that kids sometimes have—you know, where the mom sits down on the kitchen chair and the kid screams, 'Don't sit there! You just squashed Bruno!'" Liana was loath to interrupt the exchange—they were so enjoying it. But she did really need her late morning coffee. Some things didn't change. She plunked herself down at the table.

"Liana, I'm so glad you came!" Her mother's delight in seeing her reminded Liana that she had not seen her enough, so wrapped up had she been in her own gloom. For a few minutes, Phyllis chatted about topics that she thought would be neutral—the upcoming US Open at Flushing Meadows, the sprinkler heads she needed to have fixed at the house, the closing of "their" diner on Northern Boulevard. The news of the diner, though, made Liana think of Jakob—they had logged way too many hours there, eating French fries with gravy and playfully ordering the fudge brownie that was always on the menu but never available. Although Liana was undeniably sentimental about those early days of their courtship, she was more determined than ever that her relationship with Jakob would have a future and not just a past.

Her mother's voice brought her back, still filled with the excitement of the new intellectual endeavor and the people she and Irv had encountered that morning. "We met the most remarkable woman in the book group, Liana. I thought of you immediately—I think it's so important for you to meet her."

Remembering Marta's words—"Something will present itself to you, and when it happens, you'll know"—Liana stifled her reflexive impulse to shut her mother down. "Who is she, Mom?"

Taken aback by her uncharacteristic receptiveness, Phyllis continued in a rush of words, before Liana could change her mind about hearing her out.

"Her name is Margot Lattimer. She is about—what would you say, Irv? Forty-five or fifty years old, and she's fabulously successful. She went to Yale, so you have that in common." Phyllis thought that Yale was like a secret club—if you'd gone there at any time, you had a lifelong affinity for anyone else who'd ever attended the school. Liana had tried to explain to her numerous times that it didn't work that way, but her mother's faith in the power of her alma mater prevailed. "I took her card—you should give her a call."

Liana picked up the business card without reading it, put it in the back pocket of her jeans, and patted her mother's hand. "Thanks, Mom, that's very sweet," she said.

"Don't be so dismissive of your old mother—I'm not an idiot! I'm telling you, Liana, this woman is a mover and a shaker. Irv—tell her."

"She actually was extraordinary, Liana. She's the CEO of a company called Dragonfly—it's an up-and-coming player in streaming music. While we were waiting for the book group to start, she was explaining some of the issues she deals with—the conflict between the idea that music is a universal good that should belong to the world versus the need to protect the ability of musicians and everyone involved in the industry to make money. And on top of that, the question of the current situation, in which one company has been so dominant and threatens by its success to shut everyone else out of the market. She was lamenting that the attorneys she has engaged are neither sufficiently intellectually curious nor knowledgeable enough about the arts to grapple with the intricate legal problems that arise."

Liana looked at Irv in surprise. It was the most she had ever heard him say. "That was quite a synopsis, Irv!" she said, both impressed by his intelligence and touched by the obvious attention he had paid to Ms. Lattimer, with Liana in mind. "And you're right—her description of the intersection between intellectual property law and free speech and antitrust concerns is certainly fascinating. But I have no experience in any of those fields—I would be about the last attorney this woman would be interested in meeting."

Irv shrugged. "Yeah, I guess you're probably right. Actually, now that I think more about it, this work sounds like it'd be right up Jakob's alley."

For a second, the world stopped spinning as Irv's words made their way slowly into Liana's consciousness. When the idea hit her full force, she gasped. Then she stood up and kissed Irv on the cheek. "Irv, you're my angel!" Liana turned and practically skipped out of the café, forgetting entirely to say goodbye to her mother.

Liana spent the rest of the long holiday weekend holed up in her apartment. She didn't sleep, and she ate only what came out of a can and could be warmed up in the microwave in under a minute—SpaghettiOs and vegetarian baked beans topping the list.

Seventy-two hours later, she had compiled a twenty-page dossier on Margot Lattimer and Dragonfly that any Wilcox & Finney associate would have been proud to produce. Liana researched Ms. Lattimer's educational background (Yale College, Harvard Business School), as well as where she lived

(Greenwich, Connecticut), her husband's profession (cardiologist), and how many children she had and where they were attending school (two, a boy and a girl, Catholic private school). She did a profile of Dragonfly's earnings, employees, business model, and future prospects, with an entire section devoted to its current litigation docket. Liana prepared a brief overview of the industry, including the role of the major music websites, and collected online articles from the trade papers that discussed government concerns about monopoly. Finally, she profiled the attorneys and law firms that Ms. Lattimer had used in the past, and detailed, based on whatever information was public, why their performance had been deemed deficient.

When Liana finished and was satisfied she had done her best, she put the document onto a flash drive and walked up a few blocks to the Staples on Broadway to have it printed out on nice glossy paper and bound. She was so focused on her mission that she bumped into and practically knocked down an almost ready-to-pop Charlotte, who, not realizing it was Liana, screamed, "Hey, you jerk! Watch where you're going! Can't you see I'm hugely pregnant and hormonal? Are you blind?"

The handful of people that had stopped to watch the spectacle were totally perplexed when the two women locked eyes and then dissolved into peals of laughter, hugging each other and practically collapsing with the euphoria of the chance meeting.

"Where're you going with such single-mindedness that you didn't notice your Mack truck of a best friend in your way?" Charlotte asked.

"Oh, Charlie—I'm so sorry! I almost made you have those babies right here on the street!" Liana hadn't laughed this hard since before Deb died. It felt so good she didn't want it to stop.

"Are you going to tell me?" Charlotte had been infinitely patient with Liana during her funk—certainly she had a right to know if something was going well for her friend. But Liana was superstitious; she was afraid to tell her what she had planned.

"Charlie, you'll have to trust me on this. I'm on a mission. I promise you'll be the first to know if I succeed."

They hugged, and Liana hurried off, leaving Charlotte to watch her go, fingers crossed.

That night, she lay down in her bed and had the first full night of sleep since she had quit her job. When she woke in the morning, she began making the necessary telephone calls to put her plan into action.

First, she called the Public Defender's Office.

"Tony? It's Liana."

"Liana! I miss you."

"Thanks, Tony. I appreciate your saying that. Can you put me through to Piotr in the mailroom? I need to ask him for a favor."

When they had worked out the clandestine delivery of the dossier to Wilcox & Finney, she called Jakob's secretary, Gloria, who picked up the phone with her usual, reassuring, "Jakob Weiss's line, may I help you?" When she heard Liana's voice, Gloria said words that were music to Liana's ears.

"Jakob hasn't been the same without you, Liana."

"Oh, Gloria, you have no idea. I have some work to do to fix this. And I need your help." Liana asked Gloria to make a reservation at the Yale Club for one o'clock on Wednesday for three people and to put the appointment down in Jakob's calendar as a business development lunch. "I don't care what you tell him to get him there; just please get him there."

And then she made the final phone call.

"Good morning, Ms. Lattimer. My name is Liana Cohen. You met my mother Phyllis Cohen and her friend Irv Mandel in your book group. I believe that you and I both attended Yale. . . ."

On Wednesday at 12:50 p.m., Liana stood on the corner of Forty-Fourth Street and Vanderbilt Avenue, under the blue awning with the YC in interlocking white letters, perspiring in her black court suit from the heat and from nerves. She looked north, waiting to spot Jakob. Gloria had texted her when he'd left the office, reporting that he was both chipper and anxious, convinced that Frank had entrusted him with handling an initial meeting with this very important potential client.

When Jakob came into view, Liana felt a surge of love that threatened to knock her off her feet. She hadn't seen him in almost two months to the day. He was dressed in his best charcoal grey suit and the red Hermes power tie she had bought him, sparing no expense, when he was sworn into the bar. Jakob looked debonair and professional, but he had also lost weight, and there was something hollow about his face. True to Gloria's description, he was striding purposefully, walking with a bounce in his step and a confidence that Liana found riveting.

When he got within thirty feet of where Liana was waiting for him, Jakob saw her. The transformation was both immediate and jarring. In his eyes, she first read joy, which quickly morphed into panic.

"Li," he said. "What're you doing here? I don't know what to say."

"You could start by telling me you are happy to see me, but you look kind of freaked out," Liana ventured. *Maybe this wasn't a good idea at all.* She felt something crushing creep toward her heart.

"No!" Jakob said. "I've wanted nothing more than to see you. It's just that I have this really important business lunch now, and I have to focus—I can't be distracted by you." When Liana didn't say anything in response, Jakob's demeanor shifted to resignation. His shoulders slumped, and he looked past Liana toward Grand Central Station, as though he might be contemplating an escape.

"Wait. There's no meeting, right? I'm a fool." Jakob almost laughed, but the sound got caught in his throat. "This CEO I thought I was having lunch with and this company were just so exactly the kind of project I'd love to work on, and stupidly I bought that Frank believed I was the right attorney to try to bring the business in. But you didn't need to arrange this whole ruse, Liana," he said, shaking his head slowly. "I guess Gloria must've been in on it—you could have just called me."

If he had been Max's age, Jakob would have cried. As it was, he dug his hands into his pants pockets and looked down at his newly polished shoes.

Liana grinned from ear to ear.

"Come on, slugger—I have someone I'd like you to meet." She hooked her arm through his as he looked at her, astonished, and led him into the Yale Club.

"Let's not keep Ms. Lattimer waiting."

CHAPTER 27

Liana was putting together a care package of peanut-free junk food to bring to Max at the JCC when Jakob arrived at her door, a dozen roses and a bottle of chilled champagne in hand.

She put the flowers into a vase and Jakob popped the cork.

"Did you win the account?" Liana squealed as he hugged her close.

"I don't know yet, but it couldn't have gone better. If she chooses someone else, it certainly won't be because I wasn't prepared, thanks to you, or didn't make a good impression." Liana had made the introduction and sat down with Margot and Jakob for a bit, then gracefully excused herself so that they could get to know each other. Phyllis and Irv had been right—Margot was a dynamo, with a huge personality and a book of business to match. If Jakob brought her in as a client for Wilcox & Finney, his future there was assured.

As Jakob held her tight, he surreptitiously hit a button on his phone, and the room was suddenly filled with their song.

"Dance with me?" he asked.

"Did you download this legally?" Liana quipped, poking him in the ribs.

"Of course," he said, "iTunes!"

They stayed close, swaying in each other's arms long after the song had finished playing.

"Li," Jakob said, "you didn't have to do what you did for me today for us to be together. You know that I never in a million years expected you to help me directly with my work, right?"

"I know," she said, "and I don't plan on doing it again! Do you have any idea how much effort that took?"

"You did a masterful job on that dossier. Much better than I would have done. Come work at Wilcox. We could see each other all the time that way," Jakob said.

"And we'd have absolutely no other life outside of work, and we would probably kill each other. No thanks. But that project did remind me that when I put my mind to something, with a real purpose, I can accomplish a lot. I just have to figure out what kind of client deserves my time and passion."

Liana smiled at him, and then she got very serious.

"I just wanted you to know that I respect you and your career and the life you are setting up. I'm all in now, Jakob, a hundred percent, and I know that you were all along. I'm thankful that you waited for me."

When she finished speaking, Jakob took a Tiffany's box from his shirt pocket.

"Oh, no, Jay—I'm still not—" Liana stammered. "Don't you think that will look like some sort of quid pro quo? Won't people think I bought you back by handing you the Dragonfly account if you give me that on the very same day?"

He pulled her closer and kissed her, silencing her chatter.

"You hardly handed me that account," Jakob said, laughing and only slightly offended. "Relax, Liana, it's not what you think it is. Just open it."

Liana unwrapped the haint-blue box, untying the white ribbon carefully and taking out the pouch. Inside was a beautiful gold chain, attached on either side to a charm of two interlocking gold bands. Eternity in a necklace.

"It's beautiful, Jakob. I love it." He carefully put the necklace around Liana's neck, nervously fumbling, just slightly, with the clasp.

"I returned the engagement ring, for now. I think we both need to recover before we take that step." He paused, searching for the right words. "Liana, I've loved you since the first moment I sidled up to you on that booze cruise, and I will love you forever." Afraid that her emotions would run amok if she tried to speak, Liana burrowed her head deeper into Jakob's shoulder.

He brushed the curls gently from her face. "I admit that part of the reason we fell apart was because I didn't realize that I was putting my career ahead of us. I won't make that mistake again, Dragonfly account or no Dragonfly account. But however angry or neglected you felt, you lost faith in us as a couple pretty easily, and I learned that neither of us is ready to be married yet. We have time. Not everything has to happen yesterday. Let's try to enjoy each day we have together and not rush through our lives just because some people say that if you aren't engaged by thirty, your life's over."

Well, I vetoed that deadline anyway.

"I think we need to make a toast," he said, handing her a glass of champagne. "To us! To many, many years of bliss, both marital and premarital," Jakob added, winking.

They clinked glasses. He kissed Liana and pulled them both down onto the pristine white couch, champagne flying in all directions.

Thank God we're not drinking red.

EPILOGUE

Two Years Later
May 16, 2015

"Really?"

"Really!"

Liana was both surprised and touched that Jakob had thought to get her Mets tickets to celebrate her thirty-second birthday. She was especially moved that he was taking the time to go to the game on a Saturday night, the day of the week usually reserved for entertaining clients. In truth, since he had secured the Dragonfly account and made partner—at thirty-two, one of the youngest ever elected to the partnership at Wilcox—he'd been able to control his hours better and was making a significant effort to spend more time with Liana. He'd even gone to the trouble to figure out which night her favorite pitcher, Jacob deGrom, would be on the mound, and he had spared no expense on the tickets—seats on the field level with no obstructions, along the first base line, about ten rows up from the Mets dugout. Although still a die-hard Mets fan, Liana hadn't been back to Citi Field since that fateful opening day over two years earlier.

"These seats are awesome," Liana proclaimed when they had settled in. Jakob seemed pleased with himself, sitting back in his chair and surveying the view and the crowd. He turned his attention to the scoreboard and the starting lineup.

"Don't you think it's strange that Terry Collins has Wilmer Flores batting ninth, after the pitcher? I mean, isn't that a little insulting, especially since he's currently the team's leading home run hitter? I know he's made some errors at short recently, but is that a reason to humiliate him offensively?" Jakob asked.

"Did you just pose an intelligent baseball question? Jakob Weiss, you never cease to amaze me," Liana said, gazing at him appreciatively.

And it was true. She and Jakob had become even closer over the past two years—as if the trauma of almost losing each other had awakened in each of them a depth of feeling that had been hidden before. In the immediate wake of the Danny Shea episode, Liana had been afraid that he'd beat the charges again and would come to find her. She'd changed her telephone numbers and her email address, and when the Levines offered her the chance to buy Deb's two-bedroom apartment, although she was afraid of the emotional toll it might take on her to live there, with Phyllis's financial help, she'd accepted. Several months after she'd moved in, she invited Jakob to join her. In the place where Deb's comfy chair had stood and where Liana could still envision her presiding over her last birthday party, Liana had placed a used upright piano, bought with the last of her savings. Jakob filled the apartment with music, and Liana could feel Deb's approval.

After a lot of soul searching, Liana had gone to work for the Women's Justice Center, a not-for-profit organization representing women experiencing domestic violence at the hands of their husbands or boyfriends. Liana had seen enough to understand that, while taking care not to blame the victim, there were two sides to even these stories—women who some-times were unable to acknowledge their own roles in the deterioration of the relationships or who used the children as pawns to get what they needed. But for the most part, she felt she was on the side of the victim, and that was a welcome relief. Liana had come very close to danger, and she was gratified to be in a position to help these women access the court system to extricate themselves from bad situations.

Of course, she was not the only one who, if belatedly, had moved on with her life.Even her mother had made changes of the sort Liana had thought her incapable. She was still spend-ing a lot of time with Irv, to whom Liana would be eternally grateful. Neither felt the need to marry again, but they enjoyed every kind of cultural event, intellectual gathering, and food experience imaginable. Best of all, Irv had convinced Phyllis that in order to really take advantage of their golden years and everything New York City had to offer, she should sell the house on Long Island and buy a one-bedroom apartment near Lincoln Center, not far from Liana and Jakob. It was a move that Liana had thought Phyllis would never make, and she was enormously indebted to Irv, both for encouraging her mother and for all the help he'd given in going through the thirty-something years' worth of stuff that had accumulated in the house.

The two years had also brought a kind of maturation to her friendships with Charlotte and Katie. Although the three women were still fully capable of collapsing into hysterics or gossiping until dawn, those opportunities were few and far between. Charlotte and Howard had their hands full with the twins—Eliana and Katrina, named after Liana and Katie—adorable hellions who had the run of the Bromley and most of the Upper West Side as well. Charlotte was going back to teaching in the fall. Liana and Jakob had introduced Margot Lattimer to Katie, and she had become both a friend and mentor to her. Katie was on her way toward becoming spectacularly successful, managing personal wealth accounts at an exclusive private bank, traveling the world. She and Rob were happy, showing no inclination of marrying or even moving in together. When Liana would speculate on Katie with Jakob, he would gently remind her that each person needed to find her own happiness in her own way.

And what of Danny Shea? Liana had followed his case closely, through the newspapers and an occasional email with Randy. Danny had been charged with attempting to sexually assault the woman in Prospect Park. True to Ms. Wellington's predictions, the judge had allowed into evidence Danny's "admissions" in the journal that he was sometimes unable to control his urge to use force against women. But because the attack had been largely thwarted by the woman's fierce dachshund, the jury had not concluded unanimously that it had been sexual rather than a simple attempted physical assault. Liana knew that if the jurors had been privy to the entire truth—to Danny's amorous state of mind and frustrated state of body when he'd left Liana's apartment shortly before—they would certainly have found that he was out to finish with the unfortunate woman what he had started with Liana. But that interlude remained a secret, hopefully forever, between Liana and Danny. He was convicted of attempted assault in the third degree, a B misdemeanor, and sentenced by Justice Martin to the maximum, ninety days in prison. Although Liana could not have said exactly how it made her feel, she knew that Danny was out there, somewhere, and she believed he was patiently waiting for her.

Liana was so lost in this reverie that she practically jumped out of her seat when Jakob leaned over her and said, "Are you even watching? Come on, girl, get your head in the game!" deGrom, the pitcher, had just hit his second single of the night, this time to load the bases. The crowd erupted as Wilmer Flores came to the plate. "Here's his chance to really give it to Terry," Jakob remarked, and Liana laughed at his newfound enthusiasm. The Mets were leading two to nothing. On the third pitch, a ninety-four-mile-per-hour heater, Flores swung for the fences and knocked a grand slam homerun, 391 feet into center field.

Timing is everything.

The sound was deafening, the roar rocking the stadium as the fans cheered, "Wil-mer, Wil-mer, Wil-mer," over and over again. Liana could feel the ecstasy of the moment pulsating through her entire body as she jumped up and down, slapping high-fives with anyone in her vicinity. Jakob looked happier than if he had planned the whole thing himself, smiling from ear to ear. The cheering went on and on, continuing even after Wilmer had emerged from the dugout and tipped his hat to the crowd. The Mets scored four more times in the bottom of the fourth, leading the Brewers by a score of ten to zero at the end of the inning.

Liana was so transported that she was only roused out of her trance by the sudden bizarre absence of sound—an expectant hush had fallen over the stadium. She looked immediately to the jumbotron in center field, which she had been studiously checking between innings the whole game. On the screen was the following in forty-foot-high letters:

THIS IS OUR MOMENT.
JAKOB, WILL YOU MARRY ME?

Liana turned to him with unconditional love in her eyes, and Jakob put his arms around her. "I thought you'd never ask," he said, with more candor than the crowd of over thirty thousand, watching them on the screen intently, could have imagined.

Cheers of "Ja-kob! Ja-kob!" mixed with "Wil-mer! Wil-mer!" as the players clapped their hands from their positions on the field, until some curmudgeon put an announcement over the public address system that play must resume.

And at the same moment, in a small restaurant many miles away in Beacon, New York, overlooking the mighty Hudson River, Rosa and Boris raised their glasses of champagne in a toast on their wedding day, to the classy lady lawyer who had shared their taxi when they met.

"To Liana. To Love!"

ACKNOWLEDGMENTS

There are many, many people who were my angels during this process, supporting and encouraging me from the time I started to write *Unreasonable Doubts* in the summer of 2015.

Thank you to Brooke Warner, Samantha Strom, Julie Metz and the whole team at She Writes Press for giving me this opportunity. Thanks also to Jane Rosenman, my editor, for her guidance and good judgment.

Thank you to my publicist Caitlin Summie, and my social media consultant Libbie Jordan, who patiently answered my rookie questions and did everything possible to get my book out into the world.

Thank you to my brother-in-law Stephen Friedgood for generously giving his time and talent to putting together and maintaining my website.

I am so grateful to Linda Fairstein, Jimin Han, Susan Isaacs, Bill Landay and Rabbi Joseph Telushkin. I hope to pay your generosity forward to other writers if the opportunity arises.

A special thank you to Michelle Nachmani for insisting that I join her for my first class at The Writing Institute at Sarah Lawrence College in September 2014. That class, and the many that followed, have changed my life. I want to thank my fellow students and all my teachers at SLC, but particularly Pat Dunn,

Jimin Han, Annabel Monaghan, and Eileen Palma, who helped me clarify my story and exhorted me to forge ahead. Special thanks to the members of my advanced novel workshop, Carolyn Lyall, Jean Huff, Greg French, Kim Greene-Liebowitz, Brooke Lea Foster, and Elyse Pollack, whose input was incisive and given with kindness.

So many family and friends supported me in this effort, and I can't name all of the people who offered a kind word or an interested question. You know who you are, and you kept me going. I do want to single out my sisters, Dr. Karen Marder and Dr. Dova Marder, my "almost sisters," Rabbi Sharon Forman and Kim Hoelting, and my in-laws, Adele and Dr. Benjamin Gentin. I also want to especially thank those early readers who read one, and in some cases two, versions of the manuscript, and gave me constructive and gentle feedback: Floyd Abrams, Mila Bartova, Art Bell, Steve Bernhard, Rosalind Citron, Michelle Creizman, Lisa Currie, Sharon and Dave Fogel, Lea Geller, Cheryl Goldschmidt, John Horner, Shami Kini, Catherine McGregor, Esther Miles, Michelle Nachmani, Anyi Rodriguez, Emily Segal, Yonina Siegal and Anna Zolner.

I would also like to acknowledge the late Rabbi Jacob Rubenstein of the Young Israel of Scarsdale, and Kate Charap, my work colleague and friend, both of whom died too young. They understood that life is complicated, and they are missed.

There aren't really adequate words to thank Pierre, Ariella and Micah. I can't imagine a more devoted and loving crew with whom to face life's inevitable ups and downs.

Finally, I remember and honor my parents, Martha and Rick Marder. How I wish they could be here for this. When writing these pages, I felt their love.

ABOUT THE AUTHOR

Reyna Marder Gentin grew up in Great Neck, New York. She attended college and law school at Yale. For many years, she practiced as an appellate attorney representing criminal defendants who could not afford private counsel. Reyna studies at the Writing Institute at Sarah Lawrence College and her fiction and personal essays have been published in *The Westchester Review* and online. She lives with her family in Westchester, New York. To learn more, please visit reynamardergentin.com.

Author photo © Ayelet Feinberg/Stephen Friedgood

BOOK GROUP DISCUSSION GUIDE

1. At the beginning of the novel, Liana is frazzled and barely able to hold it together at work. How would you diagnose her problem? Is she burnt out? Having a moral crisis? Out of step with her colleagues? What sort of struggles have you had on the job, and how have you handled them?

2. Liana is curious about traditional Judaism. What has led her to explore her faith? How would you describe Rabbi Nacht's approach to pastoral counseling, and does his advice work for Liana? Has there ever been a time in your life when you have relied on a religious leader to provide guidance on personal matters? Would you feel comfortable doing so?

3. Jakob has chosen a career path very different from Liana's. Is there truth to Liana's perception that Jakob and the corporate attorneys at his firm look down on her work? Is it possible that Liana is creating an excuse to distance herself from Jakob? Do you think Liana is resistant to playing a traditional role in the relationship? Does her understanding of relationships change over the course of the novel?

4. At the trial, Danny Shea and Jennifer Nash describe what started out as a consensual sexual encounter—the stories diverge when they have intercourse. Whom did you find more credible? Liana's perception was affected by the fact that Danny sat in the lobby with Jennifer's purse, inadvertently leading to his arrest. What did you think?

5. In the Ethiopian restaurant, Liana tells Frank's girlfriend Marissa that rape is not sexy. What is Marissa getting at with her question? Is she asking about power, danger, seduction, or something else? Is there ever room for nuance?

6. On one level, Jakob and Danny seem to be polar opposites, and yet Liana is drawn to them both. What does Jakob offer Liana that Danny could not? What is it about Danny that Liana finds so compelling? Each tells Liana she is at the center of his world. What do they mean and how do they show it? And why is that so important to Liana?

7. Deb asks a lot of Liana. Why, when she needed help, do you think Deb chose Liana over other friends and associates? Is there any truth to the notion that "work friends" are different from "real friends"? How does that play out here, and how does Liana's relationship with Deb change? How is Liana different with Deb than she is with Katie and Charlotte? Is there a point when Deb crosses over? How does Deb's situation affect Liana's thinking about her own life?

8. What did you think of Liana's mother's cautionary advice that marriage has idyllic moments, but can also be wrenching and turbulent? What about the more retro model of marriage presented by Jakob's parents? Are these different views consistent with the concept of finding your *ezer kenegdo* (oppositional helper) espoused by Rabbi Nacht?

9. What do you feel is the difference between "getting off on a technicality," and preserving a person's constitutional right to a fair trial?

10. At the end of the novel, how have your feelings about Jakob, Danny, and Liana changed? How has Liana grown? Will she be successful personally and professionally going forward? Will she be happy?

SELECTED TITLES FROM SHE WRITES PRESS

She Writes Press is an independent publishing company founded to serve women writers everywhere. Visit us at www.shewritespress.com.

Shelter Us by Laura Diamond. $16.95, 978-1-63152-970-2. Lawyer-turned-stay-at-home-mom Sarah Shaw is still struggling to find a steady happiness after the death of her infant daughter when she meets a young homeless mother and toddler she can't get out of her mind—and becomes determined to rescue them.

The Tolling of Mercedes Bell by Jennifer Dwight. $18.95, 978-1-63152-070-9. When she meets a magnetic lawyer at her work, recently widowed Mercedes Bell unwittingly drinks a noxious cocktail of grief, legal intrigue, desire, and deception—but when she realizes that her life and her daughter's safety hang in the balance, she is jolted into action.

Last Seen by J. L. Doucette. $16.95, 978-1-63152-202-4. When a traumatized reporter goes missing in the Wyoming wilderness, the therapist who knows her secrets is drawn into the investigation—and she comes face-to-face with terrifying answers regarding her own difficult past.

In a Silent Way by Mary Jo Hetzel. $16.95, 978-1-63152-135-5. When Jeanna Kendall—a young white teacher at a progressive urban school—becomes involved with a community activist group, she finds herself grappling with issues of racism, sexism, and oppression of various shades in both her professional and personal life.

The Geometry of Love by Jessica Levine. $16.95, 978-1-938314-62-9. Torn between her need for stability and her desire for independence, an aspiring poet grapples with questions of artistic inspiration, erotic love, and infidelity.

Play for Me by Céline Keating. $16.95, 978-1-63152-972-6. Middle-aged Lily impulsively joins a touring folk-rock band, leaving her job and marriage behind in an attempt to find a second chance at life, passion, and art.